Further Associates of Sherlock Holmes

Edited by

George Mann

TITANBOOKS

Further Associates of Sherlock Holmes
Print edition ISBN: 9781783299324
E-book edition ISBN: 9781783299331

Published by Titan Books
A division of Titan Publishing Group Ltd
144 Southwark Street, London SE1 0UP

First edition: August 2017
10 9 8 7 6 5 4 3 2 1

A CIP catalogue record for this title is available from the British Library.

Printed and bound in the United States.

CONTENTS

THE LAST VISITOR

Stephen Henry

Moriarty only makes a single personal appearance in the cases of Sherlock Holmes, that brief appearance being before he tumbles down the Reichenbach Falls. Despite this single appearance he is a character that rivals all but Watson and Holmes in his presence in the collective consciousness. He is the criminal mastermind of literature, father of all nefarious geniuses. But he is never there; he is talked about, his hand is felt but never seen in the stories. To me that is what gives him his power. He is placed out of sight, manipulating and bringing devilish schemes into being by using other people. This absence makes you wonder at the limits of his abilities and power. He could be behind any mystery, pulling the strings even as our consulting detective unravels them. So, when it came to writing a story from Moriarty's point of view I wanted to show how he worked, always at a remove, always manipulating, always looking for weaknesses to exploit. I also wanted to show how his genius was different from that of Holmes. Moriarty is about action, about making things happen. Holmes is about interpreting people and what they do. They fit together, two halves of a whole at war with each other in an endless game. This is a story about one set of moves in that game, where Moriarty cannot see the human dimension in events, and Holmes does not realise how there is always a flaw that can be exploited by Moriarty.

—Stephen Henry

There is no need to look surprised, or to huddle in the corner of the cell. I am merely here as a visitor.

Do the condemned not receive visitors? The hour is late in every sense, but please be seated, and let me reassure you that I merely wish to talk. I have no doubt that this must seem strange, not least because your allotted time has almost passed, and we are strangers, but I would ask your indulgence.

My name? I am James Moriarty. And your name I know. I am familiar with your case. You are forty days condemned for the murder of the art broker Angelo Lorenzoni, and his sister Lucrecia, both killed in the early hours of Friday 28th September of this year. For that crime you will hang in a little under seven hours.

A lawyer? No, I am no lawyer. A professor, but not of the law. I am a keen student of it though. My interest is in you, and how you came to be here.

Your story? No, I do not want that. Anything I might want of that tale I know already. No, I wish to tell you something of what *I* know of your crime. I understand that this might seem strange to you, but I have gone to some difficulty to be here, and I would appreciate your attention. After all, what else have you to do?

They were an hour dead when I saw them. The room was small. The floorboards were bare. Soot and the filth of birds spattered the windows. The bodies lay on the floor, limbs lying where they had dropped when life had finally lost its grip. Blood had poured from them, and then the material of their clothes had drunk from that pool. I could make out which one was Lucrecia by the blood-soaked dress. She was face down. I do not take account of clothing, but even through the blood you could tell that her attire was poor. Angelo lay with his mouth and eyes open, his hair a halo in the congealing crimson. The garish richness of his coat was still visible in places. Canvases on easels stood around the room. Some were almost finished, others bare, and many at a point between the two. Most of them were whole, but the three closest to completion had been slashed. Blood marked the cut edges and ran down the face of one, darkening red blending with the oil-painted flank of a ship on water.

"Who did this?" I asked.

By the door Moran gave a small shake of his head.

"None of ours," he replied.

"You have checked?"

He glanced at me, our eyes met briefly.

"None of them would dare."

Then he shook his head and went back to his watch of the stairs that led to the lower levels of the building. It was disused, we had made sure of that. Sat on a stool, Moran looked bored, his face and limbs relaxed. The revolver resting in his right hand seemed almost to be there by accident. Only his eyes moved, glittering as they glided over what lay before them. I have never seen a real tiger, but knowing Moran, I feel I know what one must look like when crouched beside a jungle pool.

I looked back at the corpses, and then at the canvases.

"They only touched the Maturins," I said, and pressed a handkerchief over my nose and mouth. I confess that the smell was becoming too much. There is a smell to killing. It is the reek of open bowels and organs exposed to the air.

As a rule I do not interfere directly in endeavours. I leave action to those who carry my instructions. After all, if the heavens can be described perfectly by my pen using numbers and symbols, what need is there of me to leave my study for earthly concerns? But occasionally I choose to touch the work as it progresses. I had been coming to meet the Lorenzoni siblings that night. I was greeted by the ruin of one of my endeavours. I was angry. Seven months now lay slashed to pieces on the easels, and the only way of recovering the loss lay on the floor beside her brother. I was more angry than I had been in a great while.

Moran glanced at me for a second, and then back to the stairs.

"It could be someone beginning an offensive on your operations," he said.

"No," I said. "All those who might try are known to me, and they have no knowledge of what we were doing here."

"You are sure?" asked Moran.

I lowered my gaze to him and after a second he looked away.

"My pardon," he said.

I turned, my eyes running around the room again.

"This is something else," I said, "something new." I stared at the blood-dappled canvas.

"Someone inside?" he said.

Anger sparked in the flow of my thoughts. "Perhaps," I replied.

I had decisions to make, but I could not see the paths

clearly before me. I will admit to being perturbed. You understand this, of course. I am a creator – that is my nature, my craft and the triumph of my life. Some live in the world as it is given to them. I do not. I make the world as I want it. I do not muddy my thoughts with trying to grapple with its knots of instinct.

"Undo the preparations for the sale," I said.

Moran nodded, and stood, gun still in hand. He could read me well enough to know that we were leaving.

"And this?" he asked, nodding at the corpses.

"Leave them," I said. "Be certain to touch and disturb nothing. Once we are gone make sure word reaches the police anonymously."

He nodded, the brief shadow of a frown on his features. Ever the good soldier.

"There are signs that we have been here," he said.

"They remain."

"The bills of sale?" he said, nodding at the pile of papers resting on a stool next to Angelo Lorenzoni's corpse.

"Those as well."

"If whoever looks at this is clever they will be able to tell a lot about the endeavour…"

"I hope so," I said, walking to the door and starting down the dank staircase. "I hope so."

The clocks were ticking towards the early hours in my study. I had the window open, and the draught as the door opened rippled the flames in the fire grate. In their bulbs the gaslights dimmed and then brightened as the door shut. The first chill of autumn was in the air; but I dislike excessive heat. Cold is the spur to the body, just as ambition is the goad to the mind.

"Professor," said Moran, as he crossed from the door, and sat in one of the chairs facing my desk. It might be a strain of sentimentality, but I keep my study as it was when I taught applied mathematics. My desk sits opposite the hearth. A ring of chairs sit before it. On the walls are my books, on my desk instruments of calculation and geometry, pens, paper, both foolscap and letter. My servants keep it ready for me, night and day. It is the centre of the universe.

I looked up at Moran as I finished a line of work, and placed my pen down. He had stuffed and lit a pipe. Grey smoke wound around his sharp face. He was not young, but even haloed by lines, his eyes were flints. There has never been a man more able in the art of execution, nor more in need of another man to follow, than Sebastian Moran. He had been watching the garret in which Angelo and Lucrecia had been killed since the previous night. I am told that the landscape of London's roofs is not so different from the crags of the lower Himalayas, and a first rate telescopic sight is as useful to an observer as it is to a hunter. Amongst his other skills Moran also has a facility for reading lips. Later, when the police and you had left, he came and told me what had happened.

"Yes?" I said.

"The police came. Local, poor quality. They were going to wrap the whole thing up as a killing in the course of an argument. Family disagreement." He inhaled slowly. Moran never does anything quickly. That is, to say, apart from killing. Slowness is a discipline to him, a chain he shackles his temper with. He exhaled a deep cloud of blue smoke. "Then one of the younger ones noticed the bills of sale. From that they looked at the canvases. They were confused."

"They sent for Scotland Yard," I stated.

He nodded.

"Lestrade?"

He nodded.

"And Lestrade read the bills," I said. "He looks at the canvases, and after looking at the bodies confirms what was obvious to the first policeman who could hold his breakfast down, that there is no way Angelo could have cut his sister's throat, stabbed himself several times in the torso, and then made the weapon vanish."

"Exactly so."

"How long was it until he sent for the consultant?"

"An hour."

"And he came?"

Another nod. "And the doctor."

"What did he do?"

"Holmes walked in and stopped. Lestrade kept talking. The doctor looked at the bodies. He is capable, even though you do not think him of worth. He deduced the time that they had been killed to within half an hour, and the weapon to be a short blade, wide and sharp, but without a point."

"What did the consultant think to that?"

"He didn't, or he didn't say. You know his manner. He just gave a little smile." Moran shook his head once. "Insufferable."

"Dislike him all you wish," I said, "but never let yourself have contempt for him. He is a rare creature. Limited though he is by morality, he is still very dangerous. Forget that and you are a fool, and I have no need of a fool."

Moran did not answer, but looked away, and breathed slowly through his pipe for a second.

I waited. To use such creatures as Moran requires sharpness and subtly. He is a killer, full of skill, and the arrogance that comes with skill. Welded to that ability is a rage-filled void. He is not fully in control, he is a horse harnessed to his emotion. He needs someone to tell him what to do, because that is what happened to him through those years in the corridors of Eton, and then in the army. He wants orders, but he hates those who give them. The only thing that keeps him loyal to me is that I make sure he fears me more than he loathes me. People are simple beasts, are they not?

"The doctor thought that Lucrecia had been killed first, and then her brother. Holmes agreed, but said that the killer had been in the room with them both, and that he had slashed one of the canvases first. She had stepped close to stop him, and the killer turned on her, cut her throat with the same knife that he had used on the canvas. Antonio started forwards, and the killer let go of Lucrecia, and then stabbed Antonio in the gut. He held him and stabbed him several more times. Letting him go, he then slashed the other Maturin canvases and left."

"Remarkable," I said. "How did he know that this was the course of events?"

"The canvas nearest Lucrecia had no blood on it, and the cut was ragged, as though someone had wrestled with the hand that caused the damage. She fell back and her throat was slit. Antonio tried to grab his sister."

"You say 'he' when talking of the killer," I said, absorbing the details of Moran's report. "I presume that your choice of words is not accidental."

Moran shook his head. "Holmes said that the killer was a man."

"Did he give a reason?"

"None, though the doctor asked."

"And our presence?"

"He knew we had been there," said Moran.

"Us specifically?"

"Two men, both of mature years, one dressed in heavier clothes suitable for adverse weather; the other well dressed, but in a restrained manner, such as you would expect of a banker, doctor, or a practitioner of the bar. The first was fit, and armed; the other slight and with a cane, though he does not use it for walking. They knew the brother and sister, though were not friendly with them. They were here after the fact and stayed for ten minutes, fifteen at most."

"You are certain that you are quoting verbatim?"

Moran did not reply, which was reply enough. He has an excellent memory. It is one of the skills that makes him more than just a ruthless man with a gun.

"So he all but saw us there," I continued. "And the rest? What did the consultant make of the rest?"

"He saw the bills of sale but did not touch them. He looked at the canvases though. All of them, and for some time. He sniffed the paint palettes, even scraped some off with a knife and tasted it. He looked at one bill of sale, told Lestrade to gather the rest carefully, and said that he was going to Soho the next morning."

I listened to this, and let it slot into my mind. So far the vector of events was as I had calculated.

"He is on to us, then," I said. "Good."

At this point, I feel I should outline the endeavour that brought me to the workshop of Lucrecia Lorenzoni on the night she was killed. The operation had been in progress for some time: two years, one month and five days to be precise. It was a thing of wondrous simplicity.

Lucrecia Lorenzoni was a rare talent. She was as skilled with a brush, charcoal and pigment as any that have lived, or so I am advised. In another age that might be blind to her sex, she might have remade the world of art and sold her creations for the coin of kings. We do not live in that age, however. Her father was a deficient artist, but a good broker of art to the wealthy of Florence. His indulgence and modest fortune let Lucrecia discover her talent and pursue its growth in the cradle of great art. Her elder brother was prone to accumulating debts without care or limit. With their father gone, and their inheritance exchanged by Antonio's need for a brief thrill at the card table, they fled from the Continent to London. That is where I found them.

You see, Lucrecia was not only a sublime artist; she could look at the work of other artists and make their hand hers. She did not just imitate, she had the knowledge of techniques that are almost lost. She could make the glory of Caravaggio live again, or da Vinci seem alive amongst us. Without money, such talent only had one use.

In imitation of his father, Antonio began to sell forgeries of paintings of modest value. He set up a brokerage, drew a line of credit and loyal customers across London. In time, greed would have made him overreach, of course. Sooner or later his hunger for losing money would have made him squander what he had, and then he would have asked his sister to paint something that would have been impossible to accept as real. They would have been discovered, and then they would have paid the price.

That did not happen, however. An agent of mine noticed one of the forgeries, and traced it back to its source. I saw potential. I bought every painting Antonio Lorenzoni sold. I fed his coffers, and watched him run up debts around every gaming table in London. I bought each of his markers. I was both the feeder of his habit and the consumer of his despair. Once I owned him utterly, I made my offer: his sister would work for me. They agreed.

People are made weak by emotion. Lucrecia Lorenzoni could have walked away from her brother and left him to the end he deserved. She did not though. Love – was there ever a greater crack made in the stone of rationality?

Now, what use I put Lucrecia Lorenzoni and her brother to might seem obvious: I engaged them to produce forgeries of pictures, and then sell those pictures to the wealthy of the land. That is not all, however. Anyone could have taken Lucrecia's talent and enacted such a scheme. Indeed, Antonio had tried exactly that. No, I did not just use them to create and sell forgeries. I used them to sell genuine paintings too, and by doing so put people of wealth in my debt.

Once he worked for me, Antonio stopped selling forgeries for a time. Using various agencies at my disposal I made him party to a number of sales of several fine paintings. The sales went smoothly, and his role as the source of provenance, and his reputation for honesty, were impeccable. Through careful engineering he was instrumental in saving a number of buyers from purchasing forged works. Within a year he was not only trusted, but he was sought out by all those who deal in such matters.

His sister had not been idle. She had begun producing two types of forgeries. The first were works that were new, but produced in such a way that they could be attributed to an artist of worth. Such was her skill that these works could, and do, hang unsuspected beside the works of the authentic master. Other parts of my network provided fake provenance, and Antonio helped to sell them.

The second types of forgery were copies of works that existed and were being sold by their owners. With these sales Antonio's reputation for trustworthiness and knowledge was key. People sold and bought through the House of Lorenzoni because they believed that it was safe. During the transaction, Antonio would substitute Lucrecia's forgery for the original. No one realised what had happened, and the sale was completed to the satisfaction of all. Only later would Antonio approach the sellers with concerns that the works were forged. He would apologise but produce proofs: the blend of pigment, a subtle mistake in the wood of a canvas frame, an errant colour. He would say that he had no choice but to reveal this to the buyers of the work. He would say that he would also pursue damages and speak in court against the seller as having knowingly tried to deceive both him and the buyers.

Reputation. Reputation and vanity – to the powerful there are few more effective levers by which to turn them to thieves. I selected the targets for this method with care. All saw their position with their peers and the public as fragile. None could risk such scandal, and so they agreed to work for my interests. Words from the privy council, papers from the cabinet office, decisions from the keepers of the exchequer: all have come to me as payment for keeping quiet crimes that were committed only by me. And, naturally, we kept the original paintings, and shipped them abroad to be sold on the other side of the world.

Beautiful, I am sure you will agree.

This is what I saw in ruins when I saw Lucrecia and Antonio dead on the floor of her studio. Someone had taken one of my creations and broken it. I hope that you can appreciate the anger I felt at that. Vengeance is the only pure human instinct.

"Tell me," I said when Moran returned to my study on the second night after the killing.

He sat again and lit his pipe as before. His eyes were shards of coal beyond the smoke.

"The verbatim, or in brief?" he asked.

"As close to the reality as you can recall," I said, putting aside the paper I had been working on. He inhaled, shifting his body to relax. I could sense that the days of observing and coordinating watchers were not sitting well with him. I would have something to sate his impulse soon enough.

"Holmes went to the House of Lorenzoni," he said. "It was left uninhabited as you instructed. He spent ten minutes on the pavement looking at the front of the building. The doctor complained that if he had known they were going to be outdoors he would have brought a heavier coat. Holmes did not respond, but they did go inside."

"What did he do inside?"

"He stood in each room for a minute each time, three in the main storeroom. He looked at two paintings, smelled the paint, turned the frames over."

"Which paintings?"

"Both were Maturins, the two genuine articles from the Duke and Duchess of ——"

I nodded. Maturin was an artist who had been much in

favour several decades before. Immoderation of drink had meant that he had not produced anything new for over a decade. The last that had been heard of him, he had fled to France after striking a bailiff. Whether alive or dead it did not matter to the operation. His work was commanding a high price again, and his fondness for the bottle meant that producing plausible provenances for works that might have been his was simple.

I sat back, steepling my fingers, trying to see the lines of fact and inference connect between what I knew and what I was being told. I could see possibilities, nets of connection and opportunity. I saw how if I were an enemy I could use these circumstances to attack my operation. I saw how I could turn it to my advantage. But I could not see an answer – who could have done this?

"The Maturins were the only canvases slashed by the killer," I said out loud.

"The doctor made the same connection," said Moran. "Holmes seemed not to think it worthy of remark."

"How so?"

"He talked of the brushwork, of the style, of the use of pigment and texture to create brightness. The doctor said that Holmes had never mentioned being a connoisseur of art. The reply was that he had spent the night reading the notices of Maturin's exhibitions in *The Times* archive." Moran gave a dry chuckle.

"What is amusing?" I asked.

"The doctor said that he had not known that Holmes had gone out. That seemed to please Holmes."

I blinked away the irrelevant detail. My mind was shifting through the threads of my operation. The Maturins… Antonio had been preparing a sale of a mixed portfolio including work from the Duke and Duchess of ——, and a number of fresh works created by Lucrecia in imitation of his style. Buyers had already expressed interest. The killings could have been to prevent the sale. Of all of those involved with the Maturin sale, could the Duke of —— have discovered what was happening? Was this a way of his heading off the damage to his reputation? But the man was a sheep, for all his birth. This was an act of directness. I began to think of people connected to the duke. What other agency might have an interest in protecting his reputation that they would take this step?

My mind came back again to a traitor. It was always a possibility that there would come another human as gifted as myself, with the clarity of sight and the will to attempt what I have achieved.

"Holmes then went to Antonio's office," continued Moran. "He sat in his chair. He looked at his desk, tasted the liqueur in his cabinet, and looked at every bottle. He went along the ledgers in Antonio's office of business. He did not open any of them, just pulled them off the shelf far enough to see the edges of the pages. The doctor looked at them in more detail while Holmes roamed the offices. He wondered out loud if it could have been someone who had bought one of the fake paintings that had killed Antonio and his sister. Holmes laughed once."

Moran tapped his teeth with his pipe, stood, and moved to my own drinks cabinet and proceeded to pour himself a brandy. I did not object to the presumption. The cabinet exists for others' vices, and I have no need of deference from Moran. He knows he is mine, and I know that he knows. Moran sat again and took a drink, baring his teeth as he lowered the glass.

"'This, Watson, is an operation far too developed and finely balanced to have been conceived, let alone executed, by Antonio Lorenzoni.' That is what he said."

"The consultant is as perceptive as ever. On what basis did he make that leap?"

"The doctor asked the same question," replied Moran. "'He was a man of excess, Watson,' said Holmes. 'He also lacked good judgement or caution to maintain such a scheme once it was in motion. You can also see it in the ledgers. Not in the numbers but how they are kept. The earliest ledger dates back to when the business opened, but only those covering the past two years show any regular use. Before that the paper is fresh, only written on the once, when the fictional entries they contain were written to pull a curtain over Antonio's previous activities. After that the ledgers show the wear and tear of regular use. Someone came in and took over Antonio's operation two years ago, someone with an eye for detail, and with a lot of patience.'"

"You are certain they were not aware of you?" I asked as Moran finished his recitation.

"Certain," said Moran.

I did not press it further. I trust Moran; you have to trust someone, don't you, even if only a little?

"What else did he deduce?"

"Everything," said Moran. "The broad outline and purpose of the House of Lorenzoni. How it worked, even the reason for Antonio fleeing the Italian peninsula. All he was missing were names. He left, and sent a message to Lestrade to turn over the House of Lorenzoni and to go through the ledgers. He said that a number of the most notable sales would be of forged pictures." Moran paused, eyes glittering, fingers tapping on the arm of the chair. "They are going to undo the entire operation. If you wish to act, it must be now."

I waved the words away. "The events you describe must have occurred several hours ago. What is the consultant doing now?"

"Nothing," said Moran with a shrug. "He has gone back to his lodgings in Baker Street. He sent out a boy runner, but I missed what he told him. I set people to follow the boy. He went to a drinking house on the Southbank, then went back to Baker Street."

"What did the consultant say to him?"

"Nothing. The boy just said 'gone three nights', and Holmes gave him a coin."

I leant back in my chair. The fire flickered in the grate before my eyes. In truth I had no notion of what the words meant or how they fitted in.

"Is this drinking house known to us?"

Moran shook his head. "It is like all the rest, all the small sins and pitifulness poured into one place."

"Who did the boy ask about? If he replied 'gone three nights' he must have asked when someone was last seen there."

Moran nodded. "He asked about a seaman without a ship, using the name of Grade."

"Do we know the name?"

Moran shook his head. "Do you want the word put out?"

"No," I said, and stood. "Have the carriage brought. I want to be close to Baker Street before dawn. Make sure we have a net around the place and ready to move. When Holmes moves so do we."

* * *

I was waiting in the cold grey of the pre-dawn when Moran swung up into the carriage and told the driver to go. His breath was white on the coal-scented air.

"They are going to the East Docks," he said. "Their carriage is just pulling up."

He drew his pistol and checked the rounds, and then took the carbine from under the carriage seat and checked that. The carriage lurched into motion, and then it was swaying as the horses pulled it through the fog and lamplight.

"I want whoever it is alive. Maim them, but keep them alive."

"And Holmes?" he asked.

I shook my head, and pulled the fur collar of my coat closer. The pre-dawn held a chill that even I did not find pleasant.

"He is not to be harmed." I smiled. "He is to be thanked."

Moran frowned.

I watched as Holmes got down from the carriage and walked to the end of the Ottoman Quay, moving between stevedores unloading the ships. I watched through a hand-scope while Moran tracked him in his sights from some high vantage amongst the warehouse windows. I saw Holmes smile as the dawn began to brighten, and the winds catch the edge of his coat. I saw him stop at the furthest mooring post and look out at the river, at the ships and the colour-washed sky. I watched and waited. He stood there for a full minute, and then I saw him take a letter from his pocket and pin it to the mooring post. Then I watched him turn and go back to his carriage.

My people followed him back to Baker Street, but I

stayed, and sent Moran for the letter.

"Professor James Moriarty" the outer fold read. I will confess I was surprised. I sat there and looked at it, and then ordered to be taken back to my rooms, my office, and the purity of my thoughts. I did not read it until I was back at my desk. Even then I considered throwing it into the fire.

I opened it and read. There was no greeting. It simply began:

> The case that you have watched me briefly engaged with is concluded. That end will not serve your needs for your revenge, nor any wider purposes that you may have harboured for discovering the killer of Lucrecia and Antonio Lorenzoni. They are free of you, and what harm they did on your behalf is gone with them. The police will dismantle your web of criminality relating to the House of Lorenzoni. That consequence you must have envisaged even if you did not foresee this one. I will not explain what mistakes you made, nor those by which you revealed your hand, suffice to say that the marks were there.
>
> I will give you an answer to the question of who killed the Lorenzonis only because I know that soon it will be public knowledge.
>
> Edward Maturin killed them both. On the night of the killing he had followed Antonio from his offices to the studio. He killed Lucrecia first as she tried to stop him slashing one of the canvases of his copied work. Her brother reached for Maturin as he did the deed and was stabbed. Maturin stabbed him several times more, and then used the same knife to slash the remaining canvases. Then he fled. The knife he used had a heavy, broad blade of the type that dock loaders use to cut ropes. One can

see wounds of the same kind in any of the river margin streets if one cares to observe such things.

He had been frequenting a drinking house on the Southbank, when he had the funds, and was known for his temper and his debts. He tried to get passage on a boat the same night he killed the Lorenzonis, offering to work as a deckhand, but the blood on his clothes was enough to get him turned away. After several days he secured berth on a ship heading to Lisbon. That is where Dr Watson and Inspector Lestrade will have arrested him this morning. I do not know but I would hazard that he will not deny the charges.

Why he committed the crime he will hang for is simple: pride and jealousy. Antonio Lorenzoni displayed several of the false works created by his sister alongside genuine work by the artists they imitated. Maturin saw them. His world was inside a bottle, his talent a memory. He saw his work, and beside them work that was not his but imitated his style better than he could now create. You never looked at his work, I know, not truly. Lucrecia Lorenzoni mocked him with her talent, and so he killed her. It is that simple.

Of your presence, Maturin knew nothing, and still knows nothing. His crime was one that you did not see because you could not imagine that your web could be broken by human emotion rather than intellect or intent. For that insight I am grateful.

Yours,
Sherlock Holmes

I confess that he is correct. I was blind to the obviousness of humanity's destructive urges. But if I am blind so is he. He believes in justice, that the structures of order are strong in foundation even if their walls are crumbling.

That clink further down the corridor? Yes, I hear it too; our time must be drawing to an end. I am sorry for that. For the damage and waste you have caused my endeavours, I cannot forgive, even if I am grateful for the lesson. Why, if I had the choice I would not let you see the hangman's noose, Mr Maturin. I would give you to people I trust, people who would draw a measure of recompense for what you did to something that was not yours. That is what I would do, and I would be satisfied in that knowledge.

That must be the sound of the warden coming.

Why do you flinch? What could be coming down the corridor to this cell other than the warden with the key to open the door and the candle to guide my way out?

You hear another set of steps outside? Surely that is not uncommon?

Even if it is strange, why do you recoil? You hang in the morning. What fate could be worse? And after all a man condemned to death cannot leave his cell, can he? What would it take to make such a thing happen? What would it take to have another man take the place of a man who is going to die? What could induce the governor, surgeon and witnesses to sign that the man who drops at the end of the rope is the man condemned to make the fall? How could that be done? Who could do such a thing?

Comfort yourself. Is that not impossible? For if it was going to happen, then Sherlock Holmes would have delivered you not to the law's justice, but to mine.

And that is impossible, because the great detective could not make such a mistake.

Ah… The key turns… It is time to go.

THE DOCKLANDS MURDER

Dan Watters

Wiggins the street urchin first appears alongside the Baker Street Irregulars in *A Study in Scarlet* as Holmes's eyes and ears on the streets of London. He seemed the perfect character through which to view Arthur Conan Doyle's city from a new angle – one both physically and socio-economically lower.

The early Holmes stories, after all, take place during a time of great economic upheaval, particularly in urban areas – the Second Industrial Revolution of the late nineteenth century – which led to both great opportunity and great exploitation. The London Dock Strike of 1889, a great step towards the founding of trade unions, seemed the perfect crystallisation of these ideas.

Holmes considers the boys "sharp as needles", and so I wondered how they themselves might view the oft taken for granted wealth and privilege of Holmes and the majority of his clientele. From this, certain class-based double standards began to make themselves clear – Holmes, for one, is a habitual user of cocaine. Yet we find him in "The Man with the Twisted Lip" showing a somewhat vitriolic dislike for frequenters of opium dens. As such, I considered whether there might have been elements of society impenetrable to Holmes that Wiggins and his gang may understand all too well.

—Dan Watters

Before she died, Mother insisted that I have my letters, and I'll admit I'm proud to have them. The others, they wouldn't know to cross their 'i's and dot their 't's. But recently I was visiting Mr Holmes and I saw a cheque on the desk (not that I'm the kind of fellow to go through a man's papers; it had been casually discarded and was plain for anyone to see, once they'd opened the drawer and lifted a couple of books). It was from one of the magazines Dr Watson publishes his stories in, and blimey if he doesn't make a pretty penny off his stories, writing about Mr Holmes. So I figured, having an entrepreneurial spirit as I do, I would give it a go and see if anyone would want to pay me for the story of the Docklands Murder, which was a case that I took myself, though Mr Holmes helped (and so did the rest of the boys, I suppose, in a way).

It started when I saw the man on Baker Street. I knew he was on the way to see Mr Holmes by the way he was walking. They have a particular manner, a certain hurried hunch. They seem to be weighed down with an odd sort of guilt, though they might not have done anything wrong (and few come to Mr Holmes because they themselves have, as he's all too likely to prove it for them and everyone around them).They feel a very specific kind of guilt, I think, just for allowing their lives to have reached a place in which they require a consulting detective, especially Mr Holmes himself. Therefore they walk as though their bodies are trying to go in two different directions: urgent, yet reluctant. They desperately need to get to Mr Holmes and his help, but they don't look forward to the conversation they'll have within 221B.

This one caught my eye because he was doing that walk that they do, but he didn't look like one of Mr Holmes's usual clients at all. His boots were well worn and had recently (but not too recently) been reheeled, and his overcoat was patched and threadbare. He didn't look as though he could afford Mr Holmes's services, in short, and this is what piqued my interest. Mr Holmes and Dr Watson do miraculous things, but mostly they do them for those who can afford miracles, and most ordinary folk would never even consider being able to hire their services. Most folk worry about being able to eat the following Wednesday, rather than whether or not they can afford to hire a private detective, to pay another man's wages (even for a few days) with their own. Never mind the wages of the most famous and prestigious detective in London. Thus I wondered what could have driven this fellow to try his luck at 221B Baker Street. I also thought, being an ordinary fellow myself, I might be of some assistance to him during the case, should he choose to take it.

I followed the man from the other side of the street. Sure enough, he rapped at the door of 221B, and Mrs Hudson admitted him. I thought it pertinent, as I had already decided to offer Mr Holmes my assistance (and that of the others, of course) on the case, that I should be present for this initial meeting. I did not, however, wish to intrude nor interrupt, and so decided that it would be far more courteous of me to listen from the drainpipe that runs up and around the side of the house, and offers a near-perfect vantage point from right outside the small back window which just about grants a view of the sitting room. Ducking around the building, I scrambled up leisurely, hand over hand, my boots finding familiar footholds. I judged, by his hurried yet reluctant gait, that the man would not outpace me by any margin. Sure enough, I reached the window, happily finding it cracked open, allowing me to hear the knocking as it came at the sitting-room door.

"Enter. The door is unlocked," said Mr Holmes. I realised that Dr Watson must be absent, and probably had been for some time. The detective's voice carried the tell-tale drawl of recent morphine use, a vice that I knew Dr Watson is not in any way fond of, and one that I have a feeling Holmes, though he would never admit it, makes half-hearted attempts to keep distant from and out of the sight of his companion. As such, for him to be partaking so openly in the sitting room, in which he also conducts much of his business, was, I am sure, not too common a thing, and indicative of the doctor's being away on some travelling or other.

I removed my cap so that it wouldn't jut above the window frame, and looked in with intermittent glances so that I was sure I would not be noticed. Mr Holmes was sat in his usual chair. The man stood by the door. "Mr Holmes?" the man enquired. "The detective Mr Sherlock Holmes?" His voice was thickened by an East End accent.

"Come in, sir," said Mr Holmes. "Take a seat, Mr…?"

"Macrain. Albie Macrain."

"And how go the dock strikes, Mr Macrain? I was reading about them in the papers only this morning." I too had read of the strikes – Jonesy, one of the others, makes a few bob a day flogging papers on the corner near the station, and he always holds a few back for the rest of us. The newsagents don't seem to have noticed yet, and I make sure the rest of them keep up to date with current events. (There's no way to get ahead in life without knowing what's happening in the world, you know, and sometimes I despair that the others wouldn't get anywhere without me and my entrepreneurial spirit.) When I next glanced in, the man Macrain was seated, and his mouth was open in the familiar 'o' of surprise that Mr Holmes so oft elicits from people. (Sometimes I wonder if Mr Holmes thinks that the rest of us just sort of walk around with our mouths agape all the time, since this is how he so often sees us.)

"But, Mr Holmes. I ain't said a thing about the docks yet."

Though his back was to me, I could sense Holmes's smile. He loves doing that to people, though he acts like he doesn't. "Mr Macrain, your boots are heavy duty, hardened and reinforced leather, and, though you've filed it down and polished it, the left has a wide scrape upon the toecap from some large, heavy, but flat object. Perhaps pulled out from beneath a fallen cargo crate?"

Mr Macrain nodded, dumbfounded.

"Your clothing, if you don't mind me saying so, is well worn – worker's clothes – and your hands are calloused. Yet you take good care of yourself. Your hair is recently cut, your face shaven, your shirt clean and your jacket patched. So you've taken care to make yourself presentable. But, the patches on your jacket are all cut from the same piece of cloth, and sewn with the same coloured thread. Therefore it is likely that all the patching was done at once, in a single sitting or near enough. This suggests that you have recently begun to pay more attention to the respect of your dress. Thus, you have taken a new position of some standing, but not one with better pay, or else you'd have been more likely to simply replace the jacket. So a position of influence amongst your peers, more plausibly. The strikes of which I read this morning, now entering their fifth week, are being led by organisers who have taken charge from within the workers themselves. The kind of position of authority that'd make a man want to appear respectable to the best extent of his means, wouldn't you think?"

Mr Macrain nodded slowly, impressed I think, yet pensive. "They said you were good. That's why the boys all clubbed together for your fee. Couldn't have more gratitude for them. They're good lads, but desperate. They just want to work. A man's got that right."

"It's to my understanding, Mr Macrain, that the work is sitting there waiting for them, and your men are refusing to get on with it. That's the very meaning of a strike, is it not?"

I could see Macrain bristle through the window. "Ten thousand men there are in Tower Hamlets alone, Mr Holmes, scrabbling for work each day on those docks, and the West India Docks Company employing about a third of them each time. Getting up each morning, unsure whether they'll be bringing home a pay packet that evening. These are men with families. Wives and children to feed. And now the trading companies want to take away our plus money – that's the bonus we get for clearing a ship real fast – just so's they can offer cheaper rates and bring more ships into our docks. I tell you, Mr Holmes, it'll do them no good if their entire workforce is starved. To strike, to deprive them of our hands and bodies and sweat and blood, is the only way we can make our voices heard."

"I see your plight, Mr Macrain. But not how it requires the services of a consulting detective."

"Well, that'd be for the murder, wouldn't it? We've got a shipping man dead, and either today or tomorrow I'm like to be arrested for killing him."

Mr Holmes sat up straighter in his chair. He offered Mr Macrain a cigarette from his silver holder, which was gratefully received. He took one himself, and lit both.

"And you *didn't* kill him, I take it?"

"Would I be here if I had?"

"You underestimate the overconfidence of some who walk through that door, Mr Macrain."

"Well I didn't. And I wouldn't. His death's going to do me no good, I can tell you that."

"Whose?"

"What?"

"Whose *death*, Mr Macrain. What is the name of the deceased party?"

"Robert Gail. He was the overseer of the dock. They found him this morning in his office."

"Blunt force trauma? Shot? Asphyxiated?"

"That's the thing, isn't it. There was nothing wrong with him. Other than that he was dead."

"I'd say that's enough, wouldn't you, Mr Macrain? Poison then, presumably."

"That's what the police are saying too. Especially as the door was locked and Mr Gail had the only key."

"And what makes you the principal suspect, if you please?"

"Mr Gail… he wasn't much for the strike. And we were surprised, you know? He may have been the overseer for the dock, may have had a little more job stability than the rest of us, but that didn't mean that he was one of them. He wasn't a wealthy man, and he knew many of us pretty well. We expected him to be behind us, especially, bear in mind, since he was getting paid either way." Mr Macrain had finished his cigarette, and eyed Holmes's holder. The detective offered him another, which was again quickly accepted.

"Well, over the last few weeks, Mr Gail had been getting more and more aggressive. Making frequent mistakes with his own work, while spending all his time trying to urge the men to get back to theirs. Said that we'd all be out of a job, that the ships would use other docks and ours would close down altogether. The men refused, of course, but that kind of thing's not on. Us working people, we got to stick together and look after one another or else no one's going to do it for us, are they? So I'm afraid… I'm afraid the other day I saw red. Stormed to his office and hammered at his door, yelling at him to come out. When the door flung open, he had a face like a devil on him, teeth bared in a snarl. He didn't look any more impressed with me than I was with him. Normally Gail had such a calm demeanour; the men made fun of him for having ideas above his station. He was a tall, thin man, something of your build, Mr Holmes – in fact, if you don't mind me saying so, he had something of your general demeanour altogether. He talked the way you talk – increasingly so, in fact – though he'd only grown up in the next street over from me. His mam used to take tea with my mam every so often.

"But that was all dropped now, and I can't say I wasn't taken aback by the way he came at me. He shrieked at me to leave him alone, to get back to work. Called me a slovenly rabble-rouser and a traitor to my class. Bear in mind, Mr Holmes, that there were people watching, men who'd normally be at work alongside me, who looked to me now for leadership. Men who were holding the line though their bellies and those of their children were empty, all for a better future. I couldn't stand there and take it, is what I mean, couldn't have them demoralised like that, so I had to respond in kind and… well. I'm not proud to say that we came to blows, and I'm even less proud to admit that it was me who swung first. I struck him on the nose; not so hard that he bled, but so's he knew he'd been punched is all.

"When he hit me back was when he slipped, though. He weren't too much of a physical man, but even so when he landed a punch on my jaw I was surprised at how little it stung. He'd put all of his weight behind it, so he lost his footing. He was on the step up to his hut, and he sort of fell off it altogether. The fall didn't seem too nasty, and those who were present, having grown to a small crowd of spectators due to all the shouting and that, seemed to find it pretty amusing, and there was a fair bit of laughter. Not too cruel, you understand, but well it's always nice to see someone who thinks they're better than you put in their place, isn't it?"

Holmes didn't respond, so Macrain went on. "Anyway, I went away satisfied that Gail had made a spectacle of himself and would be too sore about it to make any more trouble amongst the workers, at least for a little while. And that was the end of it, I thought. But now…"

"Now Mr Gail has turned up dead and you fear that you will be seen to have had a motive to murder him."

"That's right. More enough, the boys fear that if the papers get wind that one of our supervisors was murdered they'll say it was a dock worker that did it, and the docking companies will find it all the easier to smear our reputations. With the weight of the public behind them, they'll force us back to work at even lower wages than we've been on before. So you can see why we need your assistance, Mr Holmes, and quite desperate like."

"Hmm." I realised all of a sudden that Macrain had lost Mr Holmes's interest altogether some way back. "I think you'll find that you don't," he said. "Tell me, Mr Macrain. This fall that Mr Gail took. Did he slip backwards or forwards off the step?"

"Backwards. In that he ended up lying on his back."

"And his head, I presume it was near the step or the door when he landed?"

"Against the door frame, I suppose. He ended up almost leaning against the hut."

"And a good man like yourself, Mr Macrain, in front of men who respect you and know that you care for the wellbeing of others, I suspect that you bent down to check that Mr Gail was not too badly harmed?"

"I did, as a matter of fact."

"And did you notice anything untoward about Mr Gail's demeanour then?"

"Well, now that you mention it, once I was leaning over him, up close, I did notice that his eyes seemed strange; there weren't really any focus in them, I guess you would say. But he seemed fine after that, scuttled back inside and slammed the door."

"Well, congratulations, Mr Macrain," Holmes sounded bored. "After the autopsy is complete, I would expect that the worst they will convict you of is manslaughter."

"Excuse me? But I told you I didn't kill him, and I meant it."

"I know you did, but unfortunately the police may not see it that way. I believe that the autopsy will reveal that on slipping from the step, Mr Gail struck his head against the wall of his hut, resulting in a concussion. Nasty things, concussions; they disorientate a man, resulting in the kind of quiet, unfocussed demeanour that you describe the victim as suffering. Furthermore, they can have longer lasting results: nausea, sickness and even death, but can take days to appear. My expectation would be that Mr Gail most likely worked late the night before his body was found, and fell asleep at his desk, never to wake. There are a few other ways it might have happened, but all along the same lines. The police will be able to fill in those blanks at the very least. It was unfortunate that you were involved in a physical altercation with the victim when he received the concussion itself, but it sounds as though you'll be able to find enough witnesses to convince the police that you didn't inflict the—"

Mr Macrain had gone very white in his chair, and I could see even from a distance that he was physically trembling. He did not, however, appear afraid, but angry. "They'll crucify us for this, Mr Holmes. The papers will. It doesn't matter if I did it or not, if there's any doubt that I did they'll run this like it was murder. The strike will be over, and the trading companies will get everything they want from us. Nothing will get better for anyone except for those who have it all already. You must do something to help us."

"That sounds terrible, Mr Macrain." I don't know if Holmes knew how disinterested he sounded, but I'd like to think that he didn't. "And for what it's worth, I shall not be charging you my fee; I cannot in good conscience, for you have taken less than fifteen minutes of my time.

But the truth is the truth, I am afraid, and we can only interpret it in so many ways before we bend it. And that, as you know, is anathema to my profession. Good day, Mr Macrain. And good luck."

Holmes waited until the dock worker had left the room and the man's dejected tread had disappeared down the stairs before he spoke again. "Do come in, dear boy. Some may consider it poor manners to eavesdrop on a private conversation, you know."

"You don't mind," I said as I pushed the window open and clambered in.

"Oh?" Holmes raised an eyebrow. "And what has brought you to this conclusion?"

"Well, for one you've had the rusted bolts replaced so that the drainpipe is less likely to break. You wouldn't need to do that, I don't think, unless there was going to be something heavy hanging from it. Something like me, perhaps."

By the detective's thin smile, I knew that I'd passed a test of sorts. He likes to set me such exercises; to sharpen my mind, he says.

"Alas, I have little to task you and the Irregulars with today," said the detective. "Everything that has come to my door has been excruciatingly dull. As dull as the untrained senses of the average man about town."

"That Macrain fellow's story didn't sound dull," I pointed out. "There are plenty of ways that man could have died other than a concussion."

"Such as?"

I fell silent.

"You are a smart lad, Wiggins, but a master detective

you are not just yet. Nonetheless, even if the victim *was* murdered, he was a man whose professional stance was unpopular with tens of thousands of men, all of whom had the same motive to kill him; blood runs hot when livelihoods are on the line. I have little inclination to begin the interview process that would be required to rule out every man who worked that dock regularly, as it would, to be frank, bring very little intellectual stimulation. If one of those men did it, it may as well have been another of them. Or all of them, for that matter."

"But figuring out which of them… the search for the truth of the matter. That's the kind of thing you do."

"*Truth?*" Holmes almost spat. "Truth is utterly secondary. What I do, young Wiggins, is stave off the darkness of inertia." I wondered whether Holmes knew how much the average man on the docks, his fingers scarred with rope burns and splinters, would dream of the stability and comfort that a life of inertia brought with it. That life for them was not a series of games to be won or lost without repercussion. I thought it best, however, not to ask in case he went into one of his moods.

"You could at least go see the crime scene."

"A scene that will no doubt by now have been well contaminated by the clumsy stomping of police boots and the eager hands of grasping officers." Holmes sank back irritably, then lurched out of his chair, suddenly cheery. "But why would I, when I could send you in my stead?" He stepped towards the mantel before turning and pressing a shilling into my hand.

"Consider this your first true task as a detective in my employ, lad. Report back anything from the scene that Mr Macrain may have missed or thought unimportant. Keep a watchful eye for anything out of the ordinary, anything at all, however negligible it may seem initially. The devil is, as always, in the details. And, Wiggins, do feel free to leave by the front door, there's a good chap."

I thought it was pertinent, in order to be successful in my enquiries, to alert the others – those whom you may know from one or two of Dr Watson's stories as the Baker Street Irregulars. It was Mr Holmes who started calling us Irregulars, which we all found pretty funny if I'm honest, for the way we see it there's nothing irregular about us at all. We're poor people, and there's always been poor people, and there always will be. We're only irregular to the likes of Mr Holmes, as he lives in a way that most could barely dream of. But it's the people who live like Mr Holmes and Dr Watson who write the papers and the books and run the government and so on, so they think that the way they live is the regular way, even though they're far more irregular than someone like me if you really think about it. This means that they can't see the world properly and don't know how it really works. I don't think this makes them altogether *stupid*, just unfortunate. And I wondered if the truth of Holmes's disinterest in the case that Mr Macrain had brought before him was that Mr Holmes knew he wouldn't be able to understand it properly on account of his being irregular, and that he was going to need my help on account of my being all too regular.

We moved the way we do, in a group but not all together, so you wouldn't notice us, across the city from west to east and into Tower Hamlets. It's not a short way on foot, but if you're looking you can take in plenty on the way, especially on this day. It was a warm day towards the end of August, and all of London seemed to be out on the streets, lazy in the heat. There was a lot more chatter than work, but it was easy to detect an undercurrent of hostility, eyes catching one another for a little longer than is generally deemed polite, or avoiding one another altogether. Everything seemed to centre around the docks, as though the river was emitting a pull. Everyone was waiting to hear whether the trading companies or the workers were going to break first. You didn't hear anyone speak it, but it seemed to sit unbidden on the tips of tongues; if the dock workers could improve their lives, why not the factory workers? The day labourers? The entire city was watching from the corner of their eye, but nowhere yet did I hear any whisper of a murder.

We arrived at the docks presently, and I have to say I've never seen the like before. Dozens of ships blotted out the sun, jostling for position, unable to unload their cargo. Sailors sat around playing cards, drinking or merely waiting, on and off board, unable to abandon their cargo. It was easy to locate Mr Gail's overseer hut on account of all the police and sailors and dock workers who were crowded around it. I knew that, unlike Mr Holmes, I was unlikely to be let in to see the crime scene. So the others and I moved amongst the crowd, keeping our ears open for gossip. I heard little of interest myself beyond what Mr Macrain had told me, and hoped the others had fared better; but when we reconvened, I was to be disappointed.

"There was one sailor there who said he saw the whole thing," Jonesy told me. "He said that a few of his fellows had come up to the door early this morning on account of seeing the lamp still burning in the window. They didn't suspect anything amiss, just wanted to harass Mr Gail as to when the strikes were going to be over – some of the produce on board was fresh, and has already spoiled. They said that though the country's other docks were overcrowded on account of London, they were about at the end of their patience and willing to try their luck unloading elsewhere. They panicked when they saw Mr Gail through the window, slumped over his desk, but couldn't get into the office. One of them ran back to the ship to get a crowbar, while another went for the police. They were talking about it an awful lot; they were worried that they were gonna be suspects themselves, I think."

I nodded, mulling over the situation.

"Odd that there was no crowbar in the overseer's tool shed," Ollie said. "Would've thought that was one of the most important tools you might need for unloading and checking crates."

"Perhaps it's in the office itself?" Alex piped up. "Perhaps it kept getting nicked from the shed so Mr Gail kept it with him."

An idea of what might have happened was beginning to formulate in my mind, but I knew that to find any evidence at all, to be able to work without obstruction, we were going to have to wait until after dark.

At night, the sailors took turns to keep watch above deck, protecting their precious cargo from thieves. It is astounding, however, how prone people are to only look at what is at head height, and how easy it is to avoid detection in the dark if one is simply able to stay low and quiet. As the others silently scaled the ladders to the nearby ships to conduct a search as per my instructions, I returned to the overseer's cabin. A new padlock had been put on the jimmied door, but the pick I keep in my cap took care of that in short order. As it clicked open, I heard a grunt from behind me that sent my heart near enough into my hat. I wheeled around and saw no one, until I followed my own advice and looked downwards. A rough sleeper was leant against the wall behind me, which separated the docks from the street. He appeared at first glance to be fast asleep, but I caught a sparkle from under his hat brim that suggested he was watching me. Confident, however, that this man was unlikely to rush off to tattle to the constabulary, I proceeded into the cabin.

I had to count myself lucky that there was a full moon in the sky that night, for I could not risk lighting the lamp, nor leaving the door open. Even so it was hard to make everything in the room out, and I knew that if my hunch was in any way correct, I'd have to proceed in my search with the utmost caution.

Mr Gail's body had of course been moved to the morgue, away from gawking eyes, early that morning, but evidence of the kind of man he'd been was strewn around the place. Sweet wrappers and smoking papers were scattered on the desk, and the shelves were full of large books, most of which appeared to be unread. There were no photographs of family, and there was little one might have construed to be of value. Staying away from the window, I moved from the back of the office around to the front of the desk. I opened its drawers, and then opened them again – as I had half suspected, Mr Gail's desk drawers contained a false bottom, allowing for a shabby cubbyhole beneath them. I gasped as the drawer's contents sparkled brilliantly in the pale moonlight.

And then a creak of the step outside the door.

I ducked down under the desk as the door swung open, and a man, heavy set by the sound of his foot and his breathing, entered the room. A gruff voice – a policeman's voice – barked out. "Lad. You were seen coming in here by one of my men. Come out and don't make this worse for yourself."

I peered around the desk. Vague fantasies flashed through my mind of managing to creep around the room and out the door as the policeman searched for me, but I knew these were folly. My only chance was to make a break for it, to wait until he was far enough into the room that I could dash past him and into the docks, and only hope that the rest of his men weren't waiting outside. He'd left the door wide open, and I could see him silhouetted against it, and behind him… a further silhouette – the silhouette of the murderer, confirming my worst fears, behind the policeman. With a yell of horror, I leapt upon the constable.

The policeman let out his own yell as I landed on him. The murderer – the spider I had seen dropping from the ceiling towards his collar – tumbled to the ground, where I just had time to stomp on it before the constable – whose stern features I could now make out and revealed him not to be a constable at all but rather *Inspector* Lestrade – grabbed my ear.

"Are you a madman?" he yelled. "Attacking an officer of the law? Who are you? You could very well hang—"

"Inspector Lestrade." A voice came from the door. There stood the rough sleeper whom I'd spotted on entering the hut, but his stance was no longer that of a down-and-out.

I realised who he must be before he removed his hat. "The boy is with me," said Sherlock Holmes, "and I believe he may have just solved your case for you." Lestrade, dumbfounded, released my ear.

"Mr Holmes? What on earth is going on?"

To neatly compound the confusion, Alex chose that moment to drop from the ladder of a nearby ship and come running into the cabin. "Wiggins!" he yelled, "Wiggins I found it just where you said it'd be!" He cut off short as he saw me standing with two adults, one of whom was clearly, by his demeanour, a police officer.

"And what is this now?" Lestrade despaired. "Breaking into ships, too? Really, Holmes, your methods tend to be unorthodox, but—"

"Unorthodox?" Holmes said. "I'd say there's little more unorthodox than not thanking a man who's just saved your life, wouldn't you, Inspector?" He nodded towards me. "Good work and a keen eye, lad. You'll make a fine detective yourself one day." He bent to examine the crushed spider, and then looked up at Lestrade. "A Brazilian wandering spider, I believe they call this breed. Enjoys hiding in dark places – say, oh, *shipping crates*, for example, and quite deadly. If young Wiggins here hadn't spotted it behind you, I don't think I'd have reached you in time, and you may have been quite dead, Inspector." He turned now to Alex. "Did you find what you were looking for?"

Alex nodded, straightening his posture, pleased to be addressed by the great man. "I did, sir. One of the crates on the ship had been jimmied open… but there was nothing in it but a brown sludge. Sickly smelling, too."

"Bananas, before they were stuck on a dock for weeks

and rotted. Meaning the ship was from Brazil too, I would care to wager?"

Alex nodded.

"So," Lestrade clearly wished to be included. "Mr Gail must have opened the crate himself, and found himself unwittingly ferrying this murderous passenger back to his hut before being bitten. But why would a supervisor be opening crates himself?"

"Wiggins?" Holmes's eye sparkled at me again. I crossed the room to Mr Gail's desk, and began to remove the objects that were inside the hidden compartment: two gems, near as big as my fist, a somewhat hefty block of opium wrapped in a handkerchief, and a pile of crumpled slips of paper.

"What are these?" Inspector Lestrade began to rifle through the papers. "Betting markers. My goodness, *all* of these? There must be hundreds of pounds of debt here, if not thousands!"

"Mr Gail lived something of a life of vice," I told the inspector, "one that he kept secret, for appearances' sake, and one that certainly would be difficult to sustain on an overseer's salary. That's why he got into the smuggling business."

"Brazilian topaz." Holmes smiled. "Each worth a good thousand pounds by the looks of them. A fortune."

I went on. "Mr Gail would have been tipped off by his contacts in the Americas, and then when the ships docked he would quietly "inspect" the crates' contents, and pocket the gems that were secreted amongst the fruit, or other cheaper produce. But with the strikes, he was unable to get to the gems… and as a result, unable to cover his debts, leading to his being banned from all of the gambling dens in town. They really don't like men who can't cover their debts."

"Which is why," Holmes noted, "he was so fiercely opposed to the strikes, and was trying to assist their end by any means necessary – so that he could get back to the gaming table."

"And," I looked at Holmes, who did not immediately meet my eye, "also why Mr Holmes thought he displayed signs of a concussion after being struck down by Mr Macrain. They weren't the symptoms of concussion, but of opium use. A man robbed of one addiction has a good chance of turning to another. I'm guessing that Gail missed his games so much that his opium intake was getting out of hand; I mean, look at the size of that block. He probably knew that such a habit was apt to get him the sack; from Macrain's story, it sounds like it was already affecting his work."

"Knowing he needed to get back to his at least more presentable addiction," Holmes picked up the thread once more, "Mr Gail decided to break into the crate himself, leading to the unfortunate circumstances you have already so kindly laid out for us, Inspector. Wiggins here has a keen mind, as I've oft said; it took me some mulling over to consider the similarity between the effects of drug use and concussion myself, at which point the fact that Mr Gail must be engaged in some sort of double life became immediately apparent."

"Then why the disguise?" I asked. "Why not go direct to Lestrade?"

"I wanted to let you have your moment, lad. And a fine job you've done. You're well on track to being one of the cleverest men in London, I'd wager." If I didn't know better, I would have thought I detected a hint of embarrassment or even contrition to Holmes's posture at that moment; but know better I do.

Everyone seemed in such jovial spirits that I said nothing of how it had not been the concussion that had tipped me off to Mr Gail's opium addiction, but that what Mr Macrain had said about his speech being similar to the detective's when Holmes's had been marred with the drawl of morphine.

Nor (and I realise that this may make my story somewhat unpublishable but I feel compelled to write it nonetheless) did I say anything of the *third* gem that had been in the drawer, which I had secreted in my left sock, and it's this that proves Mr Holmes wrong on at least one account. None of the fences I know knew what to do with such a valuable lump of topaz, so I have been left with a very pretty and expensive paperweight, which is currently hidden beneath my pillow. As such I am quite sure that I will never be one of the cleverest men in London.

SHERLOCK HOLMES AND THE BEAST OF BODMIN

Jonathan Green

Sir Henry Baskerville, Baronet, is the Canadian-born nephew and sole heir of the late Sir Charles Baskerville. Following the mysterious death of his uncle at the beginning of *The Hound of the Baskervilles*, Sir Henry is the next poor wretch to be hunted by the phantom dog. The way he is described by Dr Watson – a "descendant… of that long line of high-blooded, fiery, and masterful men" and "a comrade for whom one might venture to take a risk with the certainty that he would bravely share it" – makes him seem like the type of character who would usually be the protagonist of many an adventure story, rather than merely the excuse for the plot.

As well as being one of the good guys, a gentleman, and a brave soul to boot, Sir Henry is also a true romantic. Of course, this is the cause of his undoing in *The Hound of the Baskervilles*, when he falls for Beryl Stapleton at the drop of a deerstalker. Despite seeming to have it all – inheriting a vast fortune and the Baskerville estates – his good fortune leads to him being targeted by a ruthless murderer. And where it really matters, in matters of the heart, Sir Henry is what can only be described as "unlucky in love".

These qualities made him very appealing to someone used to writing the pulp adventures of a faux-Victorian master of derring-do; that and the fact that Sir Henry's lands border the county of Cornwall, a land rich in myths concerning mysterious beasts all of its own…

—Jonathan Green

Legends, in my experience, have a habit of persisting, and the West Country seems to have more than its fair share. Take, for example, the Devonshire legend of the Hound of the Baskervilles. That was just such a tale that persisted throughout the centuries, so much so that a villain built a plan upon it, with the intention of stealing both my life and my inheritance. And he would have succeeded if it had not been for the legend who is celebrated as the world's foremost consulting detective.

To require the services of Mr Sherlock Holmes once in your lifetime might be considered unfortunate, but to require his services more than once smacks of carelessness. But that didn't stop me from writing to him when events began to take a dark turn once again, in the wilds of the West Country.

But I'm getting ahead of myself. Before I go any deeper into my tale, I should explain the circumstances that led me to seek the aid of the consulting detective for a second time. Not that it was me who contacted him the first time, you understand – that was my friend and physician Dr James Mortimer – but it was I, Sir Henry Baskerville, Baronet of the Baskerville Devonshire estate, who had benefitted from his intervention. So, like Dr Mortimer before me, I found myself contacting Sherlock Holmes on behalf of another.

Some – namely those who have read Dr Watson's account of the case of *The Hound of the Baskervilles*, as he so luridly titled it – might consider me unlucky in love, and I would count myself among them. As a consequence of the affair of the Hound, and the duplicity of both Rodger Stapleton and his wife Beryl – whom I had taken to be his sister and with whom I had fallen deeply in love – I had not thought that I would find love again, having been so bitterly betrayed before.

But nonetheless, I had recently become engaged to Miss Loveday Trelawny of Trelawny Hall – a grim, gothic manor that stands at the heart of that bleak expanse of Cornish borderland known as Bodmin Moor, the foundations of the pile dating back to the sixteenth century and the reign of Queen Elizabeth I. Miss Trelawny had inherited the estate from her father three months previously, after Lord Tiernen Trelawny died under mysterious circumstances.

Perhaps it was the similarity of our situations, the way in which we had come by our respective inheritances, but when I first met my fiancée at her father's wake – I myself attending as was mete and right for a landowner with some interests in Cornwall, as a consequence of the precise nature of the Baskerville estate – we found ourselves drawn together immediately. At least that was what I thought at the time. But again, I am getting ahead of myself.

Miss Trelawny's family line is as old as my own Dartmoor-dwelling bloodline, and has a history just as mired in tragedy and humiliation. But let me return to the matter of Lord Tiernen Trelawny's death, for it is pertinent to my tale.

Lord Trelawny had met his end suddenly and violently. And it was clearly no accident; the injuries he sustained were so savage that some said he had been attacked by a monstrous beast, while others claimed he had been murdered by an escaped lunatic, who had broken out of Cornwall County Asylum, which was located nearby.

Mention of the Beast of Bodmin, as the locals called it, married with her grief-stricken state, had my beloved believing that she had seen a monstrous cat prowling about the estate as she sat at the drawing-room window, looking out over the grim expanse of the moor. Reports that a number of animals had turned up dead on nearby farmland – sheep and goats mainly, but also a shepherd's faithful canine companion in one instance – bearing similarly savage wounds to those her father had suffered, only exacerbated her temporary mental instability, to the point where Loveday fervently believed that a big cat was hunting her, wailing to me that her family line was cursed. She was so consumed by this hysteria, I wished that she could be rid of the name Trelawny as soon as possible.

On Dartmoor and within the environs of Grimpen Mire, it had been a hellish hound. Here on Bodmin Moor, it was a phantom cat. But tales of such a beast were nothing new, and so I return to the history of the Trelawny line.

Legend had it that the century before, one particularly roguish smuggler had brought a black panther to England aboard a ship that had sailed from Java. However, as soon as it made it to shore, the animal promptly escaped, disappearing onto the moor. The smuggler was captured and tried by the local landowner, one Squire Trelawny, who condemned him to hang for his contraband crimes. The squire himself died not long after, apparently having been mauled by a big cat whilst out on the moor hunting with his dogs.

It was Loveday's growing obsession that her ancestor's fate and her late father's death were connected. To help put her mind at ease, as well as to protect the local farmers' livestock, I organised the hunt. I did not believe in the Trelawny curse any more than I believed in the Baskerville curse, at least not since Mr Sherlock Holmes had proved the hound's haunting had been nothing more than the Machiavellian machinations of a greedy and heartless rogue. But there did indeed appear to be something on the moor – the slaughter of the farm animals attested to that – and a good landlord knows to take care of his tenants just as well as he takes care of his loved ones.

When Loveday heard of the latest attack she took to her bed in an apoplexy of fear. She was unable to bear anything more than a thin soup, strongly flavoured with cardamom, which the late Lord Trelawny's Sikh houseboy swore by, claiming it to be a remedy he had learnt from his mother.

As the future master of Trelawny Hall, I took it upon myself to pay a visit to the farmer whose lifestock had most recently been attacked. The victim on this occasion was a cow in calf that had been attacked in a pen within the perimeter of the farmyard, which had put the fear of God into the farmer, a man by the name of Bligh, and his family. Had this been Canada, rather than Cornwall, I would have said that the cow had been attacked by a grizzly.

Having seen the evidence of the Beast's slaughter with my own eyes, the hunt was convened on Saint Valentine's Day, as fate would have it.

Valentine's Day came, and with it a light but persistent mist that clung to the moor like a shroud and which provoked murmurs from the more superstitious members of the hunting party that it was the work of dark powers. Perhaps it was the devilish, dead smuggler seeking to protect his pet from the hunters who would see Squire Trelawny's descendants freed from its prowling predations. They did not see the fog for what it really was – a not uncommon meteorological effect, given the climate and the season.

We gathered on the drive in front of Trelawny Hall, in sight of my betrothed, who watched anxiously from the large bay window of the drawing room. Farmer Bligh was in attendance, a shotgun broken over the crook of his arm, as were his farmhands. Even Baghinder, the late lord's houseboy, joined us, armed with his impressive, and not a little intimidating, talwar, preferring to carry the curved blade bestowed upon young Sikh men when they reached manhood. And there were dogs too – mastiffs, not unlike the hound that had prowled the Baskerville estate not so many months before, straining at the chains the gamekeepers' gripped in their gloved hands, and even a pair of bloodhounds.

Despite setting out with the best of intentions – to drive the Beast from cover and put an end to its savage reign – the hunting party's fervour also appeared to be its undoing. We hunted on foot, lines of men stretched out across the undulating moorland and exposed rocky bluffs. The shouts of the men calling to one another were muffled by the ground-hugging cloud, although the harsh barking of the dogs, keen to be after their quarry, carried through the mist and chilled me with the memory of a savage beast with another name.

After three hours' fruitless searching I began to fear that the Beast was keeping well clear of the moor that day, preferring not to leave the safety of its lair, wherever that might be. But it was then we heard the terrified scream. I shall never forget that sound for the rest of my days. It was a desperate, blood-chilling, womanly wail, and yet there could be no doubting that it had been made by a man.

We all rushed to converge on the spot from whence the scream had come, shouts of "This way!", "Did you hear that?" and "Over here!" echoing strangely through the fog. I was the first to arrive at the scene of the slaughter and see the body lying beside a spur of exposed limestone. There was no question that the man had been mauled by some large predator, just as there was no doubting the fact that he was dead. The throat, ripped out by a fang-filled maw, attested to that, the injury visible even though the body was lying on its side, blood soaking the man's clothes.

It was only in that moment, as the other members of the hunting party gathered around me, that I became aware of the danger I could have put myself in, coming upon the scene as quickly as I did. But by then the danger had well and truly passed; the noisy approach of the rest of the hunt, and their furiously barking dogs, had driven the beast away again.

However, the shock I felt at what I saw, seeing the man's carcass opened from belly to throat by the bestial nature of the attack, when one of the bolder gamekeepers turned the body over, was as nothing to the shock I felt when I saw his face. For despite the agonised rictus of pain etched forever on his features, I recognised the wretch. And what made that realisation even more shocking was that I had believed him to be dead already!

"It's Stapleton!" I said, giving voice to my surprise, unable to contain myself, even though no one else present knew to whom I referred. For the dead man was indeed Rodger Stapleton, the same villain who had masterminded the scheme whereby he had planned to have his maltreated hound kill me and thereby claim the Baskerville estate for himself.

"It looks like he's been attacked by a bear!" I was gabbling, shock causing me to be unguarded with my words.

"Or a big cat," came a voice from one among the hunting party.

My hunter's instinct taking over in that moment, I scoured the ground for any signs of the Beast's presence, but I could see none. "Where are the Beast's footprints?" I asked.

The other hunters began looking too, but none of them could find any sign that the cat – or whatever the Beast was – had been there, just a matter of moments beforehand. Only our own footprints could be seen in the soft earth, even though something as large as whatever had killed Stapleton would have surely left its own distinct prints behind.

It was then that some helpful Bodmin man said, "'Tis the Beast! It don't leave footprints, it being a phantom an' all."

Murmurs of agreement rippled through the throng, as if the fellow who had spoken was the wisest man in all the West Country. But I had encountered a so-called phantom beast before, and Stapleton's wounds spoke to me of something very real indeed, which had to be quite literally red in tooth and claw. But I could not explain the absence of marks to show which way it had gone or, indeed, from which direction it had come.

I was reminded of the fact that, when my own uncle, Sir Charles Baskerville, had died of fright upon seeing the terrible Hound, the footprints of a monstrous dog were found nearby. But here there was nothing. And so it was that I decided to contact Mr Sherlock Holmes to ask for his help.

* * *

I wrote to Mr Holmes that very afternoon, to let him know that Stapleton had not died in the Grimpen Mire as we had all presumed, and that he had turned up again, now most definitely dead.

I must confess, I'm not sure what surprised me more: finding Rodger Stapleton dead on the Trelawny estate, or finding Mr Sherlock Holmes calling at Trelawny Hall that very evening.

"Mr Holmes!" I exclaimed, when the consulting detective was admitted by Baghinder, after the house lamps had been lit.

"Sir Henry," he replied. "I called at your lodgings at The Cross Keys but when I learned that you were not there, I decided to see if you were dining with your betrothed this evening."

"How good it is to see you," I said, shaking him furiously by the hand. "I did not expect you to respond to my letter so quickly." And then, as my surprise subsided and logic began to take over, I went on, "In fact, you have arrived far sooner that I would have imagined possible!"

"You asked for my help, did you not?" Holmes challenged me.

"I did indeed. I did not mean to appear rude or ungracious," I apologised.

Holmes's gaze lingered on the displays of Indian weaponry and hunting trophies that adorned the entrance hall of the old house, the stuffed heads of exotic animals – antelope, hyenas, a water buffalo, and even a rhinoceros – and a number of animal skin rugs as well, tigers and bears mainly. All this put the moth-eaten stags' heads and dusty antlers of Baskerville Hall to shame, all a legacy of the late Lord Trelawny's time on the subcontinent.

"Do you hunt, Mr Holmes?"

We both turned at hearing the sweet voice, with its delicate Cornish twang, to see Loveday standing at the foot of the stairs, her face as pale as the white lace dress she wore, her blonde tresses arranged in an orderly fashion on the top of her head.

"Only ne'er-do-wells," Holmes replied, his eyes returning to the imitation glass eyes of a decades-dead Bengal tiger.

Wrong-footed, I introduced the detective to my betrothed, who then continued in a similar fashion as before.

"They are a legacy of my father's time in India," she explained.

"The late lamented Lord Tiernen Trelawny," Holmes said.

"Just so," Loveday replied. "Stories of his hunting expeditions are famous throughout Uttar Pradesh, or so my father told me."

"Ironic then," Holmes mused, "that the hunter should become the hunted."

"I say, Mr Holmes," I railed. The detective's cold manner and careless use of language forced me, as a gentleman, to interject. I was no stranger to the man's bizarre and unfathomable ways, but I could not tolerate plain bad manners.

"I apologise, Miss Trelawny," Holmes said. "I meant no offence. I was merely making an observation, which is, after all, what I am famed for."

"I understand, Mr Holmes," Loveday accepted graciously.

"We have yet to be introduced," the detective said, turning to Baghinder, who hovered at Loveday's shoulder, as he was wont to do.

"This is Baghinder," Loveday said, as the houseboy bowed. "Another legacy of my father's time in India."

"That's a most distinctive ring you are wearing, Baghinder," Holmes remarked, regarding the gold ring, set with an unusual gemstone, the precise nature of which I had wondered about before, but never remarked upon myself. "A tiger's eye, isn't it?"

"Yes, sir," the houseboy replied. "It was my father's."

"Now, if it is not too impolite to ask," Holmes said, "would I be right in thinking that dinner is about to be served?"

Over dinner I recounted to Mr Holmes all that had happened since my extended sojourn at Trelawny Hall had begun. His response to which was to ask to visit the moor and the scene of the crime the very next day, but not before examining Stapleton's body, which had found temporary accommodation at the doctor's surgery in nearby Bodmin.

After breakfast, the two of us set off for Bodmin and the doctor's. A grey mist hung over the moor, just as it had the day before, and I insisted on taking my Webley revolver with me, as a safety precaution.

The local physician, one Dr Philip Thorogood, led us from his fire-warmed consulting room into the icy, tiled surroundings of the cold store-cum-morgue that he shared with the butcher next door. If Mr Holmes felt any emotion upon seeing his erstwhile nemesis laid out on the slab, with irrefutable evidence of Rodger Stapleton's death presented before him, he did not show it. He merely stared at the frigid corpse with hawkish intensity.

"Ah, yes," he said, pointing with a gloved finger at the

ragged mess of the dead man's neck, "you can see the tooth marks quite clearly here" – I followed his finger as he indicated a spot below the jaw – "and here. Stapleton was quite clearly mauled to death."

"Then he *was* killed by the Beast," I murmured.

"That I do not know," Mr Holmes replied. "But what I can tell you, with absolute certainty, is that Stapleton was killed by a big cat. The bite marks confirm it."

"I had wondered if he was the victim of a psychopath, Mr Holmes," Dr Thorogood put in, and I couldn't help wonder if his interjection was intended to impress the world's foremost consulting detective.

"Then how do you explain these claw marks here and here?" Holmes asked, indicating numerous slashes to the man's clothes.

"Someone wielding a claw-like weapon of their own devising?" the doctor suggested, his imperious tone starting to waver.

"Dr Thorogood," Mr Holmes said pointedly, "do you have many patients escaping from the Hospital of St Lawrence? Besides, as I have often said before, when you have eliminated the impossible, whatever remains, however improbable, must be the truth. Equally, when the obvious is staring you in the face, no matter how unlikely it may seem, you need not look elsewhere for an explanation."

The doctor cast his eyes to the ground, shame-faced.

"Rodger Stapleton was mauled to death by a big cat. The question is, which one?"

After a spot of lunch at The Cross Keys, Holmes and I determined to walk back to Trelawny Hall along an old sheep track, stopping off at the scene of the crime on the way.

The chill mist had lifted at last, and as we strolled across the moor, the warmth of the sun on our skin pleasantly complemented the warmth in our bellies from the spatchcock and heady ale we had enjoyed at the inn. Such a change was this compared to the day before that it felt as if the killing of Stapleton had occurred months ago, rather than the previous day. But as we neared the spot where I had first come upon the reprobate's body, clouds appeared over the horizon and the afternoon turned a drab and forbidding grey.

"This is the scene of the crime, Holmes," I said as we approached the spot through the knotty grass and heather, the spur of exposed limestone confirming that we were in the right place.

Holmes took a few moments to cursorily examine the location – crouching to inspect a few blades of grass, or so it seemed – before stating, with great confidence, "This is not the scene of the crime."

"But this is where I found Stapleton's body," I said, bewildered.

"Precisely, and I am afraid, Sir Henry, that you have made a most elementary mistake in presuming that this is also where the wretch died. You told me yourself that very little blood was found upon the ground surrounding the body and that most of what you did observe was soaking the villain's clothes. As my good friend Dr Watson would tell you, if he were here, when a man's throat is sliced open, and the jugular exposed, as in the case of Rodger Stapleton's death, the pressure of the blood within the human body is enough to send it spurting a foot or more from the wound. And yet you can see for yourself that there is no such blood patterning here. Ergo, this is not the place where Stapleton was killed, it is only where his body was moved to, post-haste, post-mortem."

I moved my disbelieving gaze from Holmes to what I had believed to be the scene of the crime and back again, utterly dumbfounded.

"Trelawny Hall lies this way, does it not?" the detective said, pointing north-east across Bodmin Moor, to which I could only nod dumbly in response.

As the house came into view beyond the undulations of the moor, and the dry-stone walls and raised embankments that criss-crossed it, the reluctant sun gave up the ghost and began to sink lower and lower in the sky.

The route Holmes had taken over the moor brought us to the gloomy depths of a gulley – that on Dartmoor they would call a "goyal" – and in this hidden hollow he found the evidence he had clearly been looking for.

"Look, Sir Henry," he said, sounding almost excited by the discovery, just as I felt a mixture of shock and appalled horror. For the hollow contained the unmistakeable signs of slaughter, dried blood still visible upon the rocks and grass, there not having been any rainfall the previous night. "*This* is the scene of the crime."

The ground at the bottom of the hollow was damp, and in the cloying black mud I could make out myriad footprints – both those left by a man's boots and those of a huge feline.

Holmes looked suddenly grave. "Sir Henry, where is Miss Trelawny?"

"Back at the hall," I replied, my pulse quickening.

"And who is with her?"

"Why, Baghinder, the houseboy, I suppose." My heart was in the chill clutches of fear now.

"Then it pains me to inform you, Sir Henry, that she is in the most terrible danger!" the detective declared, setting off at a run. Reacting on instinct, I set off in hot pursuit, not knowing what terrible danger Loveday could be in, only that I had to do all I could to save her from it.

The prints left by the Beast were as clear as day to me now, despite the failing light, providing us with a trail to follow all the way back to Trelawny Hall, I realised with ever-deepening horror.

It could not have taken us more than a quarter of an hour to reach the house, but at the time it felt like hours. We arrived as dusk was falling and entered the house to find the place in darkness. The lamps had not yet been lit. Were we too late? Had the great danger Holmes had spoken of already come to pass?

I made for the stairs, calling for Loveday, trying to keep the fear from my voice. I was halfway up them when I heard the deep rumble of a growl only a moment before a sinuous shadow as big as a mountain lion, composed of lethal strength and predatory intent, detached itself from the darkness and struck at me with a paw, claws extended.

I cried out and stumbled backwards down the stairs, grabbing for my left arm where I felt the intense cold heat of unanticipated pain and then the warm dampness of blood.

My mind had barely registered that the Beast of Bodmin was somehow inside Trelawny Hall when the monstrous cat leapt at me, snarling in fury, and I saw a flash of white as it came down almost on top of me.

It was only later that I discovered precisely what happened next. Mr Holmes, who had already pulled a spear from a display of Indian weaponry at the foot of the stairs, hurled the weapon at the beast. The tip pierced its ribcage and found the animal's heart, its leap becoming a death-dive as the huge cat crashed down on the stairs and lay there, motionless, the sword protruding from its body.

I could barely make any of this out at the time, the details, along with the truth, only being revealed to me when Holmes found an oil lamp and lit it using a box of matches he carried about his person. As the flickering lamplight danced over the prone body of the Beast, I saw the orange and black stripes for the first time, along with the white fur covering its belly, now stained crimson with the creature's blood.

Not once, not even in all my wildest imaginings, had I imagined the Beast of Bodmin Moor to be a Bengal tiger.

"I would hazard that this was another part of Lord Trelawny's Indian legacy," Holmes said, as if reading my mind.

"Loveday!" I gasped, as I slowly began to put the pieces of the puzzle together, realising that the tiger had been coming down the stairs; I feared what I would find if I continued to make my way up. But continue I did, taking the oil lamp from Holmes to light the way, my own injury put from my mind by the horrible realisation, while Holmes pulled a sword from the same display that had held the spear and followed me upstairs.

Approaching Loveday's chamber, my heart thumping in my chest, I opened the door and found the room beyond bathed in light. My fiancée was sitting on top of her bedcovers, her knees pulled up to her chest, a wild look in her eyes, patently terrified.

"Loveday," I began, but as I moved towards the bed I was suddenly aware of noise and movement behind me, and I turned to see Baghinder appear from behind the bedroom door.

As shocked as I was by his sudden appearance, I was just as shocked to see him dressed, not in his normal servant's attire, but in the exotic garb of a Sikh warrior, his talwar blade raised above his head. And he doubtless would have brought it down upon mine if it hadn't been for Mr Holmes, who saved my life once again, coming in through the door as he did at that moment, fending off the blow with the sword he held in his own hand.

Having lost the element of surprise, Baghinder was forced to retreat as Holmes pressed home his newly gained advantage, forcing the Sikh back into the room.

The two men duelled, and in one unfortunate moment – that is, a moment more unfortunate than all those that had passed already – Holmes stumbled into me as he took a step back to avoid the warrior's sweeping blade, and the oil lamp was sent flying from my hand. It landed on the carpeted floor, before rolling to a stop at the foot of the drapes that had been pulled shut across the window against the approaching night.

The drapes caught light with a *whoomp* of flame that momentarily distracted Holmes from the Sikh, who saw an opportunity and took it, bearing down on the detective, and it was in that moment that the revolver barked in my hand.

It had been an instinctive reaction more than a premeditated one, but with the sharp report of the gun still ringing in my ears, Baghinder dropped to the floor, my shot having found its mark in the middle of his forehead.

Screaming like a banshee, Loveday threw herself at me.

She was like a woman possessed, attacking me as if she were some rabid beast, tearing at my face with fingers knotted into talons. That is until Holmes knocked her senseless with an open-handed blow to the back of her neck.

By now flames had climbed the drapes and were crawling across both the ceiling and the floor, the room filling with smoke. There was no way Holmes and I could hope to put the fire out now, and so our priority became to evacuate the house as quickly as we could. With Holmes leading the way, I bundled the senseless Loveday up in my arms and carried her downstairs and out through the entrance hall as the blaze took hold in earnest behind us.

I fell to my knees on the lawn outside the house, laying Loveday down on the damp ground, coughing the smoke from my lungs, my emotions in turmoil as I gazed down at the woman I loved, through watering eyes. She looked as if she were only sleeping, the innocent I had once believed her to be. In my heightened emotional state, I tried to reconcile how my heart ached for her still with how she had reacted to my method of dealing with Baghinder.

And then, my mind and my body overwhelmed, I collapsed on the ground beside Loveday as fire consumed the Trelawny family home, the flames lighting up the Bodmin Moor night.

"Why?" I cried, momentarily losing control of my inherited British reserve. "Why?"

"I believe I can explain," Holmes said, having recovered from the effects of smoke inhalation far quicker than I. "But first I feel I must explain how I came to arrive here last night, before your letter had even left Cornwall."

My mind returned then to that moment, barely twenty-four hours previously, and the surprise I had felt at his sudden arrival.

"I began my investigation long before you were even aware of the danger you were in, when I read the announcement of your engagement to Miss Loveday Trelawny in *The Times*. Considering what happened last time, and how you were so cruelly duped by Mr and Mrs Stapleton, I decided it wise to conduct an investigation into Miss Loveday Trelawny's background, to make sure you weren't being duped again. I discovered, as you already knew, that she was indeed the daughter of Lord Tiernen Trelawny, who had spent some time in India. Indeed India was where Loveday spent her formative years, in the care of her native nursemaid – that is until she was sent to boarding school in England. However, as well as being the place where Loveday was born, it was also where her mother passed away. When Trelawny eventually returned to England, he did so accompanied by Loveday's ayah and the nursemaid's son, Baghinder."

Holmes paused in his recount then, his brow furrowing. "The tiger troubles me though."

"Could it not be that it was brought back to England as a cub, as a family pet perhaps?" I suggested.

"I'm afraid not," Holmes replied. "The animal that attacked you was a young male. Besides, even if Lord Trelawny had returned from India with a pet tiger, the species does not live long enough for it to have been the same animal."

"But how does the death of Rodger Stapleton link to what happened to us tonight, and Baghinder's crazed attack?" I asked, still trying to make sense of everything.

"I surmised that Baghinder was actually Lord Trelawny's son; when Trelawny returned to England, he did so accompanied by Loveday's ayah and her son, Baghinder.

But why bring this woman to England when Loveday had no further need of a nursemaid? I deduced that there was some understanding between Trelawny and the ayah, one which was clarified when I arrived last night and saw the signet ring Baghinder was wearing on the little finger of his left hand. A signet ring is given from father to son, and is a British, not a Sikh practice, therefore Baghinder's father must be British. Given the circumstances, Trelawny was the logical candidate, and Baghinder might want to press his own claim to inherit his father's estate above that of his half-sister and her future husband. I wanted to determine that you and your fiancée were safe, but without making the rogue aware of my intentions, fearing that with Lord Trelawny dead, his son might try to do away with you both and claim Trelawny Hall as his own.

"I took the first train I could from London Paddington and arrived at Bodmin Road station just as your letter was about to be taken to the capital. Fortunately the stationmaster, who as you doubtless know also doubles as the postmaster, recognised me from my appearance in the paper following the Baskerville case and passed the letter to me directly. I cogitated upon the contents of your letter as I made my way to Trelawny Hall, but…"

The detective broke off, and by the light of the burning house I could see that he looked troubled.

"What is it, Holmes?" I pressed.

"It is just that Miss Trelawny's reaction to the houseboy's death has caused me to reconsider my initial assessment."

The sound of sobbing, and Holmes's mention of Loveday, had me turning to look at her once more, and I saw that she was conscious again, tears running down her face.

"How did you expect me to react to the cold-blooded

murder of the man I loved?" she sobbed.

"It's alright, I'm here," I began before I realised what my fiancée meant, and it was a truth too horrible to countenance.

"You mean you had an incestuous relationship with your half-brother?" Holmes said. For my own part I was made mute by the horror of it all.

"You might call it that," she riled, "but we shared a bond few others have ever known."

I could not hide my disgust, and it was all I could do not to strike her across the face. The revelation that I had been betrayed once again, and in such a sordid fashion, became a very real knot of sickness in my gut. When once I would have happily gazed upon her beauty all day and all night, now I could not bring myself to even look at her.

"You don't understand! We loved each other!" she spat. "My father didn't understand either! That's why he had me committed to the Hospital of St Lawrence" – I knew of the place by its other name, the Cornwall County Asylum – "and Baghinder sent back to India, but not before beating him within an inch of his life."

I physically withdrew from her at the confession of her madness. But now that Loveday had started talking she seemed unable to stop. It was as if the floodgates had been opened. "Baghinder never forgot me and planned to return for me as soon as he could."

"But having been disinherited by your father, and not having the financial wherewithal to simply pay for his passage back to England, he had to find another way to achieve the desired end," Holmes interjected.

"He joined a circus in India where he studied under a big cat tamer. It took years, but we both knew that the wait would be worth it, knowing that one day we would be reunited again. And at last the circus came to England."

"So I presume he absconded with one of his charges and made his way back to Cornwall."

"With Baghinder half the world away, or so my father believed, in a fit of compassion he had me released from the asylum but kept me here instead, within sight at all times and under virtual house arrest."

"So the two of you plotted your revenge. Whose idea was it to set the tiger on Lord Trelawny when he was out walking on the moor?" Holmes asked, his tone becoming that of an interrogator.

"We did everything together," Loveday hissed, her venomous green eyes blazing. "Everything!"

"So why embroil poor Sir Henry in your schemes?"

"Upon claiming my inheritance, only then did I discover that there was no inheritance. We were poor. Our father had left us destitute. All we had left of any worth was the house."

"And so you hatched a plan to entrap my friend here," Holmes said with a sneer of disdain, "motivated by pure greed. And I suppose, having arranged one man's death already, it was even easier to countenance arranging another. By making much of your family's so-called curse you hoped to hurry the wedding, so that you might rid yourself of your cursed family name. But things were made even harder for you and your half-brother when Stapleton turned up."

Mention of Stapleton shook me from my horrified stupor. "What do you mean, Holmes?" I gasped. "Stapleton came here on purpose?"

"Yes, Sir Henry, and all because of you. He had maintained as keen an interest in your comings and goings as I had. Having escaped the Grimpen Mire, and discovering that he was believed to be dead, he had the perfect cover, which allowed him to spy on you and work out how to bring his original plan to fruition. I imagine he also looked into Miss Trelawny's background and discovered that she had enjoyed a prolonged stay at the asylum. With such information in his possession, I suspect he blackmailed her into letting him in on the plan," he turned to the weeping Loveday then. "Isn't that right?"

This provoked more heart-wrenching sobs from my duplicitous fiancée. "He said I should marry Henry, and then, in due course, my husband would meet with an accident. I would marry Stapleton and we would share the Baskerville fortune between us."

"Stapleton having first assumed a new, false identity, no doubt, considering he was still a wanted criminal. But he was unaware of the precise nature of your relationship with your half-brother."

"Baghinder had no intention of letting that happen. Stapleton came to the hall again, just after you had all set out on your futile hunt. I don't know why."

"I don't suppose you gave yourself the chance to find out. Perhaps it was arrogance on his part," Holmes suggested, "proving to himself how clever he was to be within yards of you, Sir Henry, without you having any idea. Or maybe it was just to remind you, Miss Trelawny, that there was no escaping the abominable pact you had made."

"Baghinder set the tiger on him. He wasn't expecting that." She giggled then, her laughter chilling me to the bone more than her heartfelt howls ever could.

"But Baghinder joined us on the hunt," I pointed out, recalling the houseboy's presence among the hunters gathered at the front of the house.

"Did you actually see him when you were out on the moor?" Holmes asked.

"No," I admitted. "I confess I did not." Clearly the scoundrel had done everything to give the impression that he was joining us, before doubling back.

"Where do you keep the tiger hidden?" Holmes asked. "In the stable block? In the old kennels? And I suppose Baghinder let it out from time to time to hunt the local farmers' livestock. It would have been cheaper than paying the local butcher in order to feed the animal and in turn would have avoided any awkward questions."

Loveday said nothing.

"No matter. That is not important now. Having done away with Stapleton, Baghinder must have realised that it would be easy to trace the tiger's tracks back to the hall, and so he moved the body from the hollow, while the hunting party was out on the moor fruitlessly searching for the Beast of Bodmin, hoping that no one would discover the connection or see him in the process."

"But I heard Stapleton scream," I piped up then. "I came upon the body within minutes."

"You heard someone scream," Holmes said, with a wry smile. "Logic would suggest that it was actually Baghinder. While you were running towards Stapleton's corpse, he could return to the house and cover his tracks. It's only a shame he didn't think to cover the tiger's tracks as well. And once they knew that Sherlock Holmes was on the case, Miss Trelawny and Baghinder must have realised that the game was up, and so planned to eliminate both of us. And what then, Miss Trelawny? Make good your escape back to India?"

"We realised that the money didn't really matter after

all," she replied distantly, the conflagration reflected in her moisture-filled eyes. "It didn't matter where we were just as long as we were together. And it still doesn't."

She stared at the burning house. There could be no stopping the fire now. It had become the funeral pyre of her hopes and dreams, the wretched houseboy and his savage pet cremated along with the rest of Lord Trelawny's Indian legacy.

"Let me look at that arm of yours," Holmes said, carefully pulling back my ragged shirtsleeve to assess the damage beneath. There were five clean cuts but the blood was already starting to clot.

And that was all the distraction Loveday needed. Looking back on it now, I suppose with her lover and her pet and what little that was left of her inheritance going up in flames, she decided she had nothing left to live for. Or perhaps she realised that the only future that awaited her was interment within the county asylum for the rest of her life, a prospect she could not stomach.

Whatever her misguided reasoning, as Holmes tended to my arm, she rose and, before either of us could stop her, strode through the front door of the house and into the welcoming flames.

And so it was that the real Beast of Bodmin, Miss Loveday Trelawny, died, but the legend did not die with her. As I said before, legends have a habit of persisting, and the counties of south-west England seem to have more monsters than most.

THE CASE OF THE BLIND MAN'S SPECTACLES

Marcia Wilson

My readers know I tend to use Lestrade as the John Bull, but **Gregson** demanded his turn. I don't think Arthur Conan Doyle could create a boring character if he tried, and Gregson is fascinating. Sherlock Holmes calls Gregson and Lestrade "the pick of a bad lot". The two bitterly compete for advancement within the Yard's meritocracy, and they even *look* like complete opposites. Gregson has always fought me for his voice – smug, confident, and unthinkingly brave. He runs to, not away from, trouble. I respect the man but hope he would never arrest me. He plays no favourites and never lets his emotions colour his work. I've never lost the suspicion that he thinks of everyone, even Sherlock Holmes, as a possible suspect in a crime somewhere. In a lot of fiction, you see policemen wrestle with the question "Could so-and-so do it?" Gregson never wastes time with that. As a military policeman I know keeps saying, "You've got to stop underestimating people." Gregson lives by that rule.

—Marcia Wilson

"Well, Mr Holmes," and I put it to him just like that, "if I might be so bold, why would a blind man wear glasses he doesn't need – and glasses such as these?"

"Ah, that is an excellent question, Gregson." And Sherlock Holmes smiled.

We were having this stimulating debate in the most unlikely of places under even more unlikely circumstances. I was giving my case to Mr Holmes as we sat in Dr Watson's new surgery, waiting on Lestrade's stitches. I knew it would make that runt rot from the inside to know I was consulting Holmes whilst he laid about dead to the world (Watson hadn't even needed the chloroform), but I would take that satisfaction later. I won't admit it to anyone, but if anything makes me happier than beating Lestrade, it's the satisfaction of watching Sherlock Holmes light up like a lamp when he's got a murky case before his eyes.

But I'm getting ahead of myself again.

I'd known what I was getting into, but it wasn't like I had much choice in the matter. I was in a cab under weather conditions that were better suited for sleds, and Lestrade was bleeding all over my lap. It was no simple matter, holding a compress to that fool's thick skull whilst grappling on to the seat for dear life.

But you don't hesitate in this line of work, and once I'd made up my mind, I got us to Dr Watson's surgery (I reasoned he'd be new enough that he wouldn't be very busy) and then threw twice the normal fare to the driver to go collect Sherlock Holmes from Baker Street.

Watson's a decent enough sort and he's military to the core so you can usually count on him to choose to treat a bleeding man of law over a lassitudinarian with a cold. Sure enough, it took one look at us on the step before he had us inside his surgery and asking the maid to kindly call for the locum to take the front-room patients, thank you.

By the time Mr Holmes got there Lestrade was halfway through his surgery. With no more than a brief greeting he hung up his raincoat next to ours, pulled out his already-packed travelling pipe, and sat down in the guest chair by the fire for me to give the details. This is where my story to Mr Holmes starts, and I'll tell it to you the same way I told it to him, though due to the sensitive nature of this case, some things have been altered.

If there's rubbish gadding about London, you can bet I'll find Lestrade not far from it. The man has no discretion. For all his years in the CID and the fact that he wears a suit to work, he thinks and acts like he's still a constable; even keeps his time-worn truncheon under his coat for old times' sake. It is embarrassing, and I've polished him for it. But he just glares at me with his shifty black eyes and says some of us need a bit of extra help. As if it's my fault he's a runt.

Now, the way of it is, I'm right more often than he because I see things better. I've got discretion, and I want to live long enough to be promoted. So I stop when the whistles go off around me. Six constables, all from old Parker's divisions, running with their clubs up, splashing through the puddles and emptying them almost as fast as the rain fills 'em back up. I was on my way to a cold supper at The Flying Tree, but duty forever calls, and you never know which case will be the one that recognises your hard work and dedication.

And, one ought to be alert within twenty minutes' walk of any powder mill.

I'm sure you know the exact place where it all began, Mr Holmes. That crumbly old canal on the eastern side? What a nightmare of a patrol! If you're going to run into trouble it is usually in one direction.

Those policemen were running for whatever-trouble in the direction of one of the pellet houses, and I followed with, I confess, a bit of apprehension. We cut our teeth as beat police hearing stories of the explosion at Waltham back before the Americans' war, but I couldn't hear anything suspicious. And it was rather quiet; the whole cut was shut down for repairs. Even the Irish wouldn't bother to throw tacks in the mills right now – there was nothing to damage until the mills were finalised for the Royal Artillery, and that wouldn't happen until the spring flooding dropped low enough to let the canal drain enough for dredging and patching.

It got my attention that there were a few people who weren't police headed for the trouble too. There's the usual chasers, mostly street Arabs hoping to find something to steal or information to sell to one of our own informers, but a few men were in the hurly-burly too, and they were dressed well enough that it seemed they would have better things to do than poke their noses into affairs that didn't concern them. A milk-faced little swell in a striped suit even bumped into me, nearly making me fall, and I sent him flying with a shove. He whined like a dog but kept away from me after that.

The fuss stopped and swarmed at a section of broken canal. The water was halfway down and the smell was getting through the meltwater of spring. Mr Striped Suit and his fellows in sensationalism pulled back, their fine white handkerchiefs to their prim noses.

Lying on the path along which the horses drew the powder barges was a man's corpse. He was flat on his back with a snow-white beard pointed to the heavens. He hadn't been there long; the clothes weren't yet soaked through with the rain, but there was a thin red puddle spreading from under his head. An umbrella sprawled broken by his side and his walking stick was in pieces about his feet. I wasn't surprised to see that amongst all the running and pushing and shoving of the policemen against the curious, Lestrade was there. As I said, he's always in the middle of a mess. He wasn't looking too well, and for him that's quite an achievement.

I yelled at the top of my lungs and pulled out my warrant card, managing to barge through the throng. I took another look at the body, then decided to taunt Lestrade for letting his men get out of control. Any group with Constable Smerdon in it means trouble; the man wants to get promoted so badly he doesn't ask himself how he's going to do it.

Lestrade's colour was even worse than normal, yellow like a malarial, and he was holding his head in his hands against his muddy knees. As usual, he'd put on his best-looking suit and shoes to start the day and ruined it all before the end – man can't solve a case in his head; oh, no, he has to get down in the dirt. Really. He was covered with mud from where he'd fallen face-first into the muck. I don't know how his wife can keep him.

What got me was that he was missing his hat. Lestrade's stupid, but he does answer the Yard's minimal requirement for intelligence, so he's never without his bowler. None of us would dare otherwise, as they're as good as a leather helmet and there's always someone trying to throw something at your head. I started looking for it in the weeds.

Lestrade finally noticed me. "What're you doing here?" he mumbled, and he sounded foggy like he was having trouble thinking.

"Looking for your hat."

"I think it was knocked in th'canal."

I took a closer look at him. On the back of his head was a nasty gash making a mess of his collar, coat, and probably that expensive shirt underneath. I was about to point that out when I saw there was something queer about the gash. It went straight down like someone had tried to cut a stripe on his head with a knife, and it was deep enough to score the bone. The blood was coming out like a fountain. Constable Brewster knelt and put his handkerchief on Lestrade's head to stop the bleeding.

"What happened, man?" I asked but Lestrade was all grey now and his eyes were rolling up. I'd wasted my time asking him the wrong question.

I looked around. There was a dead man, but no sign of a trail left by his murderer. Even if we'd blocked the scene off before it was trampled by muddy boots, we wouldn't be able to do a thing against the rain, which was really starting now. If a man had set out today to plan murder, it couldn't have been more perfect. The rain was so thick you could barely see to the next road marker, the roar of water swallowed up most of the sound, and every clue on the path was washing straight into the canal. Constable Smerdon was glaring over his chinstrap at me like I was stealing his case, and I could feel the temperature dropping. It takes time for the cold to settle in the lowlands, but when it does you need to be careful.

A closer look at the dead man wasn't any better. He didn't have eyes; his lids had been sewn shut long ago. The rest of him was short and fat inside a coal-black suit and matching frockcoat, with bright brass cufflinks at his wrists, which matched the tie-pin at his throat, and his brass-plated watch in his waistcoat pocket. All four items had the same stamp: a circular belt buckle. It had the look of something like the Freemasons about it, and I decided it was a clue to study later.

A finely made pair of wire-rimmed spectacles lay under his shoulder. I could see that the lenses were thick but not much so – maybe a sixteenth of an inch at the most. So far they were the oddest thing on the scene, so I wrapped them up in a wax envelope.

The man was bald, which made it easy to see how he had been killed; his skull had been opened by a single slash. He had thick, glossy white moustaches and an arrowhead beard, with none of the yellowing and staining from tobacco smoke, snuff, or that vulgar chew. His hands were clean as a baby's, nails trimmed like a gentleman's, but when I picked up the left one there were some funny little callouses on the insides of his index finger and middle thumb-joint, and some tiny line-thin callouses on the tips of the pads.

Looking at his right hand, I expected to see something to prove he was left-handed, but I was surprised to see the same callouses. You get to see a lot of strange marks on a man's hands in police work; a criminal can't hide their skin as easily as a dyed beard or a new suit of clothes. But for the life of me, I never saw anything like this. Everyone favours one hand or the other, but who favours both? And what tools would he be using to make these marks?

I was still trying to think this out when Brewster called out that he couldn't stop Lestrade's bleeding. Duty to the Brotherhood called, and I ordered a tarpaulin spread over the body and for it to be guarded until collected and taken to the morgue. The police surgeon wouldn't tolerate any nonsense; the dead man would be safe from interference of evidence.

I sent Smerdon to call a cab. Protocol prefers a wounded man in an ambulance, but cabs are faster. Somewhere in the middle of this circus, I came to the conclusion that I'd best bring in Sherlock Holmes.

Lestrade sagged like an old stocking and I had to pull out my own handkerchief to staunch the flow from his head. It was all over his back, and my wife wouldn't be pleased with the state of my sleeve. I'd almost got his blockhead bandaged up when the cab showed, and I bundled him up in it and slammed the door with a final bark loud enough for everyone to hear that Sherlock Holmes needed to meet me at Dr Watson's surgery.

I'd lost valuable time in looking around. I should have tried harder to get Lestrade's account of the attack. After a few minutes of poking I managed to get through his groggy brain.

"What happened, Lestrade?"

"Escorting Mr Holloway," he mumbled (I'm translating because he didn't sound at all that clear). "Got jumped."

"So I see. What did they look like?"

"Went. For… for… for… 'is throat… told'm't'run… forgot…"

"Forgot what?"

"H'can't see. Couldn't see t'run."

And then the fool fainted in my lap.

Mr Holmes listened to my story politely through his cloud of smoke. I could understand his snort of laughter – it was a little funny when you thought of it. Lestrade would be spitting nails once he came around – whenever that would be. Dr Watson had been listening as well, but I can imagine it wasn't so easy to pay attention while sewing up Lestrade. At least Lestrade was behaving himself, still being unconscious.

"He ought to be more like his old self when he wakes up," the doctor said. "I would give him the full day and one night; that was a lot of blood lost in a very short time. Why, he might have bled to death if you hadn't brought him here."

"Lestrade doesn't like it when the constables are too solicitous. Thinks it makes him look bad."

"He looks bad enough. That's quite a cut." Watson washed his hands in the basin as Holmes wrote in a small notebook.

"Well, I've got questions of my own. First of all, Mr Holmes, the late Mr Holloway, whoever he is, was wearing a suit and coat worth more than a two-year coal budget, yet he was wearing brass trim like a commoner trying to ape his betters."

"Ah, Gregson," Holmes said at last. He lowered his pipe long enough to blow a ring. "That is a good question. Could it be that this 'Mr Holloway' is actually Lestrade's slurred attempt to say Mr Noah 'Hollowell' of the gunpowder manufactory fortune? Members of that trade wear brass, for it cannot strike a spark like iron nor conduct electricity like gold or silver. The symbol you describe is an alchemical symbol for saltpetre, the oxidizing element in gunpowder."

I sighed – both because Mr Holmes had managed to draw what had to be the proper conclusion, but also because that still wasn't enough to solve the case. "Well, there you are. That would be more than likely. The name's familiar to me, but I can't say I've ever seen his face in the papers. Nor does it explain his odd callouses."

"Mr Hollowell lost his eyesight in a gunpowder explosion. It ended his career in grains and measurements, but after his recuperation he discovered a new talent in building fine models for the military. You may not have seen his visage in the papers, Gregson, but you have seen his work countless times. It would be his models you marvelled over at the Great Exhibition, or in the museum exhibits for artillery. Of late his fame was centred about a toy cannon that fired a cork bullet over the Tower of London with minimal reactive impact upon its base."

"What? It was in the papers as a new model for the army! Well, that explains why I've never seen callouses like that before."

"The man's life motto was discretion." Holmes frowned a little as he smoked, for he was almost out of tobacco. I offered him my cut of Cavendish, just to see if he would take it over his usual shag. He did, and leaned back. "Hollowell has spent years building models, working on as many as ten at a time. His patience is extraordinary, but so are the rewards he reaps from it. But this is all window-dressing, Gregson. You don't need to know the murderer's identity quite as urgently as all that, do you? Not if your cohort can wake up and tell you."

"I'm not happy at the idea of sitting and waiting for evidence to come to me, Mr Holmes. Not only was there a murder in broad daylight, there was almost the added attempted murder of a fellow policeman! And as for Lestrade, Dr Watson can't guarantee he'll wake up in time to find the killer."

"I fear not." Watson scowled, a little nettled, just as I would be if I felt my profession was being belittled.

"So while the facts are the facts as I've reported them to you, a policeman is taught to pay attention to things that don't fit. And of all the strange things about this murder, these funny little spectacles *do not fit*!"

"You still have them, Gregson?"

I held out the envelope. It was sticky from drying blood on the inside. Mr Holmes pulled on the thinnest gloves I've ever seen, prised the lips of the envelope apart and pulled the spectacles out with the help of a pair of Dr Watson's surgical tweezers.

The doctor whistled softly. "Genuine gold. That looks like an expensive pair of spectacles!"

"And incongruous, wouldn't you agree, with the brass accoutrements of the owner?" said Holmes. He turned his head to look at me like a hawk before a fresh mouse. "Gregson, perhaps it is time to hear the rest of this story?"

"There were deeply lined impressions in the sides of his face." I ran my fingertips from the outer corners of my eye straight to the back of the ear. "Those spectacles didn't fit at all. His nose was red from the pinch in the front. It must have hurt him to wear them at all, I'll be bound.

Mr Holmes, why would he wear glasses with clear lenses? The blind do wear spectacles but the lenses are smoked or tinted to show they are blind."

Mr Holmes didn't answer me at first. He busied himself packing more of my tobacco into his pipe with a long, cool stare into the little fire burning in the grate.

"The answer is before your own eyes, Gregson," Holmes said at last. "If a blind man does not need spectacles, why does he wear them?"

I felt myself turn red, but I cooled off just as quick when I realised he wasn't showing off or criticizing my workmanship. "I feel there is something you know but aren't telling me, Mr Holmes."

"A theory without evidence is a poor answer on its own. The facts are with you, and you have the most important clue here: these singular spectacles."

I took them back and peered more closely. Now that I was in a quiet room, out of the rain and not surrounded by shouting constables, I was able to pay better attention to the details. The arms were twisted like a pair of vines, with tiny dots cut into the metal; some sort of delicate floral engraving.

"These are a woman's!" I blurted out. I was so shocked I almost dropped them in my lap.

"If I may?" Dr Watson asked. The man is always very polite. He took up the tweezers and turned the frames back and forth. "And they would appear to be of a strength for reading glasses, not for distance." He pointed to the sides of the frames, which were thicker around the lenses. "My friend Doyle has been showing me some of the tricks of his trade in ophthalmology. Whoever bought these had a stigmatism."

"That would hardly fit the description of your murder victim, Gregson," Holmes murmured.

"No, not at all," I grumbled. "Look, if I've had all the help I'll get here, I'd best be on my way and return to the case."

"For such as it is, Gregson," Holmes smiled. "I daresay it won't take you long to crack this little riddle."

That wasn't my worry. If I didn't solve it before Lestrade woke up, it wouldn't be my case any longer. I took back the spectacles and sent a sad thought for my missed appointment with The Flying Tree's cold roasted lamb.

On the way to the Yard I went through the facts. Lestrade had been "working" with Hollowell, but for what reason? It was all too queer. If Hollowell was frightened enough for his life that he wanted Lestrade to guard him… who wanted to kill him? The killer had attacked Lestrade first. If you want someone dead really badly, you plan a way past the guards first – otherwise you waste time taking them out, giving the victim time to get away. Lestrade was covered with mud in the front where he'd fallen – a hasty killer would think he'd dispatched them both and run off.

Or a first-time killer. They make mistakes like that; their nerve fails or they kill under an impulse they regret. Which was which? Or… was it an unrelated case, with a killer operating under separate motives? It wouldn't be the first time Lestrade fell victim to his own bad luck and worse timing – his ugly face makes him a natural for work in disguise, and someone might have recognised him from those jobs.

I needed to find the answers if I wanted to solve this case before Lestrade recovered. I had stumbled onto it by virtue of being the only uninjured detective on the scene. But if Lestrade woke up on the morrow with the full story and the identity of his attacker, it wouldn't be my case any more.

* * *

I know we Yarders have a reputation for being disorderly, but at least we've lived among the mess enough that we know how to navigate in it. Somewhere on paper were the missing pieces of this nasty little puzzle. Lestrade was watching over Hollowell for a reason, and that meant the Home Office knew about it. I decided to start with the one man who was friends with us both: Inspector Bradstreet.

I found him easily enough – it would be a lot harder *not* to find him, considering you could project a silhouette theatre between his shoulders. He was perched in his usual spot in the archives, examining a book on nautical knots and trying to draw copies with the hand that wasn't holding his mug of tea.

"Still looking for that strangler?" I said as hello.

He rumbled under his moustaches. "Such as it is. How many left-handed ropewalkers are in the world anyway?"

"In the world? It doesn't matter. You just have to worry about this city of millions." I took the chair in front of him. "Hear about Lestrade?"

"Eh, terrible. Was it blood loss or a concussion?"

"Watson says blood loss."

"He'll be fine then. Better than his client."

"So you know something about his case?"

"Lestrade complained about it. A lot." Bradstreet shrugged. He's single-minded and doesn't like to think about more than his own work. "Private contract. He got approval for it because of the quality of the client. Somebody important with the government; he said he wanted an escort for a while because he was being bothered. Didn't say what, didn't tell Lestrade what either. It was driving him half to the madhouse."

"Hmph."

I got the fish eye. "Are you trying to steal his case from him?"

"I don't see how that could happen. I'm just trying to find out who attempted to kill a fellow detective."

Bradstreet is one of the most sceptical men I know, and that makes him a good policeman. He's less suspicious when it comes to other detectives, so he just nodded his approval. Well, Bradstreet wasn't being a complete mark; a blow against one of us looks bad for all of us. The attacks on both Lestrade and Hollowell were from behind, so this worm had no problem with cowardly attacks.

"Lestrade was steaming in his collar over it. Told me he hated every bit of it but couldn't say no."

I thanked him and went to the morgue. That's never a cheerful place, as they built it to be a natural ice-cave. The police surgeon already had the victim on the slab. With the blood washed off and the wound cleaned he was a sight easier on the eyes.

I took his box of personal belongings and went through it. The new staff are delightfully meticulous, so the box was divided into sections labelled by location: coat pocket; trousers; sleeve; shoe. Most of it I'd already seen: his brass bits and bobs (the watch was still running); a tooled leather *porte-monnaie* from the left coat pocket; a mechanical crayon in the right pocket; an ink pen in the left; some loose coins; and the tiniest tool kit I've ever seen in the possession of a respectable, law-abiding man.

I opened the *port-monnaie*, thinking to find something that would help; gentlemen do not carry large amounts of money about them because it is, to put it bluntly, for the lower sort of man. But if he had a large amount on him, that could imply something suspicious.

This was not the case, just three one-pound notes, carefully folded once in the upper right corner. I'd seen the blind use that trick of marking their paper money so they could price by touch. I pulled it all out and my fingers found a small square plate of metal – brass like everything else. It was an engraving, deeply cut, but I couldn't make out the image.

Rubbings are something police are expected to know how to do, but dashed if I could tell you the last time I'd had to pull that trick. I tore out a page from my notebook and went to work with a pencil. Before long I was looking at a woman in an old-fashioned bonnet. There was a book in her lap and she was wearing a pair of very familiar-looking spectacles. The letters "LB" were in the corner.

If I felt smug, it lasted until I was halfway out of the morgue. That was when I realised I'd missed a vital clue: the pen in one pocket and pencil in the other strengthened my theory about the strange callouses on Hollowell's hands. Hollowell was ambidextrous.

Well, that was one mystery solved. Off to solve the rest. If I kept on my feet, I might be able to arrest someone in a few hours. The hard part was identifying the murderer; after that it would be a matter of sending out a search. Even the French know we Englishmen are the best in a mass manhunt. That was why desperate men tried to flee for the Continent.

The rain that erased the crime scene's evidence was helping me, a little. Weather would slow the usual departure off the island, but it wouldn't cut it entirely. I had a little time yet before I could call for a manhunt.

All I needed was one shred of evidence – one good idea of the killer's identity.

I went to the archives and pulled down every directory and newspaper I could find in the right area. Our intelligence is better than most, but we're often restricted to what the Home Office thinks we should know.

Gunpowder, however… gunpowder happens to be something that makes everyone a little uneasy. And not even the Foreign Office could keep the Yard from collecting newspapers.

I soon found our Mr Noah Hollowell, a "talented inventor and patent-collector of good family". An accompanying photograph of Hollowell as a young man showed him without spectacles and with plenty of hair. One photograph led to more, and I spent the night taking books off shelves and tearing up foolscap for bookmarks.

Hollowell was a clever man according to the records of 1860, if famous for his stubbornness. He'd taken to the family business like a duck to water, but wanted things his own way from the first. This didn't sit too well with his cousin and co-owner of the family empire, Jerimiah Wentforth.

Wentforth was a man of vision, it was said, always seeking innovative ways to create different ignitions and explosive matters. Despite prickly feelings, the two were able to get along for at least five years. They shared the same grandparents, and Wentforth was planning to marry Lucinda Bateman, the daughter of a business partner in the American South, even though Miss Lucinda couldn't decide between the cousins.

"1860" and "outside business partner" and "gunpowder" gave me a sick feeling of dread. Sure enough, the tale exploded, literally, with Fort Sumter in North America. Wentforth was one of the Englishmen who supported the slave owners (like Lucinda's father), and his cousin supported the North's interests, citing old family ties in New York. The cousins were at each other's throats, both sent before the magistrate for public fighting multiple times, but neither one gave an inch until Hollowell walked into one of the family mills and a case of arson, which Wentforth claimed was saboteurs bitter about England's neutrality. Hollowell survived the blast, but his eyes and half his workers did not. He was still bedridden when Miss Lucinda swallowed poison.

That brought me up sharp. The last picture I could find was a grainy image of the woman at some social event. Her father stood on one side, Wentforth on the other.

And there my circumstantial evidence dried up, but if I needed it by that point, I would have been even thicker than Lestrade.

Mr Holmes had seen through this entire case. My account had just been a final note on a story he'd already known! Lestrade had been saying "Wentforth" not "went for". And those spectacles?

Like a clap of thunder I recalled his voice: *"The answer is before your own eyes, Gregson."*

Why would a blind man wear spectacles like that?

So they would be seen.

Smoked glasses hide a blind man's eyes, show the world he's blind but discreetly, hiding white cataracts or empty sockets…

Hollowell *wanted* his ruined eyes to be seen… by one particular person.

And when I'd bawled out Watson's address to the driver, everyone in earshot had heard me.

I swore, and then put poor Constable Georges in charge of setting all the relevant newspapers aside in one stack for later.

I issued the order for the manhunt.

Then I sent every spare man to Dr Watson's practice.

We stopped a full street back from the practice and sent the wagons on without us – with any luck Wentforth wouldn't know the sound an empty carriage makes as opposed to one loaded down with policemen. The rain was as heavy as ever; you could barely make out the halos of brown light from the streetlamps, but the lamps in Watson's consulting room were still burning, long past decent hours.

I crept to the front of the building while Bradstreet went to the back with his men. I could hear three raised voices, two of which I knew: Dr Watson's, angry and soldierly, and Mr Holmes's, cold and sharp like a pair of scissors. The third voice was high-pitched and reedy, on the edge of panic. It made a yelping sound, and I knew where I'd heard it before. I pulled back and signalled Brewster and Rees. They're big lads and used to dancing with criminals; two shoulders drove in the door with a single blow and I ran into the consulting room for the second time that day.

The heavy table was on its side, shielding a still unconscious Lestrade. Dr Watson and Mr Holmes stood before him, with Watson brandishing a poker, and Holmes didn't look any less dangerous with a shovel in his hand. They were holding off the fourth man—a little fellow in a striped suit trying to get through their defences with a nasty looking Elgin pistol—half gun, half large knife.

"Hello, Mr Wentforth," I said. "I don't suppose you remember me?"

Wentforth could hold his own against two able men like Mr Holmes and Dr Watson, but now he had a room full of men and an Elgin can only shoot once. He spun and ran wild, straight into Inspector Bradstreet. I almost felt sorry for that little blighter. One does not try to kill Bradstreet's friends when he is around to do something about it. He plucked the man off the floor like a child and coolly freed him of the Elgin and set him back down, perhaps just a little too hard, because Wentforth took a sudden nap after that.

The details were easy enough to figure out after it was all over. Hollowell always swore Wentforth had sabotaged the mill and caused the explosion. Evidence of arson had been found, but claims against Wentforth went nowhere. England was trying for "noncommittal" to the Union and Confederacy; too many people were worried about the stability of Britain while America was at war, and every mill needed to run. Wentforth was the only man capable, as Hollowell was no longer sighted. Lucinda had killed herself out of disgust at the sacrifice of life as well as the blinding of her other beau.

Hollowell never contested the ruling, but he never went outside without wearing Lucinda's spectacles. It gave Wentforth a double horror in the sightlessness of his rival behind her spectacles. Everyone else called it eccentricity but Wentforth knew what it really was: a silent accusation of Lucinda's suicide and the loss of life and limb – and eyes – in his own family's mill. A man who can spend years planning models can easily spend decades in revenge. After years of this frankly terrifying relationship, Wentforth began to crack around the edges. Hollowell had sensed the moment and hoped to catch his cousin in the act of attempted murder – or at least in an act of violence that would lead to his arrest and perhaps open up the arson case. So he asked for a temporary police escort, and this request was granted because no one wished to anger such a useful genius with so many connections in the government. He didn't tell Lestrade any of this interesting information because he knew any policeman would clap the irons on him for instigating a crime.

Mr Holmes claims he had an eye on Wentforth for some time – only for more boring crimes, what he calls "petty paperwork crimes of fraud and inventing fees for his clients" – and he knew all about that mucked-up past. He had expected he and Watson would trap the man in the act of finishing off Lestrade, only Wentforth had moved faster than he had expected, and Watson, for once, left his revolver at home (and that'll be for the last time, I bet). So when Holmes saw Wentforth coming up the steps they shielded Lestrade behind the overturned table. An Elgin can blow a hole through one man, but that leaves the blade for the next and with their own weapons and Wentforth's cowardice the three of them were at a stalemate until we showed up.

I could be angry at Mr Holmes for not telling me he'd solved the case while I was telling him the details, but that would be two-faced. I've done the same thing myself, withholding evidence because I needed to let the prey come to me. Wentforth did a lot more than return; he was determined to finish the attack on Lestrade because he knew the runt could identify him, and nothing spoils a good exodus to France like your face in the newspapers. I'm assured that Holmes relied on my intelligence to come through in time. I am the cleverest of the Yarders; he's said so.

Mr Holmes knows a lot about the circumstances that lead up to crimes. But while he could likely rival the biggest gossips for knowing scandal, the man's a professional and he doesn't blab what he knows like a truant with something to prove. Being the man's client isn't a guarantee that he'll give you everything he learns. I can't quite put my finger on it, but I think it's all part of his peculiar ethics. It isn't his fault that he misjudged my nose for gossip; I listen to it as well as the next man who works with the public, but gunpowder magnates are out of our usual jurisdiction.

Oh, Lestrade? Dr Watson moved Lestrade to his own home for recovery – he said he would be safer there. Considering the family of thugs he married into, I'd agree.

THE UNFORTUNATE GUEST

Iain McLaughlin

I like that Sherlock Holmes is a flawed human being. It's one of the things that makes him particularly intriguing. **Peterson**, a commissionaire who makes his canonical debut in "The Adventure of the Blue Carbuncle", is an associate of Sherlock Holmes and is somebody who is not particularly important in the great scheme of Holmes's life. He's someone helping on a case. That's what interests me… when Holmes is engaged by a case, what matters most? The investigation or the people? Peterson seemed an ideal character to help examine this kind of question.

—Iain McLaughlin

I am a simple man of simple needs and simple wishes. I do not need luxurious things, and neither do I seek the fame held by the likes of Mr Sherlock Holmes. For those who find fame often find themselves targets of the immoral.

I believe it a widely known truth that Mr Sherlock Holmes has a large number of agents and contacts in every avenue of life in this great city of London. We find ourselves in his service for many reasons, but we are well rewarded. Mr Holmes is never shy with coin. However, that is not my abiding reason for assisting Mr Holmes. There is a right and a wrong in this world. And in this city, too often we see only the wrong. I feel my conscience eased by the fact that in aiding Mr Holmes on occasion I have, in some way, pushed back at the dark deeds that infect this city. I will freely admit that it is also a great comfort to think that we may call upon the expertise of Mr Holmes when it is required.

That is how it came that I found myself in Mr Holmes's rooms, with occasion to ask for assistance rather than to provide it.

Dr Watson was with Mr Holmes at Baker Street on this day and it was he who answered the door when Mrs Hudson showed me up.

I was both surprised and pleased that Dr Watson should remember me. "Ah," said he, "it's Peterson, isn't it?"

"Yes, Dr Watson," I replied, removing my cap. "I was doorman at the…"

He waved me inside, a friendly smile on his face. "Ah, yes, I remember. Do come in." Dr Watson was an easy man to take to. He was a real gentleman, and carried himself as such, but did so without making those of us not from the higher orders feel that he was peering down his snoot at us. I have worked as a doorman at several hotels, and I know of which I speak. To many of the upper classes, the lower levels of society are to be sneered at or ignored. That was never Dr Watson's way.

Mr Holmes was seated by his fire, as was often his manner. He wore a dressing-gown and was smoking a long pipe. He did not care to look at me as I approached. I knew him well enough not to take offence at that.

It was Dr Watson who spoke. "Holmes, it's…"

Mr Holmes raised a hand for quiet. "I am aware of our visitor's identity," he said. "I am also aware of the reason for his calling. However, perhaps Peterson would take a seat and tell you his tale, that you may be equally enlightened."

I did as I was instructed. It was the first occasion on which I had been invited to sit while at Baker Street.

"I see you have moved to new employment," said Dr Watson. He was impressed by his deduction but I shall admit I felt it rather obvious since I still wore my doorman's uniform.

"I joined Bertrand's Hotel seven months since, Dr Watson. Mr Holmes was kind enough to give me a fine reference." I felt I had to add, "And I am very grateful for that, Mr Holmes."

Mr Holmes waved a thin hand, dismissing my thanks. His eyes were closed as though in sleep. "Simply tell Dr Watson your reason for being here," said he, before resuming his silence.

"Well, Dr Watson, Bertrand's Hotel was looking for new

staff. Word was they had new owners and they was pushing upmarket. I heard they paid well – I knew a couple of lads who work there – so I went along and they gave me the job. It's good work, I must say. Less hours for more pay and the tips are very good. Truth is I'm much more comfortably off than I was."

Dr Watson nodded again. "A better class of client?" he asked. "Their move upmarket has been a success?"

I gave that question some thought, for I paid close attention to the guests at Bertrand's. Indeed, any doorman who did not pay heed to the guests and their needs would not be worth his salt. "They have money but none of it's from old families," I told him. "It's mostly folks in business or wealthy wives and families. We don't get many titles. We get Americans and Europeans, though." We particularly notice them. Foreigners usually tip well, especially Yanks. "I've been happy there these past six months or so. Good hours, very good money."

Dr Watson said that he understood and encouraged me to continue.

"Well," said I, "two days ago I was on duty when a chap emerged from the hotel. I'd helped him inside with his luggage the day before. He was from Edinburgh, the son of a doctor I believe. He asked for directions to a few places and was about to light a cigarette for himself. I lit it for him, as a good doorman should. He said thank you, polite as could be. Half a moment later he was on the ground at my feet, gasping for air. I called for help but by the time anyone came, the poor chap was dead."

"How?" asked Dr Watson, but Mr Holmes quieted him sharpish.

"Let Peterson tell his tale," said he. And so I continued.

"When the police came they took the poor chap away and examined him. They came back to me this morning with questions. Very accusing questions, I might add. The chap had been poisoned. And it turned out that the poison was in his cigarette. The strange thing being that he was not smoking the brand he normally smoked. It did not match the packet they found in his pocket. It did, however, match the brand that I smoke, and have done for many a year. Being as I lit the smoke for him, their eyes are turning on me, Mr Holmes. I had already set mind to asking your opinion when I returned to the room where we change for duty. We all have cupboards, and inside mine I found these…"

From within my coat pocket I withdrew several envelopes, a watch and a man's ring, all of which I had carried from the hotel to Baker Street.

"I recognised the ring and the name 'McGregor' on the post," I continued. "They are those of the dead man."

Mr Holmes did not look away from the fire. "Did you steal them?" he asked.

"No, sir," I replied quickly. "I am no thief, but it is clear that someone would have me seen as such. That is why I have come to you."

Mr Holmes fair sprang from his seat. "Understandable," said he, "but you should not have moved these objects. You have deprived me of the opportunity to examine your cupboard for potentially vital clues."

"Had I left them they might have deprived me of my life, sir," I argued. I should never normally have disagreed with Mr Holmes, but in the instance of my life being in jeopardy from the noose, I felt justified.

Mr Holmes merely laughed. "I see your point, Peterson." He took the objects from me and placed them on a desk before instructing me to continue. There was little more I felt I could tell.

"Had those objects been found in my possession, Mr Holmes, I should be for the hangman. I promise you with my hand on the Bible itself that I did not kill this man. I did not give him a poison cigarette, and nor did I steal from him."

Mr Holmes had again taken his seat. "But someone has gone to some lengths to ensure that you should be suspected of this crime. Have you enemies at Bertrand's, Peterson?"

"None, sir," I replied and it was the truth. I enjoyed my time at the hotel. "These past months have been the happiest I can remember. Everyone is friendly and treats me right."

"Not everyone," replied Mr Holmes. "Evidently at least one in their ranks has taken against you."

I could raise no argument to that point. "I have no idea who, sir. Neither do I have any hope of avoiding the rope if you do not agree to help me."

Mr Holmes sat a long moment and was so silent I feared he would reject my appeal. "I am busy with a complex case," he said eventually. "But I can spare you a few hours to examine this problem. Beyond that I can make no assurance." He was then kind enough to offer compliments as to the service I had previously provided.

We paused only a mere ten minutes so that Mr Holmes might send a note to delay a meeting he had arranged for that afternoon. It is no exaggeration to say that I felt the weight lift from my shoulders when Mr Holmes agreed to offer his assistance. Considerably more than if all of Scotland Yard itself had become involved as my protector.

There were coppers at the hotel when we arrived. Mr Gartyne, the day manager, hurried to my side as soon as we entered. "Where have you been, Peterson?" he demanded. "The police have been looking for you. And why are you using the front doors? They are for guests. The servants' door is at the back as you well know."

"Sorry, sir," I apologised but Mr Holmes interrupted.

"Would you describe me as staff, sir?" he demanded. He fixed his eyes upon Mr Gartyne and gave his most intimidating stare.

As so many had before him, Mr Gartyne went pale under the gaze. "Well, no."

"And if I had asked Mr Peterson to bring us in?"

"Then I would have no complaint, Mr…"

Mr Holmes made no attempt to furnish his name. "Then I suggest that you assume that is precisely what happened. It will save everyone a considerable amount of time."

Mr Gartyne was a man the likes of which I have seen often in the hotel trade. He thought himself more important than the rest of the world did. "And you are a guest here, sir?" he asked Mr Holmes.

"No," came a solid voice from elsewhere in the lobby. "This is Sherlock Holmes."

"At your service," Mr Holmes said first to Mr Gartyne and then to the tall man who had spoken and who now approached. "Lestrade."

Mr Gartyne was taken aback at hearing the name. He made an excuse and left, after requesting that Mr Holmes and the police be discreet.

"Caught him, have you?" asked Lestrade. He looked at me with suspicious eyes. There was little doubt that Inspector Lestrade thought me guilty.

"Far from it," Mr Holmes replied. "Indeed it was Mr Peterson who requested my presence here."

"Did he now?" For sure the copper had not expected that.

"He did, and he has asked that I find the truth."

Inspector Lestrade was sorely put out by that and he did not hide it well. "Really?"

"Indeed," said Mr Holmes. "I trust you will have no objection to that?"

The copper didn't take up the challenge. "None at all, Mr Holmes," Lestrade said, "though I trust you shall remember that this is a police investigation."

Mr Holmes, however, had lost interest in the conversation and was looking around the lobby, leaving Dr Watson to reply in his stead. "Have no fear, Lestrade. Holmes will afford you the same respect he always does."

"That's what worries me." Lestrade sniffed and looked at me. "Well, if I can leave him in your hands, Mr Holmes, I have other cases demanding my attention. However, I shall return." He looked upon me with sour eyes. "Until then, this suspect is your responsibility."

Mr Holmes raised a hand, though I cannot say if it was in agreement with the policeman or a dismissal of him. I supposed it did not make any difference. Lestrade left, again promising me that he would return and warning me against taking to my heels.

Such a thought had never occurred to me, and I was concerned that perhaps I might have made a bad choice in contacting Mr Holmes rather than choosing to run. It was not unknown for the law to put an innocent man at the end of a rope. But I had played my cards, and now my fate was in the hands of Mr Holmes.

Mr McGregor's room was on the first floor. It was not one of our largest but in Bertrand's there are no small rooms. The hotel's reputation was built on luxury, and I had benefited from that fact daily by way of generous tips. Mr Holmes examined the room, then looked into the man's suitcases and inspected his clothes. From his face I could make nothing of what he might be thinking.

"Well, Watson?" Mr Holmes said after circling the room at least twice. "What do you make of it?"

Dr Watson took a moment to answer. "Very little," he replied eventually. "His clothes are of good quality. Add that to his choice of hotel, I would say we are obviously dealing with a man of comfortable means. His boots are not new but they are freshly soled, therefore he could afford new but chooses to hold onto a favourite pair. Possibly for comfort, possibly for sentimental reasons."

"Sentiment?" asked Mr Holmes. "For a pair of boots? Yes, if a man can have a favourite pipe, he might exhibit the same attachment to boots."

"Especially if they were a gift from someone important to him," said Dr Watson. "I myself have retained boots and had them repaired beyond the time they should have been thrown away because they were a gift."

Mr Holmes conceded that point to Dr Watson. "Very well. Continue."

"So that you can tell me I've got it all wrong?" I heard amusement rather than annoyance in the doctor's voice.

Mr Holmes laughed again. "Perish the thought, dear fellow."

Dr Watson took his time before giving reply. "His papers and clothing would say he is a businessman here with the intention of making final an agreement outlined in one of the letters."

"Legal or not?"

"The company mentioned has a good reputation and its owner is known for charitable and Church activities."

"That would hardly preclude him from being a criminal," said Mr Holmes.

"Oh, by no means," Dr Watson replied. "I have seen many a villain under a church roof, Holmes. However, this man's charitable acts are often performed quietly and I hear of them only through medical colleagues."

"Fair, Watson." Mr Holmes was again picking through Mr McGregor's belongings. "Would you say the dead man was married?"

Dr Watson nodded. "Of course," he said plucking a photograph from the dead man's wallet. "He carried a picture of her. The bag is quite new and carries a subtle message inlaid in the rim. 'To my beloved…' so I should say definitely married."

"Watson, you excel yourself," Mr Holmes said, a delighted smile on his face.

"How much did I get wrong?" asked Dr Watson wryly.

Mr Holmes peered out of the window. "Absolutely nothing," said he. "My compliments were genuine. At last you make progress with my methods. Not, I should add, before time."

"Thank you," said Dr Watson, sounding more than slightly surprised. "I think. So, my conclusions are correct?"

"In as far as they go, yes," Mr Holmes confirmed. "Of course, you do not answer the largest question. Why was this man murdered?"

"Robbery?" Dr Watson suggested.

Mr Holmes was not convinced. "Then why leave possessions of some worth in Peterson's cupboard?"

"To divert suspicion?" offered Dr Watson.

"Possibly." Mr Holmes sucked a deep breath. "However, objects of value remain amongst McGregor's belongings. That would make our murderer a very poor thief. Surely he would take at least some of these valuable items to throw the police off the scent? No, I am not convinced by this either."

"Then why kill the man?" asked Dr Watson.

"Why indeed?" Mr Holmes walked to the door. "Come. We will discover no more here."

I shall confess that I was disappointed to see Mr Holmes leave the room with such haste. What's more, he had left the thinking to Dr Watson and had himself done little that I saw. To any other I should have made a protest, but I should never think of doing such a thing with Mr Holmes.

Mr Holmes asked to be taken to the room where the staff changed into the uniforms. He then pulled a magnifying glass from his pocket and examined the lock to my cupboard.

"No scratches to show anything other than the appropriate key has been used and no sign of forced entry. Any kind of jemmy would leave an obvious mark."

That did not sound good for me, and I said as much.

Mr Holmes agreed. "And you maintain that you did not have any hand in this man's death?"

That question was a surprise and one to which I did not take kindly. "I am no murderer, Mr Holmes."

"The facts, however, suggest otherwise."

"Do you think me guilty?" I demanded.

He offered no reply to that, instead saying, "I think we should reacquaint ourselves with the day manager."

With that we were back above stairs, and at Mr Holmes's request the concierge Mr Wilson left his desk to track down Mr Gartyne. While he was gone, Mr Holmes seemed agitated by this enforced moment of inactivity. He picked up a pen from the desk and examined it, then looked at the vase of flowers by the guest register. He seemed in need of any kind of distraction. When Mr Wilson returned, it transpired that Mr Gartyne was in a dining room on the first floor. Mr Holmes repeated the location to Mr Wilson and was given confirmation that he had it right. Mr Holmes was in such haste to see the day manager that he all but bumped into one of the guests.

"My apologies," said he. "The fault was entirely mine. I trust I have not caused you alarm."

I shall admit now that I was fair angered by Mr Holmes talking so nice with someone he did not know when his thoughts ought to have been directed to keeping my neck from the rope. But I did not say as much. Instead I led Mr Holmes and Dr Watson up to the first floor and into the private dining room.

We found Mr Gartyne seated alone at a table in the centre of the room. Only a few of the other tables were occupied, with this not being the dinner hour. He invited Mr Holmes and Dr Watson to be seated. That invitation was, naturally, not extended to me.

"I trust you have been discreet," Mr Gartyne said in a quiet tone.

"Impeccably so," replied Dr Watson.

"We have not disturbed any of your guests," Mr Holmes assured the manager. "We have merely examined the basics of the case."

"And?" Mr Gartyne leaned forward, evidently eager that he might make moves to clear the hotel of the incident. "You have cleared Peterson of wrongdoing? None of my staff are guilty?"

Mr Holmes straightened in his chair. "The evidence is quite undeniable," he said. "Mr McGregor was poisoned by a cigarette lit by Peterson. It was not of the brand smoked by McGregor but that smoked by Peterson. Furthermore, papers and a watch belonging to Mr McGregor were found in Peterson's cupboard. That, I fear, is enough evidence to put Peterson in the dock."

I could only stare at Mr Holmes. I had sought his aid, but he had just decried me as a killer. Again my thoughts turned to how I could escape. There were many ways out of the city, but where I could go I had no idea.

"Of course," Mr Holmes continued casually, "it does not require the intellect of Sherlock Holmes to see that Peterson is not the killer."

I swear that I felt my heart beat faster as Mr Holmes spoke those words. I had not been abandoned. My cause was not lost.

"You have just said that the evidence points to his guilt," Mr Gartyne protested.

Mr Holmes lit a cigarette and then carelessly dropped the match by an ashtray. He took a deep drag before replying. "Peterson is no fool. Were he to rob a guest such as the unfortunate Mr McGregor, he would hardly steal a watch inscribed with the dead man's name when money was left untouched. Nor would he take papers that are clearly of no value to any other than Mr McGregor and his partners but leave notes of promise behind. He would be a very poor thief indeed. I would add to this the question of motive. Why would Peterson kill a guest? And why commit the act in so elegant a manner?"

"Surely," said Mr Gartyne, "that is a question better asked of Peterson."

Mr Holmes stubbed out his cigarette, slowing the ash so that it dropped onto the tablecloth. "No. Peterson is not the killer. The evidence was placed to make him appear guilty, and at first glance, the police would see him as the obvious suspect." Mr Holmes looked at the ash for a moment before continuing. "It is known to some in the criminal fraternity that Peterson has, on occasion, proved invaluable to me in my work. It is clear that if he were to fall into this manner of trouble he would seek my assistance. His evident guilt in the motiveless murder of a man would likely draw me to the case but the watch and papers being a foolish choice of items to steal were, of course, designed to ensure that I was intrigued. Therefore, my deduction is that not only did Peterson not murder Mr McGregor, but that the unfortunate McGregor was killed simply to attract my attention and to draw me here." Mr Holmes waited for a response. None came. "I took the time while idling at the concierge's desk to examine the register of guests and the rooms that they occupy. I see here that your tables are numbered for your guests.. For example Room 7 is taken by a single lady, but at the corresponding table are sat two men, neither of whom is dressed in a manner appropriate for this establishment. I therefore must conclude that the people at these tables are also part of the deception." His eyebrows raised questioningly. "And so, Mr Gartyne, may I enquire why it was so pressing for me to be summoned here that you would kill an innocent man to ensure my presence?"

Mr Gartyne seemed rather confused by the question. "Why should anyone go to such lengths to ensure your presence, Mr Holmes?"

The smile Mr Holmes gave had no warmth behind it. "I believe, Mr Gartyne, that was the question I asked you.

Before you answer, I shall warn you that Dr Watson carries his service revolver with him."

At that, Dr Watson did draw his revolver from his coat pocket, and aimed it at Mr Gartyne.

"Does he?" replied Mr Gartyne. "I will admit that I have never had a guest draw a weapon on me before." Mr Gartyne's face underwent a quite remarkable change. I had known him for nigh seven months to be pompous but in most ways decent and efficient. That man's face faded and in its place was one that wore the same features yet the expression in the eyes and mouth made him seem a different person entirely. This was, undoubtedly, an unpleasant and evil man. "Were I so devious, Mr Holmes," he continued, "then surely I would have anticipated that Dr Watson would be armed and have prepared for that eventuality?"

Again the smile from Mr Holmes. "Then I can assume I am correct that the men at these tables—"

"—are my men?" Gartyne finished. "You may, Mr Holmes."

I quickly looked around the room, as did Dr Watson. More than a dozen men surrounded us, seated at their tables. All had their gazes on us, and many had their hands in their jacket pockets, seemingly ready to pull out a firearm should the need arise.

Mr Holmes continued, as reasonably as if he was asking about breakfast. "So, will you enlighten me as to the reason for this charade?"

"You could not resist, could you?" Mr Gartyne sounded very pleased with himself. "The puzzle, I mean."

"I was intrigued," Mr Holmes admitted.

"For all that legendary intellect, you are slave to a greater ego."

Mr Holmes looked at the grandfather clock that sat in the corner of the room. "I am more than aware of my many failings, Mr Gartyne," said he. I'm damned if he didn't sound bored. "But if you could make haste. I have an appointment with my tailor this afternoon that I am loathe to miss."

"But miss it you shall, Mr Holmes." There was villainy in Mr Gartyne's tone. "You have no more need of boots."

Mr Holmes seemed no more put out. "The explanation?"

Mr Gartyne gave some thought before answering. "Some time since, you sent Frederick Parson to the gallows, Mr Holmes."

"I did," Mr Holmes confirmed, "and I regret that five innocent men died before I could deliver proof of Parson's guilt."

It was a story I remembered well. The newspapers were full of it. Parson, who ran several local businesses, was revealed as a villain, a man trying to claim a corner of London as his own. He ran women, opium dens, smuggling and gangs of thugs demanding money from local businesses lest they find themselves torched in the night. All this he did from a small shop in a side street. By use of intermediaries and agents, he kept himself distant enough from his crimes that the coppers did not suspect him. Mr Holmes had not been so easy to fool and had brought him to justice.

"Mr Parson was our leader," said Mr Gartyne. "We prospered under his wing. We earned good money and lived well. Those were good times for us, our families. You took that from us, Mr Holmes. As easily as you might snuff out a candle, you took the coins from our pockets and the bread from our tables."

"I will not apologise for taking stolen bread or money from a thief," Mr Holmes replied.

"But you shall pay for it with your life and your reputation. We had lain low since you sent Mr Parson to the gallows. We bought this hotel, improved it, and now it runs at a healthy and legitimate profit. It is widely known that Peterson is one of your network of agents. Luring him here was easy enough, with the offer of fair pay for a decent day's work. It tickled me that you even provided a character reference for him. You see, Mr Holmes, you played your own part in this."

Mr Holmes merely raised an eyebrow at this but said nothing.

"This hotel is a legitimate business. It is also the heart of every other business enterprise we run."

Mr Holmes nodded. "You could simply call them criminal activities."

"A fair point," the manager conceded. "It is a perfect location for people to travel through and conduct their business." he shrugged. "With regret, Mr Holmes, it is also the location of your final case. You will be found dead tomorrow along with Dr Watson, betrayed and murdered by one of your own agents, Peterson."

"Ah," nodded Mr Holmes. "So not only will I die but my reputation will be in ruins, my judgement open to question because I employed a murderer who then turned against me."

"A tawdry death, Mr Holmes."

"Dr Watson is armed. We could try to fight our way out," said Mr Holmes. "At least that would ruin your plan to choreograph our deaths as a murder by the desperately fleeing Peterson."

"But you won't, Mr Holmes," Mr Gartyne said, with such an arrogance that I itched to smash my fist into his jaw. "Mr Parson was not only our leader, but he was our friend. You saw him as a mere criminal. We saw him as a man who gave gifts to our children, who aided us when we had need of it. He was our friend, and you cut his life short, Mr Holmes. That is why we have played this long game with you and why our members are gathered here today to see your end."

Mr Holmes bowed as though accepting a compliment. "I am honoured to have been worthy of such a detailed plan. Just as I commend the devilled kidneys you serve at breakfast. Just the right amount of mustard. The lamb chops at supper are equally splendid. Your chef is a credit to you."

Mr Gartyne's face twisted in confusion. He had been in complete control of the situation and now he was not. "You have stayed here?"

"Yes," Mr Holmes replied, "or perhaps I should say that the elderly cleric, the Reverend Aubrey Goodchild, stayed at this hotel on two occasions in the past six months."

I remembered the gentleman of whom Mr Holmes spoke. He was bent with age, with thin white hair, a thick pair of spectacles and a wheezy voice. His nose was... I stared at Mr Holmes's profile. "The Reverend Goodchild was you, Mr Holmes?" I cried.

"Yes." Mr Holmes was fairly delighted that his deception had taken in one of his own. "Do you think that I would write a character reference for Peterson without taking an interest in his new place of employment? Particularly when I am aware that so many of the criminal underclass frequent the place?" He smiled, this time a superior and dismissive expression. "You see, Mr Gartyne, I too am versed in long-term plans. I was under no illusion that the timely and welcome end of Mr Parson's activities would stop his subordinates from seeking the opportunity to regroup and recommence their activities. My investigations revealed the identities of many of his lackeys. However, it seemed expedient to allow you to congregate and again feel at ease in your activities. That would allow us to cast a net around you all." He pointed to a corner table. "There is Eamonn Gallagher." His finger roved around the room as he picked out men by name. At each utterance, his subjects looked increasingly ill at ease. "Ronald Milne, David Carson, Wilson Kettley, Daniel Prentiss…" He paused, letting his words sink in. The men began to shift with discomfort. "You see," said Mr Holmes in a relaxed tone, "this meeting has brought to a head my own plan. As we were being brought up here, I bumped into a guest and apologised. That guest was in reality a police constable and my apology to him contained a prearranged signal that he should summon Inspector Lestrade and his men. They have not returned to Scotland Yard as they stated but have instead simply been waiting a few streets from here. Probably in the Allenton Tea Shop." He pulled his watch from its pocket. "I imagine they are here by now."

At that moment, Inspector Lestrade rushed into the room, followed by several burly constables. There were a few skirmishes and one shot was fired, but that was into the floor and the bullet hurt no one. Parson's men were cuffed and taken away. Some took a deserved truncheon about the ear when they resisted.

I myself was still in something of a shock, as was Dr Watson.

"Holmes?" asked Dr Watson as he watched Inspector Lestrade place his own cuffs on Mr Gartyne and be none too gentle about it. "It is over?"

"Indeed," replied Mr Holmes.

"And Peterson is no longer under suspicion?" asked Dr Watson again, and I was grateful for him remembering and championing my plight.

"Of course he is no longer a suspect," said Holmes. "He never was one. He was simply a convenient means to bring the matter to a head."

"Scandalous," said Dr Watson, his tone one of outrage. "Utterly scandalous, Holmes. You could have told me. Dash it, man, you should have told Peterson."

This idea was evidently one that had not occurred to Mr Holmes, and he saw no reason to regret his decision.

"If nothing else he's lost his job," Dr Watson continued.

"But the crime is resolved," said Mr Holmes as though that should provide an answer to every question, and I believe that in his mind it probably did.

For Dr Watson it clearly did not and his protests continued as he followed Mr Holmes to the door. "Peterson, I can only apologise," he called to me before leaving.

And there I was: a free man again. A free man without employment.

I made clear at the beginning of this account that I sought no fame, and that I did not relish danger. None of that changed in the resolution of this matter. What did change was the readiness with which I decided to make myself available to Mr Holmes in the future. Had he asked me, I should have proudly consented to assist him in this case. He had allowed me to work among thieves and killers without warning that my life might be in danger.

Sherlock Holmes or not, I had the right to know. However, he did not deem me deserving of such respect and he appeared to have no care for how the case should affect my circumstances. I was as much a pawn for him as I was for the villains who sought his end.

I must now ask myself if I am willing to be known as someone in Mr Holmes's employ. I felt my life in jeopardy by Mr Holmes's actions. I am no coward, but I am no fool either.

I am a simple man of simple needs and simple wishes. I have now reported to Dr Watson that I have no wish to maintain an association with, nor be in the service of, Mr Sherlock Holmes. I had thought he might object or tell me that I should take time over such a decision. He did neither. Instead he promised me a letter of recommendation for any position I should pursue. For that and for his kindness, I am grateful. Dr Watson is a gentleman.

Of Mr Holmes I shall say only that he is as great a detective as his reputation would say. I have no doubt that he has saved more lives than I can imagine. But now I am aware that my own life was put in danger's path so that he might solve his case. My jeopardy came as much from him as from those guilty of villainy. I will take that risk no more. I shall not be missed by him, for he has many in his employ.

But I am no longer among their number.

THE UNEXPECTED DEATH OF THE MARTIAN AMBASSADOR

Andrew Lane

Lord Holdhurst appeared once in the Sherlock Holmes canon, in "The Adventure of the Naval Treaty". Appointed Foreign Minister and put in charge of negotiating all treaties between the United Kingdom and foreign countries, he crossed paths with Sherlock Holmes when an important document was apparently stolen and his nephew was blamed. I had originally planned to write a story about Mrs Turner (who turns up once, bizarrely, as Holmes's landlady in "A Scandal in Bohemia") but when I started to write I found myself slipping into the persona of an irritable middle-aged diplomat, so I decided to follow and see where the story would lead. It led here.

—Andrew Lane

NOTE FOR THE RECORD

FROM: Lord Holdhurst

TO: Mycroft Holmes

DATE: 17th April 1895

SUBJECT: The Unexpected Death of the Martian Ambassador

Dear Mycroft,

This Note for the Record is being typed by me, personally and laboriously, letter by tedious letter, and is intended for your eyes only. This minimises the number of people who know the whole sorry story to you, me, your brother and possibly that parvenu ex-army doctor with whom he socialises. It should remain that way, and I suggest you file these papers in a locked cabinet in a locked room in a locked building and pretend they never existed. Isn't that what we do with all contentious documentation?

En passant, I would like to state that it has been more years than I care to remember since I last used a typewriter. I hate the damned things with a passion. For God's sake, surely this is why we have staff! I'm looking along the top row and all I can see is a random collection of letters – Q, W, E, R, T, Y and so on. I swear this machine is functionally defective. Why aren't the keys in alphabetical order? That's the British way – straightforward and logical. Still, knowing the labyrinthine complexities of your mind, I half-suspect you designed the arrangement of the typewriter keyboard yourself as part of some fiendish plot to keep the lower classes in their place, or somesuch thing.

I digress. On your recommendation I asked your brother to call upon me in my home in Chelsea late on the night of 23rd March this year. He was half an hour late. Despite his rudeness I offered him a cup of tea and some biscuits as my butler showed him in to my study.

"I am working on a case at the moment," he said, in his overly fast, overly precise tone. "I rarely eat or drink at these times, as I find the ratiocinative process can be slowed down appreciably by the transfer of blood from the cerebral cortex to the digestive system. And if I *were* to take sustenance then it would certainly not be tea. The dried leaves of the shrub *Camellia sinensis* are allegedly stimulants, but for thousands of years they have been regarded by the British as something gentle and soothing, coinciding with a period of rest and relaxation. In this respect, I trust the accumulated wisdom of the masses more than I trust the retorts of the chemists."

"I shall take that as a 'no'," I said. "Please, sit down. I wish to retain your services on a matter of some sensitivity."

"I had assumed as much," he said, falling rather than sitting into the stuffed armchair that, you might remember, I keep in the corner of my study and that I regard as my own "special" chair (i.e. I sleep there, when I work late, in order that I do not disturb Lady Holdhurst's slumber). "It is after midnight and I am summoned to the home of a man who works a stone's throw away from my brother and whom I have previously encountered in the context of another sensitive government task that I concluded successfully and discreetly. Apart from a silent butler who looks more like a bodyguard and who carries a loaded revolver in a holster beneath his jacket, there are no staff in sight, and I am specifically asked not to bring my companion and colleague, Dr Watson. The conclusion is obvious. This is not a social call."

"Indeed," I said in what I trust was a glacial tone, intended to impress upon your brother that he and I moved in significantly different social circles and that he should be more respectful of authority and the natural order of things. "If it was a social occasion I would have offered sherry."

"Alcohol is another chemical with a depressive effect on the nervous system," he said dismissively. "I rarely drink it until I have finished with a case." He was frowning, and running his fingers along the cracked leather of the armchair. "You are the third... no, the fourth owner of this armchair, I perceive. The second owner kept a small reptile."

"You can tell that just from sitting there?" I asked, genuinely amazed.

He shrugged. "There are flecks of scale in the creases of the leather – not obvious to the eye, but noticeable to the trained observer. Now, please tell me what I can do for you. Be brief, if you can. Politicians are, in my experience, rarely brief, but I would appreciate the attempt. I am currently working to save the life of a man who has been sent, through the post, a freshly severed finger that resembles in every respect his own left ring finger, down to the presence of a healed scar across the knuckle and a supposedly unique wedding band he designed himself."

"I presume it *isn't* his own finger?" I asked, intrigued despite myself.

"No, not unless said finger is severed at some stage in the future and then sent back through time – a possibility I am ruling as unlikely, despite the recently published scientific romance by Mr Wells."

"Funny you should mention Mr Wells," I said, feeling a shiver run through me, "as this is very much the kind of story that he might write." I took a deep breath. "I need you, Mr Holmes, to solve the mystery of the death of what might turn out to be the first Martian ambassador to this country."

My study was silent for some moments.

"If there is one thing that politicians are worse at than brevity, it is humour. I assume therefore that you are not trying to be funny." He stared at me with a raised eyebrow. "You have, I presume, been approached by something or someone that claims to be a representative of whatever authority is in charge on the planet Mars. Given the recent observations made by Percival Lowell of canals on the Red Planet, and indications of planned vegetation along the side of those canals, it seems a reasonable assumption that life might exist there. There is no logical reason why we should be the only planet in the cosmos harbouring intelligent life. If such intelligent life exists there, and if they are advanced enough to cross the gulf of space between us – two large and unprovable assumptions, by the way – then they would naturally attempt to forge a diplomatic alliance with whatever they perceive to be the ruling group."

"Naturally, the British," I said.

Holmes smiled a thin smile. "You may wish to check

that this presumptive Martian ambassador has not made approaches to the Germans, the Russians, the French and, at a stretch, the Americans as well. They may be covering their bets." He shrugged. "It occurs to me that Mars orbits further away from the sun than the Earth and is thus obviously much colder, despite its angry red hue. Any inhabitants are likely to be biologically very different from us."

"Indeed," I said, "and this is the crux of the problem."

"Start from the beginning," he said. "Leave nothing out, even if it seems to be unimportant. I have found that the relevance of facts to an investigation is often in inverse ratio to their *apparent* importance – a paradox around which I intend writing a small monograph at some stage."

"Very well." I closed my eyes and steepled my hands on the blotter in front of me, the better to recollect the sequence of events. "We were approached by—"

"We?" he snapped. "Be precise!"

"The Foreign Office, of which I am the head," I said heavily, "was approached by a man named Darius Trethewey. He is, as far as we can ascertain, an entrepreneur and businessman who invests in scientific developments. He told us an apparently incredible story about having received messages via some medium that he would only describe as an 'etheric force', detected by some device invented by an inventor of his acquaintance—"

"Ha!" Holmes interjected.

"I'm sorry?" I am rarely, if ever, interrupted by anyone who works for me, and the relative novelty of the experience does not make it any more pleasant.

"My friend, Dr Watson, once compiled a list of my

strengths and weaknesses. It was his opinion that I had no knowledge of philosophy or astronomy. He was wrong, of course, as he so often is, but I find it strange that we have here a case that involves both natural philosophy *and* astronomy together."

"A shame you'll never be able to tell him about it," I said.

"If you wish to find out more about the 'etheric force' you could do worse than seek out the recently published works of Heinrich Hertz and Oliver Lodge. Rather than 'etheric force', the currently accepted term for the phenomenon is, I believe, 'Hertzian waves', which rather seems a shame as 'Lodgian waves' has a certain ring to it."

"Yes," I said, "the Germans do seem to have a habit of self-aggrandisement that the British lack. Anyway, this Darius Trethewey told us that he had been, for some months, in regular communication with an entity on Mars. In the end his Martian interlocutor asked to send a representative to Earth – to England in particular – to discuss the possibility of a mutual trade treaty. After some discussion, of which your brother was a part, we agreed."

"I feel sure that Mr Trethewey refused to let you examine, or even see, his equipment?"

"Correct. He cited intellectual property rights and pending patents."

"Of course he did." Holmes nodded. "I presume my brother was suspicious?"

"He was. He muttered something about once having been asked by his superiors to negotiate a treaty with the spirit realm, which he refused to elaborate on."

"It was early in his career," Holmes said with a smile, "when I was fifteen years old. We were in Ireland, at the invitation of a peer with a strong interest in spiritualism who had suggested he was able to reliably contact ghosts and that they could be used as secret agents for the British Empire. It was, of course, a complete confidence trick meant to defraud the British government out of thousands of pounds. In a sense, I think Mycroft's exposure of that fraud boosted his career." He waved a hand. "But enough of my family history – please continue."

"Mr Trethewey suggested that the Martian ambassador travel to Earth incognito by some means, on which he was very vague. For various reasons both we and the Martians wanted to avoid the freak-show that a public announcement would inevitably create, and so the ambassador was to be brought to the Foreign Office in a covered carriage and smuggled in through the back entrance for an initial meeting, at which the ground rules and agendas for subsequent meetings would be agreed. The date was set for one week later."

"Not very much time to arrange a major diplomatic visit, albeit a secret one," Holmes observed.

"Something about the relative positions of the two planets being favourable," I said.

"Or, alternatively, a means of putting you off-guard and unable to make a full range of security arrangements."

I nodded. "The thought had occurred. Well, to be frank, it occurred to your brother. So, on the night in question – and it *was* night, at the request of the ambassador – we waited in the main ballroom in the Foreign Office building in Whitehall."

"Did you choose the location?"

"No – Mr Trethewey gave us the dimensions of the space the ambassador would need. The ballroom was the only space large enough. I confess I did wonder if the ambassador was going to be something like a whale, or an elephant."

"Quite possible. Go on."

"There were only five of us – myself, your brother and three members of my staff." I paused, recollecting the strange events of that evening. "Two others had been dispatched to the back door to arrange for the introduction of the Martian ambassador into the building. None of us knew what to expect, apart from the fact that the ambassador had – via Mr Trethewey – insisted that there be no steps or stairs between his entrance and where the meeting was to take place. It wasn't that unusual – to be fair, your brother makes much the same request. I had arranged for refreshment – some wine, some cheese and crackers – just in case the ambassador was hungry. Anyway, we heard a rumbling sound approaching the ballroom. It grew louder and louder, and we realised that something was being *wheeled* down the corridor that led to a curtained-off area at the rear of the room. Eventually the curtains were pulled aside, and the most bizarre contraption was pushed in. It was, in the words of Gilbert and Sullivan, 'something between a large bathing machine and a very small second-class carriage', comprising a rectangular iron frame, studded with massive rivet-heads, holding vast sheets of glass in place. At least, the front two-thirds was glassed, while the back third was entirely ironwork, covered in strange mechanical devices. It resembled an enormous fish tank, of the kind one might see in the aquarium at the London Zoological Gardens, except that it moved on numerous iron wheels set close to the ground. My two staff members were pushing it, while

Darius Trethewey – a tall man with a black handlebar moustache and bushy eyebrows, resplendent in evening dress, top hat and opera cloak – strode along beside it. I confess I winced as I contemplated the effect of that weight and those wheels on the black and white marble tiles that comprise the ballroom floor."

"Tiles?" Holmes queried. "How large?"

Your brother can be a very irritating man. "Does it matter?" I snapped.

"I am not yet in a position to say. Indulge me."

"Tile-sized. Perhaps two feet square."

"And was there any *smell* that you could detect?"

"A *smell*. Is that relevant?"

"I have no idea. Was there?"

"A sharp, disagreeable odour, like that of tincture of iodine, but *darker*, if that makes any sense. May I proceed?"

He nodded. "And apart from the rumbling of the wheels, was there any other noise made?"

"It sounded," I said cautiously, trying to be precise, "like several steam locomotives all moving at once, but at different speeds. There was a metallic clattering, as of wheels going over points, and a hissing and wheezing as the various pistons worked and as pressure valves were released."

"Instructive," he said. "It all sounds very contemporary. One might have expected Martians to have developed a different technology from ours – perhaps even a more advanced one."

I was shocked. "Mr Holmes – this world of ours, in the age of Victoria, is the pinnacle of scientific and engineering development. I cannot imagine that any of it could be improved upon."

"I look forward to you explaining that to those rail passengers whose shirts or dresses are covered in soot at the end of their journeys," he snorted, "or whose eyes have been burned by glowing embers, or the pedestrians in our towns and cities who regularly have to step across, around or sometimes *in* piles of horse dung left on the street. I'm sure they could suggest some improvements."

I was about to remonstrate with him, but bit my tongue. This was not the time. "The inside of this contraption," I went on stiffly, "appeared to be filled with a brownish gas that swirled around, partially obscuring but partially revealing the Martian ambassador himself."

"Probably bromine," Holmes mused to himself, "judging by the smell. Odd." He waved a hand at me. "Please – continue."

I hesitated, remembering the feeling of unreality that had passed over all of us as we saw the form within the tank. "The… *being*… inside was like a human being – two arms, two legs and a head, but its limbs were thinner and its hands and feet were much larger, like paddles. Its bald head was elongated to a point at the back. Its skin – what I could see of it beneath the covering it wore – was of a reddish hue, and its eyes were entirely black – no iris, no cornea, just pools of darkness. It sat on a chair of odd design – metallic, and comprising sweeping curves rather than straight lines."

"All of the things you have described could have been the result of disguise, of course – make-up on the skin, gloves over the hands, a head-covering coloured to match the make-up, and scleral lenses of the type recently demonstrated by German ophthalmologist Adolf Fick."

"Of course."

"And its clothes?"

"Black hessian, I believe – very flexible, with straps and buckles."

He fixed me with his penetrating stare. "I presume you had one of your men ready to sample the gas in the tank?"

"Indeed." I smiled, acknowledging Holmes's grasp of the sordid realities of diplomatic work. "We had anticipated some kind of sealed container, given what we know already from scientific observations about conditions on Mars. Indeed, the Royal Society had already anticipated the possibility of a semi-aquatic race on that planet, given the existence of the canals that have been observed. The flipper-like hands and feet would tend to confirm that those markings *are* actually canals."

"Classic circular thinking," he snorted. "Canals have been observed on Mars therefore Martians would be semi-aquatic in appearance; this Martian is semi-aquatic in appearance therefore the markings that have been observed must be canals."

I ignored his retort. "One of my men was standing by with a diamond-tipped drill. Unobtrusively, he came up behind the tank while we were talking, drilled a hole, took a sample of the gas and then sealed the hole over again with a glass patch and glue. The noise of the pistons and valves covered his activities. He was not detected. Believe me, we were not taking this ambassador for granted."

"And have the results come back?"

"Yes. The gas is bromine, as you suggest. The entire tank was filled with it, meaning that no human could be inside pretending to be the ambassador. This was, as far as everything we could see and the test told us, a real creature inside a poisonous atmosphere."

"I shall reserve judgement about that. You say you *talked* with the ambassador? There was, then, an exchange of information?"

"Of sorts. I welcomed him – it – and gave our names. It then introduced itself with a string of platitudes of the kind that are regularly given during such encounters – how glorious a moment this was, how historic, how both worlds will benefit, and so on, and so on. Tedious stuff, but it has to be said."

"This creature's voice – what did it sound like?"

"Crackly, as if it was passing through a phonograph."

"Did you see its mouth move?"

"Yes. Its teeth were pointed, and its tongue black."

"Again, effects easily produced. Did it move around inside the tank?"

"It shifted a little, from time to time, easing its weight on the chair, and it moved its hands to punctuate its words."

"And did it give you a name?"

"It told us that its name was unpronounceable in our language, and that we should just call it 'Ambassador'."

Holmes smiled. "A slip – very careless."

"What do you mean?"

He shrugged, and looked away. "I will explain later. Did these pleasantries lead to anything more substantive?"

"We agreed on areas for further discussion – mutual trade, exchange of diplomatic staff, how borders might be managed and travel arranged."

"And how long did this all take?"

"Several hours."

He nodded. "I presume that there were frequent pauses, repetitions and requests for explanation?"

"Indeed. Again, not unusual in diplomatic discussion

that crosses a language barrier. When we came to a natural break the ambassador suggested we call a temporary halt to proceedings and restart them the next day. Or, rather, the next night." I fixed Holmes with a stare. "I am aware that we come across as being, perhaps, unduly credulous, but the thought was in the back of my mind all the time that this might be a trick. I was waiting for the ambassador to ask for money for some reason, at which time I would have called its bluff, but the subject was never mentioned. Indeed, the ambassador mentioned that its planet had many resources such as gold and diamonds just lying around on the surface, and it offered us whatever we wanted."

"And what was Mr Darius Trethewey doing all this time?"

"He stood beside the tank, not speaking, not touching it, but watching events with interest. At the end he bowed, and asked for the help of my personnel in getting the ambassador's receptacle – that's how he phrased it – to the waiting carriage."

"I assume it was a large and heavily reinforced carriage with more than four wheels," Holmes said. "Your men followed it?"

"Back to a house outside London owned by Mr Trethewey. They could not see past the high walls around the grounds, but from the sounds they believe the tank was unloaded and moved inside a coach house."

"And on the next night?"

"The ambassador returned, with Mr Trethewey, in much the same way as the night before. We picked up our discussions where we had left off. The matters we talked about were more detailed, including details of what technical ideas might be exchanged, what musical or artistic performances could be mounted on both planets, and so on. The ambassador claimed that the Martians were an older race than ours, and implied that there were many wonders that were ours for the asking."

"Yes, they call it 'baiting the hook'," Holmes said dismissively. "I presume the same clanking and hissing noises were there again."

"From the devices producing a breathable atmosphere and environment for the ambassador, yes."

His gimlet-like gaze flickered across my face. It felt as if he was examining every single muscle and tendon. His attention produced an almost physical pressure, pushing me back in my seat. "I perceive," he said eventually, "from your expression and appearance, that it was on this occasion that something went wrong."

I nodded weakly. "Yes. We were discussing, as I recall, the engineering requirements for allowing British visitors to live on Mars – sealed and pressurized hotels containing a breathable atmosphere, and food shipped in from Earth would be necessary as a minimum – when the ambassador started shuddering. I asked it what was wrong, but all I heard was a series of choking noises. After a few moments it abruptly jerked and then slumped back in its chair, staring at the glass panel that formed the roof."

"And Mr Trethewey?"

I frowned. "He was fine."

"I mean: what was he doing?"

"He was obviously agitated. He pounded on the glass wall of the tank, attempting to attract the ambassador's attention, but it was no use. He was distraught. We had to fetch brandy and smelling salts to revive him." I sighed.

"Of course, such a course of action was no use for the ambassador: we could not get inside the tank without releasing the bromine gas and killing everyone."

"Indeed." Holmes considered for a moment. "Did you leave the ambassador's tank where it was, or did you attempt to move it?"

"Mr Trethewy said that moving the tank might affect the ambassador negatively. He insisted that we leave the tank exactly where it was."

"Of course he did. And this was tonight? You would not have summoned me so urgently if this had all occurred several days ago."

"Yes, it was tonight. A few hours ago." I passed a hand across my brow wearily. "I came home for a change of clothes and to think. I left the ballroom guarded." I gazed at him, and I am not ashamed to say there was a pleading expression on my face and tone in my voice. "Mr Holmes, a being that may or may not be the Martian ambassador has died in my presence, in this country. It may even have died because of some weakness in the tank caused by the actions of my man in drilling through the glass. If it had been the German or the Russian ambassador then war might result. Please, Mr Holmes – I need to know. *Is this really a Martian ambassador, and am I guilty of manslaughter?*"

He smiled a thin smile. "My brother," he said, "as you will be aware, prefers to stay in a comfortable armchair, much like this one, and have facts and evidence brought to him so that he can make his decisions. I have always thought that theorising based on reported evidence is never as productive as deducing or inferring from direct observation, but I must admit that, for the first time, I see his point. The story you have outlined leaves only one logical conclusion." He sighed, and shook his head. "And yet I do find myself curious. I would like to see the scene for myself before I give you the benefit of my explanation. That is the essential difference between Mycroft and me – he has no curiosity to speak of. He merely observes what happens, and then reacts to it."

I should point out, by the way, that I am repeating your brother's words verbatim. I would not wish to be the cause of any falling out within the Holmes family, but I believe it is important to be as accurate as possible in this record. Besides: I suspect you already know your brother's opinion of you.

My carriage was waiting outside, as I had anticipated your brother's request, and so we set off. At that time of night the journey took barely twenty minutes. He did not speak. For myself, I was paralysed with doubt and concern.

We entered the Foreign Office building, and I led the way down the opulent marble corridors to the ballroom. Just before we got there, Mr Holmes indicated a door on the right. "A stairwell?" he asked.

"Leading down to the basement." I started off again, but when I reached the ballroom door and turned to speak to your brother he was not there. The door to the basement stairs was swinging shut. Quickly, I followed him, cursing as I did so.

The basement corridors are considerably less opulent than the ones above ground. "Bare and functional" would be an adequate description. Holmes was halfway along, looking up at the ceiling.

"Is this room directly beneath the ballroom?" he asked.

I glanced up as well, as if we would be able to see through the stonework. "Yes," I said, "but close to the wall."

"And is there a room directly beneath where the ambassador's environment tank was first located, before it was moved?"

I considered the question. "I believe so."

"Please take me there."

It was around a corner, and a short walk away, that we stopped in front of a plain door. Holmes tried it, but it was locked.

"Records," I said. "We store files in there. Except that—"

"Please have the door unlocked," he interrupted.

With bad grace I returned to the foyer and commanded the night porter to accompany me back downstairs. Your brother was still where I had left him, standing in front of the door to the file room. The night porter unlocked the door and was about to open it when Holmes stopped him.

"You can come out," he called. "The jig is up, as the criminal classes say. You are under arrest."

After a few moments the door opened and a small man emerged. His teeth were prominent, rat-like, and he was unshaven. He looked dishevelled and distressed. "It's a fair cop," he said, raising his hands. "You've got me bang to rights, guv."

"This man is to be arrested for burglary and, if you wish, for espionage as well," Holmes snapped to the night porter. "Take him upstairs and call for the police." To me he snapped, "Follow!" in a peremptory tone at which I bristled. Before I could remonstrate with him he had turned around and strode off.

I caught up with him upstairs, entering the ballroom. The ambassador's body was still slumped motionless inside his environment tank, wreathed in brown smoke.

Darius Trethewey was seated on the floor, back against the glass, head in his hands.

"Mr Trethewey, I believe," Holmes called as he crossed the marble tiles. "I am Sherlock Holmes. We have your cracksman in custody." Turning to me he said, "You may wish to arrest this gentleman on the same charges. The entire thing is a hoax, designed to allow agents of some foreign power access to your archived files, and any secrets that might be contained therein."

"How can you be so sure?"

"Simple logic. Mars is further away from the sun than the Earth, therefore it will be considerably colder – cold enough to freeze water. The canals, therefore, are natural objects or illusions, and there can be no Martians with flippers for limbs. In addition, the chances of any Martian, having developed separately from humanity, sharing the same physical characteristics down to exact size and placement of the eyes, are very low. The clinching factor was the ambassador telling you that the Martians spoke a different language from us. For them to have exchanged information with Mr Trethewey and learned English via Hertzian waves is frankly unbelievable. It would be as if I had taught myself Hungarian by sending telegrams in English to a Hungarian merchant who could speak and write no English. There is no possibility of comparison of items or asking questions. It was, therefore, a confidence trick, and a fairly simple one at that, and the only question was, what was the intention? Getting the ambassador's tank into this ballroom seemed to be important, along with the deliberately large and noisy design, and these factors gave me the clue. When this contrivance was wheeled into the ballroom it contained *two* people, not one. The first – a woman, I believe, judging by the relative thinness of the limbs – was of course disguised as the Martian ambassador, and kept you busy, while the second person, hidden in the back third that was supposed to be filled with pumps, engines and tanks of bromine, cut around one of the marble tiles, removed it, then cut his way further through the floorboards to get into the file room below, where it was his job to break into the cabinets where the files are stored. The noise of the pumps and engines – which were pure flummery, of course – disguised the sound of him working. The aim was to keep you talking while he retrieved whatever files he could and resealed the floor and the tiles using materials he had brought with him."

Part of me was filled with relief that this creature was *not* a real Martian, and that we had not been party to a terrible diplomatic incident, but part of me was, I confess, embarrassed by the ease with which we had been tricked. Perhaps we just wanted to believe.

"But what of the amba… the woman *pretending* to be the ambassador?" I asked. "Surely the bromine would have killed her." I glanced at her body, the poor soul. "Well, earlier than it did."

"The glass walls of the tank are actually double-walls," Holmes said dismissively. "The glass looks thick, but that is because it is comprised of two sheets of glass with an empty space between them that has been filled with bromine. The effect is to make it look as if the entire tank is filled with the gas." He clapped his hands, and began to walk away. "I shall remit my invoice in due course," he called over his shoulder.

"But – Mr Holmes!"

He stopped and turned.

"How did the woman actually *die*?"

He frowned. "That is a trivial matter for a coroner and the police to establish."

"Can I presume there was a leak in the tank that caused the bromine to leak out of the glass walls? Did my orders cause that leak?"

He looked surprised. "No – it was murder, of course."

"Murder?" Darius Trethewey sprang to his feet and stepped forward. "Edith was *murdered*? I assumed there had been a leak in the tank as well!"

"Of course." Holmes glanced from him to me and then back again. He sighed, and walked back to where we stood. "Bromine is, like its sister gas chlorine, a bleaching agent. There is no sign of any bleaching on the Martian costume worn by the unfortunate Edith, therefore there was no leak." He glanced at Trethewey. "There was adequate ventilation?"

"There was." He was almost sobbing.

"Then she did not suffocate. As you would have seen someone else in the tank, she was not assaulted with a weapon. I deduce, therefore, that a poison was used, and it was introduced at some stage before Edith returned here in the tank." He frowned. "You may wish to suggest to the police that they examine the red make-up on her face and hands for signs of adulteration." He stepped closer to the tank. "Poison is typically a woman's weapon. Judging by Mr Trethewey's excessive grief I would suspect that he and Edith were in the middle of a passionate relationship." Glancing sideways, he said: "Are you married, Mr Trethewey?"

"I am," he said weakly.

"An adulterous relationship, then. Is your wife prone to fits of jealousy?"

"She is a very… possessive… woman," he admitted.

"Then the police would do well to start with her." He clapped his hands together. "Well, that would appear to be it. I shall leave you to sort out the details."

And with that your brother walked away.

That pretty much concludes the story, Mr Holmes. Your brother was right – the wounded Mrs Trethewey readily admitted to the police that she had laced the make-up with arsenic – she was part of the whole plot, and was particularly responsible for applying the red stain to Edith's skin. Edith was a mere commoner, a girl from the streets who had been taken on by Trethewey because of her malnourished appearance. His mistake was falling in love with her.

My fingers are aching now, from this repetitive typing, and it is late, so I shall conclude my report of events here, in the firm belief that it will be hidden somewhere and never seen again. I also find myself remembering a memorandum that you sent a few weeks ago, after Mr Trethewey had first been in contact with us but before the meeting with the supposed ambassador, in which you asked that the file rooms in the basement be relocated because you were worried about the effects of the Thames flooding. I checked with the porters, and they informed me that the files had all been recently removed to a secure building in Scotland Yard. I am left, as always, with a profound admiration for your mind, and a profound gratitude that you – and your brother – are working on *our* side, and not the side of our enemies.

Signed,
Yr obedient servant,
Holdhurst

NO GOOD DEED

David Marcum

Since I first discovered Sherlock Holmes when I was ten in 1975, I've read and collected thousands of pastiches in the form of novels and short stories, television and radio episodes, films and scripts, comics, fan fiction, and unpublished manuscripts. Since the mid-1990s, I've also organised them into a massive chronology, now over 600 pages of fine print, of both canon and pastiche, breaking down these adventures by book, chapter, page, and paragraph into year, month, day, and even hour. It represents the complete lives of Holmes and Watson, more than what is revealed in those pitifully few original sixty tales by way of the first literary agent. In those thousands of adventures, there are a great many that are not narrated by Watson, but rather by the associates of Sherlock Holmes, and they all help to provide a well-rounded view of our heroes. When George Mann invited me to participate in this new collection, I knew that I wanted to see Holmes from a different perspective than other non-Watsonian views that have been explored before – Mrs Hudson or Mycroft or the random Scotland Yard inspector. It only took a few minutes before **Jim Smith**, son of Mordecai Smith from *The Sign of the Four*, began to tell me about the previously unknown events of late April 1891 and his own subsequent encounter with Mr Sherlock Holmes. And I raced to transcribe it…

—David Marcum

I came up Baker Street that morning, 24th April it was, dodging here and there between the people already thick on the pavement. At one point I was obliged to step off into the street so that a fine lady could get by, only to get a curse yelled my way from an omnibus coming up behind me. No good deed goes unpunished, as my old mother used to say. She had cause to know; the most charitable person I ever knew, and it never helped her at all. She may be fetching her reward for it now on the other side, for all I know. She wore herself out raising five children, and putting up with her husband. She encouraged my father to do the right thing, and it lifted him up to being a better man for as long as she was able. But then she was gone, and he settled into different ways. Which was why I was making my way up that busy street, looking for a certain address and a man who I hoped could help.

It was late enough in the morning that the sun was starting to peek over the buildings on the eastern side of the street. There it was, farther north than I'd supposed. I'd never been in this part of London before – I usually navigated along the river. I'd grown up there, just across from the Tower, but thanks to my poor mother, I hadn't run that rat warren along the southern shore like the other children my age. She'd made sure that I'd stayed busy – idle hands and all that – both around the house and on my father's old boat. And along the way, I received a fairly adequate education, learned to read and write, and speak fairly well besides. I'd resented it at the time, but I certainly appreciated it now. Already, I'd been promoted twice since obtaining my current position – which would require my presence again by tomorrow night, so I hoped to get this business settled quickly.

I stepped up to the door, with mixed emotions about whether I should even be involved in this, when – before I could knock – it suddenly flew open before me. Startled, I took a step back, almost stumbling. For a sailor, I've always been slightly clumsy, especially when on land. It always vexed my father no end.

I started to mumble my excuses to the man hurrying out the door, but something caught in my throat. I suddenly felt, for no reason that I could explain, a terrible fear, like a mouse under the gaze of a hawk. On the surface, there was no reason for it at all. He was just a middle-aged fellow, such as those I see on the ship every day: tall and thin, with a high forehead, a few strands of whitish hair combed across. As he came out of the door, he was clearly angry, and muttering to himself while he placed a tall black hat upon his head.

He was snarling something about "destruction" and "promise you one, but not the other!" when he saw me. With a hiss – and it *was* a hiss, it couldn't be called anything else – he raised his cane as if he meant to strike me. Then he seemed to take hold of himself, and the rage twisting his face dropped as if covered by a falling curtain, replaced with a look of contempt. His head moved from side to side, and I almost expected his tongue to flick out like a snake. He glanced up and down at my uniform and said in a low voice, "You must be one of those damned urchins that he uses.

Take heed, boy. You'll want to get far away from him!"

He brushed past me, while I tried to take the meaning of what he'd just said. Granted, I was small, but surely I didn't still look like a boy. Maybe he'd just made a mistake because he was angry. My mother always said an angry man makes mistakes. As I wondered what other mistakes might be in store for him, I glanced up at the first-floor window and saw that I was being watched. There was a man in a dressing gown, staring intently down at me. He had surely seen my encounter with his visitor. There was a grim expression on his face, but when our eyes met, it softened, and he beckoned to me. Then he stepped away from the window.

The bald man had left the door standing open. Inside it was quiet, and with the door shut, the hallway was dark. Behind me, over the door, the fanlight let in some light, and I looked at it, with the reversed 221 showing. There was a stairway leading up, and I mounted the steps two at a time, before stopping at the door that would surely open into that room looking down on the street.

I already had an idea what to expect. Just last year, I'd come across a copy of *Lippincott's* that contained a narrative about the tenant of these very rooms. I would have been interested anyway – I'd been following this man's career since I'd first met him over two years earlier. But to see the circumstances of that very meeting reported in the magazine was almost unbelievable. The article hadn't been specifically about my father and me, but we'd both played our parts, disreputable as they were, and I was even mentioned by name. It was the closest to fame that I was ever likely to get.

All of this flashed through my mind in just a few seconds,

but it was apparently too long for the man inside. He called out, almost impatiently, for me to enter.

The sitting room of 221B Baker Street was smaller than I had expected. Mr Holmes stood before the front windows, his right hand in the pocket of his dressing gown. He seemed quite tense – not unusual, if he'd just had an argument with the man I met downstairs.

"I'm sorry," I began. "You've just had another visitor—"

He seemed as if he willed himself to relax, taking a step forward. His brow was knitted, but he made an effort to straighten his posture, whereas before he had stood as if poised to defend himself. He removed his hand from the dressing-gown pocket, and I was startled to see that it held a gun. He stepped purposefully toward the mantel, where he laid it down, then he reached for a pipe, turned, and dropped into a chair facing me, stretching his long legs out in front of the cold fireplace. I was surprised to see how tired he looked. Careworn as well, as if he had been desperately overworked for too long. And yet, in spite of his obvious weariness, there was a tightness about him, rather like a coiled spring, with all that compressed energy simply waiting to be released.

"My landlady has apparently stepped out," he said. "I can't offer you any tea, but you're welcome to smoke." He gestured toward a cane-backed chair beside him. Happy to have made it this far, and hopeful that I'd be able to tell my story and ask for his help, I gratefully sat down, fishing out the makings of a cigarette.

"I took you for a pipe smoker," he said, glancing at my pocket, where the shape of my pipe was obvious.

"I'm out of pipe tobacco."

He was packing his own pipe with tobacco from a

foreign-looking shoe tacked to the side of the mantel. "I can offer you some shag, although I'm told that my method of keeping it tends to dry it too much for most people to enjoy. But if you'll notice over there—" and he gestured toward the chair opposite him on the other side of the fireplace, "—there is some Ship's. It's not too old, as my friend that uses it is still a regular visitor."

"Dr Watson's, then," I said. "Is he not here?"

"The good doctor married a couple of years ago, and now has a practice in Paddington."

Replacing the cigarette fixings, I withdrew my old pipe, a friend to me both in port and on my travels, and stepped across for the tobacco. It was a bit stronger than what I normally used, but I felt that I would need the extra boost that it provided to convince Mr Holmes to help me.

As we both finished the tedious process of getting our pipes lit, I settled back and started to speak. But even as my mouth opened, Mr Holmes said, "Do you enjoy the London to Liverpool run better than plying up and down the Thames?"

I nearly dropped the pipe. I had seen a little bit of this for myself, during that short time I had been around him in September '88. And I knew as well from reading about it in the story in *Lippincott's*, called *The Sign of the Four*, that he did this type of thing all the time, the way that an old salt can tell the coming weather from the clouds, or judge the shallowness of the water just from the smell. But I somehow hadn't expected him to practise it upon me.

I glanced down. "I can see how you would know I'm a sailor," I said, "and this is the uniform of the Liverpool, Dublin, and London Steam Packet Company, out of the Albert Dock—"

"On the *May Day*, perhaps?"

I swallowed. "Yes. But how did you know about the Thames?"

He pulled his legs back and crossed them. "You were born in Southwark, and were raised in a brick house adjacent to the Thames, straight across from the Tower. It's since been torn down. You have four younger brothers, no sisters, and you are the eldest at twenty years of age. You are left-handed, and walked here today, rather than taking a cab or some form of public transport. You are obviously a sailor, and have been on the Liverpool boats for two years, after spending your life assisting your father on his steamship, the *Aurora*." He closed his eyes. "Black, as I recall, with two red streaks. And a black funnel with a white band."

"Ah." I understood now. "You remember me."

"Yes," he nodded. "Sometimes hard facts make deduction unnecessary. You are Jim Smith, son of Mordecai Smith. You were but seventeen when Jonathan Small hired you and your father to wait for him while he retrieved the Agra Treasure, in order to transport it downstream to a waiting ship."

I nodded. "After we ran aground that night, you and Dr Watson were quite kind to me. When the police took charge of the *Aurora* until it could be searched in the morning, and my father and I were pulled onto the police launch, you gave me your coat."

He waved it away. "I was sorry to hear about the loss of your mother."

I raised my eyebrows in surprise. "How did you know about that?"

"Your little brother, Jack. He sometimes assists my Irregulars."

Ah, Jack. I feared for him. Since my mother's death, he

had been in the care of my other brothers, who in turn were nominally under the protection of my father. However, as his situation had declined, so had their prospects. I was glad that Jack was benefiting from some association with Mr Holmes, however remote.

"I didn't know that Jack had found employment."

"That says a great deal about your brother's trustworthiness." A slight smile danced around his eyes. "I knew when the little scoundrel asked me for a shilling back in '88, and then another, that he was sharp." His expression changed, and he added, "I was also sorry to hear of the loss of your house and dock."

"Yes. When the building of the Tower Bridge was announced, we had no idea that it would swallow our little piece of property. We were given what was termed 'adequate compensation', but of course it wasn't. I believe that my mother's broken heart was what led to her early death."

"And your father?"

I sat up straighter. "That's why I'm here, Mr Holmes. It seems that my father has disappeared, and I need your help to find him."

Mr Holmes's eyes narrowed, and a pained expression crossed his face. "I'm afraid you have come at an inopportune time," he said. "My previous visitor has been pushed right to the wall, of late, and he has indicated that certain events are being set in motion that cannot be stopped. Things are quickly coming to a head, and all my attention and energy in the next few days will be occupied elsewhere."

"Perhaps," I said earnestly, seeing my chance slipping away before I'd even been able to present my case, "if you'll only let me tell you the circumstances, you might be able to at least offer a suggestion."

He closed his eyes and took a deep breath. "Proceed. Perhaps an armchair investigation might be for the best today."

At that moment, I heard the street door open and close. Mr Holmes immediately sat up, glancing toward the gun on the mantel. Then, something in the sounds below must have seemed familiar, because he visibly relaxed. He stood and crossed the room to the door. "Mrs Hudson!" he cried before bounding down the steps. In a moment he returned, stating, "Excuse me. I had to relay some urgent instructions, as well as request some tea. I had observed that you appeared to be thirsty before beginning your tale, and as you've taken the Blue Ribbon, I didn't want to offer you anything stronger."

"It's true. I took the pledge a year ago, after my father's drinking increased. It had always been something of an issue, but my mother was able to keep it in check. Since her death, he has become much worse. I believe that is what has gotten him into this situation."

Returning to his seat, he waved. "Tell me more."

I settled back. "After we lost the property, we relocated to a house farther back from the river. My father found a new place to dock the boat, but it wasn't the same. Part of what gave him any success at all was having our house – and my mother – right there at our own dock to keep an eye on things, to manage the business, and frankly to keep him out of trouble. Now that she was at the new house all day, my father was left to his own devices at the dock, and he quickly fell into the bad habits that had called to him throughout his life.

"As I said, my mother was heartbroken. My father stayed away, drinking instead of earning a living with the *Aurora*. In the end, he lost it to the creditors, and my mother died, all within the same month. I had stopped working with him long before that. I had wanted to stay and try to help him find some sort of success, and frankly to keep him on the right path, but we simply had to have someone bringing in a steady wage. I was able to get on with Liverpool, Dublin, and London, and at least that kept food upon the table.

"When my mother died, Father seemed to rally for a while, for the boys. He stopped drinking, and he obtained a job with a merchant of some sort, who needed someone to manage his imports. My father had no experience with that sort of thing, but he did know the docks and the ships, so it seemed like a good fit. He was able to feed my brothers, and I began to worry less about all of them.

"It didn't take long, however, to see that something was weighing upon my father's mind. It took several months before I could get the truth from him, and even then the details were sketchy. The short of it is that his employer was involved in some sort of smuggling, which I suppose is no surprise, and with every week that passed, my father became increasingly worried that he was being snared tighter.

"There was a sort of feeling growing within the groups that my father had dealings with, an uneasiness that it was all going to come crashing down at some point, taking everyone involved with it. Once, when I was home for a visit, Father broke down, worrying what would happen to the boys if he were arrested, and making me promise to take care of them. I calmed him, but the worry about it kept growing in my head."

"Who is your father's employer?" interrupted Mr Holmes.

"Mr Parnell. Abel Parnell."

His eyes narrowed. "And does young Jack know that any of this was taking place?"

"I'm certain that he does."

"He never told me about any of it."

"Apparently his trustworthiness and discretion run both ways."

His lips tightened in something like a smile, and at that moment, the landlady knocked on the door, bringing in the tea. Pouring a cup for each of us, she departed. I sipped mine gratefully, while Mr Holmes left his untouched. He waved for me to continue.

"A week ago, I returned home to find the boys alone. My father had gone on some errand for Mr Parnell several days earlier, and hadn't returned. Thankfully he had left them enough money, plus what remained of my wage, so that they hadn't run out of food. We're fortunate that a widow next door keeps an eye on things since Mother died, but in any case, it was of some concern that my father hadn't been home. I began to fear that either he had resumed drinking, or that his position with Mr Parnell had led him into deeper danger. I asked around at his usual haunts, but no one had seen him. Then I crossed the river and went to Mr Parnell's office, off Oxford Street, but I couldn't get past the clerk, who simply said that he had no idea where my father could be, and that if I didn't leave, he'd have me thrown out.

"I waited outside for several hours, knowing that it was unlikely that I'd see my father arrive just when I was on the scene – and I was right. He never appeared. Finally, I had to return to Southwark, making sure that my brothers would be all right for another week while I was off on my run to Liverpool and Dublin."

"And when you returned again this morning," said Mr Holmes, standing, "you found that your father was still missing." He walked behind me, to some shelves filled with commonplace books that were mounted on the wall beside the fireplace, and pulled down a volume.

"That's right," I said. "I asked at a few of my father's old watering holes, and around the docks, but it felt as if I was wasting my time again. Finally, knowing it would be pointless to return to Mr Parnell's office, I recalled meeting you and decided to see if you could offer any advice." I paused, and then said, with a lowered voice, "I'm afraid that I cannot pay what you usually receive."

He glanced up from the book with surprise. Then, with an impatient shake of his head, he said, "My fees are fixed, except when I remit them entirely." Closing the book with a snap, he returned it to the shelf. "As I will in this case." He started to turn away, and then reached up and touched the book for a moment, looking from there to several other items around the room, almost with sadness.

"I have encountered Mr Parnell before," he continued. "He is an agent of the very man that you met upon your arrival." I raised my eyebrows, and he correctly read my thoughts. "It is not so much of a coincidence as you might think. The man that was leaving today sits like a spider in the midst of a web that stretches across London, with a thousand dirty threads in every direction. These days, it would be almost impossible to meet a criminal who isn't connected with the Professor, my earlier visitor, in some way or another. It really is becoming intolerable."

"Then why haven't you done something?" I blurted out.

His lips tightened, and he turned toward the closed door behind him. Shrugging out of his dressing gown as he went, he answered, "I have."

He opened the door, revealing a small bedroom, barely

lit by the tall window that looked out toward the rear of the house. I remained seated as he began pulling on a coat. I was afraid to speak, scarcely hoping that something I'd said had interested him and that he was preparing to help me.

He returned and crossed the room, and I stood. At the door to the landing he pulled on an overcoat and asked, "What did the Professor say to you downstairs?"

"He warned me. He said I must be one of those urchins that you use, and that it would be well for me to get away from you."

His eyes narrowed. "He must have seen your resemblance to Jack. I'll need to get word to him and the others to stay out of sight for a while."

He held open the door and gestured for me to precede him. "Let us go see Mr Parnell."

Downstairs, he paused for a moment before opening the door. "I really do have some scruples about taking you with me. Just now, I'm under a rather dangerous cloud, you see."

I swallowed. "Mr Holmes, I had no real hope of any help today whatsoever. I'm very grateful, and I'll be happy to accompany you."

He nodded and opened the door. "Then we shall attempt to avoid the danger."

Outside, he paused, looking up and down the street, as if expecting something that didn't seem to be there. Right in front of us was a hansom cab. Having never ridden in one, it didn't occur to me to think that I would now, and it turned out that I was correct. As if assuming that I'd meant to walk toward it, Mr Holmes put a hand on my arm. "There are times when an urgency requires that one take the first cab that presents itself. Then, at other times, one should not take the first, or even the second. Today, if you have no objections, I think that we shall eschew horse-drawn transportation altogether – it has the disadvantage of trapping one in a box at the mercy of one's opponent, especially if the driver deviates from your chosen route. What do you say, Mr Smith, to a ramble through London?"

I agreed, a little puzzled, and we started down Baker Street. My eyes met those of the cabman, and for a moment, it seemed as if his narrowed in anger. Then, I was racing to keep up with the much longer legs of my companion.

Mr Holmes didn't cut a straight path. He led me down George Street and Thayer Street, and on into narrower William Street. He asked me a few more questions about my father, but he seemed to already know the answers, and while he listened intently, his attention was mostly turned toward keeping an eye on our surroundings. He looked toward doorways and passages and into mews, and upwards as well, towards windows and rooftops.

We were on the crossing at the corner that leads from Bentinck Street on to Welbeck Street when Mr Holmes threw out his arm and pulled me back. It was a two-horse van, driven crazily by a man who was whipping his horses mercilessly. He took the corner into Bentinck Street on two wheels before racing down the short distance to Marylebone Lane. He turned there again and vanished.

I took another step back on my own and almost stumbled. Mr Holmes, still gripping my arm, steadied me, and said with a grim look on his face, "The Professor didn't waste any time. We'll have to be more careful."

I nodded. I had thought we were already being careful. But then again, we hadn't been killed, and that was something.

Keeping away from the edge of the pavement, we soon

crossed Wigmore and Henrietta Place, and then made the short turn into Vere Street, which would lead us to Oxford Street. Somehow I felt that we would be safer on that busy thoroughfare than we had been so far.

I was soon convinced of a couple of things – one, that I probably should have taken Mr Holmes up on his offer to remove myself from this situation, and two, that I was right to want to get to Oxford Street as soon as possible. We had barely started down Vere Street when Mr Holmes gave a cry, pushing me forward at the same time. Thank goodness he had been looking up. I heard rather than saw the impact on the pavement behind me. I stumbled but kept my feet and, turning quickly, saw a shattered brick lying between us. Naturally, I looked up, just in time to see an angry rat-like face staring down at us for only an instant before it pulled back and vanished.

A constable was just down the street at the Oxford end, and Mr Holmes called him over. Explaining in general terms that someone had intentionally dropped the brick from the rooftop above, thus endangering passers-by, he convinced the somewhat sceptical officer to investigate. A knock on the door and an explanation from the policeman to the landlady quickly gained us access to the roof. Mr Holmes crawled about, looking here and there, while the policeman pointed several times to a pile of building materials nearby, explaining with some pride his theory that the wind – of which there was none whatsoever that morning – had blown one of the bricks over the side. Neither Mr Holmes nor I mentioned that we had seen the man who dropped the missile, and the policeman became frustrated when his theory wasn't praised, or in fact even acknowledged. Finally, the detective straightened, thanked the constable, and led us back to the street.

As the irritated policeman wandered away, Mr Holmes said softly, "I recognised the fellow on the roof. It was Parker, one of the Professor's men. Dropping stones is not his normal method – he usually prefers to carry out his killings much closer to the victims."

"If you recognised him, then why did you bother examining the roof?"

"To see if there was evidence of anyone else. It would appear that Parker is working alone. The Professor may have mobilised his troops, but so far they are rather disorganised. I believe that I owe you a debt of thanks, Mr Smith."

"You do? For what?"

"You've done me a good deed. For getting me out and about today, after all."

I recalled what my mother used to say about good deeds. "But why? It has only placed you in danger."

"Not any more than I would have been in Baker Street. And if I had remained there, I would have been gradually outnumbered and bottled up until there would have been nowhere to go, and no way to even summon assistance. No, by presenting your problem when you did, I was able to slip through their net before it was quite fixed. And I intend for that to remain the case. Shall we continue on our errand?"

We walked east until we reached Rathbone Place. Mr Holmes knew as well as I did where we were going, leading me around the corner. I wondered what he could tell me about Mr Parnell, and how much he'd found out about the man in the commonplace book beside his fireplace.

Not far down on the left was a doorway opening onto a stairwell. I had been here a week before, and nothing had changed. We started upstairs, and I was very happy to let Mr Holmes lead. I had the sense that my presence there wouldn't have made any difference one way or another.

We stepped into the room where I had been turned away before. The man behind the desk was lean and dangerous-looking, and he half-stood before sinking back down, a look of recognition and – possibly – fear on his face. He half-heartedly said something to the effect that we could not go inside, but it was too late, for Mr Holmes had already opened the door.

Inside, a fat man rocked back in a chair beside a tall roll-top desk along one wall. There was only one high window behind it, apparently opening onto some court behind the building. I hadn't met Mr Parnell before, but my father had described him, and I knew that we were in his presence.

He started to speak, but then collapsed into a rheumy cough, much like those of the old workhouse men. I knew that if he tried to stand, he'd probably have the workhouse legs as well. How could a man like this have ended up in an office, carrying out important business for someone? For the Professor?

"Mr Holmes," he finally wheezed. "I didn't expect you."

"I am certain of that. Has the word gone out that the inconvenience I'm causing will soon stop, one way or another?"

"I have heard something along those lines, although there isn't any question about who will be the victor."

"That conclusion is premature. Tell me about Mordecai Smith."

Parnell's eyebrows rose like those of Punch – at least, the way they do on some of the fancier puppets I've seen. His surprise was sincere. Then, for the first time, he looked past the detective and saw me. His eyes narrowed. "You're the son," he sighed. "I'd heard you were here."

"Why won't you tell me what has happened to my father?" I blurted out. Mr Holmes held up a hand.

"My friend's question stands," he said.

Parnell coughed and shook his head. "He had an attack of conscience. There is some important business about to take place, and he objected to it. He threatened to tell the police if we didn't desist." He laughed, and then collapsed back in his chair in a fit of wheezing. "If the fool felt like that," he said when he caught his breath, "why didn't he just tell the police? Why warn us ahead of time, as if his puny threat would make us change our plans?"

"I take it you are referring to the arrival of the *Lydia McGraw*, from China."

Parnell's eyes widened. "Maybe you really are as good as they say."

"I suspect my sources are better than yours. In fact, it was diverted in Marseilles four days ago, and the ladies held within have been freed."

"Impossible! I would have heard."

"You only knew what I wanted you to know. You wouldn't know now if I wasn't interested in Mordecai Smith's whereabouts."

"The Professor should have killed you years ago."

"Speaking of life and death, is Mr Smith still alive?"

Parnell waved a wrinkled hand. "He is. I hadn't decided yet what should happen to him."

"I have decided for you. Have him at Baker Street by eight tomorrow morning. Unharmed. I assume that you're keeping him in the warehouse in Whitstable. That allows you plenty of time to retrieve him."

Parnell laughed. "And why should I do what you say, Mr

Holmes? You're a walking dead man."

"Need I remind you of Helen Silsoe of Stoke Mandeville?"

Never have I seen a man lose his colour so fast. In fact, considering the man's condition, I'm surprised that Parnell didn't die on the spot. He swallowed twice, and then fumbled to open one of the drawers in his desk. He brought out a bottle of brandy and drank from it. He coughed, closed his eyes, drank again, and then set the bottle down. "Eight, you said? I can have him there in four hours."

"Eight o'clock tomorrow is fine," said Mr Holmes. "And in perfect condition. I have other business to attend to today." He looked around the office, as if memorising its features. "I do trust that Mordecai Smith is still in pristine condition."

"He's well enough," said Parnell, a whiny tone now in his voice.

"Good day, Mr Parnell," said Holmes, turning to pass through the door. My eyes met those of Parnell, and for one brief instant, I saw the fire of hate in his eyes. Then, just as quickly, it was gone. No doubt he feared that the power held over him by Mr Holmes might also pass to me. Far be it from me to disabuse him of the notion.

On the street, I found myself somewhat shaken. Had it really been that easy? Of course, it wasn't over yet. My father still had to put in an appearance.

I looked up as Mr Holmes pressed something into my hand. It was his card, upon which he'd written a man's name, along with a well-known shipping company in the East End. "This fellow owes me a favour or two," he said. "If you think that you can straighten your father out, then take him there and let this man know that he needs a job. Show that card. It should be enough."

I didn't know what to say. I wanted to express my thanks, but he waved them away. "I'll see you tomorrow morning in Baker Street," he added, starting to turn away.

"But—" I said, then stopped. He turned, looking back expectantly. "But it isn't safe for you. Can I help?"

He smiled then, the first time I'd seen him truly smile since meeting him. Shaking his head, he said, "No, although the thought is much appreciated. You should make your own way home for the night, being careful, of course, that you aren't followed. You have, after all, spent a portion of the day with me, and that carries a certain amount of risk."

He glanced around, as if to spot the very danger of which he spoke. "I'm going to spend the day with my brother at his club, and then possibly visit Dr Watson." And with that, he set off, back down Rathbone Place, and so into Oxford Street.

I watched him go, considering his advice only long enough to realise that I was about to lose sight of him. Hurrying, I saw him step abruptly into the street, hailing a passing growler. I recalled his advice about not taking the first or second cab, but assumed that this one, chosen at random on the busy street, was acceptable. I still felt that I needed to provide some sort of assistance, however insignificant it might be. I couldn't run after him, wherever he was going, and I didn't want to try and follow in a cab of my own. Finally, hoping that I hadn't grown too tall, or that my uniform wouldn't attract too much attention, and trusting that my old skills hadn't completely deserted me, I dashed forward and secured a tenuous seat on the back of the vehicle.

The cab headed south, finally reaching Pall Mall. When I felt the cab start to slow, I jumped off as I had learned to long ago. Not a moment too soon, it turned out, as the cab stopped in front of No. 78. Mr Holmes paid the cabbie and dashed up the front steps, leaving me to wonder exactly what I was doing.

I stayed hidden in an alleyway for several hours. I was considering whether to abandon my post, when the detective appeared on the steps, pulling his gloves from his pocket. He had been there but a few seconds when he and I, from our different spots, both heard a cry. Mr Holmes tensed. A man was running toward him from across the street, carrying a club, and bellowing loud enough to wake the dead. I realised that I was not suited for this type of work at all, as I had not previously noticed the fellow. I was rising to render assistance when I saw that it wouldn't be necessary. Mr Holmes had dropped his gloves and settled into a crouch. Even as the man reached him, a quick move that I couldn't even describe afterwards was all that it took to leave the attacker stretched on the pavement, clutching a clearly broken jaw. Mr Holmes called for the elderly doorman to summon the police. Then, turning toward where I was hidden, Mr Holmes called, "You can join me, Mr Smith."

I sheepishly walked up the street, where he was binding a handkerchief over two bleeding knuckles. "I suspect that the driver of the cab that brought us here – oh, yes, Mr Smith, I knew when you joined us – told the Professor where I was. I suppose that I'm quite lucky that he only sent Devereaux to kill me and not a whole pack of them." He glanced up and down the street. "They must not have ready access to Von Herder's air gun at the moment," he said softly, almost to himself. "But they'll get it soon enough."

He finished wrapping his hand and said, louder this

time, "I observed you move to defend me just now. It is much appreciated, but I assure you that I can take care of myself. You should return to your family. I've finished making my plans with my brother, and I go now to inform Dr Watson. I shall be safe enough."

I could tell that he wouldn't take no for an answer. And, as I was uncertain as to what assistance I could provide in any case, and as there was no way that I could follow him without his knowing, I agreed. I left him there, wondering if I would myself be attacked on the way home for simply having been in his company.

The next morning, I was at Baker Street fifteen minutes before the appointed time. There was a cluster of idlers standing in the street, and a fire wagon was nearby, the firemen rolling up a long hose.

I hurried forward and slipped through the lingering firemen and loiterers without waiting to learn what had happened. There were faint smoke stains on the wall above the windows of the sitting room. Had the Professor's men succeeded after all? Had Mr Holmes been killed, in spite of his confidence and many abilities?

I dashed through the open door and pounded up the steps to Mr Holmes's rooms. His door was open, and I lurched to a stop, seeing a couple of men standing there. One was a tall fellow with very blonde hair and large hands. Everything about him proclaimed that he was a policeman. The other, with his back to me, was some sort of priest. He was in a long black robe, and hanging from his hand was a wide, round parson's hat of the sort that I've sometimes seen the Italians wear when aboard my ship.

The policeman looked up and scowled when I entered. The priest turned more slowly, and my jaw dropped when I saw that it was Mr Holmes.

"Ah, Smith," he said. "The inspector and I were just discussing last night's fire. Luckily, the damage was only superficial."

The inspector's eyes kept looking at me with suspicion, something that has happened to me – and any boy growing up in Southwark – upon any number of occasions. Mr Holmes noticed it and said, "Nothing to worry about, Gregson. This is another matter entirely. Just a bit of last-minute business before the game begins."

"If you say so, Mr Holmes," replied the other man. He glanced toward a desk in the corner. "Will the papers be all right there?"

"They will. In pigeonhole 'M', and done up in a blue envelope, just like we agreed."

"I still don't know why you can't just give them to Patterson or me right now."

"We've discussed that."

The big man shrugged and put on his hat. "As you say, Mr Holmes. We've discussed it. But I'm not sure that I agree with it. Luring him to the Continent? What will that accomplish?"

"It will serve to leave his train without a conductor, right at the most crucial turn in the track. With him distracted, the train will fly off the rails, and you and your men will be there to pick up the pieces."

"It sounds dangerous."

"It is."

They looked at one another, and then the big inspector stuck out his hand and shook Holmes's. "God speed, then," he said with quiet sincerity, and then departed.

Before I had a chance to speak, Mr Holmes turned away and began fussing with a suitcase on his chair. He added some tobacco and, after careful consideration, an oily black clay pipe. Then he snapped it shut. It was then that I heard a cough. Turning, I saw my father standing in the door. Somehow he'd silently climbed the stairs. In the old days, when he was drinking, he could never have been so quiet.

I ran to him, feeling like a child in spite of my twenty years. He threw his arms about me and gave a sob. We stood like that for a moment, and then he took a deep breath and backed away. He smiled. There was apology in it, but also an unspoken promise.

"They—" he began, turning to the door, and then had to clear his throat, "they told me that I'm free because of you, Mr Holmes. How can I – that is to say, how can *we* thank you?"

"If you don't mind just a little more danger, Messrs Smith, I could use some camouflage," Holmes said.

And so, fifteen minutes later, we were in a four-wheeler headed for Victoria Station. After we had agreed with Mr Holmes's seemingly painless scheme, he had directed us towards the door. Then, placing the flat priest's hat on his head, he had picked up his suitcase and followed us. Turning, he looked back into the sitting room for a long minute. Now, after knowing what happened later, I wonder if he had a premonition, and was taking a last look around to say goodbye. But I suppose that I'm simply remembering it that way to make it a better story. In any case, he pulled the sitting-room door shut, led us downstairs, and out through the back of the house.

We walked to Dorset Square, where he hailed a cab. As

we boarded, I hurriedly showed my father Mr Holmes's card with the name of a man who would give him a job. My father started to thank the detective once again, but Mr Holmes impatiently waved it away.

"They will be looking for me," he explained, changing the subject, "and I'm not certain that my disguise will pass muster. I wore something of this sort a few years ago, when I needed to fool a woman into showing me where she had hidden a photograph. I had hired a number of people to stage a fight in the street as a distraction, and some of them had also done work for the Professor in the past. They may very well remember this disguise and be looking for it. However, it seemed like one of the best that I could assume in order to pass relatively unnoticed on the boat train. If they are looking for a priest, maybe it will be less conspicuous if I'm traveling with two other men. At least, that's what I hope. Both of you are known, one way or the other, to the Professor's people, and that could cause difficulties. We'll have to make a few minor changes to your appearances and hope for the best."

My father hung his head, looking ashamed for a moment while Mr Holmes adjusted his and my clothing. But then, remembering his second chance, he looked up with a new determination that I was happy to see.

As we made our way to Victoria, Mr Holmes watched all sides from the cab windows. He seemed satisfied that we weren't being followed. We reached the station, and he offered to pay the cabbie to take us wherever we wanted to go, but my father demurred, stating instead that, if I didn't mind, we would prefer to walk and enjoy the new day. Mr Holmes thanked us again for our help, and then vanished into the crowds streaming into the station.

My father and I stood there for a moment amidst the bustle. We were preparing to leave when I saw Dr Watson arrive in a small brougham, driven by a massive driver in a dark cape and a scarf pulled over his face. No sooner had the doctor stepped to the ground and retrieved his bag than the driver whipped up his horse and vanished into the distance.

Dr Watson watched him for a puzzled moment and then went inside. I was explaining to my father who it was that we had just seen when another carriage arrived, also in great haste. It skidded to a halt, and I was shocked to see who its passenger was: the very man that had loomed so large in my thoughts for the last twenty-four hours: Professor Moriarty.

He turned his head this way and that, in that curiously snake-like fashion, clearly looking for someone – Sherlock Holmes, perhaps, or the doctor, whom he had apparently followed. Then, not seeing them, he began to make his way into the station, cursing and swinging his stick when the crowd inadvertently blocked his way.

Telling my father to stay where he was, I followed. Over by the Continental Express, I could see Dr Watson looking anxiously this way and that. Behind him, Sherlock Holmes, dressed as the Italian priest, was climbing into the first-class carriage. Who could they be waiting for? And was it possible that Dr Watson was looking for Mr Holmes, not realising that the man was right behind him?

Even as I asked myself that question, the Professor saw Dr Watson, and headed in his direction. Not knowing what he intended, I moved without thinking. Dodging past a nursemaid pushing a pram and an old soldier with one leg, I circled back toward the Professor. He was still quite a distance away from the doctor and Mr Holmes, and there was a surge of people between them, moving toward the train. The doors were starting to slam shut, whistles were being blown, and I could see that Dr Watson was climbing into his compartment, still looking around. Then he turned with a jerk, looking at the man in priest's clothing across from him. He said something. The train started to move.

At that point, the Professor gave a cry of rage. Several people turned his way, and I observed Dr Watson look at him as well. His eyes locked with those of the Professor, even as the train gained speed. The Professor reached his hand into his coat. Fearing what he would remove, and what would happen when he did, I made a final lunge forward, knocking him to the ground. A gun fell from his hand and skittered across the platform. I ran to it and kicked it the rest of the way across the platform and into the gap beside the accelerating train, where it disappeared from sight.

I turned back to the Professor, who was getting to his feet. He raised the cane, pointing it accusingly in my direction. His eyes locked with mine, and then they flicked down toward my uniform. I knew that he recognised me from the day before. He took a step toward me, and then stopped. Seeming to make a decision, he cried aloud, "Bah!" and turned, making his way haltingly toward the office where one arranges to engage special trains.

I wanted to do something else to help, but I had reached the limit of what I could provide. If the Professor chose to engage a special, there was nothing that I could do. I prayed that Mr Holmes and Dr Watson, wherever they were bound, would be safe. Perhaps there was hope after all. Now all that I had to fear was that the Professor had marked me. That was quite enough to worry about.

* * *

Nearly two weeks later, on 7th May, I was on the run back from Liverpool when I happened to read the Reuters dispatch, telling what had happened to Mr Holmes when the Professor caught up with him in Switzerland on the fourth. The details were sparse, but it was enough, and it was absolute. I couldn't imagine how it had happened. Mr Holmes was the most capable man I'd ever met. What set of circumstances had occurred that would let a man like the Professor win?

Still, I believe that if the only way to defeat the Professor was for Mr Holmes to sacrifice himself, then he wouldn't have hesitated. From the little that I'd seen during those two days, and all that I've read and heard about him during the two-and-a-half years since that day he and Dr Watson left London, I cannot doubt that he knew what he was doing.

Just the other day, when I returned from the Liverpool–Dublin run, my father handed me the latest *Strand* magazine. It had the account of what took place on those two days in April '91, and what happened after that as well. There was no mention of me or my father – but, then, there wouldn't be, as it's likely that Mr Holmes never mentioned it.

I've thought about writing to Dr Watson, to tell him of this, one of Mr Holmes's last cases, but something keeps holding me back. Perhaps, now that I've written this account, I'll send it to him. He needs to know that, through Mr Holmes's efforts, my father had the opportunity to change his life, and he grabbed that chance and has made the best of it. It's been a good year, and we had a good Christmas, all of us, including my wife and new child.

My mother would be happy, but she would shake her

head when pointing out that, even though I now know better, good deeds are always followed by punishment. "Look at what happened to poor Mr Holmes after he helped you!" she would say, and no amount of argument from my side – that what happened to him was already in motion when he took time to aid us – would sway her, God rest her soul.

And God rest Mr Sherlock Holmes as well. As Dr Watson wrote, he was the best and wisest man – even if I only knew him for just a couple of days – that I've ever known.

THE CURIOUS CASE OF VANISHED YOUTH

Mark A. Latham

I've long had a fascination with **Langdale Pike**. We know little about him, except that he is a "strange" and "languid" character, who spends his days "in the bow window of a St. James's Street club". He is named in one story – "The Adventure of the Three Gables" – but although he does not appear directly, unusually it is he, and not Holmes, who solves the case. We know little about the man, except that Watson dislikes him. Scholars have pointed to the language used in describing Pike as perhaps an indictment of the man's sexual persuasion in the Victorian mind, and to Watson's strange disavowing of Pike as reflective of Conan Doyle's own attitudes. And yet Pike is, in many respects, the hero of "Three Gables", and it has often led me to ponder whether he was analogous to a real-life character known to Victorian society, or to Doyle. This, then, was the inspiration for my story.

—Mark A. Latham

Between the years 1891 and 1894, Sherlock Holmes was dead. Or so everyone thought. And yet, of course, his legacy lived on until the time that he returned to us from the grave, triumphant against a great evil that had plagued Europe for years. But what of the dark times between Holmes's fall at Reichenbach and his return in "The Empty House"? If one was to believe the stories of Dr Watson, Holmes miraculously solved at least one case during that period, and likely others, though careful scrutiny of the case notes makes it clear to all but the most bone-headed Scotland Yard inspector that the detective at Watson's side then was not Holmes at all.

Much later, upon the publication of "The Adventure of the Three Gables", I gave a wry smile. Watson had, as always, altered the names and locations pertinent to the case to protect the innocent. And yet he had no choice but to characterise me, because the case could not have been solved without me. And so, in the pages of *The Strand*, I found myself immortalised as a "strange" and "languid" character, who spends his days sitting in the window of a St. James's Street club (nonsense, of course, for I virtually reside at the Albemarle).

He called me Langdale Pike.

Now that the Great Detective has retired, I think it is safe to put pen to paper to record my first case with Watson, one that he never dramatised, for reasons that will become very clear by the end of the narrative. I doubt very much that I shall ever publish it however, for this is a lurid and curious tale. This, then, is my story.

It was in the late autumn of 1891 that the most alarming news reached my ears. I had long made it my business to know everyone else's, and gossip seemed to gravitate towards me quite naturally, for me to use or store away as I saw fit. Indeed, Dr Watson later painted me as a scurrilous rumour-merchant; rather an exaggeration. But this particular nugget of information was not of the usual kind, for it concerned matters rather too close to home.

It was my fellow clubman Bosie who brought the news. I was sitting in the library window of the Albemarle, ostensibly working on my latest play, but really gazing distractedly onto the street beyond. It has always been in my nature to abandon anything that becomes a chore; my humble drama, which had started as an amusing conceit, had rapidly become a commitment to a noted West End producer, and now my brain wanted nothing more than to abandon the task at hand and find something more intriguing to occupy it. Bosie's interruption brought to me what I craved, though I quickly learned to be careful what I wished for.

"Might I have a word, old boy?" he ventured.

"You needn't ask, Bosie. Take a seat."

"Not here," he said, lowering his voice. "Best to take this somewhere more private."

His youthful expression was so uncharacteristically grave that my interest was piqued at once, and I led the way to a private room. Bosie lit a cigarette with a trembling hand, and I realised that something very serious was affecting him.

"It's about a mutual acquaintance of ours," Bosie said. "Young Toby."

"Be more specific; I know several Tobys."

"You only know one Toby Cottingford."

I leaned forward, and now it was my turn to lower my voice. "What of him?"

"He's missing."

"Missing? For how long?"

"Four days certainly, perhaps a few days before that."

"A strange answer," I said. "Is it four days, or is it more?"

"I..." he paused. "I was to meet him four days ago, but he never turned up. I thought he'd just changed his mind."

"Oh, Bosie," I groaned.

"Come on, Pike, you know Toby. Anyway, he didn't turn up, and I thought no more of it. Then I was talking with Whiggins yesterday, and he mentioned something similar. And apparently Toby's sweetheart is beside herself, hasn't seen him for a week."

"Sweetheart?"

"Fiancée, actually. He's supposed to be marrying some bank clerk's daughter from Holborn."

I cleared my throat. "Now that's the most unlikely thing you've told me so far."

"It's true."

"Has it been reported to the police?"

"The girl reported it, but they told her that a young gentleman is quite within his rights to go where he pleases. They probably think he's had a change of heart about the girl, and has beat a retreat to the country."

"And what do you think?"

"I think Toby's a flighty bird, but he's not the sort to be so callous."

"So you say…" I thought for a moment. "Why come to me? You aren't implying that—"

"Oh, good grief no," Bosie threw up his hands. "I know that's old history. Besides, I tried all the… usual haunts. No one has seen him for weeks. Looks like he's taking this girl seriously, which is why I worry."

"But you were meeting him, four days ago," I said, my eyebrow raised.

"Well, that's different. Old times' sake. Look, you know everyone and everything, old boy. Thought maybe you could perhaps find something out, seeing as the police are unwilling."

"Bosie, you are a dear friend, so do not take offence at what I am about to imply. But if the police were to take an interest, would they come to your door asking the wrong sort of questions?"

Bosie went very pale, and I knew I had hit upon the nub of it. "Quite possibly," he said. "But I doubt they'd stop at just me."

I sucked in a breath. Bosie wasn't the sort to deliberately make trouble for anyone, but he wasn't the most discreet of men either. I decided to change the subject. "What about Toby's father?"

"The old goat is about to shuffle off the mortal coil. Toby's only nineteen but he's been running the family's affairs for some time already."

"And you don't think Sir Denis Cottingford might have sent Toby off somewhere having learned of his son's more bohemian habits?"

"No, he's not exactly compos mentis. Besides, he only has one son and heir—who else is he going to leave the family jewels to?"

"Certainly not to a bank clerk's daughter from Holborn,"

I mused. "Perhaps I should talk to the girl first." My mind was already churning through possibilities. Given Toby's past associates, some of those possibilities were too terrible to dwell upon. "Toby Cottingford is a friend. I shall find him."

"I don't doubt it," Bosie said. "If anyone can find him, it's you."

The next morning, I paid a visit to the girl, one Dorothea Beresford. The house was a well-presented second-rate affair, not far from Furnival's, that great Inn of Chancery. I could see why Toby would meet a girl here of all places; the inns had long been occupied by men predisposed to bachelorhood.

The door was answered by a housemaid, who was naturally reticent to allow a strange man to see her young mistress who was, I was informed, home alone. A calling card revealing my identity, and a deftly presented shilling with it, secured me access regardless, and I was ushered into a small bland sitting room.

When Dorothea Beresford entered, my impression was that she suited her environment perfectly. In my younger days I would have said something awfully biting, such as "how on earth could a blazing flame like Toby extinguish himself so in such a pool of mundanity". Nowadays, however, I understood only too well the need for the mundane, like the grounding of an uncontrollable electrical charge.

"Do you really think you can find Toby?" the girl said over tea, when she had finally shaken the stars from her eyes.

"I can try," I replied, "which is more than can be said for the police, if I understand correctly. Tell me, when did you see Toby last?"

"Last Friday, at the music hall."

"Which music hall?"

She leaned forwards, and whispered, "Mile End. The Paragon."

I offered a reassuring smile. "I shall tell no one if you don't," I said. "Toby has a predilection for visiting such places incognito. Can I presume that you have indulged this habit?"

She nodded nervously.

"You need fear no rebuke from me," I said. "I have done things ten times as rash. But tell me, was the music hall the only place you visited that night?"

She nodded yet again.

"And have you visited… other places… with Toby, of late?"

"No, sir. It was the first time we had stepped out in a week or more."

With Toby, it had always been the thrill of adventure that drove him. Though the son of a wealthy baronet, he had always sought his pleasures outside his social circle, carousing with down-and-outs in Whitechapel gin-palaces, or backstreet opium dens, from where he would sometimes not surface for days. Thankfully, he had rid himself of that particular habit, although his current situation made me wonder if he had not been sucked back into the mire. But now, with a respectable young girl to support, would he tread so dangerously?

"What did you see at the music hall?" I asked.

"A magic show. The Magnificent Balthazar. He was ever so good—he made Toby disappear in his magic cabinet…" The irony of what she was saying dawned on her, and she paled.

"What time did you leave?"

"It must have been nearly ten o'clock, sir."

"It is some distance from here to there," I said. "Would your father not have been worried, having you out so late?"

"No, sir. Two of my friends accompanied us, and I came straight home."

"In a cab?"

"Of course, sir."

"With Toby?"

"No, sir, with the other girls. Toby said he had a friend in lodgings nearby that he wished to visit, and so he summoned a cab for us and left. That was the last I saw of him."

"Did Toby name this friend?"

"He did not, sir."

"In which direction did he walk upon leaving the music hall?"

"The opposite way to us," she said. "We went over Bow Bridge."

I suppressed a shudder. That would mean Toby, on foot and alone at night, would have walked towards Mile End Gate, through the Waste. The Waste is a vibrant place to take one's pleasure, with its amusements and market stalls, but is no place to linger after dark. I could see why he would send Dorothea home first. I started to wonder if I should first look to the East End mortuaries, in case Toby's body had washed up in the Thames.

"He never called on me on the Saturday, as he promised. It was unlike Toby—he has never missed an engagement with me."

"Were any cross words spoken between you that night?"

"None, sir."

"And do you know of anyone with whom Toby might have quarrelled recently?"

Tears began to form in the girl's eyes. "None whatsoever, sir. He was always so pleasant to everyone. Do you think some evil has befallen him?"

"Do not dwell on such things my dear, for in my experience the mind always conjures worse possibilities than the truth." It was a lie, but a necessary one.

"If he is not come to harm, then perhaps… perhaps he wishes to call off the wedding."

Just looking at the girl's plain features was enough to tell me that any marriage between her and Toby Cottingford was unlikely to be successful. Unless of course it was a marriage for appearances' sake, in which case she would prove the most excellent cloak for Toby's more exotic escapades. All of this flashed through my mind. What I said, however, was simply, "My dear, it is more likely that he has been summoned away on business for his father, and that a message has simply failed to reach you. Or perhaps he and this mysterious friend overindulged in the local taverns, and he is too ashamed to call on you."

"There is a pub nearby," she said. "He mentioned that he'd been there before, but it's not the kind of place he could take a lady."

"Do you recall its name?"

"The Vine, I think."

"Excellent. If that was the direction in which he was heading to meet this friend, then there is a chance he may have gone there. I shall look for him, and rest assured I shall send him to your door post-haste once I find him."

This seemed to placate the girl, and so I said goodbye, keeping her mood as cheerful as possible, though my own was blackening by the minute.

* * *

I made sure to visit The Vine that very day. It was a Thursday afternoon, and the day was surprisingly bright and crisp given the horrid London particular that had hung over the city the past two days. It was this fortunate change in conditions that I now exploited, walking briskly, hoping not to be recognised, and dressed in a plain and modest fashion.

The Vine was a tall, narrow tavern, sandwiched between a meat-packing shop and a coffeehouse. Hardly a ray of sunshine penetrated the frosted glass and smoke-stained net curtains of the front windows. The previous night's detritus had been swept into the corners where it sat like molehills beneath poorly upholstered benches, upon one of which lay a gaudily dressed woman, fast asleep. I sidled up to the bar, shoulder-to-shoulder with several unwashed patrons.

"I'm looking for a boy," I said to the landlord. "A young man. He has been in here several times, perhaps Friday last. I am afraid he has not been seen since."

"You with the coppers?" he asked, suspiciously. I sensed ears pricking up around the bar.

"No. I am here on behalf of the lad's fiancée. She is most concerned about him."

"What's 'is name?"

"Toby. He pretends to be a local, but is actually a young gentleman. I am sure you would have seen through his ruse." I slid a shilling across the bar.

"We gets a few of that type in 'ere, time to time. If he's the lad I'm thinkin' of, he's a dandy sort. Might be he wouldn't have known what to do with 'isself when trouble came a-callin'."

"So you think you know him?"

"Seen him, maybe. Fresh-faced, dark hair in need o' a trim."

"That sounds like him."

"As I said, dandy sort."

One of the customers at the bar, a weasel-faced man, leaned toward me. "You're a dandy sort, an' all," he said, and grinned, revealing broken and yellowing teeth.

I ignored him and turned back to the landlord. "Was this youth here last Friday?"

"Can't say as I recall."

"There was a show on at the Paragon that night," I said. "The Magnificent Balthazar. I imagine you had a few people through your doors when the music hall closed."

"Too many to remember one face," he said.

I was about to ask another question when a woman's voice piped up from behind me.

"The Magnificent Balthazar! 'Ee made my Polly disappear."

"Oh, lordy," muttered the landlord. "You've woke 'er up now. On yer own head be it."

I spun around to see the woman who'd been sleeping on the bench now teetering towards me. Rouge was smeared up one side of her face and her powdered hair had taken on the aspect of a precarious crow's nest. She reeked of gin.

"My Polly's been gone three munfs," she rasped. "An' it were him, Balthazar. 'Ee made 'er vanish on the stage. Then she vanished for real!" The woman let out a heartfelt sob.

"She's not right," the landlord said. "In the 'ead I mean. She weren't right before Poll went missing. Been worse since."

"This Polly… did she really go to see the Magnificent Balthazar on the night she disappeared?" I frowned.

"So Bess says."

"She did, sir, she did!" Bess chimed in. "But the coppers, they didn't do nuffin. Said she were on the game and run off wi' some fancy man."

I looked to the landlord for assistance. He shrugged and said, "She wasn't that sort o' girl. Polly was a good lass."

"When you find your lad, will you find my Poll an' all?" the woman pleaded.

"O' course he won't," the weasel-faced man said. "His sort only care for their own."

"It's true enough what Dipper says," another man said. "Papers round here have been full o' missin' East End youngsters. Police are turnin' a blind eye, an' if they keep on turnin' a blind eye there'll be blood on the streets, mark my words. But then one young toff goes walkabout, an' suddenly we got the likes o' you askin' questions."

"Yeah!" snarled the weasel-faced man—or "Dipper"—his hands bunched into fists.

"Look here," I said, "I certainly will not be turning a blind eye, but I didn't even hear of these disappearances until just now."

"Bet you 'ave," said the other man. "But you'd have put it out of mind soon enough, 'cos they was from the East End. You wouldn't notice if we all disappeared, 'cept you'd have nobody to fetch and carry for you."

"You have made your feelings clear," I said. "But regardless, I intend to find my friend. If your loved ones are with him, I will do what I can; you have my word."

"What good's the word of a ponce?" said Dipper, leaning in close.

"I shall not stay here to be insulted," I said, doffing my hat. "I must go forthwith and find Toby… and young Polly." I stepped away briskly. I saw Dipper step with me menacingly, but Bess intercepted him.

"You leave 'im be, Dipper, you lout," she slurred. "We

need all the 'elp we can get. He's a true gent, looking for my Polly…"

I did not stop. Thankful that my plan had worked, and the woman had risen to my defence, I marched confidently from the pub.

Though my pride was somewhat bruised by my hasty retreat, at least it was the only thing injured. My head was swimming with possibilities, however. There was certainly a chance that the aforementioned disappearances had nothing to do with Toby. My suspicions that he had been robbed and even murdered still held water; he could just as likely have found his way to an opium den and spent the last week in the blissful smoke of the dragon. But Dipper had spoken of other missing youngsters…

My network of paid contacts and society spies were of little use in the poverty-stricken districts of London. If he was not dead, I would have called at once on my old associate, Sherlock Holmes, for what I had before me now was a true mystery.

I flagged down a hansom. "Baker Street, quick as you like," I said to the cabbie, and I finally allowed myself to relax as we left Mile End Road behind us.

The idea had struck me all at once. Sherlock Holmes might not be available, but Dr Watson was. Someone at 221B Baker Street would be able to direct me to Watson, and then I would persuade him to assist me, as he had assisted Holmes for so long.

"Send in the next patient please," Watson said, his voice muffled by the door.

I tipped my hat to the nurse, and entered the small

consulting room, where Dr Watson sat behind a large desk, scribbling notes.

"Take a seat," he said, without looking up.

"Thank you, Watson, but I prefer to stand."

At that he looked up at me, recognition crossing his features. "You," he muttered.

"Manners, Doctor."

He stood. "What can I do for you, Mr Pike? I doubt you are looking for a new physician."

"I am not. I am here because I need the help of a consulting detective."

"Then I am afraid you have had a wasted journey." Watson looked grave. "There was only one consulting detective in London, and he is gone."

"But his notoriety lives on through your stories, Doctor."

"Perhaps, but there are no new stories."

"There could be. For no one knows Holmes's methods as well as you."

"You flatter me. I am not the detective. Holmes was—"

"Pish! It is clear from the way Holmes spoke of you that he held you in high regard."

"He… spoke of me? To you?"

"Several times. He would want you to continue the legacy that you forged together."

"How would you know what Holmes would have wanted!" he snapped. "He was *my* friend."

"And mine also. He was not a detective out of sheer vanity. It was his vocation."

Watson's grief played across his face plainly, and then his features set again. "Mr Pike, given your somewhat… distasteful… habit of holding scandal over the heads of socialites, it has always struck me that Holmes and I should have investigated your exploits, on more than one occasion. Why should I help you?"

"I shall answer candidly. It is true that my business is intelligence, and that I have many times been the enemy to those who lack it. And yet I have never brought harm to the doors of any who did not deserve it."

"Now I say 'pish'!" Watson retorted. "Lady Devonshire, and the scandal of the ruby coronet?"

"Simple. She had attempted to blackmail a member of the royal family, placing in jeopardy a diplomatic visit to Turkey. I used the information that I held for the good of Britain."

Watson narrowed his eyes. "Do you think you are the man to make such moral judgements? After all—"

"I am sure I don't know what you're talking about, Watson. What I do know, however, is that a young gentleman has been missing for the past week, and that his disappearance is somehow linked to a spate of similar incidents amongst the poor of the East End. I need help finding the lad, if he still lives."

"Have the police been consulted?"

"They have. They care not for the paupers, and do not deem even a wealthy boy's whereabouts to be of concern to them at present. He leaves behind a heartbroken fiancée."

Watson rubbed at his chin; his attitude softened. "What makes you think the boy's disappearance is linked to these poor East End folk?"

"Magic," I said, trying to suppress a smile. Watson stared at me like I were an imbecile. "One of the girls vanished on the very night she had attended a magic show, performed by a man called the Magnificent Balthazar. My missing lad, Toby, attended the same show on the night he disappeared in Mile End. I doubt I could persuade the police to trouble themselves, but two men, acting covertly, might be able to observe something untoward at this conjurer's show."

I saw a gleam in Watson's eye, and I knew that I had his interest sufficiently piqued. "Holmes would have said there is no such thing as coincidence..." he mused.

"Indeed."

"I may be willing to help you, Mr Pike, but only insofar as lending my modest observational skills at the theatre. If anything is amiss, we go straight to Scotland Yard."

"Of course."

"Then we must find out when this 'Balthazar' is set to perform next."

I handed a playbill to Watson, which I had obtained from a ticket-seller en route. It was emblazoned with several dates for the travelling magic show, the next being on Saturday, at the Hoxton Varieties.

"Are you available this Saturday?" I asked.

"It would seem so," said Watson.

"I shall send a hansom for you."

I have spent a great deal of my life around the theatres of London and Paris, and counted thespians as my own people. The Hoxton Varieties, however, colloquially called the "Sod's Opera", was a world apart from the stages of the West End.

Watson and I entered through the smoky tavern along with the rest of the audience. "I thought you said we should attend incognito," Watson grumbled.

I looked down at my blue suit, tartan cravat and polished white shoes. "What, this old thing?" I said, innocently. "This is one of the dowdiest suits I own." I stifled a snigger at Watson's expense; he was resplendent in a drab brown suit, plain overcoat and flat cap, as though a country squire had stumbled into the music hall.

The back of the tavern was arranged in the semblance of a traditional theatre, though the stage was low and small and the curtains tatty. Small tables made up the bulk of the seating area, and I was surprised to note that several ushers were on hand to show people to particular seats. Our own table gave us a good view of the room but a poor one of the stage.

"Do you see how the audience is being arranged?" I asked.

"Indeed," Watson replied. "The youngest members of the crowd are being ushered to the front. Everyone else is left to find their own place."

"I haven't seen anyone in the boxes yet." I nodded to the private booths, little more than tiny balconies reached by a flight of steps hidden behind heavy drapes.

"Nor I. Mind you, I don't suppose they see much custom. This is hardly the sort of venue to attract the well-heeled."

Customers were still noisily entering the music hall when the lights were dimmed and the act began. A voice from behind the stage curtain announced the entrance of the "Magnificent Balthazar, purveyor of the most profound mysteries", and the magician himself then pranced into view. Balthazar was a diminutive man of middle age, with lank hair scraped over a bulbous head, and moustaches styled in the most ridiculous tight twists. As music sprang up from a lone pianist, the magician launched into a tired routine, making sparrows appear from beneath handkerchiefs, and pulling bunches of silk flowers from his sleeves. Watson and I applauded politely, our eyes scanning the room, though the gaslights were so low we could barely make out anyone beyond the first few rows of tables.

Soon, Balthazar ordered the rear curtains to be raised, revealing his more ambitious paraphernalia, along with a "beautiful assistant", who was a woman who had seen too many winters for the role she now played. For the next hour, Balthazar astonished at least some of the crowd by levitating his assistant and passing a steel hoop—inspected by two members of the audience—over her, to demonstrate that there were no wires at play. He had another audience member lock a set of manacles about his wrists, from which he escaped in seconds. He had a young girl come up and inspect a guillotine for its sharpness, which he then used to supposedly chop off his assistant's head, only to reveal her waiting in the wings. Each time the volunteers from the audience were selected from the first few rows. Balthazar chose male and female spectators seemingly at random, but they were always young and at least moderately attractive.

Watson leaned over to me and pointed to the private box closest the stage. I squinted against the gloom, and sure enough saw the embers of a cigarette glow bright, and a plume of pale smoke waft from the box. Someone now occupied it, although we had seen no one enter; most likely it was the manager taking a look at his investment.

Balthazar's final feat was the "vanishing cabinet", the announcement of which caused both Watson and I to shift in our seats and lean forward in anticipation. Another young girl was plucked from the crowd. For all her obvious poverty, she was a truly beautiful young woman. Her skin was pale, her cheeks rosy, and golden curls fell to her waist.

"Ladies and gentlemen," Balthazar announced. "I present to you the cabinet of instantaneous relocation!

Our brave volunteer…" he paused and craned close to the girl, who whispered her name, "…Lucy, will step into the cabinet, whereupon she will vanish into thin air! Lucy will be magically transported to the spirit realm, until I call upon the mystic powers to bring her back."

The girl was led to the cabinet by the magician's assistant, and was asked to step inside. The door of the cabinet was closed, and at once the magician wheeled it around in a circle, to show that there was nothing beneath it. To the shock of the audience, he then took up four swords, and thrust them through the cabinet. Finally the swords were withdrawn, and the cabinet opened to reveal nothing within.

There was some posturing as Balthazar drank in the applause. A girl on the front row screeched, "Bring 'er back!"

Balthazar bowed low and announced, "I will do exactly that, my good lady." Here, he began a low chant, raising his arms, his unintelligible muttering growing louder, until finally he shouted, "Ala-kazam!" There was a loud crack, and a puff of smoke from the right-hand side of the auditorium. When it cleared, the magician pointed up to the private box where we had earlier observed the cigarette-smoker, and the girl was there, beaming with delight.

As the girl returned to her table, I caught the briefest glimpse of a pale face in the box, which quickly vanished. Watson turned to me—he had seen it too. As the house lights came up, I was quite certain that the box was now empty—whoever had been there must have exited via some unseen means.

"What do you say we steal a word with this Balthazar?" said Watson.

"I think not," I replied. "I have a feeling that we should

look for the possible victim, and follow them."

"How could we possibly know who the victim will be, if there even is one?"

"Because, Watson, the two previous victims of whom I know were called up to take part in the Vanishing Cabinet illusion, and both were of exceptional beauty, by all accounts." I nodded towards the girl who had vanished from the cabinet as she passed by us. "We should follow her to ensure her safety, and if we find nothing we shall return."

"By then Balthazar will have gone," Watson said.

"A touring stage magician with several dates left to play will not be difficult to find. A random poor girl amongst all the poor girls of East London is, however, a needle in a haystack. Shall we?"

Watson was forced to concur. We left our seats and followed the girl as she left the tavern and headed along Pitfield Street, weaving our way through the groups of theatregoers, keeping our target in view. The young girl was fearless, marching towards the even more unsavoury environs of Whitechapel. She crossed the road opposite an almshouse garden, and slipped into a quiet side street.

Then the girl began to falter, her steps becoming suddenly uneven. She put a hand to her head, and reached out to steady herself against a wall. As she did so, I saw movement in the shadows on the side of the street. Two figures, large and powerful-looking, lurched from an alleyway and set upon her, clapping hands upon her mouth before she could scream, and lifting her off her feet. My heart lurched—never had I been so dismayed at being proven right.

Watson was off like a shot, racing along the street and shouting, "Here! Leave her be!" I saw one of the men peel away as the other carried the girl off. Watson landed a blow upon the ruffian's chin, and received payment in kind for his trouble. As I reached them, with the intent of shoving into the man with all my might, I was hit with great force from the side; all I saw was the onrushing of black shadow from the alleyway, and then I was sprawled upon the cobbles, utterly bewildered.

By the time I cleared my head, I saw Watson fending off not one, but two assailants. The gallant doctor swung his cane, landing a blow upon the cheek of one villain, but immediately fell to a clubbing from the second. Both men stepped forward and swung vicious kicks at Watson as he curled up on the pavement. One of them then patted Watson down, taking his wallet and growling, "So we know where to find you, should you give us any trouble later." The men were all dressed in dark clothes and polished shoes, and had mufflers pulled up over their faces.

I heard hoofbeats and a carriage pulled up at the end of the road. All three men piled inside, dragging the struggling girl. I noted a flash of gold paint upon the door as it closed, and then the carriage was gone.

I finally managed to haul Watson to his feet, and saw with some pity the horrid scrapes down the side of his face, and blood oozing from his nose.

"What now?" Watson said.

"I suppose we must adopt your plan," I replied. "Let us find the Magnificent Balthazar."

It was not without toil that we tracked down the magician. The hour was late when finally we were admitted to a squalid Hackney flat by the man himself.

"Balthazar" was in fact one Cecil Blaylock, an engineer's son from Portsmouth. His stage assistant was his older sister, Alice, with whom he now shared a humble dwelling. Both Cecil and Alice still wore their greasepaint, although their costumes had been exchanged for housecoats and slippers.

"We don't hang about," Blaylock said by way of explanation. "Don't want the punters coming over, asking how it was done."

"What about the equipment?" Watson asked. He was in a foul mood, and had barely spoken to me as we had traipsed around town looking for the Blaylocks.

"You mean the cabinet, and so on?" Blaylock asked. "It is all sent to storage after every show, sir. I have a cousin who works the warehouses in Pimlico."

Watson looked askance at me. I was certain our thoughts were aligned—a warehouse was the ideal place to keep prisoners. Or bodies.

"Of course, once I would have afforded a larger premises of my own to store my apparatus," Blaylock went on. "Once they spoke of me alongside Mr Maskelyne; but now I can barely fill the sixpence taverns."

"Mr Blaylock, I am afraid we are not here merely to discuss your show," I said, seeing the dreamy look of the loquacious bore in his eyes. "We wish to talk to you about vanishing ladies of a different kind."

"Eh?"

"There's no need to be coy. The young attractive people who take part in your act—they are planted there by your people are they not?"

"No, sir, they are not!" Blaylock looked indignant. "They are strangers to me, drawn from the audience. There is no trickery on my part—they inspect my apparatus for themselves and find it inscrutable. Look about you, sir. Does it look as though I have coin to spare for stooges? If you find the appearance of my volunteers comely, then it is testament to the good eye of the theatre manager. It is an old stage trick, sir, which I am sure you are familiar with—put the pretty girls and handsome lads in ready view of the rest of the clientele, and a more favourable impression of the whole show will be given. Years ago I might have picked the right volunteer from anywhere in the crowd, but alas my eyesight is failing me, and so now I must rely on the staff to seat the most eligible subjects near the front." He tapped at the rim of his pince-nez spectacles, which he certainly had not worn on stage, to illustrate his point.

"What if I told you that the golden-haired beauty who you made disappear tonight has been kidnapped?" I asked.

"Kidnapped?"

"Yes. The good doctor here received his injuries near Spitalfields. We were unable to stop the thugs who took her."

"Why… that's terrible!" The shock appeared genuine. Alice Blaylock clasped her hands to her mouth and gasped theatrically.

"A week ago, outside the Paragon in Mile End, a young lad also disappeared. He, too, had taken part in your show that night."

"I… Wait a minute…"

"You may remember him. Smooth features, with long dark hair and striking blue eyes. He is the son of Sir Denis Cottingford, who is very well connected in Parliament. That is what brings me to your door, you see."

"You cannot possibly imagine that I—"

"And of course, upon the trail of this strange disappearance, I also learned of a young girl named Polly, who was snatched immediately following your show in Whitechapel last month. You made her disappear that night, too. A frightful coincidence, don't you think?"

"I resent these accusations!" Blaylock spluttered, as his sister broke down in tears. "Who do you think you are?"

"You know me, sir, from the newspapers, which is why you do not fear my interrogation. But it is clear that you do not recognise my associate here. This is Dr Watson. You have doubtless heard his name in connection with the late Sherlock Holmes?"

Blaylock paled.

"I have secured the formidable deductive powers of Dr Watson," I continued. "They brought me here, to you. Mr Blaylock—what happened to those poor young souls? What have you done with them?"

"I have done nothing. I swear it!" Blaylock gasped for breath.

"If you have something to confess," Watson said, "then say it now, or we shall be back within the hour with a Scotland Yard detective." Watson's glower, along with his battered features, certainly put the fear in me, never mind Blaylock.

"I have nothing to confess!"

"Then maybe we should talk to your cousin in Pimlico."

"Why? He has nothing to do with it."

"To do with what?" Watson growled.

"I… I… oh." The man took a deep breath. "I swear I have nothing to do with kidnapping. The only thing I can think is that a certain patron—a private patron—might know something."

"Speak plainly, man," I said. "Who is this patron? Why do you suspect him?"

"I don't… I mean, not until now. He comes to my shows

maybe a few times each year. Each time he provides some of his servants to help with the act—getting the disappeared volunteers from backstage into his private box, y'see. He insists on seeing the act close up, and throws a little extra my way for the privilege."

"He occupies the box in which the volunteer miraculously reappears?"

"He does."

"He was there tonight?"

"Yes."

"And his men were backstage, with ready access to the girl?"

Blaylock nodded as an awful truth dawned on him.

"I suspect the girl was drugged," I said to Watson. "It would appear that someone slipped her something during her time backstage."

"The man's name," Watson said to Blaylock. "A girl's life may depend on it."

"I never spoke to him direct, sir. His men call him Sir Algernon Dinmont. But that's not his real name. I don't know his real name."

"Then how do you know he's using an alias?" Watson asked.

"I am not a fool, Doctor. I have spoken with the theatre managers who secure the boxes for Sir Algernon. With them he goes by Monmouth. I looked him up, in the book of peerage. I read a lot, you see. There is no Sir Algernon Dinmont, and all the Monmouths I could find are dukes or earls, and I thought if he'd lie to me, he'd as likely lie to the managers, wouldn't he? I didn't care, long as the money came. Oh, God, have I done wrong?"

"That remains to be seen," I said. "For now, I want you

to say nothing of this conversation should you have any contact with Sir Algernon's men. Do you understand?"

He nodded.

"We are done here for now."

"Pike, I don't think—" Watson began.

"No, Watson," I said. "We have all we need."

I managed at last to usher Watson from the flat, leaving a devastated magician and his sister in our wake.

"What do you know?" Watson pressed as we returned to our cab.

"I know the identity of Algernon Dinmont," I replied.

"How?"

"I know every secret of note within the upper echelons of society. Blaylock may have guessed that Dinmont was an alias, but not the real reason behind adopting it. The man behind the name is far more important than his title would suggest—we must tread carefully."

"Title matters not," said Watson. "We should root out this villainy and strike while the iron is hot. I can call upon Inspector Lestrade, and—"

"No, Watson, we cannot rely on the police in this matter, believe me. I will not tell you what I know, not yet, because you are like to run off half-cocked and get us both into terrible trouble, and this poor girl harmed in the process. No—you shall go home to your wife, and tend to your injuries. Be ready in the morning, for we shall go to confront our man, refreshed and prepared."

"Now will you tell me where we're going?" Watson demanded.

The carriage had rattled towards the city limits, until

the open space of Bexley stretched before us. In that time, I had said nothing to Watson about our objective, for I had no idea what his reaction might be.

"We are travelling to the estate of Lord Percy Montagu." I said.

"The high court judge?" Watson looked aghast.

"The name 'Monmouth' is often used by *The Gazette* in place of several of society's great luminaries—Montagu chief amongst them. What most common folk may not know is that Lord Montagu is a fancier of terriers—specifically, a small breed of dog called a 'Dandie Dinmont'. Indeed, in chambers as in his club, Montagu is known as Dandie, a nickname not altogether undeserved."

"It sounds convincing, I'll grant you," said Watson. "But it is thin grounds to put ourselves on the wrong side of a law lord."

"True enough. But think back to those thugs we encountered last night. Far too well-dressed to be common rabble. When they made their escape, it was in a liveried carriage. I could not make out the heraldry, but it gleamed gold. I am not as expert on the peerage as Mr Blaylock, but I do know that the coat of arms of Lord Montagu prominently features two golden griffons. We can only hope we will be granted an audience; you look dreadful, Watson, like you've been brawling in the streets."

Watson shot me a glare, and then sat back in his seat. "I hope you know what you're doing, Pike."

We were greeted at the door of Lord Montagu's palatial estate by a pack of diminutive, tuft-headed terriers, which yapped at us relentlessly until the butler ushered us into a vast reception room.

We waited there for some minutes, before Lord Montagu

or, more correctly, the Earl of Torrington, appeared. He was a large man, wrinkled of features and prodigious of girth. He was pushed into the room in an invalid chair by his valet—a valet who sported a graze upon his chin.

"Pike, you rogue!" Lord Montagu exclaimed. "I should have you horse-whipped after that snippet in *The Gazette* last October."

"Lord Montagu." I bowed. "It has been too long. And to which snippet do you refer? My sources always provide anonymous scandals—if you would be willing to put your name to one, I imagine my readers would simply faint with excitement."

The old man barked a laugh. "Incorrigible as ever! What brings you to my door?"

"Among other things, I came to invite you to a soirée. I hope you are not housebound?"

"Gout, damn it. Never you worry, Pike, it'll take more than that to put me down. Came here in person to invite me to a party, eh? Must be more to it than that."

"My lord is most astute," I replied. I noted Watson's dumbfounded expression at my familiarity with the earl, and took pleasure in it. "I come here with my learned colleague, Dr Watson, to seek that most vulgar of things."

"What, marriage?" Lord Montagu laughed again.

"Alas, Lord Montagu, I have already taken those vows, though for what reason puzzles me to this very day. No, I speak of patronage."

"Patronage? You strapped for cash, Pike? Surely you haven't been frittering away your fortune at the gaming tables?" He wheeled himself a little closer. "Or is it your other… appetites?" He winked, and I masked my nausea with all the skill of an experienced thespian.

"Not at all. It is not money I want for, but influence in the right channels."

"Go on."

"This is the same Dr Watson who formerly associated with Mr Sherlock Holmes. I imagine a man in your line of work would have run into Holmes more than once."

"I did. He sent a goodly number of crooks through my dock."

"It is not common knowledge that I was a friend to Holmes. I was rather hoping to pick up where he left off, and accompany Dr Watson once more into the detective business."

"You wish to become a consulting detective? You? Ha!" he laughed again.

"For once I am entirely earnest," I said. "But of course, what many people do not know is that Holmes was vouched for by his brother, Mycroft, and thus given certain freedoms within the legal system that I myself cannot command."

"Mycroft, eh? An odious toad." Lord Montagu fixed me with a withering gaze. "And you would not have some ulterior motive for placing yourself above the law, Pike? Not in any trouble yourself?"

"You wound me, Lord Montagu. Why, we have already run afoul of a group of criminals as a result of our amateur sleuthing. Sherlock Holmes could call upon any police constable in London without fear of refusal. I only ask for a similar privilege, and I am certain your influence could secure it."

"And what were you investigating to get yourselves in such a pickle?"

"A series of kidnappings, culminating in the taking of a young girl last night in the East End."

"Young girls go missing in the East End all the time."

"Ah, but this one is a real mystery. Several victims, all taken within hours of attending a magic show. And by a gentleman, no less."

"A gentleman? What makes you so sure of that?"

"The men with whom Watson here had his altercation were almost certainly household servants. The carriage in which the victim was abducted was a private one. You see, Lord Montagu, if this matter becomes one of extreme delicacy, it would be useful to have the backing of an influential man such as yourself."

The earl held my gaze for a moment, with the same hard stare from beneath his bushy eyebrows that I imagine he reserved for the condemned men in his dock.

"I am not by nature a charitable man," he said at last. "But our association stretches back some years. Send me a business proposal through more official channels and I'll think on it."

"I can ask no more, Lord Montagu. You are too kind to give us your time."

We turned to leave, and I realised I had made a misstep when Lord Montagu cleared his throat and spoke again.

"This soirée, Pike. When and where?"

"Ah, yes, I almost forgot. Next month, at Apsley House," I lied. "I'll have a messenger send the details along with the proposal."

"Apsley, eh?"

"You know me, Lord Montagu. Only the best is good enough."

"Yes, Pike, I know you well. Too well."

The butler appeared to escort us out. I paused and turned again to Lord Montagu.

"I have only just realised, Lord Montagu. Your taxidermy—there is none on display. When last I visited this room was resplendent with exotic birds, was it not?"

"It was."

"I trust your collection is still intact. Some say it is the finest in Europe."

"Not any more. Sold it, y'see. Grew bored of it. I find my pleasures elsewhere these days."

"Then you must have found a great diversion indeed."

"Oh, indeed I have, Pike. Now, I must bid you good day."

And with that, we left the invalided earl and returned to our carriage.

"What on earth was that about?" Watson asked as we set off. "If he's guilty of these crimes you've put the cat amongst the pigeons."

"I certainly hope he's guilty," I remarked, "otherwise I have a function at Apsley House to organise, and very little time to do it."

I rapped on the roof of the carriage and called to the driver.

"As we turn the next bend, slow so that we may depart, and then carry on to the gate. Wait for us at the allotted place. If we do not return in an hour, go directly to Scotland Yard and deliver the letter I gave you."

The driver did as he was bid, and once out of sight of the house I alighted from the carriage, leaving Watson no choice but to follow.

"As you said, Watson," I explained, "the cat is now amongst the pigeons. We must see if any of them take flight."

We trod carefully through the small copses that lined the long drive, until we found a secreted location at the end of a large rose garden, affording us a good view of the house and grounds. My suspicions were proven correct almost immediately, when Lord Montagu's valet left the house in a great hurry, and shouted directions to several servants, before setting off on foot across the grounds carrying a lantern.

"Hullo, where is he going?" Watson whispered. "And why does he have a lantern in broad daylight?"

"We must follow him, but have your wits about you, Watson—I am certain he is the man with whom you tangled last night."

"I have more than my wits about me," Watson replied, and revealed a revolver in the pocket of his overcoat.

"Full of surprises! Let's hurry, before he gets out of sight."

We followed the man through a grand orchard, past a large orangery, and through an ornamental garden, until finally we saw the man descend into a hollow, whereupon he entered a tumbledown folly.

"Aren't these things normally facades?" Watson asked.

"Yes, but he must have gone somewhere. Come, we must get closer."

We stumbled down into the hollow, until we reached the rough-hewn walls of the folly. The door through which the valet had entered was made in the semblance of a castle entrance. Ivy clung to the stones around it, climbing up a cylindrical tower, open at the top in the style of a ruin. Even as we paused near the door, sounds reached our ears—a muffled, angry male voice, almost drowned out by moans and pitiful wailing.

"An underground chamber?" Watson whispered.

"With prisoners," I replied.

Watson and I shrank back as the door swung open and the valet reappeared. The man seemed to sense my presence, and stopped dead. In a trice, Watson stepped up and hit him hard on the back of the head with the butt of the revolver. The valet fell in a heap.

"Watson! We needed to question him," I said.

"Time for that later. If there are prisoners down there, we can ask *them* our questions."

Watson searched the man and found a set of iron keys. Taking up the lantern, he led the way into the dark portal.

The eerie moans had quietened, though the muffled sound could still be heard as we descended a flight of uneven stone stairs. The smell of mould and damp mingled with a stench so foul that I covered my face with a kerchief. The stairs terminated at another wooden door, which Watson unlocked. Nothing could have prepared us for what we saw.

Within the folly's foundations was a circular basement with an earthen floor. Around the room were people shackled to the walls. Illuminated in the yellow flicker of the lantern, emaciated, blank faces stared at us. Some moaned and whined, others tried to form words. Most appeared to be young, beneath the grime and dishevelment. A few stick-thin corpses were still chained to the walls, while other bodies littered the floor. I turned away from the hellish sight.

Watson, being of sterner constitution, entered the room and released the prisoners. He urged them to leave the cell, but only two were able to stand, and one was so terrified of leaving her confinement that she screamed until Watson allowed her to shrink back to her place against the wall. The other, a young man, staggered towards the door. As he reached me, I cupped his face in my hands, praying I had found Toby, but it was not he. I entered the cell and looked at the others, then breathed a sigh of relief to not find Toby amongst them.

"Watson—we have to leave them," I said. He stared at

me dumbly. "We can send help, but now we must question the valet, and find out the extent of this operation."

Even in the meagre light I saw a darkness cross Watson's features and I saw the steel of the man on whom Sherlock Holmes had depended.

Outside, we found the valet coming to. Watson grabbed him by the lapels and shook him hard. "What were you doing down there? What did you do to those people?"

"Just checking how many had croaked," the man said, groaning with pain. "The master doesn't have the heart to put down the waste, so I has to clear out the refuse from time to time."

"How many others?" Watson growled. "Where do you keep them?"

The man coughed, and the cough turned into a ghastly laugh. "You would do well to leave this place, and never speak of it, if you value your life."

Watson looked at me with a face like thunder; for once, I was at a loss for words. He turned back to the valet. "Your master cannot get away with this, for all his influence."

"You have no idea," the man croaked. "Do you think no one knows? We are *protected.* Do your worst."

Before I could say anything, Watson had dragged the man to his feet, hoisting him towards the door. The valet let out a cry, but too late, as Watson shoved him down the stairs. He followed him down into the darkness, and I heard sounds of a struggle, and then the slam of a door. Presently, Watson returned.

"He's locked away for now," Watson said. "But what do we do next, Pike? How do we find the girl, or your friend?"

"The tower," a thin voice said.

We both turned to see the youth who alone had escaped

his confinement. He knelt in the damp grass, face turned to the sky. Who knows when last he had seen it?

"What tower?" I asked, gently.

"In Lord Montagu's hall there is a tower. That is where he... keeps them."

Although Watson seemed all set to recreate the Siege of Kandahar single-handed, I had eventually managed to persuade him that stealth was the order of the day. It was no easy task to steal into Lord Montagu's home, as there were so many servants about. I was on this occasion thankful for my modicum of fame, for the two occasions upon which we were discovered I first managed to spin some yarn about a surprise for His Lordship, swearing a young housemaid to secrecy, and then crossed the palm of a potboy with sufficient silver to buy his silence, for a short time at least.

After a laborious climb up several flights of stairs, we reached the uppermost room of the mansion's tower. The door was, unsurprisingly, locked, but after trying half a dozen of the valet's keys, we finally gained access.

In the centre of the room was a large chair, almost a throne. Around it, arranged in a circle, were four large gilded cages, almost like gibbets but for their polished lustre.

Three of the cages were occupied.

I gasped in horror at what I saw. The girl from the previous night was slumped in the first cage, dressed in a fine satin gown, and staring vacantly into space. Next was another young girl, gaunt and frail, with her face painted like a mummer. And finally, there was Toby Cottingford, his dark hair shorn, blue eyes gazing to the ceiling, so devoid of life that at first I feared he was dead.

"Opium," Watson said. He pointed to the tubes that descended the exterior of the cages, and fed into the veins of the languid dreamers before us.

"It keeps them compliant, as I like them."

Watson and I spun around, and before us stood Lord Montagu, with a brutish footman in tow. The earl had abandoned his invalid chair, and now leaned heavily upon a stick.

"Lord Montagu," I said, "tell me you have some explanation for this madness!"

"Madness? I thought you of all people would call it decadence, Pike. Is your work not full of dark passions, and the mockery of their limitations? Of there being neither good nor evil in this world?"

"It is, and I believed it, but this…"

"You lack imagination, Pike. For all your witticisms and artistry, you are too afraid to truly embrace your passions. I am an artist, Pike. I seek beauty and I shape it into the most perfect form of itself."

"By shutting beauty away in a tower? By watching it wither and die?"

"Ah, you have seen the failed subjects then. That is unfortunate. And it leads me to think that my first great passion, taxidermy, may still hold some appeal. These three beauties are the best I have found to date. Each one represents some facet of perfection that I must possess. I am a collector of beauty, Mr Pike. Look here—does this girl not have the most lustrous hair you ever saw, and on a pauper too! This one, her smile is the prettiest in England, I'll wager. And this youth, a wastrel perhaps, but with eyes as sparkling as any damsel. They are dolls, no more, no less."

"That boy is no wastrel," I snapped. "He is the son of Sir Denis Cottingford. You have made a grave error, Lord Montagu."

Lord Montagu's face fell for a moment, and then a sardonic smile returned to his lips. "It is no matter, for no one will ever know he is here."

"How will you prevent us from telling anyone?" I asked. "Do you mean to kill us? Or add us to your collection?"

"Do not flatter yourself!" he cackled. "And I do not need to kill you, Pike. You might fancy yourself the gatherer of gossip and scandal, but I am a gatherer of evidence. One word out of you, and the details of your jaunts to every molly-house in the city will be made public. I don't believe prison life would suit you, would it? And as for Dr Watson, I believe this might stay his hand." Lord Montagu held up a photograph of a woman.

"Mary…" Watson muttered.

"The doctor's wife is perhaps too plain for my tastes, but that hair! Almost a rival for this pretty creature, I'd say. I would have to stuff and mount her to preserve her looks—"

The deafening noise that interrupted Lord Montagu fair made me jump out of my skin. My ears rang. In the middle of the earl's forehead, a crimson circle appeared, the size of a sixpence. Time itself seemed to stop for a second, and then the earl fell to the floor in a heap. The footman turned as if to flee, but Watson fired again, through his overcoat pocket. The bullet struck the man in the small of the back, and he fell, writhing in agony.

"Watson," I said, with no small effort. "What have you done?"

Watson said nothing. He trembled, and stared in disbelief at the bodies before him.

I thought quickly. Though I had never before dealt with murder and kidnap, I had proved time and again capable of removing myself and others from the grip of scandal.

"Watson, go downstairs immediately. Leave the gun. When the servants come running, you will tell them there has been a terrible accident, and they are not to come up until the police have had a chance to inspect the crime scene. Under no circumstances give them your name. Do you understand?"

Watson nodded.

"Do it now. Hand me the gun. Go, man!"

Watson, in shock, did as he was told, while I surveyed the room. There was much to do. I have said before that my methods were singularly different from those of Sherlock Holmes. My business is the affairs of others, and that often means causing trouble for those I dislike, or cleaning up the most horrendous messes for those I like. It has been said that my ability to make problems vanish is almost magical…

"You must never speak of what happened today," I told Watson as we neared Kensington. "And nor shall I. As far as anyone is concerned, the only crime that has been committed was by Lord Montagu. My contacts have seen to all other details. Be in no doubt, however, that I have ensured no one could ever connect me to the mysterious disappearance of Lord Montagu, or the murder of his footman. You, on the other hand…"

"What do you mean?"

"I mean, the day may come when I require a favour of you, Watson."

"You would blackmail me?" A dark look crossed his face.

"No, Watson, I would *obligate* you. That is my business—not blackmail or gossip-mongering. Lord Montagu thought himself to have influence in the upper echelons of society; he did not know the half of it."

"You are beyond the pale!"

"I know."

The coach pulled up outside Watson's house. I took a wallet from my pocket—the one that Lord Montagu's man had taken—and put the photograph of Mary back inside. I passed it to Watson. "Say nothing of what has transpired. If you find your conscience in turmoil, remember those poor souls in the folly. Now go to your wife, Watson. Remember that by your actions you saved her life too."

He nodded, and stepped out of the carriage. I leaned over to shut the door, and said, "Oh, and, Watson. I shall call on you again soon. I think we make a rather good team, don't you?"

After this tale, I embarked on two further adventures with Dr Watson, both of which he fictionalised as being the work of Holmes. The name of Langdale Pike stuck, though few ever guessed it referred to me, so I suppose he did me a favour. It is a singularly ugly name, derived from a place in Windermere, an unsightly pun at the expense of one of my finest plays.

Lady Windermere's Fan deserves, I think, a more fitting tribute than Watson's dull wit. I shall add that slight to my ledger, also…

THE CURSE OF THE BLUE DIAMOND

Sam Stone

The character of **Dr Watson** is the narrator for all but four of the Sherlock Holmes stories: he first appears in the very first chronicle, *A Study of Scarlet.* The subtitle in this work – "Being a reprint from the Reminiscences of John H. Watson, M.D., Late of the Army Medical Department" – would suggest that Watson himself was the focus of the story, but really he is the eyes through which the reader sees Holmes for the first time. His opinion shapes the reader's perception of the detective. I wanted to write from Watson's viewpoint because I was fascinated with how he viewed Holmes and with their relationship.

Because Watson is an intelligent character in his own right, I also aimed to explore his sense of ego as I've always felt that it would be easy to be somewhat resentful of Holmes's intellect and deductive skills. Juxtaposed with this, and equally important, is Watson's clear admiration for Holmes's accomplishments for which I also sought to pay tribute.

In my story, Watson is surprised to be invited to help a young socialite investigate the sudden death of her parents. His self-esteem is massaged by the fact that the letter is addressed to himself and not to Holmes… So some of what I'm playing with here is, would Watson let his ego affect the investigation?

I think he'd be a rather good sport about it in the end. Don't you?

—Sam Stone

It was a dark winter morning when a hand-delivered letter arrived at 221B Baker Street.

My friend and colleague, Sherlock Holmes, was away on some family business that he, in his usual style, refused to divulge to me. I was left holding the fort, so to speak, and so Mrs Hudson brought in the letter on a tray that also held a fresh pot of tea and one teacup, markedly reminding me that I was quite alone.

"Arrived a few moments ago," said Mrs Hudson. "It smells like expensive perfume too…"

I took the envelope from her and, on instinct, raised it to my nose. Of course Holmes would most likely have known which perfume it was, but "expensive" covered it for me at that point. I met Mrs Hudson's curious eyes and felt a moment of anxiety that Holmes wasn't there to comment upon the mysterious note himself.

"Aren't you going to open it?" Mrs Hudson asked.

"Not at all. Bad form to open another chap's letter," I said.

"My dear doctor… it is addressed to *you*."

"Oh!"

I read the writing on the front and discovered that my name was indeed on it.

"But who…?"

Mrs Hudson smiled and waited. I realised then that she was as curious as I, a trait I had noticed she was developing of late, and I wasn't about to encourage that curious nature of hers any more than was unavoidable.

"Thank you, Mrs Hudson. I'll enjoy my tea and get to this sometime this afternoon," I said.

I placed the letter down once more upon the tray.

Mrs Hudson frowned, then turned and left the room. I poured myself some tea, but my eyes strayed constantly to the envelope until finally I gave in to my own excessive interest and I lifted it up, smelling the paper once more, before turning it over and breaking the red wax seal on the back.

As if the perfume were not enough evidence as to the gender of the writer, the letter inside had been written in an unmistakably female hand. The writing was elegant and curved, with no sign of the aggression often found in male penmanship. However, I felt the hand rushed, and a smudge of ink on the corner of the page confirmed my suspicions.

> Dear Dr Watson,
>
> I am writing to you to ask for help. I believe you are the trusted friend of the detective Mr Holmes, and a respected physician.

The letter went on with praise for me and Holmes, and referenced how the writer had heard of us through a mutual friend, though the name of the friend was not given. Then it reached the reason for the missive:

> A mysterious sickness took my mother some months ago. Since then we had barely begun to grieve when my mother's health began to fail, until she too was no more. I'm sure that you are, by now, wondering how you may

be of assistance. This, as you may be able to tell, is very difficult for me. You see, my fiancé has recently fallen to the same affliction. However, our doctor can find no cause. What appeared to be an age-related illness in my parents cannot be the same in Jeremy's case, as a man of barely thirty years of age. Until now he has been fit and well; he remembers suffering few of even the most common childhood ailments.

It is peculiar that this all happened around the same time: when we received, or rather my father did, a parcel containing a blue diamond. A rare and expensive jewel that was left to him by his brother, my uncle…

I was startled that the lady had sent the letter to me instead of to Holmes. Maybe she was aware that he was unavailable, even though his private life was always kept undisclosed. I, as his closest friend, did not even know precisely where he was or how long he would be gone. So how would a total stranger know more? Then, when I reached the end of the letter, I discovered that the lady in question was none other than Hope Ballentine, a socialite of some repute – a lady I had met briefly some twelve months earlier. I was both surprised and flattered that she remembered me. I decided that I would help Miss Ballentine, even though I wasn't sure what I could do without my partner.

After dictating a quick reply by telegram, I was soon on my way to Brighton, on the south coast of England, as the letter instructed.

A few hours later my train pulled into Brighton station. I looked out of the window of my first-class carriage for

Miss Ballentine's driver, but no one waited on the steam-filled platform.

Taking my travel bag and my medicine case down from the rack above my seat, I made my way onto the platform.

"Are you Dr Watson, sir?" said a small voice.

I looked down to find a boy of around ten. Intelligent eyes stared at me from a somewhat grubby face.

"Yes I am," I answered.

"I'm to take you outside to your carriage, sir. The driver said you'd tip me for me trouble…"

I doubted that the driver had told the boy this, knowing full well that any driver of Hope Ballentine's would most likely have paid the urchin already for his trouble. But I knew that such young ears and eyes were always valuable in an unknown town. And so I gave the boy a penny, which he tested with his teeth, before placing it surreptitiously in the pocket of his short trousers. Then he led me outside to the front of the station, and I saw the carriage and driver waiting.

"Dr Watson?" said the driver as he climbed down from the front of the carriage. "Please forgive my having to send a stranger to find you inside. My horses were skittish and I couldn't risk leaving them alone."

He took my bags and heaved them up onto the back of the carriage, where he secured them with a piece of thick rope.

"I'm Samuel," he told me. Then he proceeded to open the carriage door so that I could climb inside.

The carriage pulled away, rattling over the cobbles. I glanced out of the window, noting that we were not headed, as I had been told, to the townhouse owned by the Ballentines on the seafront. We were heading, instead, away from the promenade and back inland.

An hour or more later, tired and sore from the jostling

carriage, I was relieved when the driver turned off the main road and began to follow a long dirt track that soon developed into an established driveway. I leaned out of the window as I caught a glimpse of an imposing house through the trees. The carriage turned and weaved towards it, and we pulled up at an impressive frontage with white marble steps leading up to a huge oak double front door.

As soon as the carriage had stopped I climbed out before the driver had time to dismount.

The front door opened, and I saw impressive white marbled archways, and a notable staircase that dominated the centre of the hallway of the house. The driver removed my bags from the back of the carriage and then led me up the stairs towards a waiting butler and, I presumed by her attire, the housekeeper.

Introductions were made. The butler was Anders, and the lady beside him Mrs Anders.

"Miss Ballentine is waiting for you in the drawing room, but first you are to go and see Mr Richmond," Anders said.

"Who is Mr Richmond?" I asked.

"Miss Ballentine's fiancé," Mrs Anders explained. "The patient."

"Ah. Then I will need my—" I turned and saw Samuel holding my medical bag out to me. I found his anticipation of my request quite disconcerting but took hold of the case nonetheless and turned to follow Mrs Anders up the stairs.

But for a sliver of light filtering through the drawn curtains, the room I was led to was in complete darkness.

"I will have to light the lamp," Mrs Anders said.

"Of course… or I shall not be able to see the patient…" I mumbled.

"Is that all right, Mr Richmond? Will you cover your

face?" Mrs Anders continued.

There was a groan from the bed in the centre of the room. A rustle of sheets, and Mrs Anders struck a match and lit an oil lamp that stood on a dresser by the door.

"He cannot bear any light," Mrs Anders explained. "This is the nearest that we can bring the lamp."

"But I must be able to see in order to examine him properly..." I said.

"I can creep closer once he becomes a little more accustomed to it," Mrs Anders said. "But you'll see..."

I approached the bed, stumbling against a chair that I couldn't see in the gloom, and then Mrs Anders turned the lamplight upwards.

The patient groaned in the bed, pulling the covers up and over his face even as I drew near.

"Mr Richmond?" I said. "I'm Dr Watson. I'm here to help you."

Richmond groaned again. It was the sound of an aged and dying man who could barely articulate his pain and suffering.

I reached for the covers and pulled them back. Richmond was too weak to fight me; although he tried to hold onto the material, it slipped easily from his frail fingers and I came face to face with the reality of his affliction for the first time.

"Good lord," I gasped, as I couldn't hold in my shock at the sight of the man.

His skin was deathly white, and as the light from the lamp hit him, his flesh seemed to react to it. It blackened and began to char with a sizzling sound.

"Pull the light back for the love of God!" cried Richmond.

Mrs Anders responded and turned the flame down once more. My eyes had adjusted enough for me to still be able to just make out the other peculiarities in Richmond's state, and as the light dimmed further it became even more apparent that Richmond's eyes were flawed. Whatever colour the irises had once been was now bleached out. The man's eyes were as white as his flesh and they glowed somewhat in the gloom, oddly luminous.

I didn't dare bring the light closer now for fear of injuring him further but I leaned in and touched his skin. It was rough, scarred: it was the flesh of a victim severely burnt.

"What happened to you?" I asked.

Richmond shook his head as though his previous outburst was all that he had left in him, and now he could no longer speak.

"Can you see at all?" I asked.

Richmond nodded. "A little. If it's dark…" he gasped. "The light… it… it…"

"Turn the lamp off, Mrs Anders," I said.

Mrs Anders complied, and I took the seat beside the bed of my patient and waited for my own vision to adjust. I could make out Richmond's shape in the bed, could hear his laboured breathing. I fumbled in my medical bag and extracted my stethoscope. I explained myself to Richmond, so as not to frighten him, and he allowed me to press the instrument against his chest.

I listened to the man's heartbeat for a moment and then looked into those peculiar eyes. I tilted his head so that I could observe the way the lenses captured light and reflected it, in much the same way that a cat's eyes did. But these were no cat's eyes. This was the symptom of some rare and frightening disorder.

"Are you in much pain?" I asked, but I knew the answer could only be yes and so I prescribed a dose of laudanum to help Richmond sleep.

"I must speak to Miss Ballentine," I said to Mrs Anders as we left the now resting patient.

"She's expecting you," the housekeeper replied, and I followed her back down the stairs and into the drawing room.

Hope Ballentine sat upright and stiff on a Chinese-style sofa. I was struck by her incredible handsomeness and paused in the doorway. When she looked at me it was as though I was released from some form of hypnosis. Miss Ballentine was ethereal. Like a muse, or a nymph, caught in a moment of complete reflection, as if by a pond and not in a place as ordinary as a drawing room.

"Dr Watson. It is good to see you," she said, and then she indicated a chair near hers and I sat down beside her. "You must be thirsty. The maid has just brought in this fresh pot of tea."

"Thank you," I said, though I felt in need of something far stronger after my initial examination of Richmond. I had seen many things during my investigations with Holmes, but this one had rattled me. Maybe because Holmes and his ever-present confidence were absent.

I took the proffered teacup and tried to hide the trembling of my hands.

"So, tell me what is going on here," I said, placing the cup back down on the tray after a few slow sips.

"Well that is why I've called you in," said a familiar voice behind me. "I wanted to know what you would make of this from a medical viewpoint."

I turned to find none other than Holmes standing in the doorway.

"Good heavens, man!" I said. "You gave me a turn!"

I stood and shook his hand then. I was glad to see him despite my surprise.

Holmes took a seat on a sofa some distance from me and Miss Ballentine, and I waited patiently as the lady composed herself enough to explain what symptoms had first manifested themselves in the patient.

However, I found it difficult to concentrate on Miss Ballentine, as beautiful as she was, because, despite my pleasure at seeing him, I was somewhat irritated by Holmes's appearance. And his declaration that *he* had sent for me, and not *she*, brought about a feeling of some disappointment: I had not been sent for merely for my own abilities.

"Come now, Watson," Holmes said and I turned to him, noting how comfortably he sat in the drawing room, as if the house were his home from home. This clearly indicated to me, knowing Holmes as I did, that he had in fact been in the Ballentine residence for some time, perhaps for all of the absence that he had conveyed to me was due to a family crisis.

Now he placed his long, musical fingers like a church steeple under his chin, and he watched me closely.

I felt a pang of guilt and wondered if he did indeed see the slight resentment I was harbouring. Holmes wasn't always the most tactful of people, nor did he care much for the emotions of others if they impaired his ability to work effectively on a case, and so I knew my antipathy would have to remain unacknowledged for the time being.

"Come now, Watson," he said again. I blinked. Then I turned my attention back to the beautiful Miss Ballentine and began to question her at length.

"My parents went the same way. The colourless eyes, the skin so sensitive to light that it burned and scarred," she said. "But it was diagnosed as some sickness of age…"

"Which quack diagnosed that?" I asked, and then

remembered myself. "Forgive me. But there is no illness of age that I have ever witnessed to cause such… deterioration as this. Age often equals frailty, but not some sudden aversion or inability to tolerate light."

I looked to Holmes for some endorsement of my words, but he appeared to be in his own thoughts. I noted how he tapped his fingers on the edge of the seat as though he were listening to his favourite opera. Was he perhaps composing something inside that magnificent mind of his, even as I struggled to make sense of a medical matter?

"I thought this myself," said Miss Ballentine. "That's why I invited Mr Holmes here in the first instance. But the day after he arrived, Jeremy fell with the same affliction."

"What do you think this is, Holmes?" I asked, growing impatient with his silence, even while I knew that deep down his genius was cooking something up.

"My dear Watson, I'm more intrigued to know what you think," he said. "I'm not a medical man. This is a medical matter."

I frowned. So that was how it was. Holmes was holding all of the cards close to his chest. Or perhaps, and I preferred to believe this, he really did need my input after all.

"All right," I said. "Your note told me that your father received a diamond? A blue diamond?"

"That's correct," said Miss Ballentine. "Some months ago from my uncle who had recently passed on. My father's brother. It was peculiar because Father hadn't heard from him for years and had already thought him long gone. Then an Indian servant arrived one day, carrying the package, and we learnt that Uncle John had been living in India all the time. The servant told us that he had left him strict instructions to bring the jewel to my father. I remember they spent a long time in Father's office, and then the servant just left."

"What happened then?" I asked.

Holmes was examining his nails as though he had heard this story so many times that it bored him.

"Father called Mother in, he showed her what was in the box and then he stowed it in the safe. A short time later he was just as Jeremy… Mr Richmond… is now. It wasn't long before he…"

Miss Ballentine halted, tears in her eyes, and I pulled out my handkerchief and held it out to the lady. She took it gratefully and dabbed at her eyes until she was composed again.

"Then you say your mother took ill…" I coaxed.

Miss Ballentine nodded. "After the reading of the will she took me into Father's study and opened the safe. Then she pulled a box from there. When she opened it I saw the diamond for the first time. It was like… an eye. If that doesn't sound too strange. A blue iris. Only large. As large as my palm.

"Mother took the diamond out of the box and held it, but I was too in awe to touch it. 'It's not in the will,' she told me. 'Your father had no time to change it before his sickness, and so I'm going to keep it to pass down to you. You are, after all, the only remaining heir of this family.'

"I forgot about the diamond as we continued to grieve, and then when Mother became sick it was the last thing on my mind."

"That was some time ago?" I asked.

"Two months. And Mr Holmes came here a few weeks ago."

Ah! Just as I had suspected: Holmes had been there all the time.

"Yes," she paused. "Mrs Anders reminded me that the servants were due payment and so I went into the safe to fetch out the yearly salary book and the money to give her to pay everyone. That's when I saw the box and recalled what Mother had said about the diamond. It all seemed so peculiar that I had completely forgotten about it. I didn't know what to think. So I sat at the desk merely looking at it.

"A while later, Jeremy arrived. We had planned to go for a drive to the seaside and I had forgotten that also. But he was quite used to me being like that since my parents died and so he came to find me in the study. I had the diamond box on the table, and Jeremy saw it. I saw no reason to keep the secret from my fiancé and so I let him look at it. That was the second time I saw the diamond," Miss Ballentine halted as though this realisation was somehow important.

"And Mr Richmond took the diamond out of the box?" I asked.

"No. Not then. But later when we returned to the house after our day out he asked if he could see it again. This time he examined it closely."

"So, why did seeing the diamond again make you suspicious? Why did you send for Holmes?"

Holmes shifted in his seat and reached over to pour himself a cup of tea.

"Oh dear," said Miss Ballentine. "I really ought to get the pot refreshed."

"No need," said Holmes. Then he stood and rang the servants' bell himself, confirming his comfort in the house once more.

"You see, when Jeremy opened the case and removed

the diamond a piece of paper fell out. It was written in a foreign language. Jeremy, fortunately, found someone to translate it and we discovered that it was Hindi," Miss Ballentine continued.

"Of course it was!" said Holmes. "And here is the tea! Come in, Mrs Anders."

Mrs Anders was indeed on the other side of the door holding a fresh tray. Holmes held the door open and the housekeeper came inside and placed the new tray down on the table, and then collected the old one.

"So what do you know, Holmes?" I asked, impatient to hear his prognosis.

Holmes remained quiet. He waited for Mrs Anders to leave, before closing the door and taking his seat again. Now with a fresh cup of tea and a plate of sandwiches, Holmes behaved as though he was alone in the room as he worked his way through two cucumber sandwiches.

I noted Miss Ballentine's distress and returned my attention to her after frowning once more at Holmes. His behaviour was more confusing than usual.

"So… erm… what did the paper say?"

"It was a warning," Miss Ballentine said, "of a curse."

"It seems," Holmes interjected, "that Miss Ballentine's uncle was a thief. Or knew one."

"Whatever do you mean?" I asked.

"The diamond was stolen. From a religious artefact. It was once known as the Eye of Shiva," Holmes said. "This very artefact is currently in the British Museum – sans its eye." He indicated a place on his forehead. "The third eye."

"Mr Holmes is right. My mother told me that my uncle's servant, Rani, was incredibly circumspect when he was questioned about the origins of the diamond. He told them that my uncle won it in a poker game. However he warned against 'holding' it for too long. I thought that meant *owning* it. But maybe it meant..." Miss Ballentine said. "I can only assume, as Jeremy and my mother held the diamond, that he meant not to touch it."

"So, the common factor is the diamond," I said, trying to keep my mind focused on the problem at hand.

"Yes," said Miss Ballentine.

"Mmmm. What do you think, Watson?" asked Holmes.

"Well. I suppose I should take a look at it. Wearing my gloves of course," I said.

Miss Ballentine led us to the study. Wearing outdoor gloves, she took the suspect box from the safe and placed it on the desk. Then she stepped back, as though she were afraid of the contents.

I pulled on my own leather gloves and lifted the box, turning it over in my hands. I noted a smear of white and smelt a distinct scent on the contents.

I placed the case back down on the desk and opened the top, being careful not to lean over it. A burst of white powder emitted into the air.

"Step back," Holmes warned. Then he threw his jacket over the case.

"What on earth was that?" asked Miss Ballentine.

"A lucky escape for Watson!" Holmes said. "And how curious that this did not happen when you showed the diamond to me. Watson, did you recognise that odour?"

"Yes, Holmes. It was lime sulphur, and that would explain the damage to your fiancé's eyes and skin. It is highly corrosive. But how was this possible?"

I held Holmes's jacket above the case, as he attempted to open it again. This time, no sulphur was released from the box, and I was able to remove the diamond from the case. I noted that it was now smeared with the white powder. Crystallised lime was covering the stone, and this could have certainly found its poisonous way onto the skin of anyone handling it with unprotected hands.

"How intriguing," said Holmes, examining the box. "It's an occasional emission. Guaranteed to catch the owner unawares at some time or other. See here, Watson, there is a small clockwork mechanism that winds itself back up as the case is opened and closed. At full wind this coil releases. Then the powder bursts out through these small holes."

"The lime would act as an irritant in this form," I said, indicating the debris on the diamond, "though wouldn't necessarily blind you without direct exposure – that would have to happen with the initial burst. Even so, it certainly wouldn't kill you."

"Then what did kill my parents? And why is Jeremy so sick? I didn't see him sprayed with that concoction," Miss Ballentine said. "So how…?"

"We must ask him," said Holmes. "For certainly he entered your study, went into your safe and examined the diamond when you weren't present."

Miss Ballentine was clearly overcome by Holmes's words. The implications that her fiancé may have been planning to rob her of the diamond hung in the air along with the smell of lime sulphur.

"One thing is for certain," I said. "The diamond must be washed and this container destroyed. Or a maiming may occur again."

I went to check on my patient and found Richmond sitting up in bed in the dark.

"How are you?" I asked.

"Sleep helped." He was groggy but better on the laudanum than without it and so I gave him another dose.

As he began to drift off to sleep I asked him a few questions about the diamond, knowing that it would be difficult for him to lie to me in his drugged state.

"I just wanted to see it again..." he murmured.

Back downstairs I reassured Miss Ballentine that her fiancé was not a thief but had been merely fascinated by the diamond.

"Thank you, Dr Watson," she said. "What an awful punishment to receive for mere curiosity."

I met Holmes again in the study. He was sitting opposite the desk, looking at the closed safe.

"The Hindus have very strong beliefs on crime and punishment, which has much to do with penance. Although I have no evidence to support this, this case reminds me of the Sanskrit Dharmaśāstras. In this document, Hindu law says that thieves should be maimed for their crimes, and sometimes even killed. Maiming is supposed to be self-inflicted too. But if the criminal refuses then the king must choose the punishment, and it often isn't pretty."

"But these people aren't thieves, Holmes. They inherited the jewel. How can they be held accountable for its original theft?" I said.

"The Hindus believe you can also be punished for crimes you committed in a previous life," Holmes continued. "We need to discover what killed Miss Ballentine's parents. That way we may avoid the murder of Mr Richmond."

"An autopsy might help," I said. "If we could gain permission from Miss Ballentine, of course."

"Since she brought us in to help, it would be odd if she refused," Holmes observed.

* * *

"Absolutely not!" said Miss Ballentine. "I couldn't possibly let you defile my parents' graves!"

"Even to save the life of your fiancé?" I asked.

Hope Ballentine's hands wrung in her lap. She was torn between her respect for her parents and love for Richmond.

"But how can you help him?" she asked. "Surely in his condition he is better off…"

"Dead?" Holmes finished.

"No. Of course I don't mean that. Oh no. This is just too awful!"

Miss Ballentine's tears fell and, once again, I found myself handing over my handkerchief.

"You must do as you feel appropriate, naturally," she said. "It's just that it is so…"

"My dear girl," I said, "don't take on so. Your parents won't know. This is not a desecration, but a search for the culprit. A way for the guilty to be punished for their crimes."

"Yes. Yes… certainly."

With the aid of her driver and a footman, Holmes and I were soon at the Ballentine family graveyard towards the back of the extensive estate.

The body was decomposing but I immediately saw signs of emaciation: Mrs Ballentine's sickness had given her a poor appetite towards the end. There was some pigmentation visible on her skin. Localised oedemas prominent on both calves. We took the body out of the casket, and lay it on a white cloth on the ground so that I could have better access. Then I examined her thoroughly.

"I hoped this would confirm my suspicion," Holmes said as I opened up Mrs Ballentine's chest. We both looked inside and I saw the degeneration of her heart.

The obvious state of the body confirmed my fears without the need to do further testing. It was surprising that these symptoms had gone unnoticed by the coroner assigned to Mrs Ballentine's case. However, I was used to investigating the unusual and the symptoms I saw gave me good reason to believe that Mrs Ballentine had been the victim of arsenic poisoning.

"A victim of arsenic poisoning rapidly loses their appetite, hence the overly slender frame. Oedemas and the brown pigmenting are other symptoms, but the condition of the heart was the final confirmation to me. If Mr Ballentine is in a similar state then I would be definite in my assessment that they were indeed both murdered," I said.

I closed up Mrs Ballentine's chest and, with the help of the driver and footman, placed her body carefully back into her coffin.

Sometime later Holmes and I left the driver and footman to re-bury the bodies of Mr and Mrs Ballentine and set off on foot back towards the house. It was then that Holmes saw a man lurking in the woodlands surrounding the house. He was wearing a thick overcoat, and a hat was pulled down over his eyes as though he did not wish to be recognised.

"There's our culprit!" I said, drawing my gun from the pocket of my overcoat.

"Maybe he is, maybe he isn't," said Holmes mysteriously. "Put that thing away for the time being. He doesn't know he's being observed, and so we will wait and see what happens."

Crouching down out of sight, we watched as the man approached the house at the rear. Then the back door opened to him as though he was expected, and the man entered the property.

"The picture becomes clearer," Holmes said.

"Well I do wish you would enlighten me, old boy," I said. "Only, the way I see it, there are several people who could have opened that door."

"Precisely," said Holmes.

It was Mrs Anders who opened the door to us when we arrived at the front door after first heading back to the graveyard. From there, Holmes had taken the driver aside and directed him on an important errand. While he did so I helped the footman to lay the last of the earth back over the coffins of Mr and Mrs Ballentine.

"Mrs Anders, can you please tell Miss Ballentine that we need to see her?" Holmes said.

"Certainly, Mr Holmes," she replied and turned to leave.

"Oh, and, Mrs Anders… I would also like you and your husband to join us."

"Us, sir? But why, sir?"

"It will all become clear. We will be upstairs checking on Mr Richmond," I said.

"Very good, Dr Watson," said Mrs Anders, and then she hurried off in the direction of the kitchens.

"Interesting," said Holmes. "Miss Ballentine is usually in the drawing room, is she not?"

We entered Richmond's room to find him still sleeping off the laudanum that I had administered. Holmes went to the curtain and peeked out through the crack but did not make any attempt to bring light into the room. I lit the lamp, but kept the light down low as we waited for

Miss Ballentine and the Anders to appear. It was quite some time before they presented themselves, but when they finally arrived, I made them all sit around the bed of Mr Richmond.

"Did you learn something that can help Jeremy?" asked Miss Ballentine.

"Certainly," I said. "It seems that your parents did not die due to the lime sulphur exposure. They were helped along."

"Helped along?" said Mrs Anders.

"Poisoned," said Holmes. "A rather common poison at that too. Disappointing that it wasn't more inventive actually. However, most poisoners are opportunists and these things are rarely thought through."

"Oh my God. My parents *were* murdered!" Miss Ballentine said. "But how? By whom?"

"That is what we need to learn. And Jeremy, here, is the means by which we will have that truth…"

Holmes whipped back the heavy curtain and the remaining light of the afternoon burst in and fell across the bed. Jeremy, however, was not in it. What lay in the bed was something that resembled a scarecrow, wearing a fine white mask that gave the aspect, in the gloom, of the wounded man.

"This whole thing has been a charade!" Holmes said.

"Where is Jeremy?" asked Miss Ballentine. "What have you done with him?"

"My dear girl, he was never injured. It was all faked for your benefit. A simple chemistry trick that even a newly indoctrinated apothecary might know. You mix certain chemicals together to create a particular effect. That, coupled with a modicum of acting ability, is enough to fool anyone in dull enough light. Even my dear friend Watson."

"But *where* is he?" asked Miss Ballentine.

"I don't know. But I suspect he is hidden in the kitchen. Or cellar. Wherever his parents want him to be."

Holmes looked directly at Mr and Mrs Anders now and the two fidgeted in their seats.

"Now, Mr Holmes. What are you implying?" asked Anders. "I'll have you know…"

"Please make it easy on yourself, Mr Anders. Richmond is your son… by adoption. But he is the proper son of Mrs Anders, isn't he?"

"Look here. I won't stand around to be insulted…"

"It's no use," Mrs Anders said. "I told you he'd know."

"His hands gave it away, Mrs Anders. Just as yours do. Sometimes the arsenic bleaching doesn't always work in all of the grooves. You see, Miss Ballentine, you have been the victim of a hoax. I dare say that the Anders family hadn't planned to take things so far. The plan was probably to get you to fall in love with their son, and when your parents died, he, as your new husband, would have access to the family fortune," I explained. "I suspect when you invited Holmes here to investigate, they rather lost their nerve."

"Watson is quite right," Holmes continued. "You see, Anders worked in India before he came here. I took the trouble to research you soon after I arrived. And after searching your room, I discovered a photograph of Mrs Anders in a sari, looking faintly darker in skin than she does now. Never truly Indian, but enough to have raised eyebrows had she not discovered how to lighten her skin with a common arsenic compound easily available from any local apothecary."

Holmes pulled a piece of paper from the pocket of his jacket and held it out to Miss Ballentine.

"Here is a receipt for the compound. Found in Mrs

Anders' possessions this morning," he continued.

"We've done nothing wrong!" said Mrs Anders. "We're hard-working. I wouldn't have been employed if Mr Ballentine had realised I had Indian blood in me… More so that Joe had married me, even though he knew that."

"Good lord!" said Miss Ballentine. "You've lied to us. But, Mr Holmes, the other things you've said. About Jeremy. Surely that is a mistake."

Holmes had the evidence to hand and he held out a photograph for Miss Ballentine to see. I glanced at it also, but I already knew that it was a picture of Mrs Anders with her son, a young boy at the time, wearing the garb of an Indian. He was smiling in the photograph, and the face, even though I had only ever seen it supposedly damaged, was without doubt Jeremy Richmond.

"This isn't possible," Miss Ballentine denied.

"I'm afraid he's telling the truth," Richmond said. "And in a way, Mr Holmes, you have done my family a favour. I was wondering how I could easily disentangle myself from this situation."

Richmond was standing behind a Chinese screen at the other side of the room, and, I now noticed, it covered a door, probably leading to a dressing room, which in turn would lead onto the landing. He was wearing the overcoat and hat that we had observed him in as we had followed him through the woodland to the rear of the house, where, we now knew, Anders or Mrs Anders had let him back inside.

"Jeremy!" Miss Ballentine gasped as he raised his arm to show that he was holding a pistol.

"Mother, Father… get behind me. Don't try to stop us leaving, Holmes. I have no inhibition towards shooting you or anyone else."

"I have no intention of stopping you," Holmes said even while I slipped my hand into my overcoat pocket and found the butt of my own pistol. "But first, clear something up for us. You planned to marry Miss Ballentine and then your plan changed. Why? You could have easily disposed of her parents in a less brutal fashion once you were married. Or merely lived happily under their roof until they died of natural causes."

"No one wanted to kill anyone," Anders said. "Then Rani turned up. He had worked for Mr Ballentine's brother. And so had Mrs Anders once. She thought Rani recognised her."

"So you killed him as he left?" I asked.

"No," said Mrs Anders. "Jeremy followed him. Found out where he was staying… We wanted to know what he'd told the master."

"There was no plan to kill him," Anders said. "It were an accident. And Jeremy weren't to blame."

"Then Mr Ballentine got sick. He opened the casket and blinded himself," said Mrs Anders.

"You saw it happen?" Holmes said.

"I was passing the study door. He always left it open. That stuff shot up into his eyes and I went in an' tried to help him… I would never have hurt him. He were a kind man."

"That's when you saw the diamond, though," I said.

"I didn't steal it. I put it back. Closed the safe – just as Mr Ballentine told me to. He didn't want anyone to see it, or that letter that Rani had given him… But I could read it and I knew what the diamond was."

"So you played on the curse?" Holmes said. "And the plan to kill Ballentine and his wife was formed."

"That's enough talk," Richmond said. "We're getting out of here."

"You still haven't explained why you didn't carry on with the marriage, Richmond. Surely that would have given you access to everything. Including the diamond," Holmes said.

"Watson was right on that score. Your presence changed everything, Mr Holmes. I had to take any suspicion away from myself. I had lost interest in the charade anyway. Why bother going through all that when I can just take everything that's hers anyway?"

At that moment I raised the gun in my pocket and aimed it at Jeremy. Without hesitation I fired, intending to injure him and make him drop the gun. The pistol in his hand went off, and Mrs Anders fell as her son's bullet pierced her in the back.

"Mother!" Richmond yelled.

Anders caught his wife as she fell, then Richmond's handsome face turned to rage as he pointed the gun at me and prepared to fire again.

"Don't do it!" Miss Ballentine cried. "Jeremy, if you ever had any feelings for me at all…"

Richmond's face turned and glared hatred at Miss Ballentine, and she crumpled in tears when she finally realised that everything she had believed in was a lie. Jeremy Richmond was the brains behind this crime. I didn't believe that Rani's death was an accident. I was certain now that Richmond's cold-blooded scheme had drawn in his parents as much as it had taken in Hope Ballentine.

At that moment we heard the approach of pounding feet. Samuel, the coach driver, entered with a posse of policemen. They overwhelmed Richmond and surrounded

Anders as he sat holding his wife. I bent to examine the woman as she breathed her last. Anders collapsed. He was a man ruined in every way.

"I cannot believe I fell for it all," Miss Ballentine said.

"Richmond was certainly plausible, and, who knows, perhaps you would have been happy if the diamond had not appeared and the family's greed had not been so encouraged," said Holmes.

"What will you do with the diamond now, Miss Ballentine?" I asked. "It isn't cursed and, now that it's cleaned, no longer dangerous to hold."

"Even so," Miss Ballentine said, "I feel like it brought us bad luck, and so I will pass it on."

"Where to?" I asked.

"The museum. To be reunited with the original artefact," Miss Ballentine said.

"A good idea," said Holmes.

On the dresser, the blue diamond glittered in the sunlight. So beautiful, and yet so deadly.

THE PILOT FISH

Stuart Douglas

It's one of the great gifts given to Conan Doyle that he is capable of creating real characters with more economy of description than almost any other writer. Irene Adler appears in person just once, Sebastian Moran the same, and even Professor Moriarty only turns up in the flesh twice in the entire canon. And yet, these are amongst the most famous characters in detective literature.

I obviously wouldn't make quite the same claim about **Fred Porlock**, but there is something tantalising about the unseen spy. In a few brief paragraphs, Conan Doyle sketches a character neither good nor bad but somewhere fascinatingly in between – a man, in Holmes's own words, "with some rudimentary aspirations towards right" though also one "encouraged by the judicious stimulation of an occasional ten-pound note".

That Porlock is no fool is plain; he has survived (figuratively) all but in the teeth of Moriarty, and can work a cipher as well as the next man. That he thinks well of himself is clear; few others would dare challenge Holmes to identify them. And he is not lacking in bravery; even fearing Moriarty suspects him, he still gets word to Holmes. Combine that with a surname with a definite literary antecedent, and I never hesitated when asked to choose someone to use in my story. If there's one person in the canon I'd like to know more about, it's the pilot fish, Fred Porlock.

—Stuart Douglas

Readers of *The Strand* magazine will be aware that I had intended my last entry therein, in which I laid out the truth regarding the death of my friend Sherlock Holmes, to be my final word on the career of that exceptional man. That remains the case even now, more than a year later. I find that, in his absence, I have no appetite for writing of our time together, though I would do anything within my power to have him back by my side.

Perhaps it was that which prompted me to pay a visit to Baker Street earlier this week. I had no particular reason for being there, but Mrs Hudson, I think, understood my motivations better than I. She left me alone in our former rooms, where I sat by the fire, smoking a pipe and flicking in a desultory manner through a collection of papers Holmes had piled by his chair in the days before he left for Switzerland. Each related to the late and unlamented Professor Moriarty, a man whose very name filled me with revulsion, and I was on the verge of consigning them all to the flames when I realised that the document I held in my hand was of a different type to the others.

Where the others consisted of barely legible notes and pages clipped from newspapers, the package I found myself opening was evidently a diary, stamped as such on its cover and tied shut with a length of string. A date two years before our first meeting was stamped in the leather of the cover.

I cut the string with my pocketknife, and carefully opened it, allowing several loose sheets of paper to fall from the back of the book into my lap. Laying them to one side, I turned eagerly to the first, undated page and began to read Holmes's account of a time in his life before our paths crossed. The events I found recounted within I now present untouched, just as my dear friend wrote them, in the hope that readers will find the same solace as I in "hearing" his voice once again.

Barring a period of three weeks in my youth, when I used such an item to track the progress of certain Clostridium spores I was cultivating, I have never felt the need to keep a diary. Public attention is anathema to me, and I can conceive of no reason for keeping a journal, other than the gratification of future publication.

That said, I am intrigued enough by a recent article on the subject of memory to attempt to jot down those tangential, apparently inconsequential, thoughts and experiences that – so the article insists – will in due course come together with similar thoughts and so form new connections that may prove of utility in the profession to which I have decided to dedicate myself. To that end, I shall record in these pages any interactions with my fellow man, however minor they may seem, and so in time build a permanent catalogue of my experiences, which may prove useful one day.

The next few pages had unfortunately been torn out, causing me to wryly ponder Holmes's definition of "permanent", but my friend's spidery handwriting reappeared thereafter, on a fresh and undated page.

MORNING

The morning was cooler than it had been in recent weeks, and though the London air was never fresh, the earliness of the hour did at least provide a certain crispness that necessitated my wearing a heavy coat as I strode along the length of Great Cumberland Place, deep in thought.

Similarities in the reporting of two distinct, apparently unconnected crimes had niggled at the edge of my mind to a sufficient extent that I had been troubled in my sleep, and so found myself, at the ludicrously early hour of six am, deep in cogitation on the edge of Hyde Park.

In the first case, several flourishing businesses had been razed to the ground in seemingly motiveless arson attacks: a papermaker's, a chandler's, an ironmonger's and an insurance office. The police had taken little interest, and indeed the first attack had been assumed to be an accident until the discovery in the debris of a badly scorched lantern that did not belong to the insurers. A spate of ever more destructive attacks had finally led to the matter being treated more seriously, until a body was discovered in the ashes of the final fire: the arsonist, according to Scotland Yard, and the case had been closed. The identity of the dead man had caught my attention, however. Nathaniel Ward was a notorious and successful cracksman, if one no longer in the first flush of youth, and not an obvious pyromaniac.

The second case involved the disappearance of a young engineer, Matthew Clute. This man, in the prime of his life and seemingly happily married, had allegedly absconded with a waitress he had met in a tearoom near his home. The evidence for this theory, according to the scant news reports, consisted of the fact that the girl had served him the day before he vanished, and she herself had not been seen since. The fact that the girl had only started in her position a few days previously was, the police believed, further evidence of a sudden mutual passion. I cannot say exactly why I believe a link exists, but the fact remains that I do, and this morning my thoughts were much absorbed in the matter.

I admit, therefore, that I was not paying as much attention to my surroundings as is my wont, but I was not so dead to the world that I failed to feel a slight tug at my jacket, nor so slow that I was not able quickly to grasp the dipper by the collar. I had only a moment to observe my captive, however, before he slipped from his own jacket and, leaving it still gripped in my hand, escaped down Edgware Road. A flash of dirty brown hair and an impression of youth were the sum of my observations at the time, but I resolved to examine the boy's coat more thoroughly at home, as a useful test of my powers of deduction.

EVENING

Having spent the majority of the day making use of the university laboratories to conduct certain chemical experiments that I believe will prove interesting if run to their conclusion, I returned to my lodgings at about ten thirty, still carrying the jacket. My intention had been to examine it in close detail, teasing out, as it were, any indications of its owner's idiosyncrasies and even identity, as was increasingly my habit with every new acquaintance. More than one sceptic has been surprised by the amount of information to be garnered simply from close observation of his shoes, cuffs and collar.

In the event, however, I was so tired that I simply threw the jacket over the back of my only chair and repaired to bed, exhausted. It would wait until morning, I believed.

* * *

In that, I was mistaken. Late that night, I was wakened by a noise coming from the sitting room. A quiet scraping, which I knew from experience indicated the main door opening, was followed by a stealthy footfall and, as I crossed to the bedroom door and pressed my ear against the wood, the sound of rapid breathing. With nothing more fearsome to hand, I took hold of a walking stick, which had been left by a previous occupant, and quickly threw open the door.

Fortunately, the light from the street lamps outside illumined the room enough for me to make out the young miscreant I had tangled with that morning. He stood near the fire, transfixed by shock, eyes wide and darting around like some cornered animal. Oddly, I had the fleeting impression that I had seen his face before, in a different context.

"Good evening," I said with what I pride myself was an admirably even tone. "My name is Sherlock Holmes. Can I help you?"

Any hopes I might have had of engaging in conversation with the boy – for, seen close to, he was no more than sixteen, pale and thin, and obviously no physical threat – were quickly dashed. He darted towards the main door, pushing my chair into my path as he did so. For a second I fancied I saw his gaze alight upon his jacket, and certainly he made a slight movement towards it, but it fell to the floor by my feet. With a grunt of disappointment, he pulled open the door and was gone. I heard the heavy thud of his steps on the stairs and then silence. I crossed to the window in time to see him running away down the street, soon to be swallowed up by the darkness.

Of course, there could be no thought of further sleep. Not that I foresaw any great mystery in the night's events. Clearly, even a garment as soiled as this was of value to a penniless street urchin. Furthermore, if he were so determined to retrieve his jacket that he would risk the penalty for burglary, then he must believe that its pockets contained some great treasure. Equally clearly, what a half-starved child considered a treasure might appear less impressive to a gentleman of even such paltry means as myself. I lit a lamp and a cigarette, and spread the jacket out on the table, expecting to uncover a wallet in one of its pockets or some such minor, illicit prize.

Even viewed in less than optimum light, much could be read from the jacket. For a start, if there was a wallet secreted within, it was a small one, for no bulge betrayed its presence. Instead, the jacket lay completely flat on the table, the material thin as tissue, with a sleek shine and greasy feel to it that spoke of poverty and filth. Bringing my nose close to a sleeve, I made out the scent of cigarette smoke, cheap food and the general stench of London's streets.

The outer pockets, when emptied, offered up little of assistance. The snapped-off blade of a rusty knife, a short length of knotted string and a smooth stone were striking only in their anonymity. I placed the stone to one side for later testing, before examining the front of the garment.

The first thing I noticed was that the three front buttons of the jacket were missing. Closer scrutiny with a magnifying glass added the detail that while one button had been torn off, whether by accident or misadventure, the other two had been carefully snipped away with scissors or a sharp knife.

Of course I understand that dippers rarely fasten their jackets, for the simple reason that, in the extremis of a policeman's grip, they can more easily shed an unbuttoned coat, but I was not aware that the complete removal of the buttons was considered necessary. Far more likely that one button had been lost and, with no money for a replacement, the owner had chosen to remove the other two rather than go about in a garment so obviously damaged. Adding a little flesh to the bones of this theory was the fact that a tiny tear in the material where the original button had been ripped had been carefully sewn. That the ragged urchin who had just fled my rooms should be so precious about his appearance seemed improbable, but I have always felt that the improbable is too often confused with the impossible.

As it happened, my theory was confirmed as soon as I opened the jacket up. Generally speaking, the homeless children who populate London do not wear overcoats, the expense of such an item causing them to settle for a tattered shirt and a thick layer of ingrained dirt to keep them warm. There are, of course, some who affect a jacket, either for comfort or due to their several pockets, but in every case the garment is a cheap one, handed down from a now-absent father or stolen from a careless working man. This jacket, however – though it was battered almost beyond recognition – had begun life as a gentleman's summer coat. A label had been partly torn away, leaving only a few letters – "Nor" – but those were sufficient to allow me to identify the tailor as Norton & Sons of Savile Row. That was interesting in itself, but of far greater import was the fact that the style of the jacket was one of only two years since. A jacket such as this might make its way naturally to the gutter – from master to servant, and from there in descending charitable stages to its present owner – but such a journey would be a long one, spread over many years. How it had contrived to make its way from a society home to a street Arab's back so quickly was, I thought, a pretty puzzle indeed.

The puzzle proved less pretty than I had expected, however. Tucked into a rent in the lining was a small square of paper, folded several times and carefully secreted so as to remain safe from a casual glance as well as unlikely to fall and so be lost.

Even before I spread open the paper and read its contents, it was clear that the boy I had so recently chased from my rooms was no ordinary urchin. By the time I had completed my reading, I had recalled who he was and – more interestingly – come across a minor and potentially diverting mystery.

All I have to do now is find him!

At that dramatic point, the first entry ended. I flipped the page over, fascinated to learn more from this younger version of my friend, but to my disappointment, the succeeding few pages were a mixture of the commonplace and the implausible, as Holmes used the book for everything from a reminder to buy new shirt collars to a note regarding various types of cigar ash. I almost skipped the following page, where a faded and smudged carbon copy of a letter had been pasted, but fortunately the word "runaway" caught my eye and drew my attention to its fascinating – if occasionally illegible – contents.

Dear Mr Hamilton,

I write to you as a stranger, but in hopes that I may be able to provide assistance to someone once known to you and, in doing so, provide you with certain information that may be of interest to you and your lady wife.

I will come straight to the point, if I may. My name is Sherlock Holmes and I work as a consulting detective. Yesterday, as I walked in Hyde Park, I encountered your son, Frederick, who, I believe, has been estranged from you for some time.

Forgive me for raking up memories that may be painful to you, but my understanding is that Frederick absconded from the family [word faded and illegible] some two years since, along with several valuable items, and that neither yourself nor your wife have heard from him since. That being so, I hope it will give you some consolation to hear that he is alive and in reasonably good health here in London. Fortunately I remembered reading a newspaper report of the theft that included a sketch of your son, and so was able to befriend him to an extent.

I understand from Frederick that he fears that any attempted reconciliation on his part might be rebuffed, but I hope most earnestly that this is not the case and some form of entente might be reached between you. As a token of his own contrition, he asked me to enclose [the words here were smudged beyond recognition] in the expectation that you will recognise it and comprehend its meaning.

I speak not as an especial confidante of your son, but simply as one whose path crossed his own recently and who would like to help a young boy gone astray, if he might. To that end, I wonder if Frederick had any particular friend in the capital to whom he might listen and *whom I might convince to add his voice to my own in persuading Frederick to return home.*

I am your servant,
Sherlock Holmes

Pasted beneath the letter was a short snipping from a local newspaper, regarding the unpleasant case of one Frederick Hamilton, a fourteen-year-old boy who had run away from his parents' comfortable middle-class home with a quantity of the family silver on his person. Police had apparently made enquiries, but had failed to find him. Holmes, however, had recognised him from his description – his prodigious memory for crime and criminals evidently already in place even so early in his career.

I laid the book to one side and considered this extraordinary missive. The Holmes I knew would not, I was sure (or, at least, hoped), have stooped to outright deception in order to progress a case, far less from mere curiosity, but there was no denying that he had done so in this instance. He had been a younger, more impetuous man, of course, but still, the thought was a troubling one.

I wondered what item Holmes had sent to establish his bona fides, then felt a familiar tightness in my throat as I remembered that I would never be able to ask him that question in person. In need of distraction and, I admit, eager to discover Holmes's next move, I resumed my reading.

18th February 1879
Several days have passed without reply from the Hamiltons. I fear that my tone was too forward. No matter. I am certain

that some fresh avenue of investigation will occur to me in due course, and in the meantime I have experiments in grave need of my time. I shall put this diary to one side for now.

19th February 1879
MORNING
A letter has arrived from Mr Hamilton! I admit to a certain relief at his response, which makes it plain that neither he, nor his wife, have any desire to be reunited with their errant son. Thus relieved of the painful task of admitting that I exaggerated Frederick's desire to return to the bosom of his family, I can utilise the other significant revelation in the letter – the last address where, Hamilton tells me, the police were able to track the boy.

I say address, but perhaps location is a better word, for Hamilton states that it has neither name nor number, but lies within an area of the capital I do not recognise, a rundown section of Whitechapel named George Yard. Situated mere yards from the high street, according to my street map, the entire area is a den of thieves and army deserters, if one newspaper report I uncovered at the library is to be given credence. I am certain that no gentleman would last more than a moment or two in its grip before he was hounded back into the light of the main thoroughfare. How then might I gain uninterrupted access? I will smoke a pipe or two and give the matter some thought.

LATER
I have never considered myself a great thespian, though I did some backstage work at school, but I believe that I would be proficient at disguising my appearance sufficiently to pass as a vagabond and so gain entry to George Yard and the hovel

beside it where Frederick was last spotted. At worst, I will be uncovered and forced to flee, but the information contained in the document I found in Frederick's tattered jacket is of great enough import to render that risk one worth taking.

I have resolved to visit this evening.

20th February 1879

I doubt if I shall ever again be involved in such a perilous endeavour as that of last night, or enter so squalid a dwelling. I arrived in Whitechapel at a little after ten o'clock, having spent the majority of the evening preparing myself. Throwing an old suit on the ground and walking over it repeatedly had given it a suitably down-at-heel condition (and gained me no end of perplexed looks from passers-by), while the application of a little stage make-up and grime from the London streets took care of the visible portion of my face and neck. Finally, what could barely be recognised as a hat, purchased from a tinker's cart, completed my tramp disguise. I would pass muster amongst the poorer sort who lived in George Yard, I was sure.

The street itself is a dark, narrow lane off Whitechapel High Street. The walls ran with water and my breath turned to steam in front of me as I shuffled along its length, eyes alert, aware that even at night places such as this remained as busy as during the day. Not that such busyness is obvious to a stranger to the area, but, as I have pointed out frequently, almost nobody truly observes his surroundings – a capital mistake, in my opinion. To look but not see is a trap into which I am determined never to fall.

So it is that I can say that as I made my way along the cobbled ground, I saw a man planning a burglary that would fail and lead to his capture (the uncovered tip of a jemmy protruding from a bag and a pronounced limp did not argue for either great cunning or fleetness of foot); a confidence trickster and card sharp (that he was the only sober man amongst his drunken victims was plain to anyone versed in the physical signs of genuine inebriation); and a myriad of children who could and should be set to bettering themselves rather than being left to rot away in the Whitechapel dirt (the intelligence on each face was matched only by the degree of filth – cunning need not, after all, be an evil thing).

Beyond these incidental observations, however, I was most aware of the crushing poverty in which every man, woman and child lived, here in a street mere yards from the centre of human civilisation. I had more pressing matters to attend to, however, and so leaned back against a wall, every inch the loafing ruffian, and cast my eyes about for the rundown building described by Hamilton.

The lane had by this point opened out into a small square, and across the way, I made out a break in the darkness, a narrow opening formed in the gap between one derelict building and the next. Though it was a good ten feet away, I felt sure that the air inside would be cold and taste foul. For a moment I considered turning back and letting the matter drop. Was the information in Frederick's letter truly worth this? But mine is a mind that requires stimulation, and I would get none back home, so I slipped my hand inside my coat pocket and wished I had a revolver to hand.

It would be an exaggeration to call the damp space I entered an alleyway. Though approaching three feet wide at the start, by the time I was five paces inside it had narrowed to less than two, and the sensation of claustrophobia I felt building in me was only exacerbated by the fetid water underfoot, the slippery mould that coated the walls and the increasing lack of light. The crooked tenements along both sides bent in toward one another like gossiping old women. I recoiled as something ran across my foot but did not let it distract me, for I could see that the tenements came to an abrupt stop only a few yards hence. I had travelled the length of the "alleyway" and, leaving it behind me, now stood directly in front of a squat, crumbling two-storey building of indeterminate use. This must be the place.

A sheet of rusted corrugated iron blocked the only entrance, but a firm push moved it and I ducked inside. There was some light within, cast by the full moon through an upper window, which illuminated a wooden staircase directly in front of me. Each step was bowed in the centre by the passage of decades of unfortunate inhabitants, and what railing had once existed was now reduced to a series of iron stumps, the remainder long since having made its way to one of London's many scrap merchants.

It was plain that the building had not been built for habitation. A rusted sign at the foot of the stairs directed visitors to a reception area on the first floor and a rotten cork noticeboard on one wall still bore the label "Announcements". But like so much of London, its abandonment had been only temporary. Close down a factory one day, and the poor in need of shelter will move in the next. Such is the way of this great metropolis.

Having come so far, I had no thought of turning back. I edged up the stairs, shoulder braced against the wall in the darkness, listening carefully for any sound from the upper floors. All was silent.

I reached the first floor and saw a long, wide, empty space without doors or windows. Incongruously, a candle shone in one corner of the echoing space, but its dim light shadowed rather than brightened the grey walls it reached. Layers of compacted filth littered the floor, with here and there a puddle of dark, still water reflecting the flicker of the candle. A set of railing-free stairs leading upwards, matching those I had just ascended from the ground, were the only other exit that I could see.

The stench was indescribable, and I pressed a hand to my nose as I stepped onto the next flight of stairs, kicking aside the desiccated corpse of a cat. The stairway doubled back on itself after a dozen steps, forming a small rectangular landing where the direction changed. Two women were slumped against the wall there, not sleeping but not completely awake either. Their eyes were open but red-lined and unseeing, and their mouths hung slackly down. Each woman held a battered tin cup in her hand – the source, no doubt, of their current incapacity. I considered the vile nature of their lives, and shuddered at the thought that only oblivion offered solace to such unfortunates, then squeezed past the nearest of the drabs and climbed the last few steps to the top floor.

The sight that greeted me was one such as I hope never to see again. The space before me was of similar dimensions to the lower floor, though slightly narrower, where a wooden partition had been built along one side, creating a series of small rooms. The air was fetid, warm and stale, as if I had stepped into an underground cavern rather than the hallway of a building in a modern city. The reason was obvious.

All along the walls silent people huddled together, every one as pale-skinned and grime-encrusted as the next. I tried to judge their number, but the moon hid behind a cloud and in the darkness I recognised that mere numbers were unimportant. That even one Englishman should live in such squalor was one too many. What I took to be a family had lit a small cooking fire, the smoke thus generated creating a "fog" that glowed in the light of the flame and billowed around my head, adding to the hellish aspect of the space. As I slowly walked forward, all the while casting an eye in the gloom for my quarry, hopeless faces peered out from beneath dirty shawls, and babies, miraculously able to sleep even in a place like this, stirred and moaned in their mothers' arms.

I reached the back wall without a sign of Fred Hamilton and stood, irresolute and dispirited, unsure what to do next. The decision was taken from my hands, however, when one of the lost souls near me detached itself from the wall and stood in front of me.

"Whatcher starin' at?" I snarled angrily, there being more to a disguise than mere face paint and rags. Failure to stand my ground would mark me as a potential victim, even if it did not unmask me as something rather more than I seemed to be. "Gerrout my way, damn yer!"

I made to shoulder past the shadowy figure, but a surprisingly strong hand grasped my shoulder and squeezed hard, stopping me in my tracks. "What's yer rush, mate?" a man's voice grunted roughly in my ear. "Got some place you'd rather be?"

I grasped the man's wrist and pulled it from my shoulder, while simultaneously twisting round to confront him. The moon remained hidden amongst the clouds so that I could not make out his face, but he was of average height and well built considering the life of deprivation he presumably led. His voice suggested a man of middle age, but beyond that I could make out nothing more. Fortunately, the moon chose that moment to pass briefly into clear air and by its fleeting illumination I was able to examine my new friend.

"Watcher gawpin' at?" he snarled, violence clearly uppermost in his mind. "Think yer better than me, do yer? D'yer even know who I am?"

He jabbed a thick finger into my chest, but I was expecting such a move and stood my ground. The thought occurred to me, however, that he might have a knife, for which I was wholly unprepared. As the moon slid once more into the clouds, I therefore decided to put my rough persona to one side and deal with the man as Sherlock Holmes, consulting detective, instead.

"You are a former army sergeant," I said automatically and without conscious thought, "who spent the bulk of his service years in this country, though you saw active duty in India in your final years. You left the army within the past three years, honourably and with a small pension, but you also had some savings of your own. This place is not somewhere you would be found in the normal way of things, but you remember the army fondly and still think of the men who were under your authority as being your responsibility."

I paused for breath, balanced on the balls of my feet, ready for any attack that might come, but the man simply stood and stared at me for a long moment. My eyes had become accustomed to the gloom by now and I could make out a look of incredulity on his face. What to me seemed the most elementary of deductions obviously struck him as an altogether more impressive feat.

"How'd yer know all tha'?" he asked. "I'll swear you've not been followin' me."

"No, I have not. I am looking for someone else entirely, in fact. Perhaps you can help me find him?"

"Tell me how yer knew all that first, then maybes I'll see if I can help yer."

He moved round to block my access to the stairwell and crossed his arms, evidently happy to remain there indefinitely if I did not explain myself. With little choice but to do so, I began to speak.

"It is simple enough, Sergeant. Your greatcoat, though now without insignia, is of a type used exclusively by the army up until roughly two years ago, when it was replaced with a lighter style. Your diction rules out your being an officer, but your bearing

and the confidence in your voice suggest a position of authority, hence my suggestion of sergeant. Your skin has none of the weathering one would expect from an extended period spent in Her Majesty's warmer dominions, but you have a distinctive limp caused by a bullet wound to the right knee, suggesting some time spent fighting abroad. I cannot be more precise than that without resorting to guesswork. It is possible, of course, that you were wounded in a clash with Irish rebels, for instance, but on the balance of probability a foreign posting seems more likely. Either way the wound led to your being invalidated out of the army, hence it occurred late in your service."

"And the rest? How could yer tell I had some money put aside, or that I still try to look after my boys when I can?"

His voice had softened and I sensed that any thoughts of violence towards me had abated.

"The greatcoat you wear for sentimental reasons, but the remainder of your dress is of reasonable quality, while your face, hands and nails are spotlessly clean. You therefore have a home somewhere beyond these walls, and, as an army pension famously is barely enough to live on, you must have some other income. Savings seemed most obvious. As for your feelings towards your men, that gentleman sitting in a gin stupor over there has the cap of the Northumberland Fusiliers on his head. You speak with a northern accent and you approached me from that direction. The deduction was a straightforward one."

I hesitated, unclear whether this was sufficient information to placate my interrogator, but any trepidation I might have harboured of the man dissipated completely as he held out his hand.

"Peter Gilham," he said as we shook, "Sergeant in Her Majesty's Northumberland Fusiliers as was, wounded by a Xhosa spear in '77 and chucked out on me ear soon after."

He sighed and looked round the filthy room. "Still, mustn't grumble. There's plenty as would bite off me hand for a billet cosy as mine."

"You come here to keep one eye on a former comrade?" I asked quietly, already knowing the answer but keen to keep him talking.

"I do. Yer wouldn't think it now, to look at him, but that lad there once held off twenty rebel natives for an hour, all on 'is own. Allowed the rest of us to push up and out, so 'e did. 'E paid the price though. Only just survived 'is wounds, and was pushed out 'isself right after." He shook his head, the sadness in his eyes visible even in the half-light. "Look at 'im now, sir. Dyin' with the drink, shaking fit to bust without it."

"You come here often?" I asked. "You know the unfortunates who call this place home?" Hamilton's absence had rendered my journey fruitless, but I wondered if Sergeant Gilham might yet be able to assist me in my search.

He nodded. "I do," he replied. "They lead rough lives, them as live 'ere, and they're at risk from all sorts. I'll not 'ave one of my lads abused by no man, police or not, and the rest… well, since I'm 'ere anyway it'd be un-Christian not to look out for 'em too."

"Police? Are they often seen?" There was a note of doubt in my voice, I knew, but it seemed unlikely that London's overworked constabulary would have the time or the inclination to patrol such derelict buildings as this.

Gilham was adamant, however. "For a while they was, though I've not seen a sign of 'em for a year since. Tends to be folk with a bit less scruples as comes 'ere now. Rougher types even than these," he concluded, gesturing to the lost souls about us.

There was nothing to interest me in the lives of such people, but Gilham's mention of a police presence a year previously did pique my curiosity, for obvious reasons.

"These policemen – were they looking for someone in particular?" I asked, as casually as I could.

Men do not rise to the rank of sergeant if they are fools. Gilham examined me carefully for a moment or two before he spoke again. "Might have been," he said finally. "It ain't like folk come down 'ere looking for diamonds and emeralds. There ain't no gold in Whitechapel, only copper and paper, and precious little of that too." He laughed, but there remained a little of his earlier suspicion in his eyes. "But whatcha want to know for?"

Here I knew I must tread carefully. Gilham would say no more if he believed that I meant the boy any harm. "I am looking for a young man named Frederick Hamilton, a runaway, who has caused his family great grief," I began. I would need to choose my words carefully, for I was sure that Gilham would know if I lied outright. "His parents are not yet ready to welcome him back into the family home, but they fear for his safety and would at least know that he was alive and well."

"Thought you was a copper," Gilham said thoughtfully. "All that figurin' out about me. Only a copper'd be able to do that." He paused, considering his options, then shook his head. "Can't 'elp you, on account of never 'avin' 'eard of the bloke."

"No, no!" I hurriedly exclaimed. "I am not with the police, I assure you. I am merely a private citizen who is keen to give peace of mind to a dear friend and his wife."

I wildly exaggerated my relationship with the Hamiltons, but other than that every word was true (to some extent, at least), and it was this core of near truth that caused the sergeant to believe me and let down his guard once more.

"Fair enough, yer not a policeman. Sorry to have said so. But

there's men 'ere who wouldn't thank me for pointing the police in their direction. And maybes young Hamilton's one of them."

Gilham hesitated once more, then seemed to come to a decision and, beckoning me to follow, led the way down the stairs and out into the street.

To my dismay, it seemed that Holmes's narrative ended there, for all that remained of the diary thereafter were the ragged edges of pages torn from its spine. Nothing daunted, I placed the book to one side and rifled again through the mass of loose papers that had accompanied it, soon uncovering several fresh pages that Holmes, for reasons of his own, had ripped from the diary. Unfortunately, there was no sign of the text that would have immediately followed the section I had just read. As a consequence, I was forced to resume the tale at a later point, with Holmes face to face with Frederick Hamilton and no direct indication of how he had got there or how much time had passed.

I held out a hand. "The letter, if you please, Mr Hamilton," I said, for I had no intention of leaving it in his hands, once he had satisfied himself as to its nature.

He handed it back quickly enough, perhaps still recollecting the painful bruise I had been forced to inflict on his wrist not half an hour before. "Might I be told what you intend to do with it?" he asked, with something like the spirit with which he had initially greeted me. "Or is that too a secret to which I may not be privy?"

He spoke properly, as one might expect from a boy from his background, but I admit I found so well-spoken a voice emanating from so grubby a figure incongruous to say the least.

And yet he had survived for two years on the hardest of London streets, amongst killers and worse, with nobody suspecting he was anything more than another unfortunate waif. Clearly, Fred Hamilton had the gift of appearing what he was not.

No matter how good his diction, however, the fact remained that he had stolen from his family, then absconded to take up a life of petty crime. The good Sergeant Gilham had left me in no doubt that Hamilton was not someone to be trusted, and I was not minded to tell him everything I knew until I was certain of his own role in the matter.

"Better that I should ask what you intended to do with it, after you lifted it from Dr Laidlaw's pocket?"

His reply was instantaneous and insolent. "Who said I did?"

"Come now, do not play the fool, Mr Hamilton. We are agreed, are we not, that the letter you just returned to me is from a Dr Laidlaw of Curzon Street to a mathematics professor by the name of Moriarty. The letter accuses the professor of professional misconduct and plagiarism and threatens to unmask him to the university authorities if he does not at once resign his position. How else do you claim to have come into possession of such an item, other than by the pickpocketing that is your daily labour? Or do men of learning often entrust you with their most private correspondence?"

Hamilton shrugged, but knew he was beaten. "And if I did, what of it? A man needs to eat, Mr Holmes, and there's nobody likely to put meat on my plate if I don't do so myself."

"Whether that is true or not, it is no answer to my question. What did you intend to do with the letter?"

The boy scowled, but I had the distinct sensation that whatever anger he felt, it was directed not at me, but at himself, for ending up in such a position. "I was hoping to extract a few quid from this Moriarty. Show him the letter and point out that I could burn it as easily as show it round the university – and for a fiver, say, I'd be more than happy to buy some matches."

Any respect I had for Hamilton almost evaporated then. It is one thing to be a criminal, after all, another entirely to be a stupid one. "And why would Moriarty pay you for a worthless letter?" I asked, with some irritation.

"So that I don't let his employers know they've a cheat in their midst, of course!"

"And he would not have realised – as you obviously have not – that the letter is of little matter, for Dr Laidlaw could easily write another, and another after that, should the first go astray."

"Oh. I hadn't thought of that."

The look on Hamilton's face was so forlorn that I almost felt sorry for him. I pride myself that I am an excellent judge of character, and I would hazard there's no real malice in him, and perhaps even a yearning for good. Certainly, when I suggested returning the letter to Dr Laidlaw, he was not averse to the idea and agreed to accompany me. We would claim to have found the letter in the street and, recognising the return address on the envelope, thought it our duty to return it. A weak story, perhaps, but in truth, now that I had found Hamilton and confirmed that the letter really was nothing but academic sniping, I had begun to lose interest altogether.

Moriarty! The unexpected sight of that hated name caused my heart to beat more loudly in my chest. I quickly turned to the next page, but to my dismay Holmes's story came to a halt once again, and on the reverse of this page were no more of my friend's words, only an undated clipping from a newspaper, pasted into the centre of an otherwise blank space.

HORRIBLE MURDER OF
UNIVERSITY DON

Between eleven and twelve o'clock last night, the well-known mathematics lecturer Dr Hamish Laidlaw was brutally slain in his own home by persons unknown.

Police are unwilling to release further detail on this terrible crime, but it is understood that the doctor was strangled in his bed while his wife lay sleeping beside him. The motive of the killer remains unknown, as no valuables are believed to have been stolen, nor was Dr Laidlaw known to have any enemies.

Dr Laidlaw is survived by his wife and two grown children.

Thankfully, Holmes took up the tale on the succeeding page.

25th February 1879
Hamilton and I arrived at Dr Laidlaw's home at around ten in the morning, only to find the house locked up and deserted. A neighbour was kind enough to inform us that there had been a substantial police presence in the dead of night, and that Mrs Laidlaw had departed in the company of one of her sons not an hour previously. With no means of making further enquiries, we left, purchasing a newspaper on the way back to my rooms, a clipping from which I have attached overleaf.

Hamilton is not entirely without wits after all, I was pleased to see, and immediately grasped the import of this unexpected death. "This is Professor Moriarty's doing, isn't it?" he said as soon as he read the journalist's report. "He's found out about the letter somehow, and killed Laidlaw for writing it." Panicked, he slapped his hands against his head and moaned the single word "mother" in despair, reminding me with this childish reaction that allowances must be made for his youth.

"Yes," I said as kindly as I could, "but there is no reason to suspect that he has even heard your name, far less knows that you hold the instrument of his ruin in your hands. Or rather," I concluded, for accuracy is of the utmost importance in all things, "in my hands, since I have the letter here in my pocket."

If Hamilton took any consolation from my words, he gave no sign of it. "What do you intend to do with it now?" he asked miserably. "Hand it to the police? Send me home? Because if I have any say in the matter," he continued, anger replacing misery in his voice, "I'd prefer it if you told the police I'm a dipper instead of forcing me back home. I'll not spend another night under the same roof as my father!"

I had no particular interest in his home life or the conduct of his father, but in any case I had never intended either to send him home or give the letter to the police. I told him as much as we arrived back at my rooms.

"I believe there is good in you, Frederick, but it has been obscured by certain poor choices you have made and—" I held up a hand to forestall the objection I could see forming on his lips, "—perhaps an upbringing that was not ideal. With this in mind, I have a proposition to put to you."

I explained my idea to him: that he should take Laidlaw's letter and give it not to the police but to Professor Moriarty himself, delivering it as originally intended by its author, but not in quite the manner in which the late doctor had desired. Better by far to present the letter already opened to this larcenous (and, it seemed possible, murderous) professor. "Explain that you have come across this missive through your own enterprise," I said, "and recognising the potential for harm it contained, you thought it best to present it to its intended recipient. Perhaps add a knowing word about poor Laidlaw, so tragically struck down, and even a hint that the letter came to you by less than honest means. Ingratiate yourself, Hamilton. Convince Moriarty that you are his man. Be the pilot fish to his shark and let me know what scraps he lets fall."

At first he was not wholly enthusiastic. But in time I was able to convince Hamilton that this path offered his best chance of achieving something worthwhile with his life. No more a shiftless pickpocket or a despised son, but a man engaged in vital, honest work. Professor James Moriarty, whatever else he might turn out to be, was a character worth keeping an eye on, I felt, and Hamilton was just the man for the job.

I have sent him to rest in my bed while I make some minor arrangements for his first meeting with Moriarty. A nom de plume is required, so that I always know that it is he who contacts me (assuming that he ever in fact needs to do so). I think I will suggest Fred Porlock, in commemoration of the person from that village who interrupted Coleridge and thus caused him to lose the thread of his thoughts, much as Hamilton did when attempting to rob me of my wallet.

I should also record here that I have proven a better man than Coleridge, for a comment of Gilham's had knocked a thought ajar in my head. "No gold in Whitechapel, only copper and paper," he'd said, and though it had meant nothing to me at the time, the phrase would not remove itself until, with a start, I remembered the arson attacks and the vanished engineer with which I had been absorbed at the beginning of this whole affair.

Obviously it is incorrect to say that there is no gold in London. Indeed, there can be few cities on earth that contain more of that precious metal. But almost all of it is locked away, safe from criminal intent. Banknotes are another matter, however. The Bank of England produces new notes constantly. Crucially, however, the paper the notes are printed on is the only thing that the Bank does not manufacture itself, but instead buys from a supplier. A quick glance through the report on the arson attacks confirmed that the first fire – the one that looked very like an accident – had burned down the offices of the self same paper manufacturer. But what if that fire had been exactly as first suspected? I could readily picture the elderly cracksman Nathaniel Ward carelessly knocking his lantern to the ground as he opened a safe in the dark. And a fortuitous fire would neatly cover the fact that certain documents concerning the constitution of Bank of England banknote paper had been stolen. So long as the fire was thought to be an unfortunate accident, that is.

Once the police had reason to suspect something else, however, a cunning man might think it better to encourage those suspicions by carrying out a series of random arson attacks, thereby allowing the significance of the first fire to be lost in the mass. Perhaps – though this is the merest conjecture which I would not repeat in public – Ward was killed for his mistake and his placement in the ashes of the final fire was merely a neat tying up of two loose ends.

So much for Nathaniel Ward, but what of the missing engineer, Matthew Clute? A visit to his widow, ostensibly to offer my condolences, swiftly revealed that Clute had recently been engaged on a prestigious and confidential new commission – to work in a team designing new forms of security for Bank of England banknotes!

Obviously, there is more to be learned than this, but it is a starting point for further investigation. The struggle of the Bank to stay one step ahead of the criminal fraternity is well-

known and still causes suspicion of "paper money" amongst many of the older generation. Though I cannot yet identify the exact use to which they will be put, ownership of the means to manufacture the correct paper stock and knowledge of upcoming security measures provide an obvious advantage to whoever is behind these crimes.

It is a clever plan, I must admit, requiring both the loyalty of a large gang and an ability to plan for the long term, which is rarely seen in the common criminal. Could there be a dark mastermind at work in London? If so, I hope one day to test myself against him.

At this horribly ironic point, the diary ended completely. There were no more pages to be read. All that remained was a smaller notebook in which Holmes had entered the name Porlock followed by a column of figures, obviously a record of such small payments as he had made to Hamilton over the years. It was only then that I recalled hearing the name before, in an earlier case involving the late Professor Moriarty, and recalled Holmes claiming to have had no knowledge of his spy's real name or even how he came to be called Porlock in the first place. Nothing was ever as it seemed with Holmes, I mused as I crossed to the open door and, passing through, pulled it sadly closed behind me.

THE CASE OF THE SCENTED LADY

Nik Vincent

Everyone knows **Mrs Hudson**. But the truth is that Conan Doyle seems hardly to have known her at all. He gave her no first name, no physical description, and only occasional appearances in his stories.

We know Mrs Hudson, chiefly, from the screen. Una Stubbs has become many people's idea of who Mrs Hudson is, but she has also been portrayed as the young widow of a pilot, an alcoholic ex-exotic dancer, and transgender.

I wanted to find my "real" Mrs Hudson, and this story gave me the opportunity to do that.

As far as possible, I wanted to follow Doyle's lead, such as it is, but I hope I gave my Mrs Hudson a little fire in her belly.

If Watson's description of her in "The Adventure of the Dying Detective" is to be believed, she must have been quite an extraordinary woman, and nobody's fool.

—Nik Vincent

It was the very best time to enter the rooms of the great man, take possession of them for an hour or two, and create some order in the chaos that was left in dear Mr Holmes's wake.

It is perfectly possible to divine the condition of Mr Holmes's faculties from the manner of his leaving. A slow, measured stride, the murmur of the door swinging open, and the considered click of the lock re-engaging on its closing suggest a calm, possibly reflective humour. On that day, at that hour, I heard a stampede, succeeded by a bang of the door, and the judder of the house resettling in the aftermath signalled a mind at full-tilt and heaving with purpose.

Note, gentle reader, that I am constant in my regard for my lodger, whom I hold in high esteem, however mercurial his humours might seem to those who know him less well. He saves much of his glee and not a little of his opprobrium for his long-suffering and venerable colleague, Dr Watson, of course, but I am privy to a measure of his bountiful spirit in my turn.

Mr Holmes is apt to eschew routine in favour of spontaneity. Great demands are made on both his time and his deductive capabilities, and housekeeping is scarcely worth his attention. I attend; it is my function, as far as I have any significance in his sphere.

On his ferocious departure on some grave new exploit, I donned an apron, and took up my bucket and duster.

Mr Holmes might not clean for himself, but domestic necessities must be seen to.

The furious flurry of his leaving was precisely echoed in the pandemonium of his rooms, as if a maelstrom had been trapped within. I had seen his rooms in this condition many times before, and was unperturbed by the results.

The sitting room was gloomy, the curtains tightly shut. The great man had, quite clearly, been at his cogitations through the night. His bed had probably not been slept in. I allowed my eyes to adjust to the darkness, and then made my way to the window. First, in all endeavours, there must be light.

When I drew the curtains, the light was as dismal as I'd expected. Great, grey clouds loomed, and the rain came down in sheets at a most improbable angle. Mr Holmes must have been in the most dreadful hurry, for I had not heard the clatter of an umbrella being taken from the hallstand as he departed.

I checked the curtains, as I always do. Blood is better removed before it dries. I have administered salt-paste and carbolic to curtains, carpets and upholstery on a number of occasions when clients have arrived bleeding, or when some regrettable altercation has taken place. On this day I found no blood, but the motion of opening them disturbed the air, wafting a sweet scent into the stale atmosphere, unlike Mr Holmes's usual aroma of strong tobacco.

A woman had been in the room. Her perfume was concentrated around the window, so she must have sat in the armchair close by. Perhaps she had stood and clutched at a curtain. There was no doubt that she must be a lady. The scent remained strong and clear, redolent of satin and velvet, of fine hats and good grooming. No lady that might wear such a perfume would venture to a single gentleman's rooms at night, or else, she must be very desperate to do so. Perhaps her plight had resulted in Mr Holmes's urgency. And yet, surely he would have seen the woman to her carriage?

No, indeed. No carriage had drawn up to the house while I was around to hear it, either last night or this morning. The lady had come very late in the evening or during the night, after I had retired. The urgency had surely come from Mr Holmes's nocturnal cogitations.

She was a lady. The perfume indicated as much, and she was desperate to have come to Mr Holmes at night, but the cushion had been straightened on the chair she had sat in, so she was both meticulous and not above tidying after herself. Who could such a woman be? And how might she come to require the services of Mr Holmes?

I put such nonsense from my thoughts, for neither Mr Holmes nor his client had need of my idle reveries. I turned to the work at hand. There was only so much I could do. Mr Holmes was ever particular about his belongings, so there were areas of the sitting room that I could flick a duster at, but heaven forbid I should interfere with anything. I noted that his violin had not been moved. It was on the same shelf where it had been the day before, the bow lying undisturbed beside it. So, the woman, whoever she was, must have arrived in the evening, at about the time Mr Holmes might have been expected to take up his instrument. I certainly didn't remember hearing him play. Mr Holmes had not slept, therefore he must have spent much of the night giving consideration to whatever case the lady had brought him. I glanced at the log basket, and, just as I thought, it was empty. I held a hand to the grate, and it was long cold, but there was a greater quantity of ash than on a regular morning. Mr Holmes's work had kept him up until dawn, and he had become so intent on the matter at hand that when the fuel for his fire was used up, he had allowed the room to grow cold rather than disturb his process by collecting more wood.

I brushed out the grate, filling the dustpan twice, my bucket brimming as I came to the final layer of fine ash. As I swept the hearth clean, something rang against the dustpan, some small metal object. I took the poker up, and moved its end gently in the ash. When I lifted it out, a ring slid down its length, almost into my hand. I dropped it into my apron and rubbed gently with a thumb and forefinger to dislodge the worst of the soot.

The ring was made for a man, a large signet with a bold and very beautiful piece of lapis lazuli filling the mount. I did not recognise it as belonging to my lodger, or to Dr Watson. It must have been brought here by the lady, and yet it could not have been worn by her. Was it simply lost, or had she discarded it? Thrown it in the flames in an act of desperation, or in a fit of pique? This was a mystery, indeed. No doubt Mr Holmes was hard on the heels of some new discovery that would neatly solve the case.

The inside of the ring remained black with soot, so I twisted the corner of my apron around my finger, and wiped the worst of it away. After a turn or two more around my shrouded finger, I examined the ring more closely, and found an inscription on the inside. I had some education as a child, but girls were not instructed in Latin in my day, so I could not fathom what it said.

I dropped the ring into my apron pocket for safekeeping, and went to the desk, picking up a smoking jacket and closing the lid on a tobacco jar, before removing Mr Holmes's

Prince Alberts, propping the slippers against the hearth-rail ready for them to be warmed ahead of his return. The embroidered monogram on the tops of the slippers reminded me of the signet ring in my pocket. I took it out and rubbed the blue stone, but when I looked at it, I could see that it had not been engraved. It was a gentleman's ring, so why did it not bear his crest or monogram? And yet it was engraved within the band. How very strange.

I wondered at my own curiosity, for it was none of my concern. I could not help but tut at my musings, and I dropped the ring back into my pocket and continued with my tasks. I pulled the cushion from Mr Holmes's customary chair, and dropped it on its end onto the floor, to ruffle the feathers within and plump it up. I turned it and dropped it again, on its side, and repeated the process until it had returned to a pleasing shape. As I settled it back in place, I spotted a slip of paper on the rug that must have fallen from the cushion. It was just a corner of a piece of good writing paper, the rest having been torn away. Perhaps the remainder had found its way into the fire.

The fine white paper was expensively made with a green border. There were a few elegant, precise letters in violet ink; an unusual colour. None of the words were complete or readable. I slipped the corner of the paper into my apron pocket along with the ring. I learned long ago not to discard anything that I might find in Mr Holmes's rooms. The smallest object might prove the most important, though I never could see any rhyme or reason to his curious intellectual meanderings.

I flicked the duster over the bookcase and noticed that several volumes had been removed. A considerable pile of them was tucked beside Mr Holmes's chair. Several were closed, and I flicked through them to make sure that no pages had been marked, before returning them to their rightful places on the shelves. Two, one on top of the other, lay open. I marked the pages, closed them and put them on the corner of Mr Holmes's desk. Two of the closed books had markers in them, so they went on the pile, too. I glanced at the titles: a political treatise on East India, a biography of a Lancashire cotton magnate, an almanac and a romance novel. What could any of these things have to do with the lady who had written the note in violet ink? For surely none but a lady would use such a feminine style. The romance novel, perhaps, but what of the other references that Mr Holmes had marked so diligently?

Green, white and violet!

I had it. My mind had done its work, while my hands were busy, without my even noticing. These were the colours of the suffragettes. Green, white and violet: Votes for Women.

Had Mr Holmes's visitor been a suffragette? That band of irrepressible women who not only espoused the cause, but who put themselves in peril fighting for it? Of course, given my position, I could not possibly demonstrate my own political bias. I must remain discreet. But that others campaigned was of singular interest to me, and I applauded them.

I also applauded Mr Holmes for taking a case brought to him by a suffragette. Mr Holmes was not known for his political awareness. Dr Watson might tell you that he hadn't a political bone in his body, that Mr Holmes took little interest in philosophy, politics or social thought. I bow to his better judgement in such things.

Mr Holmes is concerned only with the case in hand, and the conundrum it poses. The lady suffragette's case must have been an interesting one indeed. As intrigued as I was, I could make no sense of what it might be.

By the time of Mr Holmes's return, I had swept the rug, dusted the mantel, and cleared the glasses from the evening's visit, both water and brandy. Of course, it might be considered unusual for a lady to drink brandy, but this was a forward-thinking woman, and besides the brandy might be considered medicinal: a restorative.

Mr Holmes's supper tray was hardly touched, the liver curled at the edges and the gravy congealed, but the large ashtray was full. He must have tapped out his pipe a dozen times, something he did a great deal when deep in thought.

I sorted Mr Holmes's post, hopeful that I might see more violet ink, but it was not to be, and I put the most urgent-looking letters on the top of the pile, including one with an interestingly peculiar seal.

I was cleaning the gas lamps when Mr Holmes swept back into the house, Dr Watson hard on his heels.

"Since twilight is precisely five hours and forty-seven minutes away," said Mr Holmes, consulting his timepiece, "perhaps you could interrupt your task, and furnish us with a tea tray, Mrs Hudson?"

I returned to my own rooms, and, whilst boiling the kettle, I removed my apron. As I hung the garment in its usual place on the pantry door, I noticed a smudge of soot on the hem, and recalled the signet ring and the slip of paper that I had put in the pocket. I retrieved them at once, in order that I might not forget to restore the items to Mr Holmes's possession.

As I returned to the gentlemen, I caught a little of their conversation.

"There must be a train from London to Preston this

afternoon," said Dr Watson. "I shall telegraph the Grand Hotel to expect our arrival."

I placed the tea tray on the card table at Dr Watson's elbow, and crossed to the credenza. It took the matter of a moment to pull the railway timetable from its customary home, turn it to the page for Euston station, and hand it to the good doctor.

"There you are," said Dr Watson. "There's a direct train from Euston at a quarter to four o'clock."

I wondered whether the lady had come all the way from Lancashire to see Mr Holmes. Perhaps she too had travelled by train such a distance to meet the man himself. Perhaps Mr Holmes had shredded the letter when it had arrived in the post. I tried to recall seeing a matching envelope among his correspondence in the days prior to the lady arriving, but could not.

"It's a dashed distance to travel," said Dr Watson, reaching for the teapot.

"Should you prefer a passenger ship to the colonies?" asked Mr Holmes.

"Indeed, I should not," replied Dr Watson.

"Then we must needs visit the cotton mills."

While the gentlemen stirred their tea in silence, I crossed back to the tray to top up the pot from the steaming kettle. When that was done, I put the ring and the slip of paper on the tray where they would not be missed.

"What have you there, Mrs Hudson?" asked Mr Holmes.

I might have known that he would detect my movements.

"When I was cleaning this morning—"

"Yes, yes," said Mr Holmes, eager that I should come to the point. "Whatever it is, bring it here, will you?"

"It's a ring that I found in the ashes of the hearth," I

said, "and a slip of paper lodged in a cushion."

Mr Holmes pocketed the ring absentmindedly, and put the slip of paper back in my hand. I was astonished that he took so little notice of the evidence that I had so carefully saved, and which might be at the centre of this case.

"But what of the lady?" I asked, unable to contain my thoughts. If the lady could be so bold as to associate with the women's suffrage movement, then surely I could speak out on her behalf.

"The lady?" asked Dr Watson. "What lady?"

"There was a lady here, last evening," I said. There was no turning back now that Dr Watson had taken an interest, though I was surprised he didn't know already. "I smelled her perfume in here while I was tidying up."

Mr Holmes handed me his cup and saucer, and went to his desk. He picked up his post and rummaged for the paper knife, which I had earlier returned to his pen tray. I crossed the room to retrieve it, and handed it to him. He sliced open the first envelope with its seal, before Dr Watson spoke again.

"Well?" he asked. "What of the lady, Holmes?"

"It was nothing," said Holmes, not looking up from the letter, "a trifle."

"Then I shall not pursue it further," said Dr Watson, whose eyes seemed almost to twinkle.

A gentleman's privacy is paramount, of course, and I had always afforded Mr Holmes his seclusion. I had never interfered in his affairs, nor did I care to, but this was too much.

"She is a suffragette," I said.

"Oh indeed," said Mr Holmes, setting down his letter, "and what brings you to such a conclusion, Mrs Hudson?"

I did not know whether I was being mocked, or whether

Mr Holmes had genuine interest in my opinion, but I had come this far. I opened my hand.

"This," I said. "This slip of paper. There is a lady's handwriting upon it, in violet ink. The paper is bordered in green..."

Dr Watson took the paper from me and examined it. "She's perfectly right, you know, Holmes," he said.

"Brava, Mrs Hudson," said Holmes. "Then what did you make of this?" he asked, plucking the signet ring from his waistcoat pocket and holding it out. Dr Watson half-rose from his chair and took the ring from Mr Holmes's hand.

"I found it in the ashes—" I began, but Mr Holmes urged me to my point once again.

"Yes, yes," he said. "I believe you mentioned that, Mrs Hudson, and what of it?"

"It's a man's ring," I said. "Perhaps belonging to the father of the lady, her brother, or her husband."

"And how might it have come to rest in the hearth?" he asked.

"Perhaps she discarded it," I said.

"So, you deduce that last evening I was visited by a suffragette with a grudge against a male relative?" asked Mr Holmes.

"I thought that it might be some such," I said.

"And where, then, is the case to answer?" asked Mr Holmes.

"A lady in dire straits might require your help," I replied.

"And what straits might she be in?" asked Mr Holmes.

"Take it easy, Holmes," said Dr Watson, under his breath.

It was chivalrous of him to come to my defence, but I can stand up for myself. "What little understanding I have of your work, Mr Holmes," I said, "leads me to believe that you have come to the aid of a great many persons in distress during your career."

"She's right," said Dr Watson, "you have."

"So, you detected a lady," said Mr Holmes, "and you were correct, but what else, Mrs Hudson? What else did you discover that you have left unsaid?"

I thought for a moment, thinking back to that morning. "Two brandy glasses," I said. "A woman rarely drinks brandy, except as a restorative."

"That's true," mused Dr Watson.

"The slip of paper, of course, and the ring," I said, enumerating what was already known, while racking my brain for anything new.

"Is that everything, Mrs Hudson?" asked Mr Holmes.

"Is that not enough?" asked Dr Watson.

"It is not nearly enough," said Mr Holmes, returning to his chair.

"You make sport of Mrs Hudson, and I wonder whether it isn't unkind," said Dr Watson.

"No, indeed, my dear Watson," said Holmes. "We have a little time before embarking on our escapade to the cotton mills, and I am interested in the turn of Mrs Hudson's mind. I wonder if she can't come to the truth with a little encouragement."

"You were up all night," I said. "You did not rest, so I must presume you had some case to consider."

"Indeed I did, Mrs Hudson, but must it, by necessity, have been the case of the scented lady? Do we subscribe to the principle of '*Post hoc, ergo propter hoc*'?"

"After it, therefore, because of it," I said. I may not have learned Latin, but we are all familiar with the meanings of the most common axioms. Finally, I was reminded of something new.

"There's an inscription inside the ring," I said. "I wondered if that might be a clue. If the lady tossed the ring into the fire, you might not have known of the inscription."

Dr Watson held the ring up, and turned it so that he could read the inscription inside. "She's right, again," he said.

"*Ad usque fidelis*," said Mr Holmes.

"A family motto, perhaps," said Dr Watson.

"But what does it mean?" I asked. "It talks of loyalty, surely?"

"'True to the end'," said Dr Watson. "It's rather beautiful."

"Is that another piece in the puzzle, Mrs Hudson?"

"And the stone is left blank," I said. "It is not engraved with a coat of arms or monogram."

"How very observant you are, Mrs Hudson," said Dr Watson.

"There seems to me a great divide between observation and deduction," said Mr Holmes, "but do go on, Mrs Hudson. Did you discover any other clues in this room? Evidence of anything or anyone else?"

His emphasis fell so heavily on "anyone" that I truly began to feel that my lodger must be mocking me.

Mr Holmes stood and took a turn around the room, glancing from the credenza to the hearth, to the seat by the window, glancing at his desk, up to the mirror over the mantel, and then into the hearth again.

"Come, come," he said, "even after your domestic ministrations, clues abound. What of the hearth, for example, or the rug?"

I looked down at the rug that I had swept only half an hour previously. It had been lightly soiled, a little dusty, before I had cleaned it, but I could see nothing nor remember anything very unusual about it.

"The tassels are in disarray, Mrs Hudson," said Mr Holmes. "I wonder that you did not notice, and straighten them."

He was right, of course, the tassels at the corner of the rug furthest from the hearth formed a swirl of curving strands.

"I wonder what might cause the rug to be disturbed in such a way?" asked Mr Holmes. "And the hearth; you must see the hearth?"

I looked again. I cast my eyes into the grate, and then along the rail where Mr Holmes's slippers still lay. Then I did see something. There was the finest line of dried earth against the far end of the rail, about the width of my hand.

"There," I said, "a line of dirt on the rail."

"Brava, again, Mrs Hudson, but how did it come to be there? And what relation does it bear to the rug?"

It had all become rather too much for me. My thoughts were in turmoil, and I could make no sense of these tiny signs, signs that I had not previously seen. Perhaps my observation was as limited as my facility for deduction. I could do nothing but sigh and shrug.

"Take a seat, Mrs Hudson," said Mr Holmes.

"Yes, dear lady, do sit down," said Dr Watson, who rose and moved the chair that stood beside the window closer to the hearth, that I might sit, yet still be able to see the hearth and the rug. "I fear we are to be schooled."

"It was a simple matter," began Mr Holmes, "of a personal nature, but since you take so great an interest, allow me to enlighten you. I was visited last evening by a young gentleman of my acquaintance, from a great family. I have previously worked for his father, and he saw fit to consult me on the matter. He was accompanied by a lady, his fiancée, whose presence you noticed. You did not see that he stood at my hearth, his foot upon the rail, or that he stepped and turned, suddenly, to address the lady, hence the smudge on the rail and the swirl in the carpet. You were correct in your assumption that the brandy was supplied to the lady, for she was in some consternation that her beloved had thrown his ring in the fire, but there were more used glasses than there were people you had decided were in this room. Her fiancé took only water.

"The ring belonged to him, given as a gift by his father. What does the inscription tell you, Mrs Hudson? Or the empty cartouche?

"No, no… no need to answer.

"The young man was torn in his affections between his father and his sweetheart. His father is a rather well-known politician, who heartily disapproved of his choice of bride. The ring was given to remind his son of whence he had come, and to prick his conscience, the cartouche left blank until the lady was forsaken, when the family shield would be engraved upon it."

"No gift at all, then," I said, unable to contain myself.

"No, indeed," said Dr Watson.

"And what did you do?" I asked Mr Holmes.

"Why," said Mr Holmes, "I did nothing, of course."

"You did nothing!" exclaimed Dr Watson. "But what of your deductive powers, Holmes? Surely there was something to be done?"

Dr Watson voiced my own amazement, for I had never known a time when Mr Holmes was incapable of making a deduction that might aid a cause.

"Might you not have intervened, Holmes?" Dr Watson continued. "Was the lady not, in other regards, suitable?"

"Indeed, I made a great many deductions," said Holmes. "I deduced that the young man was besotted by the lady, and that he was therefore immune from any advice I or anyone else might furnish him with. I deduced from the lady's dress, demeanour, poise and manners that she was the young man's equal in all things, including intellect and breeding. I deduced that the suffragettes might win their cause, and having won it that the lady would be free from its shackles. I deduced that the young man's politician father would remain gracious in defeat, as politicians must if they are to continue on and succeed in their careers. And, I deduced, or rather I knew, that affairs of the heart are not my bailiwick. Give me facts, give me a mystery, but do not ask me to navigate the finer feelings of a young man in love or of a lady.

"I deduced that the young man would come to his own conclusions, make his own decision based on his emotions, and that having done so there was nothing left for me to do but to support him… for his own sake, for his father's and for the sake of the lady. I deduced that there was some truth in the adage, 'He also serves who only stands and waits'."

"And what was the outcome of the romance, Holmes?"

"The young man talked himself into a rage, threw the ring in the fire and turned into the embrace of the lady," said Mr Holmes. "She, in her turn, scolded her lover, and made him promise to make amends with his mother, should his father decide to carry out his threat of cutting off his son.

"In all regards, these two are suited, and peccadilloes are easily overcome by doting parents, such as most fathers must surely be, given a little time and the right kind of feminine persuasion. The social order might change, but that has little or nothing to do with families. Besides, the lady is so very suitable that, should the young man find himself cut off, they would still be very well provided for. It was a romance, nothing more."

"And the letter?" I asked.

"It was a note that the young woman had written to her lover, excusing him of any obligation to her. He tore it to shreds and threw the pieces onto the fire, declaring his constancy to her. A piece must have been kept from the fire in the flurry."

"Then all is well?" I asked.

"I anticipate being invited to a society wedding within the month," said Mr Holmes, "if I am returned from Lancashire by then. Indeed, since I had deduced that my support was wanted, I offered to stand up for the groom at the altar in order to appease his dear father.

"This was a delightful interlude, Mrs Hudson," he finished, "but there is work to be done, so perhaps you wouldn't mind packing my overnight bag."

"No, indeed," I said, rising from the chair. I took his words to mean that I was dismissed.

"One more thing, Mrs Hudson," he said, rising, and fingering the pile of books that I had placed on the edge of his desk. "How did you reconcile my choice of reading material with your deductions?"

I thought for a moment. "I didn't," I said.

"You didn't wonder how a political treatise on East India, a biography of a Lancashire cotton magnate, an almanac and a romance novel might provide answers in the plight of a lady suffragette?" Mr Holmes asked.

"I must have wondered for a moment," I said, "but I failed to connect the clues."

"Mrs Hudson, I am working on the case of a missing industrialist and his East Indian factotum. Time is of the essence, and my research must be thorough."

"But the romance novel?" I asked.

"Belonged to the factotum, and was the last book he was known to have read," answered Mr Holmes. "And that is my first lesson to you, Mrs Hudson. Every clue contributes to the whole. We cannot ignore evidence because it fails to fit in with our own imagined scheme."

Mr Holmes was generous in his lesson, but he need not have given it, for I had no intention thereafter of allowing my curiosity or my interest to get the better of me, ever again.

HARLINGDON'S HEIR

Michelle Ruda

Violet de Merville appears only in "The Adventure of the Illustrious Client" (1924). She is the daughter of a general, and is engaged to an Austrian murderer called Baron Adelbert Gruner. Gruner has manipulated every public scandal he's been a part of in such a way that Violet thinks he's the one who's been mistreated. A friend of the general's hires Holmes to thwart the relationship. It is only upon receiving Gruner's "love diary" from Holmes that Violet de Merville disengages herself from Gruner.

—Michelle Ruda

The carriage lurched as a fresh barrage of rain beat against the window. Trees towered over us from either side of the narrow road, thick and unrelenting, blotting out the sunset's light. I glanced at Millie, my maidservant, who was shaking, either from the cold or the rumours about the orphanage we were approaching.

I was numb. The past month had whizzed past in a blur. The funeral, the lawyers, the bureaucracy of it all. Not to mention the scandal it was as the fruit of my association with Gruner.

And now, this.

I had sat opposite Mr Valler, our family lawyer, in his office like one swimming through a dream.

"You should sell," he said emphatically. "And sell right away. Sever your connection with Harlingdon as soon as you possibly can; your father never wanted you to have any association with your Aunt Penny, which is why he never told you she was residing in Bristol. And now, with these disappearances, do you really want your family name to be attached to such a place? Regardless of its sponsors the property is yours. It used to be a manor. Your father would've sold it; he would've wanted you to sell—"

"And how precisely would you know what my father would have wanted?" came a languid drawl, which took me a moment to realise that it was my own.

The carriage sharply turned and Millie gasped.

Through the flecks of rain was a clearing, and on its edge, a large red-brick manor gleamed in the sunset. Harlingdon. So pristine, so picturesque, it was the first time I laid eyes on it. It was hard to believe the supposed goings-on within its walls.

I glanced out of my window. Opposite the building and across the clearing, the sun was melting into a sharp precipice that gave way to the Avon Gorge. The expanse of orange-pink sky was deceptively welcoming as it distracted from the steep, jagged plunge below, right down to the Avon River.

The carriage pulled up in front of the door. A plaque read *Harlingdon Boys and Girls Home*.

The porter rushed out to meet us with umbrellas and ushered us in to the entrance hall where I was greeted by a young lady, no older than myself, wearing a severe black dress.

"Welcome, Miss de Merville, to Harlingdon Boys and Girls Home. I'm the matron of this establishment. It's so wonderful to finally meet you after all our correspondence."

"Mrs Eade," I acknowledged, surprised at how young she was.

"Lillian, please. Now. You must be awfully hungry after your journey. How about some refreshments and then a tour of the orphanage?"

The food was nowhere near as edible as that of my London home, and I ended up having a meagre meal of soup and bread. But despite the need for a new cook, the orphanage completely met my expectations.

"The Harlingdons' dream of having a home for the homeless manifested itself in this orphanage," Lillian explained, as we walked down a corridor. She gestured to a classroom where children were having a mathematics lesson. "The teaching is second to none, as I'm sure you're aware. This orphanage is prestigious. Its main sponsors are the Royal Navy Institute and the Corporation of Bristol. Many of the children here are sailors' sons and daughters."

She interrupted the class and I met some of the pupils and the teacher, Mr Trenor. I also met two other teachers, Miss Jenkins and Mr Ardham. I found the orphanage most satisfactory. Everything was clean, the staff were friendly but not overly so, and the children were polite and well-behaved.

As the building used to be a manor house, most of the rooms had been converted into classrooms or rooms for the girls to learn domestic service and for the boys to learn shoemaking. Upstairs were the dormitories and also a strongroom, and a couple of empty rooms. Lillian showed Millie and me to my room, which had been the master's bedroom.

"Where is the master?" I asked.

"He… left. We have not yet found a replacement."

It had stopped raining, and Lillian also gave us a tour of the grounds, pointing out the gardener's shed and also warning us to stay a good distance from the cliff face. We went as close as we dared, and upon turning we had full view of Harlingdon. To the left of the main house, tucked away was a picturesque cottage adorned with different coloured flowers.

"Who lives there?" I asked.

"I do," Lillian said, "with my husband, Mr Eade. I would like you to meet him but he broke his leg not long ago and hasn't left the cottage since."

We returned to the house and entered through a side door that led into the kitchen.

"There was a fire here, not long ago," Lillian explained, pointing to burn marks on the wall. They had been painted over but you could still tell where the fire had eaten away at the wall.

"Caused by the last cook—but not on my watch!" said a plump lady whom I discovered to be the current cook, Marie. "I get up in the night sometimes because of my arthritis anyway, you see, but I always have a check. It's a habit now but I don't mind; better safe than sorry! As long as the ghost doesn't come in the kitchen—"

"Marie."

Lillian did not shout but her tone was like a knife. Marie blushed and apologised before shambling away, mumbling about dinner. My maidservant, Millie, who already had been behaving like a deer in an open field since the moment we arrived in Bristol, now looked like she'd seen a wolf.

"I'm very sorry about that, Miss de Merville." Lillian smoothed her skirt. "Perhaps we should sit down and talk? In private?"

"Millie, go to our room and prepare our things for tonight. I'm sure we'll be tired after dinner."

Millie curtsied and scuttled off. I followed Lillian to her office on the ground floor, and took a seat before her at the desk. When she sat down she sighed and it was then that I noticed the bags under her eyes, the air of tiredness that exuded off her as soon as she wasn't being overly hospitable. "How much do you know, Miss de Merville?"

"I know that there are eighty children here and that fifteen have gone missing within the past month, and that these disappearances started after the deaths in the winter, after a bout of influenza struck the orphanage. The family who ran this place, whom it is named after – the Harlingdons – all passed away. Penny Harlingdon was my aunt; she used to be a de Merville. I don't know if you knew her—"

"Unfortunately not. I came in as matron just after Anna, their daughter, passed away. They died before her. Gregory and Penny Harlingdon were master and matron of the establishment."

"Tragic."

"I know."

"I've heard that the police have been here and that staff have left due to the missing children, and that the committee is thinking of closing Harlingdon down as its sponsors are considering withdrawing support. All their hard work, all this acclaim, down the drain because of some ghost."

I wasn't sure if I was imagining it but I thought I saw Lillian wince ever so slightly.

"You… don't believe it is a ghost?" she asked me, her voice even.

"Of course not! People die all the time everywhere; there are more dead people on this earth than those alive. It is obviously some fanciful story that small townsfolk wish to indulge in and I do not have time for. You seem like a level-headed woman, Lillian; there must be some logical explanation for all of this? The children have run away. Or they are playing a game, hiding in the woods—"

"We've searched the surrounding areas. Staff have slept in front of the doors of the dormitories and seen no one enter. There is no other explanation."

I stared at her. Her gaze did not waver; her expression was open, honest.

"You're not telling me you believe this is what's been happening here?"

Lillian closed her eyes briefly. "We've been in touch with another orphanage. They don't have space for the remaining children here but there is a ship setting sail for Canada—"

"Canada! They're no safer in Canada than they are here! No, children can't vanish into thin air. We need more staff, first of all—"

"We've been advertising for weeks."

"And?"

"There is no interest. The public have found out about this; journalists came sniffing around and the newspapers have been calling us 'Haunted Harlingdon' since December. And the committee are questioning hiring new staff if they're thinking of closing Harlingdon down anyway."

"Haunted Harlingdon?" I couldn't help but laugh. "On what grounds? So children have gone missing and everyone assumes—"

"There have been sightings," Lillian said. There was a slight tremor in her voice.

"Sightings?"

"A ghost child. Standing right at the cliff edge."

"And you've seen it?"

"No. But Marie, the cook has. And Mr Duncan, the gardener. Some of the children too. The other staff members who saw it left including the most recent master."

"I'd like to talk to Marie again and meet Mr Duncan. And if anyone from the committee is visiting soon I'd like to meet them too."

"William Pearson. He's the relieving officer. He'll be here tomorrow."

"Excellent. As for sending these children to Canada, I must protest. Some of these children have fathers in the navy, am I correct? They should stay here in Bristol; perhaps we could sponsor them into other homes."

"As you wish," Lillian replied, though I could tell there was a whole barrel full of protests going on in her mind.

* * *

Later I conversed with Marie while she was preparing dinner.

"We've had priests here, and still I saw it!" Marie shivered.

"When?"

"About three weeks ago. I was sleeping, that door there, that's my room—" She nodded to a door on the other side of the kitchen, and then pointed to the one closest to us. "This door leads to outside, and someone was knocking. I thought it must be Lillian, coming in from the cottage. Strange! I thought. Why isn't she using her key? So I got up and opened it – plain as day, I saw him! Standing there, as pale as the moon, with his head hung low, right at the edge of the cliff, almost falling into the gorge!"

"Did you call someone?"

"Call someone? I fainted! Right on the spot!"

Mr Duncan, the gardener, had a similar story. He was a stork of a man, tall and grey, thin but strong-looking. He had a thick Bristolian accent, and said he saw the ghost of a child three weeks ago, standing by the cliff. Although he thought he was imagining it because one minute it was there and the next it was gone.

"Its head hung low, lolling across his chest. It was a terrible sight."

I pondered on these accounts for the rest of the day. Impressed though I was with the orphanage and the way it was run, I did find it strange how none could prevent the disappearances of the children, and the ghost sparked a possibility that I could not snuff out.

Apprehensive of dinner, I was relieved to find Marie had

prepared a separate meal for Millie and me, of chicken broth and bread. Supper was served with a doom and gloom that reminded me of the days before my father's death. No amount of candles or strained conversation from the staff could hide the strange atmosphere that descended upon the orphanage that night and, I presumed, every night. Lillian, Marie, and Mr Trenor kept me company during the meal, which tasted like bitter nettles, but Millie's constant restlessness by my side, and the suffocating tension in the hall, started to gnaw at me. The children ate in the eeriest silence, and their sense of dread was inextinguishable, even when a teacher tried to engage them in song, and reward them with sweets. The curtain closed; the show they had put on for me had ended, and the reality of the situation could not be masked any longer.

After the meal I felt so tired that I had Millie prepare me for bed in our room on the second floor. They had arranged two beds in our room, one close to the door and one by the opposite wall beside the window.

A fire crackled in the fireplace, casting the room in a warm yellow. I nestled into the bed nearest the door.

"You hardly ate at dinner, are you not hungry?" I asked Millie.

"No, Miss." She settled into bed. "What do you intend to do?"

I closed my eyes. "Hire more staff from somewhere other than Bristol. Find the children."

"How?"

"I… don't know."

"Will you not just sell?"

"Seeing as I own this property I feel like I am responsible for these children and the orphanage. Besides, I'm not sure where home is anymore. I couldn't stay in London. I needed to get out."

I'm not sure who fell asleep first but what happened next neither of us could have anticipated.

I was woken by a thud or some other loud noise, in the middle of the night.

"What was that?" Millie whispered.

The room was dark apart from a stream of moonlight that came in from the window and fell across my bed. The fire had somehow gone out and the room was freezing. I still felt half asleep.

And then, out of the darkness, from somewhere in the room…

"Violet." A child's voice.

Millie cried out. In the silvery shadows she gripped the covers and cowered in her bed.

"Miss, where is it? Miss?"

I scanned the room, my heart beating against my chest. There – in the corner – what was that?

"Violet."

I climbed out of bed and stood up. There *was* something in the corner.

"Look at me." A boy's voice.

Millie whimpered.

I couldn't take a step closer. "Where are you?" I said. "What do you want?"

"The window."

Millie screamed. She jumped out of bed and ran to me, as far away from the window as possible.

"The window?" I echoed, walking towards it.

"Miss, no!" Millie grabbed my wrist. Then I saw him.

The master bedroom's window overlooked the cliff edge, and like a beacon on the horizon, he stood there glowing, as white as the moon, his head hung low, a step away from plummeting into the gorge. Could it be? Such things did not exist! But I could see the ghost with my own two eyes, hear his voice in my ears.

Like an unyielding pull, I had to move closer, I had to go to the window, even though my mind was screaming at me to flee, and Millie tugged at my arm. He'd said my name, he was calling to me—

A scream filled the room – Millie dragged me away from the window and to the door. My limbs felt heavy. I was tired, so tired…

"Someone help us please!" she wept.

"He's trying to say something."

But all I could hear was Millie crying. I wrenched myself free from her grasp and ran to the window again.

"He's gone."

Millie could not be calmed or consoled no matter what I said to her and in the end I had to exert my authority as her employer, which, in light of a supernatural being versus a human, did not do much. She wanted to fetch someone even though I assured her whether porter or police, the ghost would not care about their status.

I admit I expected, even wanted, the ghost to appear again or to hear his voice. The fact that both Millie and I had seen and heard the same thing made it all the more real. And yet, how was it possible? I did not believe in such things. A part of my brain still questioned it all, still could not rationalise it.

"His voice was in this room," I thought aloud. "But his body was at the cliff."

"Miss, stop."

"How is that possible? Yet we saw it and we heard it. And how did he know my name?"

Millie put her hands over her ears.

"They have had priests here," I continued. "And police. But there must be someone—"

And suddenly I remembered a tall man sitting across from me at my house in London last year, composed, rational, unfeeling.

I'd never before been to 221B Baker Street. It was filled with books and newspapers and smoke. Dr Watson, whom I'd never met before, led me to an armchair. Sherlock Holmes sat opposite me, his pipe in his hand.

I was anxious, not from the ghostly encounter but rather from the news that morning: another child had disappeared. Jim Carrison, the son of a navy officer, ten years old.

Even more upsetting was the way the staff reacted. The relieving officer, William Pearson, who Lillian boasted had held the post for Harlingdon for twenty years, visited the same morning. He solemnly nodded at the news, collected receipts from the matron, and filled out documents relating to the missing boy. I overheard two teachers talking about funding cuts, and their current job applications to a private school. Millie was mothered by the cook, and her cries were the only legitimate reaction out of all that I witnessed; the teachers' passivity enraged me, so much so that I felt even more determined to do what I'd intended: I told my staff I'd return to Bristol with Sherlock Holmes.

Millie was in no condition to travel back to the orphanage with me. I left her at my father's house and travelled to Baker Street alone.

The famous detective and I looked at each other. He appeared exactly the same as when I had previously met him.

"Mr Holmes."

"Miss de Merville."

"Not the Miss de Merville?" Watson exclaimed. "My condolences about your father, the general."

"Why, thank you."

"Whatever is the matter?"

"It is rather a strange situation."

"Well, we have heard many a strange thing here haven't we, Holmes?"

Mr Holmes watched me. "Please begin."

And so I talked. Watson interjected with questions here and there but the detective only listened intently, puffs of smoke rising occasionally from his pipe until I'd finished.

"Now, Miss de Merville," Holmes began, "your staff. What do they sound like?"

"Sound like, sir?"

"Their accents. Are they regional? Bristolian?"

"A few are. Most sound like they are from other parts of the country."

"And this ghost has never been spotted amongst the dormitories or within the orphanage? Only outside?"

"Yes, although I heard his voice in my room—"

"And these children only started going missing after the death of the Harlingdon family?"

"Why? Do you think it is a ghost from that family?"

"Of course not, Miss de Merville! How does a non-physical entity remove a physical entity from a room with walls? How can these children vanish into thin air? How is a ghost that is only sighted *outside* the orphanage, taking children from *within* the orphanage? It's not possible. You know this and you believe there is a rational explanation otherwise you wouldn't have come to me. Is there somewhere Dr Watson and I can hide outside the manor house, where we can observe the cliff edge?"

"There is a cottage on the grounds where the matron and her husband live and also the gardener's shed."

"Excellent. Dr Watson and I will follow you to Bristol on a later train, but for now you must return, and when you get there, tell no one when we are coming."

I returned to the orphanage and did as Mr Holmes asked. That night I couldn't sleep. I stood in the master's bedroom at the window, eagerly watching the cliff edge.

Suddenly, a scream pierced the night.

Movement, footsteps, outside my door. I ran out. Mr Trenor, one of the teachers who watched over the boys' dormitory, was in the corridor, ghostly by his candlelight. Further down the corridor, the door to the girls' dormitory opened.

"What was that?" Miss Jenkins' shaky voice called down to us.

"It came from downstairs," Mr Trenor whispered.

Bang, bang, bang.

"Miss de Merville! You shouldn't go down there!"

But I was already at the landing, flying down the stairs, and on the ground floor. It was pitch black except for the end of the corridor; a door was ajar, and light peeked through. The kitchen. Someone was crying.

"Open up or we'll break down the door!"

I knew that voice.

I dashed down the corridor and burst into the kitchen. Marie was quivering in the middle of the kitchen, holding an oil lamp, pointing at something on the wall.

Bang, bang, bang.

I ran past her to the door that led to the outside and threw it open.

The tall figure of Sherlock Holmes stood in the doorway. He paused when he saw the scene, and smiled. Dr Watson followed, and faltered, shocked. "Holmes! How is that possible?"

I turned.

High up on the wall, written in blood, were the words: SHERLOCK LEAVE.

Fear gripped my heart like an iron fist clutching a tiny bird. I took a step back.

"How?" I said. "I told no one. You must leave – you are in danger!"

"Danger?" Holmes stepped forward, a trace of amusement in his voice. "No. Closer to an answer? Yes."

Holmes took the oil lamp from Marie and held it up to the wall. He was tall enough to stretch out a hand and touch the substance the words were written with.

"A child's blood!" Marie sobbed.

Holmes brought it to his nose and sniffed. "Paint," he said.

"Paint!"

"Tell me. What ghost buys a pot of paint to ward off a detective? Now, we must rest. We have a long day ahead of us tomorrow. Miss de Merville, if you don't mind, I'd like to stay in the room where you heard the voice."

* * *

I slept in a spare bed in the girls' dormitory and found Holmes and Watson alive and well the next morning – with not a single child missing.

I acquired a set of keys from the porter. Holmes took us to the corridor outside the master's bedroom.

"The fireplace," he said, "connects to an attic."

"An attic?" I said. "And where are the stairs to this attic?"

"I'll show you."

He led us across the corridor to the strongroom. From the set of keys, he immediately chose the correct one and opened the door.

"How did you—?"

It was a small room, and compared to the rest of the building, it was surprisingly untidy. The room was bathed in light from the window.

"Look!" Mr Holmes pointed to the floor excitedly and then to the wardrobe against the opposite wall. "What do you make of that, Watson?"

"What do I make of what?"

"Dust!" He pointed to the floor in front of us. "There are large footprints, a man's; he was wearing boots." He took out a magnifying glass and crouched down, then spun around and inspected the carpet behind us. "Tiny flecks of mud… came from outside." Holmes then followed the trail into the strongroom and to the wardrobe. "The footprints stop here, and look, on that side of the wardrobe there is no dust, which means…" He pushed the wardrobe aside to reveal a door. "The wardrobe has been recently moved."

I was stunned. Holmes was too excited to notice. Again he selected a key and opened the door to reveal a set of stairs. We ascended. My astonishment mounted as there, indeed, was a large attic with windows that spanned the entire width of the building, full of furniture and bric-a-brac covered in sheets. All along the perimeter of the attic were the necks of chimneys and many had been fitted with grates.

"Aha! I thought so." Holmes made his way to an open grate. Beside it was a bucket with black ash and a watering can. Holmes lifted up the watering can and examined it before turning to the grate. "This chute leads down to the room you stayed in, to the fireplace. And this is how the culprit was able to put out the fire and call your name. The water would've extinguished the fire, and the ash would've masked it." Holmes then put on a child's voice, and called my name down the chute. It was horribly familiar. He took a coin from his pocket and dropped it. "If you require more evidence, you may go back down and take a look. You will find the coin in the grate. You said you also heard a thud…" He walked over to a sheet-covered chair nearby, lifted it and dropped it to the floorboards. Holmes looked at me. I nodded.

"And now," continued Holmes, "to the dormitories."

"Wait. If that person was up here… how did I see a ghost by the cliff edge?"

"Because, my dear, the criminal wasn't working alone."

I followed Mr Holmes and Dr Watson down the hidden attic stairs, and from thence we weaved our way through the rooms on the floor below. I was astonished as Holmes revealed a series of hidden doors and open doorways that connected the dormitories.

"This is absurd!" I exclaimed, after Holmes had pushed aside a thin wardrobe in an unused room next to the boys' dormitory to reveal a gaping hole in the wall.

"There was a door here; look, hinge marks. But the door was removed quite some time ago now."

"How has no one noticed this?"

"Well, I suspect it's not common practice here to rearrange the furniture."

"But why are there so many interconnecting rooms?"

"The person who built the house must have requested it. Perhaps some paranoid Harlingdon during the Civil War. And now I wish to see the orphanage's accounts."

Incredulous, I followed Mr Holmes and Dr Watson to Lillian's office. She was happy to show the detective the books.

"These are just the records of purchases. Where are the rest of the accounts?" asked Holmes.

"With Mr Pearson, our relieving officer, and Mr Jeffreys, the clerk," Lillian replied. "They're based in an office on Clifton High Street."

Holmes studied the written accounts with a ferocious intensity, taking out his magnifying glass and tracing his fingers along the letters.

"What is this?" He pointed to a large sum for Jones & Co.

"The pharmacist," Lillian replied.

"For what?"

"For laudanum."

"Laudanum?"

"For Marie, our cook. She has bad arthritis."

"I see. That'll be all. Thank you."

Lastly – and with a strange sense of anticipation – I took them to the cliff edge. Approaching the scene, even in daylight, and even after Holmes had shown me the attic, the fireplace and the dormitories' secret doors, the hairs at the back of my neck stood on end.

"Who lives there?" Holmes asked, pointing.

I followed his gaze. "The matron. That's the Eades' cottage. Lillian lives there with her husband, Charles."

"That's quite a lot of flowers for a cottage. Rather superfluous, isn't it?" Watson commented.

"I agree. It did make me wonder how much money and effort is spent sustaining them."

"Indeed," said Holmes, deep in thought. "But the ghost."

"This was where I saw him," I pointed. "Right at the precipice."

Mr Holmes dropped down, flattening himself against the grass, and took out his magnifying glass. He then slithered to his right and peered over the ledge. Without warning, he swung himself round and disappeared.

I screamed.

"Holmes!" Dr Watson shouted.

"I'm quite alright," came a voice not too far away.

Cautiously, Dr Watson and I crept closer to the edge.

Mr Holmes was standing on a clump of rock, which jutted out from the side of the cliff, low enough so that he was hidden. Below him were more protruding platforms of rock at regular intervals down to the Avon. Strange, faint white markings dotted some of the stones. Mr Holmes inspected the white mark closest to him.

"It is as I suspected," said he. "Now, both of you, go back to the orphanage. Do not tell anyone what I have found. Watson, search more rooms. Note anything unusual you find. I will be back by dinner."

Dr Watson started walking back to the orphanage, but I remained by the cliff edge for a moment longer.

"Why has no one noticed that before?" I asked aloud. "Why has no one looked over the cliff edge?"

"For fear," came a voice from below that deceitful place. "If you want someone to stay away from something, teach them to fear it."

* * *

I'd had dinner, and still Holmes hadn't reappeared. Watson, too, had disappeared some time after lunch; I had not seen him since. The sun was setting. I decided to walk around the grounds, perhaps meet the detective on his way back to the orphanage.

Just as I exited the house I saw, down the path towards the woods, two people carrying oil lamps walking hurriedly towards the trees. It looked like Lillian and Dr Watson.

"Dr Watson!" I called out.

He turned, as did Lillian, and I could tell, even from this distance, that both of them wore anxious expressions. I felt a knot tighten in my gut.

I darted over to them. "What's happened?"

"We found a child," Watson said, agitated. "In the woods. Bloodied. Barely alive. He'd escaped somehow. He'll be able to tell us who the ghost is."

"Is Mr Holmes…?"

"He ordered that you stay inside, Miss de Merville."

"But the child!"

"Go inside. Do not leave. Holmes's orders."

They half-jogged away from me, hastening to the trees. Holmes's orders or not, I was about to follow them when—

"Miss de Merville! Miss!"

I whirled around. Through the darkness came Marie, puffing heavily, her oil lamp bouncing with her. "Mr Holmes requires you at the cottage."

"The cottage?"

"Yes. He says there's someone he wants you to meet."

"So Holmes is in the cottage? I thought he was in the woods?"

"All I know is that early this morning he told me to find you after dinner and tell you to go to the cottage."

"What on earth is going on?" I said, but Marie just shrugged. Baffled, I made my way round the house and to the small cottage.

It was overwhelmed with flowers of every colour, sprouting from the ground, hanging in baskets, spilling from pots. I walked up to the door to knock but found that it was already open. I stepped inside.

It was decorated in a rustic fashion, yet quite lavish for the matron of an orphanage, even one as prestigious as Harlingdon. There were voices coming from upstairs. Male voices. I ascended the wooden stairs and followed the sounds to an open door to find Mr Holmes in his travelling clothes, standing in a cosy bedroom with a man in a bed, his leg up and encased in a cast.

"—been like a father to her. This whole time. He actually gave her away at our wedding…"

"Ah! Miss de Merville, do come in," Mr Holmes genially gestured me into the room. "This is Charles Eade, Lillian's husband. Charles, this is Violet de Merville, the one who inherited it all. Penny's niece."

"Ah! Well, as my wife's employer, a pleasure to meet you!" he laughed. He had a Bristolian accent.

The sound of coins on wood. Holmes felt in his pockets.

"Oh dear, I've dropped some change. I think it may have rolled under the bed; could you pick it up for me please, Miss de Merville?"

I was about to decline but something in his eyes made me crouch down and look under the bed. I saw the coins. And I also saw—

I froze.

"Right, Charles, Miss de Merville and I will be back within the next hour. There's someone else I'd like to speak to. Come, Miss de Merville."

I snatched up all the coins I could and handed them back to Mr Holmes.

"Pleasure to meet you!" Charles called, as Holmes and I left.

It was dark outside.

"I knew we'd need these." Holmes withdrew two short candles from his pocket, and then a box of matches. As he proceeded to light them with my help I was still thinking about what I had seen under Charles's bed.

"Please don't tell me—" I began.

"Wait," he said, as he handed me a candle. "There's something else."

He handed me his candle also, and then knelt by the flowerbed. He started digging with his hands in between two clumps of flowers. He didn't have to dig long before he pulled forth a bottle.

"Laudanum," I read the label by candlelight.

"There'll be more," he said, "given all this recently dug earth. There'll be bottles and bottles. But another critical thing…" He dusted himself off and stalked around the cottage.

There was a barrel full of water with a cup, and beside it a rope. There were white markings on the rope.

"Why are you showing me this?" I asked him.

"This is part of the crime scene. All will be revealed in time, but for now we must hurry, and time is of the essence before we confront the criminal. I need you to stay discreet and improvise. There's just one more person we need to speak to."

We made our way as quickly as we could across the clearing towards the gardener's shed, shielding our candles from the wind. Mine went out and so I closely followed Holmes.

"The child," I said, breathless. "Who is it?"

"You're going to tell Mr Duncan about the child," was all Holmes said, knocking on the shed door. "From what Watson told you."

Mr Duncan emerged, holding up an oil lamp.

"Who knocks at this hour? Oh. Miss de Merville. My apologies—"

"We found a child," I said, panting. "In the woods. Bloodied but alive."

Mr Duncan's face dropped. He steadied himself. "Bloodied? What do you mean?"

"I don't know. Watson and Mrs Eade are there now. The child's alive, but barely; he escaped somehow—"

"Barely alive?" Duncan nervously chewed his lip, and looked from me to Mr Holmes.

"I know it's awful but at least he'll be able to tell us about the ghost."

Even in the lamplight, he looked frenzied.

"I did it." He looked me straight in the eye.

"Sorry?"

"It was me. I've been kidnapping those children."

"Duncan!"

"It's no use, Duncan," Holmes said softly. "We know. We know who you did it for. All those years, her suffering in the orphanage, neglected, pushed aside with the arrival of a new family. Only the sympathy and care of others such as yourself helped her. I know you were trying to be kind. But she has committed far too many crimes."

This was too much for Duncan; he started to cry. "She's with child, Mr Holmes!"

"Who is?" I asked.

"Lillian," Mr Holmes said.

"Lillian?" I breathed.

"You can't turn her in! Not now! Not after everything that girl has been through—"

"She should've thought of that before taking children from their beds," Holmes remarked.

The matron. She said she believed it was a ghost.

"Lillian," I said again in disbelief.

"You don't know what it's been like for her. All these years in this wretched place, the torture of it all, worse than any orphan I'd ever seen! She's the rightful heir." Duncan looked at me with contempt. "Not you."

"Lillian? How can Lillian possibly—" I began.

"Because of that man – Gregory Harlingdon – blaming that child for the death of his wife! No child wishes their mother dead in bearing them. None!"

"Calm yourself, Duncan!" Holmes warned.

"What do you mean?" I asked.

Duncan sobbed. "Gregory never stood up for her even when she was being bullied by the other children. All he cared about was Anna, as if Anna didn't have enough! Brilliant, Lil was. Absolutely brilliant. Ask any teacher in this school who taught her! A genius if ever I saw one. When she taught chemistry Gregory didn't even pay her properly, can you believe that? Who can blame her? Who can blame her for what she did…"

"Talk sense, Duncan!" I cried.

"You helped her, didn't you, Duncan?" Holmes offered. "You helped her take the children. You hid in the attic, put out the fires with water and ash and pretended to be the voice of the ghost to scare people. You agreed to assist Lillian, but you wouldn't kidnap the children yourself. Your conscience wouldn't let you."

"It was to stop the children ending up on the street," Duncan sniffed. "If the land were sold, the children would end up homeless."

"Is that what she told you? Feeding into your conscience to make you think you were doing a good deed?"

Mr Duncan wailed. "She's not normal, Mr Holmes, but she's not a bad person!"

"But she has done bad, if not terrible things. I think it's time we talk to Lillian. Mr Duncan, we'll escort you to the house, and someone should stay with you. Miss de Merville we need to find Mr Trenor and get back to the cottage immediately."

After we had left Mr Duncan in the care of Mr Trenor, Mr Holmes and I hurried back to the cottage. Right on time, as we reached the front door, we heard footsteps approaching behind us. We turned to find Lillian, holding up her light, and in the distance, Dr Watson.

If I had questioned or doubted that Lillian was guilty, I didn't now. Her face was full of masked worry, and I could smell the fear coming off her like a trapped rat.

"Where's the child in the woods?" I asked.

"There was no child," she responded, staring at Mr Holmes. "He made it up."

"What?"

"May we speak with you inside, Mrs Eade?" Mr Holmes asked.

"My husband is resting from a broken leg. I'd appreciate it if—"

"I know. I've already met him."

Lillian's eyes flashed. "You have?"

Mr Holmes pushed the front door of Lillian's cottage open.

"That door was locked," Lillian said. "If you've been inside my property I'm calling the police!"

"The police will be called, Mrs Eade. As to when, you may decide. Shall we?" Mr Holmes gestured to the cottage.

For a moment, it looked as if Lillian might run.

"We've already spoken to Duncan," Mr Holmes said. "Your husband is waiting for you."

Lillian strode into the cottage. "I don't want to disturb my husband," she said, and went upstairs and closed the door to her husband's room, assuring him that she had guests and would be back. When she returned downstairs, Mr Holmes placed an empty bottle of laudanum on the kitchen table.

Lillian and Mr Holmes locked gazes and never had I seen a stronger clash. Beneath her calm exterior I could sense the bubbles boiling and felt that she might lash out at him at any moment.

"Laudanum," he said. "A potent narcotic, administered carefully, though perhaps without difficulty if you knew your chemistry. One dose administered to staff and one for children to create immediate sleepiness after dinner. That way you could move freely in the dormitories, lifting a drugged child, and guide him or her downstairs to the back of this very cottage. Miss de Merville, what did we see under Charles Eade's bed this evening?"

Lillian's snake-like eyes glided to me and I met her gaze head on.

"Chalk," I said. "Boxes and boxes of chalk and a bowl full of the stuff, crushed. There were also pipettes and empty beakers and flasks."

"Utensils to measure dosages and chalk to whiten the drugged child to give them the appearance of a ghost. Behind this cottage you would powder the child with chalk, before bringing him or her to the cliff edge. Timed with Mr Duncan's attic movements, your targeted victim would be awakened by a loud noise, and in their drugged state be induced to look upon the cliff edge by the voice of the ghost, where you would hide just below, on a protruding rock, with a rope tied around your waist and around the child's.

"You would then either hide the drugged child on the rock underneath while you returned here to the cottage in case you were summoned, or lead the child down the cliff to the riverbank. Along the riverbank, not far from here there is a rowing boat tied to a tree. There are hoof marks and large and small footprints in the grass. Most noticeably, on the rope and in the boat, is soot and sooty fingerprints. You stole these children and practically gave them away to someone who would put them to work as chimney sweeps."

I closed my eyes. "You didn't, Lillian." I didn't want to believe Holmes's words but I knew they were true. When I opened my eyes and looked at Lillian her face was livid.

"Who was the man you sold them to?" Holmes asked.

Lillian didn't respond, merely clenched her fists.

"Who was the man? Otherwise I may go upstairs, and ask Charles, as he is a chimney sweep—"

"Jack Barnell," Lillian replied through gritted teeth.

I glanced at Dr Watson. He was making notes in a small notepad.

"But there is no fortune in selling children as we have an abundance of them and you know this, Lillian, which is why you didn't take these children and create this spectacle for money. As we know from this—" From his inner coat pocket Mr Holmes took out some pieces of paper and passed them to me.

I saw a page ripped out of the accounts we had seen in Lillian's office earlier that day, and also some goods receipts and bills of exchange. One of the bills was for repair work following the fire in the kitchen.

"These are forged documents," Holmes stated. "The hand and ink used in the accounts book wrote these receipts and bills of exchange. They're fake, forged by Lillian, and she's pocketed the money. All of these were fabricated after the death of the Harlingdons."

"You heartless man!" Lillian spat.

"Heartless?" I said. "Was it not heartless when you sent those children off to a life they didn't want? When you snatched them from their beds?"

"He thinks he knows everything but really he knows nothing about any of this."

"I'm merely expounding your criminality to Miss de Merville, Mrs Eade, which is what she hired me to do. Unless, of course, you'd like to explain it to her yourself?"

Lillian pursed her lips in anger.

"I thought so," Holmes said. "And here we have the final piece to our puzzle."

From his coat pocket Mr Holmes withdrew a small framed sketch and handed it to me. It was a family portrait of a husband and wife, holding a baby.

"I think you should hand it to Lillian."

I frowned but did as Holmes requested. That sharp icy wall Lillian had put up suddenly melted away as her eyes fell on the picture and she clutched it with a sudden surge of emotion. She looked up at Mr Holmes. "Where did you get this from?"

"William Pearson, your relieving officer. After I climbed down the cliff this morning and followed the trail to the small boat and the Avonmouth Docks. I was able to take a cab to Clifton High Street. His office is quite small. I learnt a lot of things from visiting William Pearson. He's a very meticulous man. He's been with the committee for twenty years and has kept a record of everything from receipts, to salaries paid to staff, to visits to the orphanage. He had this picture on his wall, and was happy to tell me that it was of Gregory and Margaret Harlingdon, and the baby: Lillian Harlingdon. It was drawn while Margaret was pregnant."

I looked at her. Tears were streaming silently down her face. She did not look up at us, but kept staring at the picture, staring at her mother.

"I don't know many employees who keep sketches of their employers framed on their walls but the way he spoke about Margaret, your mother, well, it became very clear very quickly. They were childhood friends, and she was the reason he took the job in the first place and despite her being married, throughout 1881 he came to Harlingdon almost every other day. When I asked him the date of Margaret Harlingdon's death he said effortlessly, '5th December 1882. Lillian's birthday.' His visits dramatically decreased after her death. He said that everything that happened to Lillian wouldn't have happened if Margaret had been alive. If she had had a mother."

"So Gregory Harlingdon married Margaret first," I said, "and had Lillian. But then when did he meet my Aunt Penny?"

"At least a year later. They met on a trip he made to London."

"How do you know this?"

"William Pearson. Is he wrong, Lillian?" Holmes asked her, but she lifted her tear-filled eyes and didn't respond.

"So my aunt and Gregory had a daughter called Anna?" I asked quietly.

"And Gregory's perfect family was complete," Mr Holmes said. "As we've heard from Duncan, and I from Mr Pearson, Lillian was cast aside, blamed for the death of her mother in childbirth and Gregory wanted nothing to do with her."

"Now, Holmes," Watson spoke up, "I know that she's a criminal—"

"It's alright," Lillian's voice rang out. She sank to the floor, still grasping the picture frame, and looked up at us. "Please continue, Mr Holmes."

"And so this young girl was placed in a room away from the rest of her family: the room in the kitchen where Marie now resides. And throughout her whole adolescence she grew up alone and isolated, always second to Anna, and Penny. It was only the staff members, the teachers, Mr Duncan and Mr Pearson, who secretly disapproved of Gregory's treatment of his daughter and took it upon themselves to care for her instead.

"One summer a young chimney sweep called Charles Eade came to work in the orphanage and struck up a friendship with Lillian. Friendship blossomed into romance and the two of them fell in love. Unfortunately, Gregory Harlingdon found out and disapproved of the union, thinking that the low-born Charles only wanted to marry Lillian for her inheritance. Gregory threatened Lillian, saying that if she married Charles she would never see a shilling of Harlingdon money. He sacked Charles and Lillian left with him. According to Charles, Mr Pearson paid for your wedding?" Holmes addressed Lillian.

She nodded. "And Mr Duncan walked me down the aisle."

"Lillian worked as a teacher and Charles as a chimney sweep, but when he fell and broke his leg badly they couldn't survive on Lillian's income alone. At the same time there was an influenza outbreak at the orphanage. Lillian had no choice; even though she hated it here, she had to come back. And when she arrived—"

"Anna was dying," came Lillian's faint voice. "Father and Penny were dead. Finally, finally, they had got their comeuppance. Justice had been served and I, as the firstborn daughter of Gregory and Margaret Harlingdon, would inherit what was rightfully mine. But I did not realise until after Anna died that they hated me so much as to ensure that I would not get a single piece of either of their fortunes, that all of it would go to Anna, entailed thereafter to her uncle, General de Merville. I could not let them win. Their dream to create a legacy… the name Harlingdon… all their work, their charitable deeds, their accolades were hypocritical in their treatment of me. And if I wasn't going to have Harlingdon, then no one would." She smiled sadly. "Well. If you hadn't shown up, Mr Holmes."

"You wanted to ruin your parents' legacy and take everything you could in the process."

"In my shoes, wouldn't you have done the same? Please, Violet," she looked to me and then to Holmes and Watson. "Give me one more night to tell my husband. He doesn't know."

"Miss de Merville?" Holmes turned to me.

"The police will be called first thing tomorrow morning," I said.

"Thank you," she breathed in relief.

"Dr Watson, please could you find two teachers who will

stand guard outside the cottage tonight."

"Of course, Miss de Merville." Watson slightly bowed at me before exiting the cottage.

"Is it true you're with child?" I asked her.

"Yes."

"Where will we find the missing children?"

"Across country homes in Gloucester."

"And Jack Barnell?"

"Tomorrow night. He expects me then."

"Lillian," I said. She looked at me. "If I'd have known, I would've given Harlingdon to you."

Her face crumpled and I had to turn away.

"Mr Holmes," I said, "your work here is done."

He nodded. "Very well, Miss de Merville. Watson and I will return to London on the last train tonight."

Watson returned with Mr Ardham and the porter, who had agreed to stand guard. Then Mr Holmes, Watson and I returned to the orphanage. I thanked both gentlemen profusely and told them to name their price as this was the second time they had helped me. We said our goodbyes and they left to walk to Clifton where they'd be able to catch a cab to the station.

I slept in the master's bedroom that night, strangely unable to shake off the feeling that Lillian going to prison was wrong.

The next morning I was going to call the police when I discovered that the cottage was empty except for the porter and Mr Ardham, who were lying on the floor insensible. They'd been drugged with laudanum. Mr Duncan too had escaped and when I asked Mr Trenor he said he couldn't help falling asleep. The police were still looking for them.

As Lillian had said, that night Jack Barnell was caught and arrested. Fourteen out of the fifteen children that were kidnapped were recovered; the fifteenth had died in a chimney accident. This left me with mixed feelings about the whole affair.

I sold the property to a philanthropist on the condition that he would keep Harlingdon as an orphanage and I returned readily back into my London life and society.

Even in London, I still thought about Lillian Harlingdon occasionally, more so her child, and hoped that he or she would have a better life than their mother had.

THE NOBLE BURGLAR

James Lovegrove

You should never dare me. I'm not saying that as a warning; I'm saying it as a plea. I'm begging you not to dare me, because I'm rash and bullheaded enough to go through with the dare, come what may. For instance, one afternoon at a pub, my editor at Titan Books, Miranda Jewess, dared me to write a story for this anthology that would spotlight **Toby**, the ugly but redoubtable sniffer dog who plays a significant role in *The Sign of Four*. "A Sherlock Holmes story told from a dog's point of view?" I said to myself. "Absurd! Can't be done! Only a crazy person would try." And lo and behold…

—James Lovegrove

Marking my Territory: Doorstep of 3 Pinchin Lane, Lambeth

Yes, it's me. Toby, of Pinchin Lane. My master is Mr Sherman, the taxidermist and menagerie keeper. This is our house, which lies near the river in a street full of identical two-storeyed houses. Number 3. Smells of fouling and sawdust inside. Every kind of animal lives there, from snakes to stoats, cats to cormorants, some in cages, the rest roaming free – those as Mr Sherman hasn't eviscerated and turned into sawdust-stuffed statues, that is. There's even a giant rat that he tells his customers he imported from a distant land called Sumatra but I reckon comes from no further afield than the banks of the Thames.

Not a bad man, my Mr Sherman, as they go. Has a temper on him, fond of a drink, but he's kind enough to me, especially when I've earned him a bob or two, as I did just last week.

The tale attached to that piece of profit is still fresh in me and I'll be giving it out in dribs and drabs while Mr Sherman takes me for a walk around the neighbourhood. Follow the trail and you'll catch the lot.

The leash is on. Front door locked. Off we go.

First Instalment: Corner of Pinchin Lane and Park Street

It began, as my best exploits do, with the arrival of a certain person by the name of Sherlock Holmes. I always know when Mr Holmes pays a call that there's adventure afoot, and I get fair excitable at the prospect. Wouldn't you? Nothing compares with being useful to good humans, not least if it involves bringing bad humans to justice.

I knew he was coming. I smelled him a mile off. That coarse tobacco he likes to smoke. His clothes reek of it. Hangs around him like a brown haze.

His friend Dr Watson was with him, too. Nice fellow. Smells warm, like gunpowder and old leather. They always go around in a pair, a pack of two. Mr Holmes is the alpha, but only by a small margin.

Well, as is my wont I became agitated when I caught wind of them approaching. Whined and danced, such that Mr Sherman fetched me a couple of kicks and snarled, "Pipe down, you mangy mongrel!" But I couldn't pipe down. I pawed at the front door, whimpering. He soon got the drift.

"Company we're expecting, is it?" said he. "And would it by any chance be a famous consulting detective and his faithful companion?" He licked his palm and neatened down the fur on his head, then straightened his collar. A bottle of something cheap but potent was swigged from and stowed away.

Then came the sharp rap at the door, and in stepped the aforementioned two gentlemen.

Second Instalment: Railings on Park Street

Mr Holmes immediately bent down and proffered me the back of his hand to sniff. Once I'd wagged my tail to show him I accepted him on my home territory, he ruffled my ears, just the way a dog likes it.

Dr Watson was a bit more circumspect around me. He wasn't that way when we first met, but since then something has happened to make him mistrust our species. Once, a couple of years back, I caught a whiff off him, such as belonged to an enormous hound from somewhere out in the countryside. That beast had been trained to kill humans, which is a wrong thing if ever there was one, and, if I'm not much mistaken, it had pursued Mr Holmes and Dr Watson with a view to causing them grievous harm. Dr Watson has not forgotten that. I have tried every time to reassure him that I am friendly and would never so much as growl at him, let alone bare my fangs, but he remains hard to convince.

Mr Holmes slipped me a morsel of dried beef from a pocket of his overcoat. It was gone down my gullet in a heartbeat. Delicious!

Then it was down to brass tacks.

"Mr Sherman, I require the loan of Toby once again."

"Of course, Mr Holmes, of course. Wery happy to oblige. Usual rates apply, eh?"

Money changed hands, and in no time I was on the leash with Mr Holmes at the other end.

"Now, Toby, you look after these gents," my master said, patting me on the head. "Use that magnificent nose of yours to track down another willain. He's knocking on a bit," he confided to Mr Holmes, as though I couldn't hear.

"Eleven's a ripe old age for a dog. But he still doesn't miss a step, does Toby. His powers haven't dimmed, not one jot."

Mr Sherman is only free with the compliments when there are customers to be impressed, but I don't mind. Praise is praise.

I strained at the leash, impatient to get going.

Mr Holmes took the hint and we were off.

Third Instalment: Lamppost on the Corner of Sumner Street and Southwark Street

Popular spot, this. Just about every dog in the vicinity leaves a dribble here when passing. Basil the beagle, of Tabard Street. Isambard the Labrador cross, of New Cut. That Jack Russell from Gravel Lane, Georgie I think she's called. All the local characters, plus the strays as loiter around Bethlehem Asylum, those slouchy semi-feral curs.

And there we are. Leg cocked. My business done too, giving all-comers the next portion of the story.

So it turned out that Dr Watson had only just then joined Mr Holmes on the case and had no idea what crime they were investigating. As we walked westward – me happily lolloping along at their heels – Mr Holmes caught him up.

"Have you heard, Watson, of the Honourable Jeremy Farnaby-Coutt Esquire, sole son and heir of Viscount Harrington of Warwickshire?"

"I have heard of the *Dis*honourable Jeremy Farnaby-Coutt. A scoundrel and a rogue, by all accounts. One of those young aristocrats who shames the nobility with his scandalous behaviour. He has left a trail of ruined women in his wake, has he not? They say he has sired so many illegitimates that he ought to found a school to educate them."

"His offences against morality are great in number, but so are his offences against the law."

"Yes, he has a reputation as a thief."

"A gentleman thief, the worst kind," said Mr Holmes. "One who robs not because he is short of money but because he is short of entertainment. He does it solely to amuse himself and bring excitement into what is otherwise a life of idleness and indolence. Yet he has never been caught. That is the remarkable thing. He carries out audacious burglaries, stealing from the homes of the wealthy, sometimes right under their noses, but no one has been able to pin the blame on him."

"At least it would seem he targets his own kind, taking only from those who have plenty, those hailing from the same refined circles in which he himself moves," said Dr Watson. "I would rather that than him preying on the poor. Tell me, is it too much to hope that you have evidence on him, proof that will finally see him brought to account for his misdeeds?"

"Patience, Watson, and I shall explain."

Fourth Instalment: Heywoods the Pie Makers, on Stamford Street

Always nice to take a pause for relief outside a pie makers' shop. The aromas of meat, lard and pastry wafting out through the door – heavenly.

Now, where was I? Oh yes.

Mr Holmes related to Dr Watson the latest events surrounding the Honourable Jeremy Farnaby-Coutt and how he had been called upon to involve himself in the affair.

It went like this.

In recent months Farnaby-Coutt's crimes had grown both more frequent and more bold. Time and again a diamond necklace would go missing from some duchess's dressing-table drawer; a safe belonging to Lord Such-and-such would be cleaned out; a priceless portrait hanging in the hall of a grand mansion would vanish. And on every occasion the finger of suspicion would point firmly at Farnaby-Coutt. He was the common factor in each crime because just days before he would have been a guest at that particular household, attending some swanky soirée or lavish dinner. In other words, His Nibs was using these parties as cover while he indulged in what is known in common parlance as "casing the joint". He'd craftily identify where the valuables were, then return a week or so later, usually on a night when he knew the owners were going to be absent, and break in and help himself.

Very cunning, but what baffled me when I heard about it was that, if he was known for this racket, which he was, why did these noble folk ever invite him round? Wasn't that asking for trouble?

Dr Watson put this query of mine into words, and Mr Holmes replied that Farnaby-Coutt was notoriously charming. The same rakish looks and fine speech that he used to seduce his female conquests he also applied at social gatherings. Put simply, nobody believed that someone so handsome and nicely spoken could possibly be a crook, and even if they did have their suspicions, they were too constrained by politeness and etiquette to voice them. Farnaby-Coutt relied on the good manners of the well-bred to continue having his devilish way with their belongings. Perhaps they even liked the fact that he had something of the dark about him. It introduced a thrill into their safe, staid lives.

Moreover, it had lately become apparent that Farnaby-Coutt was more innocent than he was generally held to be. For, since the middle of last year, every single one of the burglaries for which he was the likeliest culprit, he could not have perpetrated. He had a cast-iron alibi each time. He would be seen out and about at the exact same moment the felony was being committed. He would be sitting in a box at the opera, twirling gaily at a formal dance, or telling jokes at his club. His metaphorical fingerprints were all over the crime, but there was no way he could have committed it.

"Remarkable," said Dr Watson, and I had to agree.

Fifth Instalment: Outside the Main Entrance to Waterloo Station

However, all that had changed. Just last night, Farnaby-Coutt was finally caught in the act.

It happened at the home of Sir Reginald Theakswood, the parliamentarian and industrialist who had made several fortunes in the wool trade. A no-nonsense Yorkshireman with a forthrightness to match the size of his bank balance, so Mr Holmes described him.

Sir Reginald, Mr Holmes said, had played host to a literary salon last week at which Farnaby-Coutt was a surprise attendee. The knight of the realm had been reluctant to let the arrogant, caddish son of a peer in through his door. Rather than turn him away, however, he had been persuaded by his wife, Lady Angela, to act hospitably, so as not to cause a fuss and upset the proceedings. He had watched Farnaby-Coutt like a hawk the entire evening, but the latter had behaved impeccably throughout, applauding the poetry recitals and the literary readings with the appreciation of a true connoisseur.

Then last night Farnaby-Coutt had struck.

Sir Reginald was a collector of rare Ancient Egyptian artefacts. He owned, amongst other antiquities, a set of Canopic jars, which are clay pots containing the dried-up internal organs of some long-dead king, Pharaoh Somesuch – I did not quite catch the name. Worth a pretty penny, those jars, and they were openly on display in the drawing room of Sir Reginald's Kensington home, the same room in which the literary salon had been held.

Sir Reginald had supposedly gone up north to a place in Yorkshire called the East Riding, to visit his voters. But that was just a lie he had put about so as to make it seem as though his house would be unguarded. Instead, while the rest of the household had indeed upped sticks and headed to Yorkshire, he remained in London. He was dead set on bringing about Farnaby-Coutt's downfall.

So it was that the man who sneaked into the house shortly before midnight, having eased open a casement window at the rear, was in for a rude shock.

Sixth Instalment: Parapet of Westminster Bridge

Sir Reginald, Mr Holmes continued, caught the miscreant red-handed. In flagrante delicto, as the lawyers have it. Lying in wait in his study, he heard furtive noises coming from the drawing room, and sure enough, as he burst in, there was the Honourable Jeremy Farnaby-Coutt, busy stuffing the Canopic jars into a knapsack.

The Yorkshireman let out a roar and lunged. Farnaby-Coutt was too quick for him, though, and managed to trip him up so that he fell hard against the fireplace. Farnaby-Coutt then fled, heading for the selfsame window he had entered by. Sir Reginald recovered and, pulling out a revolver he had taken the precaution of arming himself with beforehand, gave chase. Farnaby-Coutt was at the far end of the garden and clambering over the back wall by the time Sir Reginald was finally able to take aim. He had a clear shot. He loosed off a round, which struck Farnaby-Coutt in the calf. The wounded man gave a yelp of pain but nonetheless managed to scramble over the wall into the garden beyond and, though limping, made good his escape.

Sir Reginald summoned the police, who accordingly went round to Farnaby-Coutt's house in Chelsea.

But here is the queer thing. Farnaby-Coutt had, it appeared, just returned home from an evening carousing with friends. The policemen found him dishevelled and definitely drunk, preparing to turn in for the night.

And he did not have so much as a scratch on him. His leg was intact – no bullet wound.

Not only that but two of the aforesaid friends were present and swore they had been with Farnaby-Coutt all evening, accompanying him from pub to pub and onward to a private members' club where they had gambled at cards until just past midnight.

In short, Farnaby-Coutt could not have been the one who had stolen Sir Reginald's Canopic jars. It was simply not possible.

And yet Sir Reginald swore blind that the man he had confronted at his home had been him.

Naturally, with the police at a loss what to do, Sir

Reginald travelled to 221B Baker Street first thing the next morning to engage the services of Sherlock Holmes.

Mr Holmes told Dr Watson that he had driven with Sir Reginald in the latter's private brougham to Kensington and immediately conducted an inspection of the crime scene.

"As ever, the policemen had trampled over everything like a herd of cattle," said he, "erasing much that could have been useful in the way of clues. But," he went on, "I was able to procure a small piece of evidence that, with Toby's help, could prove crucial in securing a conviction."

"And what is it?"

"You shall see shortly, Watson. In the meantime, perhaps you might care to advance a theory as to how Farnaby-Coutt could be in two places at once and, more to the point, recover almost instantaneously from a bullet wound so that it left not the slightest trace on his body."

"You wish me to offer a few blundering, misguided suggestions that you can then mockingly dismiss."

"It does you good to exercise your brain."

"And it does *you* good to vaunt the superiority of your intellect over mine. Well, I will oblige. First of all, perhaps Sir Reginald's shot missed. In the heat of the moment he only thought he hit Farnaby-Coutt."

"No, there were definite signs of injury at the scene. Fresh bloodstains on the garden wall."

"Then he misidentified the burglar. It wasn't Farnaby-Coutt at all. He wanted so much to see Farnaby-Coutt that that was who he imagined he saw, but it was in fact someone else."

"It was unquestionably him. Sir Reginald was quite adamant. 'Wouldn't mistake that cocky little whippersnapper anywhere' – those were his very words."

"What if Farnaby-Coutt is one of identical twins?"

"Really?" said Mr Holmes, arching an eyebrow. "And all this time he has kept his brother under wraps? No one has ever seen this other Farnaby-Coutt? Even if that were so, a quick check in *Debrett's* would dispel the notion that he is anything other than an only child."

"So you admit you considered the possibility and looked him up?"

"It was, I will allow, a conjecture I briefly entertained – but for no more than the few seconds it took me to eliminate it. And no, Watson, don't you dare say what you are about to say next."

"What am I about to say?"

"That Farnaby-Coutt has some supernatural gift that enables him to appear in two places at once. I have seen those books on mediumship and spiritualism in your library."

"They are Mrs Watson's."

"And yet they sit on a shelf directly adjacent to your preferred reading matter: Dickens, Thackeray, Scott, Trollope. It is suggestive that you yourself like to peruse them."

"I may have dipped into one or other of them now and then."

"Pray do not let their charlatan content infect you."

"But it has been well documented that certain people, saints not least among them, have been shown to display the power of bilocation and—"

Mr Holmes held up a hand and barked, "Watson! Enough! We are not going to consider even for a moment a non-rational explanation for this mystery."

"Farnaby-Coutt's leg healing so swiftly does, if nothing else, seem miraculous."

"It is fraud, old fellow. Fraud and subterfuge, nothing

more. As you yourself will soon discover, assuming my inferences are correct and Toby's nose is still the sharp forensic tool it has hitherto shown itself to be."

At the mention of my name I pricked up my ears and gave a little wag of the tail. Humans always like to be rewarded with a sign of acknowledgement when they bring you into the conversation. They'd feel neglected otherwise, wouldn't they?

Seventh Instalment: Pavement of Victoria Embankment

Nice long stroll Mr Sherman is taking me out on today. I love it when he exercises me properly and gives me a chance to stretch my legs and take in the air. I spend so much of my time cooped up in 3 Pinchin Lane. Sometimes I think my master forgets that I'm half spaniel and half lurcher – both of them breeds as relish the great outdoors.

My journey with Mr Holmes and Dr Watson, which covered at least as much distance as this one looks set to, took us across the river at the Albert Bridge and northward up into Chelsea. Lots of scents unfamiliar to me there, the markings of dogs I'd never met and would likely never meet, their histories splashed piecemeal everywhere. I would have loved to stop and sniff, learning about who they were, where they had been, what they had done. But that would have been possible only if this had been a leisurely amble. The three of us were, instead, engaged on a mission. There was no time to pause and check the chronicles these other dogs had left behind, nor add commentaries of my own – a dash of opinion, a sprinkling of advice.

Presently we arrived at a huge house just off the King's Road, a dwelling fully five times the size of Mr Sherman's humble abode. Outside, we were greeted by a police inspector I had not previously made the acquaintance of, although Mr Holmes and Dr Watson both bore old residues of his scent on them, in such quantity as to indicate they had had numerous dealings with him in the past. Lestrade was his name, and his pointed, pale features put me in mind of one of the weasels in my master's menagerie.

"Mr Holmes, Dr Watson," said he, "I trust this is not going to be a waste of my time and that of these two constables with me."

"Very much not, Inspector," said Mr Holmes. "I fully anticipate an arrest."

"But Farnaby-Coutt is as slippery as an eel. We've never been able to lay so much as a finger on the fellow. We're not even sure where and to whom he fences his stolen goods."

"I doubt he does. I imagine he keeps them all for his own pleasure, perhaps even on these very premises. Farnaby-Coutt does not steal for a living. He is comfortably well off as it is. He steals for the sake of stealing. It is more a hobby to him than a profession."

"We have nothing on him that would furnish us with a warrant to search his house. No grounds on which to nab him other than hearsay."

"Give me ten minutes, Lestrade, and I will rectify that situation."

Eighth Instalment: Corner of Upper Thames Street and Southwark Bridge Road

Mr Holmes knocked on the front door, which was opened by a frosty-faced manservant. Mr Holmes presented his card, saying that Mr Farnaby-Coutt would surely agree to see him, if only to exonerate himself once and for all from guilt for the robbery last night at Sir Reginald Theakswood's.

He was playing on Farnaby-Coutt's pride and egotism, and sure enough it worked. Farnaby-Coutt instructed the servant to invite us in, and soon we were in a handsomely furnished drawing room with Farnaby-Coutt dancing attendance on us as though we were honoured guests.

He uttered a few unflattering words about me, I must confess. "What the deuce is that!" he ejaculated as I loped into view. "I have never seen a dog so ugly."

"Don't let Toby's homely appearance fool you," said Mr Holmes. "He is deceptive in his plainness. Unlike you, who are deceptive in your sophistication."

"You do me a disservice."

"On the contrary, I am paying you the highest of compliments. You have succeeded in hoodwinking some of the best and brightest this country can boast."

"But obviously not you, the great Sherlock Holmes."

"That remains to be seen. What I would like to do, if I may, is conduct a quick test."

"I cannot see the harm."

"It will determine once and for all if you are the perpetrator of a crime or entirely blameless."

"I am quite certain I know the outcome already. I will be exculpated."

"Very good." From his pocket Mr Holmes produced a wadded-up handkerchief. He unfolded it to reveal specks of human blood soaked into the fabric. He held it before me and I duly took a long, hearty sniff. "Good boy, Toby," he said. "Now, would you care to perform the same function upon Mr Farnaby-Coutt?"

He led me over to the aristocrat who, with something of a haughty sneer on his face, permitted himself to be thoroughly examined by me. I ran my nose up and down his leg, gleaning all the data I could about him.

Then I looked up at Mr Holmes in puzzlement.

"So, Toby," said he, "what is the verdict?"

"Yes, Toby," said Farnaby-Coutt. "The verdict."

I made it perfectly clear that the blood on the handkerchief did not come from the man in front of me. My eyes were wide, my head cocked to one side. I could not fathom why Mr Holmes had thought the two – the bloodstains and Farnaby-Coutt – were connected. The bloodstains had a meagreness about them, redolent of a poor diet and too much gin, whereas Farnaby-Coutt exuded ripeness and refinement, like banknotes and lavender.

"Shouldn't this canine monstrosity be barking, or lifting a paw, or something?" said Farnaby-Coutt smugly. "Isn't that the result you were hoping for, Mr Holmes?"

"Far from it. Toby has confirmed what I already thought."

"That I am not the culprit. That Sir Reginald Theakswood has falsely accused me."

Without replying, Mr Holmes bent and offered me the handkerchief a second time. "Take another sniff, Toby. Does this scent set any bells ringing at all?"

It did not.

Then it did.

Oh, it did!

The scent was already in the house. I had smelled it, amongst a myriad of others, as we crossed the threshold.

Whoever's blood this was, was in the building with us.

Ninth Instalment: Southern End of Southwark Bridge

Nearly there. If you've followed this tale so far, trickle by trickle, congratulations – especially if you've managed to visit all the instalments in the correct order, treading in my pawprints. Hope it's been worth your while.

As soon as I realised what Mr Holmes was driving at, I leapt up at him, barking frantically.

He immediately detached the leash, and off I raced. I heard Farnaby-Coutt behind me yelling in protest. "What is this? Where is that beast going? I demand that he be stopped. This is outrageous. He is running amok!"

I charged upstairs, Mr Holmes and Dr Watson following as fast as they were able. Within seconds I was outside a bedroom on the second floor, turning circles and letting out a volley of loud, urgent woofs.

Mr Holmes barged through the door to the bedroom, Farnaby-Coutt still remonstrating volubly as he joined us on the landing.

On the bed lay a man with a heavily bandaged leg.

He was the absolute spitting image of the Honourable Jeremy Farnaby-Coutt.

Tenth Instalment: Doorstep of 3 Pinchin Lane, again.

Full circle. We end where we began.

Suffice to say that the jig was up as far as Farnaby-Coutt was concerned. Inspector Lestrade and his constables were summoned from without, and the noble burglar was swiftly clapped in handcuffs, as was his accomplice.

The latter was only too ready to make a confession, once

it was explained to him that the courts would look leniently on him if he incriminated Farnaby-Coutt.

His name was Bill Jervis, and he was a petty larcenist of no great breeding and no great account. What had elevated this fellow to Farnaby-Coutt's company was the fact that the two of them looked to all intents and purposes the same. Farnaby-Coutt had encountered Jervis one evening while trawling the stews of the East End in search of paid female companionship. Jervis had attempted to pick Farnaby-Coutt's pocket, but Farnaby-Coutt, sensitive to the illicit activities of others, had seized hold of his hand as it dipped inside his jacket. He had taken one look at Jervis's face and immediately spied an opportunity. Jervis was his perfect double. The two were alike as pups in a litter. Other than a certain roughness of speech, the Cockney commoner could have passed for the aristocrat in any light. Even their own mothers might not have been able to tell them apart.

Farnaby-Coutt hatched a plan. He had begun to feel that his sins were catching up with him. He was pushing his luck further than was wise. He was not going to be able to get away with his burglaries much longer. Sooner or later his winning streak was going to come to an end.

He could not, however, bear to abandon the habit. But this other man, this twin from another set of parents, provided the solution. Farnaby-Coutt would carry on selecting the targets for thievery, but Jervis would commit the actual felonies while Farnaby-Coutt paraded about town garnering unimpeachable alibis everywhere he went. In return, Jervis was rewarded with a sizeable wage from the nobleman's own pocket, worth around half of the proceeds, along with the assurance that if Jervis were ever caught, Farnaby-Coutt would use his influence as an aristocrat to get him off the hook. I'm not sure that promise would have been worth anything if put to the test, but it had seemed acceptable to Jervis, who, one can assume, was not the freshest dog biscuit in the tin.

Theirs was a cosy little alliance, and would have continued despite the bullet wound. The plan had been that Jervis would lie low until he recuperated, whereupon the stealing would resume as before. At the same time, Farnaby-Coutt's bona fides would be maintained and even strengthened, for how could he be the burglar Sir Reginald had winged if he was demonstrably, palpably unhurt?

As for the loot, there I played a vital role again. Mr Holmes invited me to seek more of Jervis's scent around the house, and my nose led us to several rooms before finally we ended up in the wine cellar, where the smell was at its strongest. I found a wall, which appeared to be solid but which I knew was made of plasterboard not brick. I whined and scratched at it, and sure enough Mr Holmes discerned that it was a false partition, and behind it lay Farnaby-Coutt's ill-gotten gains, a treasure trove of stolen property, all neatly arranged upon shelves like trophies.

That clinched it, and currently the Honourable Jeremy Farnaby-Coutt is languishing in a police cell at Scotland Yard, facing trial and possible transportation.

"A lengthy stretch in gaol awaits him," said Mr Holmes as he, Dr Watson and I wended our way back to Lambeth. "Perhaps his father might intervene, pull some strings, have the sentence reduced or even quashed – but equally Viscount Harrington may wish to disavow his wayward offspring and wash his hands of him. I know, were Farnaby-Coutt my son, which of the two options I would choose. At any rate, thanks to Toby here, justice is going to be served and all the items that Farnaby-Coutt purloined are going to be restored to their rightful owners. Which reminds me… Would you do me the favour of holding Toby for a moment?"

He passed my leash to his companion and ducked into a nearby butcher's shop. Dr Watson stood gingerly by me, every so often offering me a timorous "Good boy. Good dog." Shortly Mr Holmes emerged from the shop with a big, juicy hambone wrapped in waxed paper. I started salivating, and didn't stop until I was back home and sinking my fangs into that crunchy, marrowy treat.

Thus concludes my tale.

Do you know, it never ceases to amaze me what a dull instrument the human nose is. Mr Holmes's seems keener than most – I suspect all his senses are keener than most – but even so, by comparison with me he might as well not have the use of that organ at all. He cannot smell a hundredth of what we dogs can. Something that to him and all humans seems an incredible feat is, to us, mere pup's play.

Never mind. As long as he has need of my nose, reliable old Toby will be here, ready and willing to lend a paw.

THE SECOND MASK

Philip Purser-Hallard

I'm fascinated by the scope of change the human lifespan can encompass – that someone born, say, when Wagner was writing operas in the 1870s, might live long enough to hear The Beatles. For my story I wanted to write about a child known to Holmes, so I could follow him or her into old age. I settled on **Lucy Hebron**, the little girl in "The Adventure of the Yellow Face".

Lucy is perhaps five years old sometime in the 1880s, so would be in her seventies during the 1950s, when "The Second Mask" is set. She's the daughter of an African-American lawyer, and the mystery in "The Yellow Face" arises from her English mother's attempts to conceal her dark-skinned child from her new husband, fearing his potential prejudice. Though Effie Munro brings her daughter to live in a nearby cottage, she insists Lucy always wears the mask that gives the story its title.

It's an unusual case because Holmes's theory – that the mask at the cottage window conceals Effie's first husband, not dead but blackmailing her – is completely wrong. In the event, though, Holmes is the one who unmasks Lucy, and he's as surprised as anyone else by what he finds.

—Philip Purser-Hallard

I remember you; of course I do, though it was a lifetime ago. Your quiet laugh of realisation when you saw me; your slim fingers reaching for my face; your kind eyes glinting with amusement as you removed my mask. I thought the whole thing was an enormous joke, and you were there to share it with me.

It was the day I met my stepfather, the man who would adopt me as his own, and claim me with fierce pride whenever some client or visitor asked what this strange foreign creature – this capering savage – was doing in his house. I loved him, of course. I was too young to remember my real father, Mr John Hebron of Atlanta. And from the moment of my unmasking, when he made his decision about me, Mr Grant Munro of Norbury adored me with all the devotion he had already given to my mother.

But it was you who showed him my true face, and for that I loved you, too.

"Of course it *was* very charitable of you, my dear," Elizabeth Goodge tells me shrilly, not because she has strong feelings on the matter – although she evidently does – but because everything she says is shrill. "You have *such* a charming garden, it would be a waste not to use it more, and they were all so conscientious about tidying up after themselves. It's only that it *was* a little noisy, and so very *conspicuous*. We're just a little concerned about the tone of the neighbourhood, if you understand my meaning."

"I believe I understand you very well," I say quietly, as I pour another cup of tea for her stern friend Maud Stokes.

It seems to me that, if anyone should worry about the tone of the neighbourhood, it should be me. I lived here comfortably for some sixty years before Elizabeth and her husband arrived, but it hardly seems gracious to point that out. Charles Goodge is something in the city (though surely not anything wildly successful, or they would have moved somewhere more impregnably affluent), Elizabeth the doyen of the neighbourhood book groups, flower-arranging rotas and sewing circles.

"Please don't misunderstand me, dear," Elizabeth goes on. "We couldn't be happier to have *you* as our neighbour. But we all have to consider the area's *reputation*."

"For pity's sake, Lizzie, it was a church picnic." My other next-door neighbour, Annabel Finch, is far more forthright than I am, which is why I asked her here. "You can't get much more respectable than that."

"You're not a member of the church in question though, Miss Hebron," Miss Stokes declares. "It is a nonconformist denomination." Her voice is deep and flat, a contrast to her friend's agitated trilling. Another neighbour, though not so near, she teaches at a nearby girls' grammar school and sits on the parish council.

So many neighbours, now. I can still remember a time, before the end of the last century, when my family's house stood almost alone among fields. Over the decades the houses that once clustered by the railway station have spread along the road, crowding us in, bulldozing the cottages and felling the fir trees, turning the pastoral playground I grew up in into this smoky, traffic-clogged outcrop of London.

Well, times change. These days few of us are left who see past the houses to the landscape beneath. For the likes of the Goodges – who arrived, half my age then, soon after the end of the last war – this area might as well have always been its grubby yet genteel suburban self.

Sometimes, I am ashamed to admit, I wish they'd all go back where they came from.

"It's a Pentecostal church," I admit now, "and no, the worship isn't to my taste. But the minister asked me, and I was glad to do them a kindness. As Elizabeth says, I have a large garden. Their congregation meets in an old air-raid shelter down by the railway line."

"Rather there than here," Miss Stokes deems.

"That is unworthy of you, Maud Stokes," says Annabel stoutly.

"I would have thought you of all people would have some concern about the character of the neighbourhood," Miss Stokes suggests coolly.

But Elizabeth Goodge is still giving us the benefit of her wisdom. "It was just such a *worry* having so many strangers on the street, my dear. They could see *right* into our back upstairs windows – yours too, Annabel. And of course they saw far more of *your* house, Miss Hebron. We're rather vulnerable here, I'm afraid. It's well known that ours are the houses in Norbury worth burgling."

I know the reason they are making a fuss, of course, and I detest it. I do not feel myself under any obligation to make it easy for them.

"It was a church outing," I say. "Surely you can't suppose that anyone was taking the opportunity to case the joint?"

* * *

I *was* a savage, certainly, when I first came to live here: unruly, wayward, inquisitive, volatile… little different, in fact, from any other child of that age, although perhaps it is true that my upbringing had done less than usual to tame me.

Yet people – our few neighbours, my stepfather's business contacts, friends of my mother's family – responded to me as something quite out of the ordinary, just as you and Dr Watson did, that day we met. After my mother's early lessons in human nature, it was easy for me to understand why.

In his reminiscences of your cases together, Dr Watson – seeking, no doubt, to make the most of his moment of revelation – described me as "a little coal-black negress". In that, he exaggerated. My mother was white, as you know, nor was my real father's blood unmixed (I was never able to establish the precise details of his ancestry, and it is possible that he never knew either). Had he been consistent in his language, Dr Watson might have called me a "mulatto", like the voodoo-worshipping cook in the affair at Wisteria Lodge, but that would have rather undercut the tender emotion of his dénouement.

I am certainly dark of complexion, though – darker than my father, based on my mother's memories and the single photograph that survived him – and there was never any likelihood that I would be mistaken for the child of Grant and Effie Munro.

Still, my adoptive father was wealthy and respectable, and that makes up for a great deal. As I grew older I found that, given certain cues, adults (a handful of boors and imbeciles aside) would treat me like any other young Englishwoman, though many did so rather self-consciously. Provided I comported myself in a manner consistent with my upbringing, I found that those I met, from my stepfather's wealthy partners and their debutante daughters to servants and tradesmen, generally fell into line and treated me with the deference appropriate to our respective stations. I might enter a haberdasher's to be faced with scowls and intakes of breath, but as soon as shopkeeper and customers saw the cut of my clothing, heard my speech and observed my manners, they were able to fit this exotic object into a familiar slot, and act accordingly. Despite my mother's fears, it seems that here in Britain, class takes precedence over race.

I was excessively fortunate in the class that claimed me, of course; I have no illusions on that score. Had I been a cook like that nameless man at Wisteria Lodge, or a street-thug like Steve Dixie, who threatened you when you investigated the burglary at Three Gables, society's reaction would have been very different.

Even you were not so kind to Mr Dixie as to me, not by a long chalk. I do not think you would have been so rude to a woman, or Dr Watson in describing one, but when I read that case study it made me wonder how real your pleasure had been in the resolution of my own story. Though you both acknowledged me a child, and to be loved as one, you allowed those men to be as defined by their blackness as poor leprous Godfrey Emsworth, your "blanched soldier", was by his excessive whiteness.

But those black men, like the Indians, lascars and Chinese who so colourfully occupy the margins of your cases, lacked the advantages I derived from my mother's family and marriage. In the hierarchy of British society, still barely changed since those days, they had not even reached the lowest rung: they were, at best, holding the ladder in place, and at worst, trying to kick it over. Convention told you what to think of them and of me, and, like everyone else, you treated us accordingly.

I might have hoped for better from you, but for all your percipience you were never infallible. That, after all, was Dr Watson's point in publishing my story.

"It's not that I've anything against their *colour*," Elizabeth Goodge explains, very earnestly. She is speaking still of the congregation I hosted here the previous Sunday, and has finally reached the crux of her objection.

"I was not expecting you to tell me you had," I say, perhaps too pointedly.

"Oh, not in the *least*," Elizabeth agrees, oblivious. "After having you as my neighbour for so many years, I don't think there's a racialist bone left in my body." She helps herself to a custard cream, although there are plenty of bourbon biscuits available. "But there are just so *many* West Indians these days, don't you feel? They seem to be *everywhere*. And they keep coming, ship after ship of them, expecting to find work here. There won't be any jobs for British workers soon."

"The West Indians are British subjects too," says Annabel Finch. "And they mostly do the jobs our own people don't want to."

"That tells you all you need to know about the attitude of the British labourer," Maud Stokes states flatly.

"You can hardly blame men returning from a war if they don't want to go back to working in a factory or on the buses," Annabel objects. "Those who came back at all, that is." Her own husband Peter, a dear man whom I liked a great deal, was one of those who did not, although the job his death left vacant was in the civil service.

But Elizabeth is not to be deflected from her track. "It's just that they haven't had the *advantages* you have, Miss Hebron," she says, as if this should come as news to me. "They come from a very backward part of the world. If it was just the one occasion I'm sure we wouldn't mind, but there's the *girl* as well."

"I'm entitled to invite who I please to my own house," I tell them sharply. I want to remind them that it has been standing here far longer than any of theirs, but that would seem petty. "I'm interested in Miss Youngblood. I've been helping her learn French and Latin during the school holidays." It has been many years since I last tutored, and I have greatly enjoyed revisiting the experience; the effort of grappling with the O-level syllabus, less so.

"Taking on a poorer pupil *gratis* speaks volumes for your generosity, Miss Hebron," Miss Stokes judges, "but not your good sense. Having such a person regularly visiting so prominent a house cannot be good for the reputation of the neighbourhood. You should consider yourself lucky your sons no longer live at home, Annabel. I cannot imagine that this young person's influence on them would be beneficial."

"She's a good girl," I protest. "She's very able. She wants—" I pause, aware that Harriet's ambitions are not mine to share with these terrible busybodies. "She wants to make the best of herself," I finish rather feebly.

"But those people have their own *place*, you know," Elizabeth says. Seeing my look, she quickly adds, "Of course I mean the houses down by the railway line. They don't belong up here."

Annabel is indignant. "You're suggesting an elderly lady should trudge all the way over there to give lessons in some squalid terrace?"

"It's not squalid," I protest. "It's a perfectly nice house." But Harriet has no space there that is not shared with her brother and sisters; finding a quiet place for our tutorials would certainly be a challenge.

"Then let Miss Hebron correspond with her," decides Miss Stokes, addressing Annabel as if she were my keeper, "or better still, donate to educational charities, rather than imperilling the value and security of other people's property with her private projects."

I am beginning to tire mightily of this conversation. "I can imagine no possible objection to my taking an interest in a young person, nor to my hosting a church picnic in my garden," I say. "If we were speaking of the congregation of St Oswald's, none of you would bat an eyelid. There is only one distinction I can see, and I object most strongly to it."

"My dear Miss Hebron—" Miss Stokes begins in a superior tone, but my patience is exhausted.

I say, "Dear be damned! It's because these people are *the same colour I am*—"

Then the front door slams, and a young voice calls out, "Sorry I early, Miss Lucy! Me mother doing her cleaning and she nah want—" It stops abruptly as its owner reaches the door to the drawing room. We all see a teenaged girl, very dark-skinned – a coal-black negress, if you like – with bright intelligent eyes and untamed hair. "I'm very sorry, Miss Hebron," she says, switching immediately to correct English, though still accented, "I didn't know you had visitors. Shall I come back later?"

"Not at all, Harriet," I say. "Mrs Goodge and Miss Stokes were just leaving, weren't you, ladies? Mrs Finch may stay if she pleases."

* * *

I do not know how far, if at all, you interested yourself in my life after our fleeting encounter. To judge by Dr Watson's account, you felt my stepfather's case to be rather an embarrassment, and may well not have wished to follow it further. (I do wonder, though. You have been in my thoughts so often over the years – did I ever play any further part in yours? When Watson whispered "Norbury" in your ear, like a Roman slave reminding a triumphant general of his mortality, did you remember my laughing face, or only your own discomfiture?)

You may have learned, then, that I did not marry, nor embark on the career I wished for, which was that of a schoolmistress. Though I was academically able, my closest approach to employment was to supplement my generous allowance with intermittent tutoring. However polite they might have been, it seemed my parents' compatriots were reluctant to entrust their children to a person of my complexion, whether as a teacher or a wife.

In the end my parents' wealth meant I needed neither a job nor a husband. Since I was in truth a frivolous and unreliable young person, a good many schoolchildren – as well as a few young men – must have had a fortunate escape, but that is scarcely the point.

Instead I lived the life that had been offered to me, that of a socialite. I went to London frequently, for dinner parties and balls, concerts and exhibitions. I danced with young men and smiled at their jokes. I made small talk with young ladies and incurred their friendship. I learned to play whist and gin rummy, and to avoid speaking my mind or behaving spontaneously. Provided I took pains to fit in at all times, society knew my place and so did I.

I travelled, too. I saw the Pyramids and the Parthenon.

I visited the northern United States, where a wealthy lady of my appearance was not so great a novelty. During the Great War I drove an ambulance in France.

It was during the war that my stepfather died.

Annabel stays only long enough to be introduced to Harriet and to powder her nose, before pleading an appointment elsewhere. (The bookmakers' on the high street, if I know Annabel. She has been falling back into old habits since her younger son Gerald left home.)

She is polite to the girl, friendly even, but I sense a reserve, which is unlike her. I knew before today that she was pro-immigration, but the reality of this dark stranger with her peculiar speech may be more than she is prepared for. I remember, also, that the experience of being the only person of one's race in a room is a novelty for most white people in Britain, and not a welcome one.

After Annabel leaves, Harriet proves herself as attentive a pupil as always, quick and intelligent. She has learned her latest set of Latin verb declensions with very few errors, and her conversational French continues to improve *par excellence*.

"*Tu fais de grands progrès*, Harriet," I tell her, although in truth I have little idea of what the oral examiners will make of her accent. Passing her O levels will be challenge enough for her, and her ambitions beyond that are considerable.

Her aspiration, which I did not confide to my visitors earlier, is to study law at university and qualify for the bar. Quite why an immigrant child should settle on so specific and so grand an aim somewhat baffles me, but I admire her hugely for it. The obstacles to its attainment are obvious, but if any young woman I have met has the determination and persistence to surmount them, it is Harriet Youngblood. I first met her on one of my rare visits to her parents' church, and mentioned that my father practised law in the United States, since when she has impressed on me the importance of her goal. I have done all in my power to assist her, although she has never yet asked me for money. I suppose we will cross that bridge when we come to it.

Now we arrange that Harriet and I will meet again the next morning; she says she needs some extra coaching in mathematics, and I agree to give it my best, though my recollections of the subject are somewhat hazy. In truth, I suspect that, as much as my teaching, she appreciates my company, or perhaps, given the size of her family, the imperfect solitude of conversing with one person, rather than with a crowd.

As soon as I am alone, I find myself worrying once more about Annabel. I wonder whether Maud Stokes's unkind comments have unsettled her. She is, I know, feeling lonely and somewhat at a loose end in her sons' absence, and it may be that the family home has become rather too large for her.

I should be sad if she felt she had to move elsewhere; she is the only one of my close neighbours whom I truly like. And I have lived in this house for so long I can no longer imagine moving away. Even when I was roaming the world, my home was always here.

I suppose that when I die, or move into a nursing home – I am still fit and healthy, but that cannot last forever – my house will be sold, to be broken up into flats or demolished. It is out of character for the street now, among all these smart modern houses, and it has no great architectural or historical value. Even those peculiar devotees of yours, who contact me occasionally to clarify details of your exploits, which I could not possibly know, have shown no interest in the house that you never even entered. (Did you know, one of them even asked me once for the address of your retirement home in Sussex, so that he could search the nearby parishes for your grave! It is undocumented, apparently – a holy grail for these enthusiasts. The foolish fellow imagined that in your final years you might have kept up an active correspondence with a child you met once during the 1880s. Can you imagine it?)

I am awoken, in the depths of the night, from a confused dream. It had me at a cocktail party, back in the twenties, where Maud Stokes had just thrown a champagne flute in anger at the young Louis Armstrong, with surprisingly loud results. In my befuddlement, it takes me some moments to understand that the crash of breaking glass was a real sound, and came from a window on the same floor as my bedroom.

Some further furtive thumps and bangs assure me that someone is in the house.

To my shame, my courage fails me and I cower under the bedclothes – not daring even to cross my room and turn the key in the lock, remembering my mother and the terror of racial violence that arose so horribly in her old age. My earlier idle thoughts about the future now feel like a reckless invitation to fate.

I hear no more movement, but as I lie paralysed in panic I imagine someone – a thug, a burglar, an assassin – creeping silently towards my room, a gun or knife in his hand. I cringe, and try not to imagine how badly it will hurt.

* * *

My stepfather was not a combatant, of course; when the war broke out he was sixty-five. He died five minutes from home, run over by a brewer's van while taking an awkward corner on his bicycle. I mourned him, of course, but when I returned from France I found that my mother had succumbed to a heartbreak that would break her down gradually, mentally and physically, over the next twenty years.

Towards the end of this prolonged decline, she would not leave the house, or on some days even her bedroom. She believed that we were both back in Atlanta; that a lynch mob had murdered my father (who in fact died of yellow fever – I have his death certificate still); and that they would come for us next, to kill her for her crime of miscegenation and myself for being its product. In her last years she refused even to open an envelope, for fear of messages from the Ku Klux Klan.

I stayed at home to care for her, of course – although it did occur to me from time to time that she had shown little of the same solicitude for my health, when I was an infant suffering the same ailment that killed my father. Her needs meant that the vistas of my youth shrank back to the landscape of my childhood. My friends of those days had left the area long since, and our new neighbours had no sense of Norbury as a place of its own, rather than an outflung limb of London.

When Mother died, I was not yet an old woman, but it became clear to me that it was only a matter of time. For a while I had hopes that I might travel again, but the last war put paid to that. My social round had settled into an endless cycle of bridge clubs, jumble sales and church coffee mornings.

* * *

"I heard the window break," Annabel Finch tells me, settling a blanket around my shoulders as she bustles around my kitchen looking for the wherewithal to make hot, sweet tea.

Five minutes ago, as I lay in bed quavering in terror, I heard a hammering downstairs at the front door, and Annabel's voice shouting, "Miss Hebron! Lucy! Are you all right in there?" When no sound of alarm or surprise came from outside my room, I finally realised that the intruder must have left already. I fled my bed and on shaking arms and legs I half-crawled down the stairs to let my neighbour in.

Now she continues with her own story as she hands me a small glass of the brandy she has found in my cupboard (more restorative than tea): "I was awake – insomnia, I suppose. I heard the noise. I looked out of my back window, and I saw a man climbing down your trellis. He had two others waiting for him in the garden. The buggers made off through my hedge! I'd left the side-gate unlocked, I'm afraid. I waited till I was sure they were gone, then I dashed round as quickly as I could. I thought he might have murdered you in your bed!"

"He didn't come near my bed," I murmur, sipping timidly at the warming liquid. I am not much of a drinker these days, except in the youthful parties of my dreams. "I heard the window too – it must have been in Mother's dressing room." That room faces onto the back garden, and is directly across the corridor from my own.

"We must look and see if anything's been taken," Annabel says. "Once you feel up to it, of course. What do you keep up there?"

"Oh, just some of her old jewellery," I say vaguely, then I remember: "Oh!" I try to stand up, but my legs are not yet ready for such a pioneering venture. "Oh, but her locket! The one with Father's photograph! It's in a drawer up there. I don't even keep it locked. Oh, I couldn't bear to lose it! Oh, Annabel, go and check for me, please."

"We'll go together," she says sternly, helping me to my feet. "You'll need to see the room, so you can describe the state of it to the police. My impressions won't be any good. I don't know what it looks like normally."

"Oh, I suppose so," I agree, grateful for her clear thinking. With her support I climb the stairs.

It does not appear that the room has been ransacked. Of course the floor is showered with glass shards, glittering in the moonlight coming through the denuded window-frame, but everything else looks as it should. Only the drawer where I keep Mother's jewellery is a little open. I stare anxiously while Annabel hurries about and eventually finds some heavy bath-towels, which she lays down between the door and the dresser. Gingerly I cross it, glass crunching beneath my feet like snow, and open the drawer.

My mother's locket, the silver one with the cameo photograph of my handsome father, is gone. So great is my distress I barely notice that the rest of her jewellery – more obviously expensive, but with none of the locket's value to me alone – is still in place.

"They've taken it?" asks Annabel from the doorway. "The *bastards*."

"You said you saw them," I say weakly. "What did they look like? Will you be able to tell the police?"

"Well, there were three of them, as I say." She seems suddenly hesitant – reticent, even. "I didn't get a good look at them in the moonlight, but from the way they ran I would think they were young men. Two were tall – one was slim, one had broad shoulders. The other one was shorter. I—" she stops abruptly.

"What else?" I ask.

"Oh, Lucy," she says. "I didn't see them clearly, but I can be sure of one thing. All three of them were black."

During the years that followed the war, West Indians began to arrive in London.

I have never visited the Caribbean, and my earliest experiences of its émigrés were not promising. Every few months, some young Jamaican or Trinidadian or Barbadian man, come to London to make a living by honest work or otherwise, would come to hear that there was a rich old coloured lady living in Norbury, and would turn up on my doorstep with a carefully prepared tale of woe – asking either for money that I was disinclined to offer him, or a job that I was in no position to. I turned them away politely; if they persisted, I shut the door in their faces, and on one occasion even called the police.

Later, though, when others like those young men had established themselves, and begun to bring their sweethearts, sisters, mothers, aunts and nieces to join them, and these immigrant families began to congregate in particular parts of London – when, in short, the coloured population ceased being a loose scattering of individuals and became small villages within the patchwork of our capital – then I began to introduce myself, cautiously, to those who lived nearby, and to extend such offers of help as I was willing to make.

It is not that I feel especial spiritual affinity with the newcomers. Though American-born with African ancestry, I have been English since I was a little child, and Caribbean culture has little attraction for me. Weak tea, not spiced rum, flows in my veins. There is no mystical quintessence of "blackness" that I share with these people: that is nothing but the segregationists' view in a more insinuating guise.

Among them I can be myself: a self neither "English" nor "American", nor "black" or "coloured", but simply Lucy – Miss Lucy Hebron.

Among them, I can set aside my second mask.

Harriet arrives the next morning just as Annabel and I have finished giving our statements to Detective Inspector Critchley of the Metropolitan Police. If her family had a telephone I could have warned her not to come, but their only link to the exchange is a telephone box at the end of their street.

"What's happened, Miss Hebron?" Harriet asks me with great interest, speaking careful English in deference to the other people present. "I saw a policeman outside in the road." She looks cautious, yet also excited, as well a budding lawyer might on finding herself at the scene of a crime. "Has there been a break-in? Are you all right?"

"Ah. Harriet Youngblood, I presume," the detective inspector says. His tone is not a sympathetic one. "Miss Hebron has been telling me about you."

It was Annabel who first mentioned the poor girl, of course, impelled by her conscience when DI Critchley, noting her description of the burglars, eyed me cautiously and asked how common it was for other coloured people to call at this house.

Harriet looks mildly alarmed, so I do my best to reassure her: "I've told him we're friends, and that I've been tutoring you. He was asking about the visitors I have here, so he can eliminate them from his enquiries. I'm afraid there has been a break-in, dear, yes. Some of my mother's jewellery was stolen, but I'm quite all right."

"Oh, good. Hello, Mrs Finch." Harriet waves hello to Annabel, who gives her a weak smile. "I guess we won't be doing any maths this morning, then. But I can stay if you'd like."

"I don't think that would be a good idea," I tell her. I have just seen the self-satisfied expression on DI Critchley's face.

"I'll be the judge of that," Critchley says pompously. "You've got some questions to answer, miss."

"Me?" Harriet looks indignant at first, then scared. "What questions?" Her accent is suddenly far more pronounced. I feel faintly sick.

"The young men who broke in here last night knew exactly what they was looking for," Critchley tells her sternly. "They knew what room a certain item was in, and even what drawer. That room's right next to the lavatory on the first floor. I expect you let her use the lavatory here, don't you, Miss Hebron?"

"Of course I 'let' her," I say indignantly. "Why ever wouldn't I?" He studiously fails to meet my glare. "What *on earth* do you mean by this, Inspector?" I demand, although I can guess all too well.

"You think I tell them where to find this thing?" The poor child's idioms are slipping now. "You think I come here looking for thing to steal? Miss Hebron is my friend. I don't know any boy who do burglary. How would I?"

"That'll do, miss," says the detective inspector. "We can talk about all that down at the station."

"Inspector, this is ridiculous and I won't have it!" I say, actually stamping my foot in anger. "Harriet is my student and my friend. She's a good girl, studious, a churchgoer. I trust her. She'd no more arrange to have somebody's house burgled than… than I would!"

"Well then, let's just see about that, miss," says Critchley nastily. "Tell me something – was this jewellery insured? Do you stand to benefit at all, if it's not found?"

"You're not suggesting—" I am at a loss for words.

"Well, let's just hope it doesn't come to that, eh?" he sneers. "With luck, she'll give us the names of those three young men and I won't need to say no more to you about it. Now come on, you."

Grasping the struggling Harriet by the arm, he marches her out of the room, leaving Annabel and myself in silent shock. My heart is thumping no less violently than during the break-in.

"My word," says Annabel eventually. She, too, looks seriously shaken. "That seems a bit extreme. I mean, I quite see that she has some questions to answer, but…"

"Of course she doesn't," I snap. "That man's being absurd and prejudiced. He thinks she's guilty because she's black."

"Well," Annabel says awkwardly, "those boys were black too. And he's right that they knew exactly where to look. Not many people could have told them that. Unless… when the church people came round for that picnic, did any of them go upstairs? I mean… I suppose some of them must have needed to, while they were here."

"I locked Mother's rooms," I mutter. "I locked all the upstairs rooms except the bathroom. Many of those people were strangers to me, church or not. I'm not a complete idiot, Annabel."

"Well, then," says Annabel. "I suppose it could be some completely unrelated gang, who were lucky enough to find your mother's jewellery drawer. But, Lucy... it's not terrifically likely, is it?"

"If Harriet's found guilty it will crush her," I tell her. "No law school would accept her after that."

"She wants to go to law school? Here in England?" Annabel looks shocked. "Good heavens. Well." She is silent for a while, then says, "Perhaps this will bring her back down to earth a bit."

After much protest on Annabel's part, I persuade her to go. I sit, alone with my thoughts and the cup of tea she insists on leaving me with.

I cannot stop thinking about poor Harriet, alone and at the mercy of that ignorant bully. After a few minutes, I jump up and curse my slowness. I telephone my own lawyer, Mr Singleton, whose family have served the Munros for several generations. I instruct him to send someone to the police station immediately, to advise Miss Youngblood at my expense.

And then I sit, and drink the cold tea, and realise that I am exhausted. I have not slept since that first sound of breaking glass, many hours before. Trembling with shock and fatigue, I take to my bed, although it is only early afternoon.

At first I add an extra blanket, but then I find myself unexpectedly hot. Though I have been shivering, it is, I realise, a warm day. I open the window, and retire again beneath the covers.

* * *

It is only a short time later – though at first I have no idea of how long – when a new set of sounds wakes me. They are the voices of men, gruff and querulous with age. My own bedroom runs nearly the length of the house, and the window I have opened faces the front, where a narrow lawn and fence separate my property from the public highway.

"This must be the place," says one of the voices. It is deep but husky, and sounds strained, like someone hoisting an uncomfortable weight. I think its owner must be someone near my own age. A car door slams and the voice continues, breezier now. "Been a long time since you was in these parts, sir."

A second voice says, "It's good to see you both." This one sounds older, wavering up and down as very elderly men's voices do. Whereas the first was cockney, this voice sounds more educated, though my finely attuned ear can detect equally working-class origins. "I've had a word with the powers that be, as you asked. I found some sympathetic ears, even after all this time. If we can find anything, I should be able to pass it along."

"Thank you, Hopkins." This is the oldest voice of all, withered and rattling like a snake's shed skin. I know of no one still alive who might have a voice like that. "And, Billy, I can assure you I take little pleasure in returning here."

There is a long pause, and I wonder whether the men have left. "These parts" probably means Norbury, after all, not my house. None of the voices were ones I recognised, but there was something in the timbre of the third… the faintest ghost, perhaps, of a voice I might have heard once, a long, long time ago.

It comes again, then – the oldest voice, smoke-seared like an ancient oracle. "Look at this house now, both of you, and tell me – if you intended to trespass at the rear for felonious purposes, how would you approach the task?"

The second voice, the one the oldest called Hopkins, says hesitantly, "Well, you can see how they did it. Through Mrs Finch's front garden to the back, via her side-gate, which she hadn't locked, then through the hedge into Miss Hebron's back garden. Mrs Finch saw them running back the same way afterwards."

The leathery tongue clicks. "I did not ask how DI Critchley believes it was done. I asked how you would do it."

"Well, I'm a bit out of practice." Hopkins' laugh is like the squeak of a door-hinge, but for a moment his amusement gives his voice the lilt of a younger man.

"And you, Billy?"

"Well, sir," the first voice says, the gruff one, "if it was me I wouldn't go in that way, not unless I knew Mrs Finch's side-gate would be unlocked somehow. I'd try Miss Hebron's first. And if that was locked – and if I was a younger fellow, and all set to climb that trellis out the back – I'd not be fussed about shinning over that way too. Going through next-door's grounds would mean more people had the chance to see me."

"As Mrs Finch evidently did," creaks the oldest of the men. "My thoughts also, Billy. Except that from our point of view you *are* a younger fellow. You may have the honour."

Billy's reply is couched in the kind of language I would not care to repeat at my time of life. A moment passes, and I hear his footsteps approaching the wall at the side of the house.

Up to this point I have been lying in bed like someone in a trance, wondering whether I am really hearing this or whether it is just another dream. When I realise that the owners of these voices are actually trespassing on my property, however, I sit up in indignation.

Another of the room's windows overlooks the side of the house. I cross to it and stare down as a figure – a big man, old but sturdy, his body of a piece with the gruff voice I know belongs to him, dressed in a long trenchcoat and with thinning grey hair – clambers over the gate beneath me. The gate is the kind that can be opened readily from the inside, and as I watch incredulously, he lowers himself to the ground with a cautious grunt, then turns and does so.

"You'll get us all arrested," says the owner of the unsteady voice as he comes through. This Hopkins is a wiry old chap, dressed in practical tweeds, and steady on his feet as he supports their superannuated friend through the gate.

"I think not," the third man gasps between breaths as they walk. "I fear DI Critchley would find us inconveniently white for his purposes." Though he supports himself on two sticks, he still leans heavily against Hopkins. He must have been a tall man once, but now he is stooped and hunched upon himself, his head sunk low between his shoulders as he hobbles along. His posture and his great sharp nose remind me of some great bird of prey – a bald eagle perhaps, since his liver-spotted scalp is so entirely devoid of hair.

The three men vanish around the side of the house, and I hurry to Mother's dressing room to listen.

"I'll not be doing that again, sir," I hear Billy saying, "however much you paid me. That there's a young bloke's game."

"We're none of us as young as we were, Billy," Hopkins points out, amused. The men are out of sight – they must be standing below the broken window, at the foot of the trellis.

"That's what I mean. You want to get some new irregulars, sir. Those of us as are left aren't up to this no more."

Their ancient companion grunts in exertion, and I imagine him crouching between his sticks to peer painfully at the ground. There is a long pause before he at last says, "Do you observe these splinters of glass on the ground, Hopkins? And the fixtures by which this trellis is attached to the wall?"

Hopkins whistles. "You're right. Critchley really should have spotted that."

"DI Critchley lacks an inquiring mind. A window is broken, a valuable item of jewellery stolen, a trellis offers access. Means, motive and opportunity are present, so all that remains is to identify a suspect – or in this case, a scapegoat."

I hold in a gasp. A rising relief fills my chest as I realise that others – this mysterious triumvirate, at least – realise, like me, that Harriet is innocent.

The men become visible from the window now, Hopkins walking alone across my rear lawn while Billy assists his ancient employer – for such, surely, is their relationship – to the bench beneath my pergola.

The oldest says, "I am told that DI Critchley's chief suspect has aspirations to the bar. It is an unlikely enough vocation for an immigrant woman, but it would be peculiarly self-defeating for the girl to imperil it further with a spot of burglary."

"That's true, sir. But people can be stupid the whole world over."

"If this were a question of succumbing to a momentary temptation, Billy, I might agree with you. But Critchley's accusation is that the young woman took note of where Miss Hebron kept an item of value, then shared this information with three acquaintances who then stole it. Miss Youngblood is welcome in the house, and trusted by the householder, so why would she resort to housebreaking?"

"Well, I suppose she'd have been the obvious suspect..." Hopkins begins, but quickly trails off as his friend coughs a laugh. It sounds like footsteps in fallen leaves.

"A fate she has hardly escaped, my dear Hopkins. But if no housebreaking in fact took place, what we are left with is one act of theft and another of vandalism. We might prefer it if the two were connected, but this is no longer certain. That they were unrelated is a possibility I might have expected the investigating officer to entertain, given Miss Hebron's ancestry and the current state of racial discontent."

The three stay silent for a moment, then Hopkins continues, "If it wasn't a burglary, though, whoever stole the necklace would have to be someone with access to the house."

"I see no difficulties with that," his friend observes. "Miss Hebron is by all accounts hospitable, and trusting of her visitors. Let us suppose that one of those guests fell to temptation and stole the locket, then later tried to cover their tracks by sending these young men to break the window. That is, I think, as generous as we can be to DI Critchley's hypothesis given the evidence... and yet we still have nothing to implicate Miss Youngblood as the thief and conspirator."

Hopkins made an awkward throat-clearing noise, but Billy was more forthright: "They was Jamaicans, though, Mrs Finch said. Who else round here's likely to know a bunch of coloured kids?"

"She said only that they were coloured, not that they were Jamaican. Nonetheless, the point is worthy of an answer. Help me over to the gap in the hedge, please." There is a protracted silence as the three old men delicately negotiate the contours of my garden. "Yes, here."

I watch as Billy and Hopkins between them gingerly lower

their friend's fragile form to the ground, where he lies spread like a fallen eagle. Billy produces a magnifying glass from a pocket of his overcoat, and hands it down to him.

For several minutes they stand quite still, watching his minute observations, and watched in turn by me. Hopkins gazes rapt at the ancient man as if he hopes, even at his time of life, to learn from him. Billy shifts his feet and huffs his hands. As I have said, it is a warm day, but I too am old. I sympathise with him, and worry for the oldest of us all, lying on ground that may still be damp. Then, at his signal, Billy and Hopkins raise him laboriously to his feet.

"A creditable effort," he gasps, once he has his breath back. "Three sets of prints most certainly, each walking with a crouching gait, once in one direction and once in the other. The shoes are different in each case, yet oddly all are size eleven, and display similar patterns of wear. Furthermore, all were worn by persons of similar weight – surprisingly light for such a shoe – and stride. Remind me, Hopkins, how did Mrs Finch describe the three intruders, aside from their skin colour?"

"One large and well-built. One slim and tall. One slim and short." Hopkins sounds thoughtful.

"Indeed." His friend cackles like a saucepan boiling dry. "And now," he says, "the rockery, if you please."

He spends some minutes studying the stones my stepfather's gardener laid down last century, then gasps out a "Ha!" He indicates a flat oval stone with one of his sticks. "You see that, Hopkins? Fresh scratches in the surface, with no signs of weathering."

He continues under the pergola, after another protracted peregrination and a few more moments of recovery. "If anybody climbed that trellis," he states, "they can have weighed no more than a cat. It *might* bear the weight of a slight adult – both coming up and going down again, if they were lucky – but some of these fittings would have been pulled loose from the wall even by the ascent of a child."

"So how'd they break the window?" Billy asks.

"Most of the glass fell inside the house," his employer creaks, "but some large pieces ended up beneath. The scratches in that stone are quite consistent with being dragged across the sharp edges of a broken pane. I would imagine that the offender tied it securely to some gardening twine, then threw it through the window from beneath. The withdrawal would be noisy, accounting for the banging Miss Hebron heard after the breakage, but would leave nothing in the room to suggest that the window was broken by a projectile. It would, however, pull down any loose glass that still stood at the bottom of the frame. Such a method of deception relies on the householder being too frightened to investigate the noise immediately, but when the subject is a lady in her seventies that is not so great a gamble."

I can see Hopkins shaking his head. "Critchley should have checked the windowsill for marks. He should have photographed the floor. The man's negligence is bordering on the criminal."

The old man shrugs. "He has what he believes to be an obvious suspect. For a deplorable few in your erstwhile profession, Hopkins, that is the beginning and the end of a case."

Billy says, "Didn't Mrs Finch say she saw a bloke climb down the trellis, though?"

That question has occurred to me as well.

"Indeed," the old man says. "And what, I wonder, was the late Mr Finch's shoe size?"

* * *

Across most of the dressing-room floor I can see large pieces of glass, the smallest the size of my hand. I lift the towels to reveal smaller slivers, fragmented into pieces by my passing footsteps. Elsewhere in the room the fragments are large, intact since their first breakage: triangular segments following an altogether larger pattern. I cannot see it clearly from here, but the paint on the windowsill seems to be marred by a faint scrape. I think more carefully than I have thought in a long time, more deeply even than I expected to for Harriet's mathematics lesson.

Annabel Finch has been in my house on many occasions. She certainly visited the bathroom before she left yesterday, while I was downstairs with Harriet.

The thing that was taken was carefully chosen, not for its price but for its value to me. It was the possession that I would have been most distressed to lose. I cannot positively recall having shown Annabel the locket, but I do show people from time to time, and Annabel has lived next door for many years. Even if she found it while snooping, its significance would have been obvious once she realised who the handsome dark man in the photo must be.

She has been feeling isolated in her house, a widow whose family has left home. Of *course* she is thinking of selling up. And of course Maud Stokes was right that the kind of person who would want – who could afford – to buy a house here, is likely to be disconcerted by regular visitations of coloured people to the neighbourhood.

An elderly dark Englishwoman they might tolerate as a neighbour – as they might some other well-behaved curiosity (a Russian exile, perhaps, or a defrocked priest) –

but West Indian immigrants calling round, having picnics and taking lessons in how to better themselves in British society? That, surely, would discourage any discerning house-buyer from any interest in the Finch family house, or at least cause them to reduce their offer substantially.

Unless, of course, Annabel found a way to discourage my association with such people.

I rush back to my bedroom, and the window at the front of the house, in time to see the man named Hopkins conclude his farewells and drive away. I watch, faintly dazed, still with a sense of unreality about the whole of this visitation, as the other man, Billy, hefts his employer's weight back into their own car.

"Surprised you had me haul you over here for this, really," he huffs. "Bit of an easy one for you, wasn't it, Mr Altamont?"

The ancient figure settles into the back seat of the car, and the oracular voice croaks: "I saw Miss Hebron's name in the morning papers, Billy. It reminded me of an incident in my past, a lifetime ago now. A face at a window. A whisper in my ear."

And he turns his head, and looks directly up at me, and smiles a withered, toothless smile.

It is hours later, when the sun is finally setting, when once more I hear a knocking – quiet, yet insistent – at my front door. Wearily I open it, and there stands Annabel, beaming at me, holding up my mother's somewhat muddy silver locket.

"It was in my rosebushes!" she cries. "They must have dropped it when they ran away. I switched my light on when I saw them, you see – they must have realised they'd been spotted, and made a run for it. Imagine going to all that effort and not even getting away with what they came here for!"

I take the locket. Annabel's grin falters as she sees my unsmiling face, but she rallies.

"I expect they'll let poor Harriet go now," she says breezily. "They won't be able to prove anything now, I shouldn't think."

Quietly, I say, "They certainly will not. Because you are going to tell them what really happened. For Harriet's sake."

Annabel flushes furiously, but her voice is almost as weak as the old man's. "What... what do you mean?"

"Nobody climbed my trellis," I say. "No one was in my house. You didn't see any black men. To do you justice you didn't steal any of my other jewellery, although I suppose you must be in financial need. I'll even do you the courtesy of believing you meant to find the locket all along. But even so, you were prepared to damage my property, terrorise me in my bed, waste the police's time and see Harriet wrongfully arrested."

"Oh, God." Annabel's hand is at her mouth. "Oh, God, Lucy. I'm *so* sorry. I'm afraid I've been a frightful shit. I hoped you'd never find out. But... I've been so stupid. I lost a lot of money on the horses... well, a little at first. But then I tried to win it back, and I kept trying, and now it's far too much. I can't afford not to sell the house, and I can't afford..."

Her self-justification ebbs away on the beach of my disinterest.

"The police know, Annabel," I tell her. "Or they will soon. It's out of my hands. If you go and tell DI Critchley what happened, I won't press charges. I'll even act as a character witness, if it comes to it. But I will not have Harriet suffer any more, do you understand?"

She nods, starts to say something, then stops and nods again. She turns away. There's guilt in her expression, and despair for the future, but there is also something in her face I recognise.

Annabel Finch is relieved to have been unmasked.

I am not, as you may well understand, a woman to harbour illusions. I know that Harriet Youngblood will always suffer the effects of colour prejudice, just as I have done for all of my life, just as my parents did last century in Atlanta. I do not know whether the London Harriet grows up in will allow her to exercise her mind in the law, or force her into some form of drudgery, domestic or industrial.

I cannot begin to imagine what kind of Britain she will inhabit when she reaches my age, although I can only hope that it will treat its immigrants with more respect and humanity than the likes of Critchley do now.

I know, though, that today Harriet is spared the worst of what the present can offer, and for that I am profoundly grateful to you.

Because I recognised you; of course I did. Your laugh, a hoarse echo of the clear peal of my childhood; your slender fingers, gnarled and arthritic; your eyes, the skin around them creased and soft like old crepe paper. I recognised the names, too, as any of Dr Watson's readers would have done: all three of them, but especially the name you were addressed by as you were leaving.

And yet I wonder, still.

I was asleep when you arrived. One hears of inspiration coming to poets in their dreams, but also of scientists finding there some crucial piece of analysis that has eluded their waking minds. Had I already realised subconsciously that Annabel had betrayed me? Fond though I have been of her – though not any more, I am afraid – she has never been exactly reliable.

Your passing left no evidence; none, at least, that I am competent to detect. All that you left behind was a truth I might have stumbled upon myself, given time.

The alternative – that the world-renowned detective who briefly went by the name Altamont is not, as all his devotees have long imagined, dead, but has survived into extreme old age, and is once again dabbling in his old line of work – is surely no more plausible, and would be far more sensational if it were known.

What was it Billy would have had you doing that was more important? Not beekeeping, surely. That job carries its own physical demands, and a man who is – as you would have to be by now – over a hundred years old, would surely need to find some less active, more cerebral way to occupy his time.

In that case, I can understand your need for an alias in your second retirement. If it were known that you were once again practising criminal investigation in the second half of the twentieth century, the world would trample a path to your door.

I could make my own enquiries – we old ladies have a knack for being inquisitive, and our information networks are spread widely. Given your state of health, I cannot imagine that you travelled far to come here. There cannot be many centenarians in the world named Altamont, and I dare say I could find with little difficulty where you are living – if you are alive outside my dreams at all, and not in some untended grave in a quiet churchyard in the Sussex countryside.

It would be such a pleasure if we could meet again. I would talk with you properly this time. We might reminisce together about all that happened then, when we were both so very young.

But, no. If you are real, then you are entitled to your privacy.

Yours is one mask that I shall leave in place.

About the Editor

George Mann is the author of the *Sherlock Holmes: The Spirit Box* and *Sherlock Holmes: The Will of the Dead*, the *Newbury and Hobbes* and *The Ghost* series of novels, as well as numerous short stories, novellas and audiobooks. He has written fiction and audio scripts for the BBC's *Doctor Who* and *Sherlock Holmes*. He is also a respected anthologist and has edited *Associates of Sherlock Holmes*, *Encounters of Sherlock Holmes*, *Further Encounters of Sherlock Holmes*, *The Solaris Book of New Science Fiction* and *The Solaris Book of New Fantasy*. His new novel, *Wychwood*, is out in September 2017. He lives near Grantham, UK.

About the Authors

Stuart Douglas is the author of the Titan Books Sherlock Holmes novels *The Albino's Treasure* and *The Counterfeit Detective*, as well as the forthcoming *The Improbable Prisoner*. He is the founder and owner of Obverse Books and is responsible for the official resurrection of the character of Sexton Blake after fifty years. He has written numerous short stories, novellas and non-fiction pieces, in addition to editing over a dozen anthologies. He lives in Edinburgh with his wife and three children.

Jonathan Green is a writer of speculative fiction, with more than sixty books to his name. Well known for his contributions to the Fighting Fantasy range of adventure gamebooks, he has also written fiction for such diverse properties as *Doctor Who*, *Star Wars: The Clone Wars*, *Warhammer*, *Warhammer 40,000*, *Sonic the Hedgehog*, *Teenage Mutant Ninja Turtles*, *LEGO*, *Judge Dredd*, and *Robin of Sherwood*. His work has been translated into eight languages.

He is the creator of the Pax Britannia series for Abaddon Books and has written eight novels, and numerous short stories, set within this steampunk universe, featuring the debonair dandy adventurer Ulysses Quicksilver. Steampunk and dieselpunk have left their mark on his latest gamebook publications as well, *Alice's Nightmare in*

Wonderland and *The Wicked Wizard of Oz*.

He is the author of an increasing number of non-fiction titles, including the award-winning *You Are The Hero: A History of Fighting Fantasy Gamebooks*, and he has recently taken to editing and compiling short story anthologies, including the critically-acclaimed *Game Over*, *Sharkpunk*, and *Shakespeare Vs Cthulhu*.

To find out more about his current projects visit www.jonathangreenauthor.com and follow him on Twitter @jonathangreen.

Stephen Henry is an author of many parts who has worked in the tabletop games and video game industry for over a decade. He lives and works in Nottingham, England.

Andrew Lane is the author of twenty-four novels and nine non-fiction books, along with over thirty short stories. He is probably best known at the moment for his series of eight YA novels about Sherlock Holmes's adventures as a teenager.

Mark A. Latham is a writer, editor, history nerd, proud dogfather, frustrated grunge singer and amateur baker from Staffordshire, UK. An immigrant to rural Nottinghamshire, he lives in a very old house (sadly not haunted), and is still regarded in the village as a foreigner. Formerly the editor of Games Workshop's *White Dwarf* magazine, Mark dabbled in tabletop games design before becoming a full-time author of strange, fantastical and macabre tales. His Apollonian Casefiles series, and his first Sherlock Holmes novel, *A Betrayal in Blood*, are available now from Titan Books. Visit Mark's blog at thelostvictorian.blogspot.co.uk or follow him on Twitter @aLostVictorian.

James Lovegrove is the author of more than fifty books, including *The Hope*, *Days*, *Untied Kingdom*, *Provender Gleed*, and the *New York Times* bestselling Pantheon series . He has written four Sherlock Holmes novels, *The Stuff of Nightmares*, *Gods of War*, *The Thinking Engine* and *The Labyrinth of Death* for Titan Books, and a Holmes/Cthulhu mashup trilogy, the first volume of which – *Sherlock Holmes and the Shadwell Shadows* – came out in 2016, with a second, *Sherlock Holmes and the Miskatonic Monstrosities*, to follow in late 2017. His latest series is the Dev Harmer Missions, an outer-space action-adventure series, beginning with *World of Fire* and *World of Water.*

James has been shortlisted for numerous awards, including the Arthur C. Clarke Award, the John W. Campbell Memorial Award, the Bram Stoker Award, the British Fantasy Society Award and the Manchester Book Award. His short story "Carry The Moon In My Pocket" won the 2011 Seiun Award in Japan for Best Translated Short Story. James's work has been translated into fourteen languages.

His journalism has appeared in periodicals as diverse as *Literary Review*, *Interzone*, *SFX* and *BBC MindGames*, and he is a regular reviewer of fiction for the *Financial Times* and contributes features and reviews about comic books to *Comic Heroes* magazine. He lives with his wife, two sons, cat and tiny dog in Eastbourne, not far from "the small farm upon the Downs" to which Sherlock Holmes retired.

David Marcum plays The Game with deadly seriousness. Since 1975, he has collected literally thousands of traditional Holmes pastiches in the form of novels, short stories, radio and television episodes, movies and scripts, comics, fan-fiction, and unpublished manuscripts. He is the author of

The Papers of Sherlock Holmes Volumes I and *II, Sherlock Holmes and a Quantity of Debt*, *Sherlock Holmes – Tangled Skeins*, and the forthcoming *The Papers of Solar Pons*. Additionally, he is the editor of the three-volume set *Sherlock Holmes in Montague Street* (recasting Arthur Morrison's Martin Hewitt stories as early Holmes adventures), the two-volume collection of Great Hiatus stories *Holmes Away From Home*, the pre-1881 *Sherlock Holmes: Before Baker Street*, and the ongoing collection *The MX Book of New Sherlock Holmes Stories*. He is a licensed civil engineer, living in Tennessee with his wife and son. Since 1984, he has worn a deerstalker as his regular-and-only hat from autumn to spring. In 2013, he and his deerstalker were finally able make the trip-of-a-lifetime Holmes pilgrimage to England, with return pilgrimages in 2015 and 2016, where you may have spotted him. If you ever run into him and his deerstalker out and about, feel free to say hello!

Iain McLaughlin was born in Dundee on the east coast of Scotland. He still lives there in a house filled with books. He has written more than twenty books and over fifty plays for radio. He has also written short stories and TV scripts. Iain has written for many famous characters and shows including *James Bond*, *Doctor Who*, *Blake's 7*, Richard Hannay, *Wallace & Gromit* and *Sherlock Holmes*. He has also written several original thrillers. For a time he was the editor of the *Beano* comic and has written the Scottish icons *The Broons* and *Oor Wullie.*

Philip Purser-Hallard is the author of the trilogy of urban fantasy thrillers beginning with *The Pendragon Protocol*, which envisages the successors of the Knights of the Round Table as a paramilitary group fighting for the soul of 21st-century Britain. He edits a series of anthologies about the City of the Saved, a technological afterlife created for humanity beyond the end of the universe, in which Sherlock Holmes has been known to appear. His short story "The Adventure of the Professor's Bequest" (in *Further Encounters of Sherlock Holmes*) deals with the posthumous papers of Professor Moriarty.

As well as writing various other books and short stories, Phil edits *The Black Archive*, a series of monographs about individual *Doctor Who* stories published by Obverse Books. For variety (and money), he spends four days a week editing official documents for a non-governmental public body.

He has a wife, a son and plenty of books, but is temporarily between cats.

Michelle Ruda is a bestselling international Nobel prize-winning author – all in her mind. She actually works in TV as a development researcher, the media equivalent of a consulting detective. She discovered Sherlock Holmes in 2013 and her life has never been the same since. This is her first published short story and she is delighted that it's about Mr Holmes. She has won two short film script competitions with scripts that have been made into films, and has had a number of articles and poems published. In her spare time she enjoys South Korean TV drama, air guitar and haggling.

Sam Stone began her professional writing career in 2007 when her first novel won the Silver Award for Best Novel with *ForeWord Magazine* Book of the Year Awards. Since then she has gone on to write several novels, three novellas and many short stories. She was the first woman in thirty-one years to win the British Fantasy Society Award for Best Novel. She also won the Award for Best Short Fiction in the same year (2011).

Stone loves all types of fiction and enjoys mixing horror (her first passion) with a variety of different genres including science fiction, fantasy, crime and steampunk.

She currently resides in Lincolnshire with her husband David and their two cats Shadow and Freya.

Her works can be found in paperback, audio and eBook.

www.sam-stone.com

Nik Vincent began working as a freelance editor, but has published work in a number of mediums including advertising, training manuals, comics and short stories. She has worked as a ghostwriter, and regularly collaborates with her partner, Dan Abnett, writing novels, and in the games industry. Nik was educated at Stirling University, and lives and works in Maidstone, Kent. She tweets @ VincentAbnett.

Dan Watters is a London-based writer, primarily of comic books. His debut graphic novel, the weird neo-noir *Limbo*, was released through Image Comics in 2016. He is currently working on various comic book titles, including *Assassin's Creed* and *Dark Souls: Legends of the Flame* for Titan Comics, and *The Shadow* for Dynamite Comics.

Marcia Wilson is a former saltpetre cave tour guide and lifetime advocate of karstic environmental protection. She's currently in an exercise regime for the Dragon Boat races and holds down the day job in an optical shop between commissions for her illustrations. She's always reading the SH canon as annotated by Leslie S. Klinger. She is a contributing writer to all but two of the ongoing *MX Anthology of New Sherlock Holmes Stories* for the renovation of Undershaw and is finishing her third Sherlock Holmes pastiche for MX Publishing.